The First Murder

THE FIRST MURDER

A Historical Mystery
By
The Medieval Murderers

Susanna Gregory
Bernard Knight
Karen Maitland
Ian Morson
Philip Gooden

**SIMON &
SCHUSTER**

London · New York · Sydney · Toronto · New Delhi

A CBS COMPANY

First published in Great Britain by Simon & Schuster UK Ltd, 2012
A CBS COMPANY

1 3 5 7 9 10 8 6 4 2

Simon & Schuster UK Ltd
1st Floor
222 Gray's Inn Road
London WC1X 8HB

www.simonandschuster.co.uk

Simon & Schuster Australia, Sydney
Simon & Schuster India, New Delhi

A CIP catalogue record for this book
is available from the British Library

Hardback ISBN: 978-1-84983-736-1
Trade Paperback ISBN: 978-1-84983-737-8
Ebook ISBN: 978-1-47110-272-1

This book is a work of fiction. Names, characters, places and incidents are
either a product of the author's imagination or are used fictitiously.

Typeset by M Rules
Printed and bound by CPI Group (UK) Ltd, Croydon, CR0 4YY

THE MEDIEVAL MURDERERS

A small group of historical mystery writers, all members of the Crime Writers' Association, who promote their work by giving informal talks and discussions at libraries, bookshops and literary festivals.

Bernard Knight is a former Home Office pathologist and professor of forensic medicine who has been publishing novels, non-fiction, radio and television drama and documentaries for more than forty years. He is author of the highly regarded Crowner John series of historical mysteries, based on the first coroner for Devon in the twelfth century; and of the Dr Richard Pryor series.

Ian Morson is the author of an acclaimed series of historical mysteries featuring the thirteenth-century Oxford-based detective, William Falconer, and a brand-new series featuring Venetian crime solver, Nick Zuliani.

Philip Gooden is the author of the Nick Revill series, a sequence of historical mysteries set in Shakespearean London, including *Sleep of Death* and *Death of Kings*, and also writes 19th century mysteries, most recently *The Ely Testament*.

The author of various non-fiction books on English, his newest title is *Idiomantics*, and he blogs on language at www.philipgooden.com. Philip was chairman of the Crime Writers' Association in 2007–8.

Susanna Gregory is the author of the Matthew Bartholomew series of mystery novels, set in fourteenth-century Cambridge, the most recent of which are *Mystery in the Minster* and *Murder by the Book*. In addition, she writes a series set in Restoration London, featuring Thomas Chaloner; the most recent book is *The Piccadilly Plot*. She also writes historical mysteries under the name of Simon Beaufort.

Karen Maitland writes stand-alone, dark medieval thrillers. She is the author of *Company of Liars* and *The Owl Killers*. Her most recent medieval thrillers are *The Gallows Curse*, a tale of treachery and sin under the brutal reign of English King John, and *Falcons of Fire and Ice* set in Portugal and Iceland amid the twin terrors of the Inquisition and Reformation.

Medieval
Murderers

ThE PROGRAMME

Prologue – In which Ian Morson tells of Prior Wigod of Oseney Priory writing *The Play of Adam*, and how the world's first murder – of Abel by his brother Cain – is enacted with equally murderous results.

Act One – In which Susanna Gregory relates how *The Play of Adam* travels from Oxford to Carmarthen in the year 1199, and the castle's constable and his wife encounter murder among rival clerics.

Act Two – In which Karen Maitland tells how the towns-people of Ely fear that *The Play of Adam* has unleashed a demon upon the town, after a gruesome discovery is made in the cathedral.

Act Three – In which Philip Gooden tells the story of a playwright who wishes to obtain revenge on William Shakespeare and comes to an unfortunate end, while player Nick Revill faces the secret agents of the Privy Council.

Act Four – In which Ian Morson writes about Doll Pocket satisfying her yearning to become an actress, while Joe

Malinferno struggles with the mystery of Egyptian hieroglyphics. Unfortunately, the rehearsals for the newly discovered *Play of Adam* result in a murder. But has it to do with thespian jealousies, or something much more arcane?

Epilogue – In which Bernard Knight recounts how *The Play of Adam* is revived by an academic department during the Second World War, which provides an unexpected finale.

PROLOGUE

I am gracious and great God without beginning.
I am maker unmade; all might is in me.
I am life and way, unto weal winning.
I am foremost and first; as I bid, shall it be.
The bliss of my gaze shall be blending
And flowing from hardship protecting;
My body in bliss still abiding,
Unending, without any ending.

Prior Wigod carefully put down his quill so as not to splash the ink from the nib, and leaned over his work to admire it. He muttered the words he had written to himself, then with an improper sense of pride, got up from his chair and stomped around speaking them out loud. He grunted with pleasure. The words sounded fine echoing round his private parlour. So he knew they would be even more portentous carrying out over the assembled crowd of common people who would come from nearby Oxford to stand before the main doors of Oseney Priory on Easter Sunday in the year of our Lord 1154. Perhaps he would play the part of God himself. Why not? He was prior of the recently augmented Augustinian community, and this play was to be performed to mark their first twenty-five years.

He looked at the words he had written once again, some admittedly borrowed, it was true, but some his own. Mostly his own, he liked to think. And they were written in the ver-nacular in order to reach the hearts and minds of the

ordinary people of the town. The community he led, insti-
tuted by Robert D'Oyly, was of the Canons Regular of St
Augustine, and part of their role was preaching and teaching. Feeling an unseemly swelling of pride in his breast,
before retiring for the night he hurriedly kneeled before the
large crucifix that hung on the eastern wall of his parlour.
Bowing his head, he prayed to the Lord for His forgiveness
for the sin of pride.

At daybreak, Brother Paul, who was designated the 'careful
brother' by the prior because he could be relied on to see that
all things were done at the appointed time, rang the bell to
rouse the brethren. This was the call to dress and enter the
church for prime, the first daylight service of the seven offices
ordained by the psalmist. Paul muttered the relevant words
under his breath as he cheerfully and lustily tolled the bell.

'Seven times a day do I praise Thee because of Thy righteous judgement.'

On that cold March morning, Brother Wilfred was the
last of the brother canons to rise, and had to hurry from the
dormitory, through the cloister court, and into the church
transept, where he received a severe look from the prior.
Wilfred was often late and regularly chastised for his misde-
meanour, but it made no difference. He was young and still
not used to breaking his rest at midnight to the sound of
Paul's sleepless bell, only to return to his austere pallet and
rough blanket after singing matins and lauds in a dark and
cold church. He felt he had only just closed his weary eyes
again when the prime bell rang. This morning, like so many
before, he found himself stifling a yawn. On the other hand,
he could not help but notice the bright fervour that shone in
Paul's eyes at the final exhortation to 'let everything that
hath breath praise the Lord'.

The careful brother was no older than Wilfred, but had been rewarded for his zeal by the prior. His recent appointment as the toller of the bells that regulated the daily affairs of the priory had filled Wilfred with envy, though he did not know why. The last thing he wished for himself was to have to be awake before everyone else in order to rouse the Augustinian community out of their beds. It's just that envy was Wilfred's natural state. He envied the rotund Brother William, who had long held the position as kitchener, because he obviously filled his belly with extra food. He envied Brother Alfred the infirmarian, because he had an easy time tending the sick and elderly monks, which kept him indoors on cold and inclement days such as today. And he envied Brother Roger, who was the cellarer and had access to the stores where the casks of wine were kept. From Roger's sometimes unsteady gait, Wilfred suspected him of 'sucking the monkey', as the novices called it. This practice involved sticking a long piece of straw in the bunghole of a cask and sucking out the contents without apparently broaching the barrel.

Wilfred knew why he envied all these people, but he could not say why he especially envied Brother Paul. Perhaps it was not because of his position, but due to the fact that he and Wilfred had begun as novices on the same day. And yet Paul had progressed so much further and faster than Wilfred. Even the next ritual of the long day reminded Wilfred of his junior status. For it was in order of seniority that the canons silently processed out to the cloister to wash their hands and faces at the stone trough that ran the length of one side of the court. Wilfred was in the rearmost echelon, preceding only the young novices who had just begun their long journey towards priesthood. As he stood in the lengthy queue for these ablutions, Wilfred heard one of the novices behind him, unused to the rules on silence, whispering to the young boy next to him a choice piece of news that Wilfred had not heard.

'I heard it said that the prior has written a play to be performed as part of the Easter liturgy.'

The other novice must have been more concerned with observing the Augustinian rules. Wilfred heard only a noncommittal grunt from him before the novice-master scurried past him towards the original offender. Wilfred, his eyes still looking ahead, heard the crack of an open palm on tonsured head. The offending novice had been duly reprimanded for his infraction. But not before he had planted a seed in Wilfred's head.

Of course, it could be nothing but the exaggeration of an overwrought boy, this talk of a play. For many years the canons of Oseney Priory, built on the southernmost arm of the water meadows close by the walls of the university town of Oxford, had included small dramatic episodes in the Easter liturgy. On Easter morning, after the third responsory of matins, two canons clothed in albs walked to where a wooden cross had been laid on the floor of the church just below the altar. It represented a grave, and they seated themselves there until three more canons carrying censers and representing holy women, joined them. At this point one of the seated canons in the guise of an angel asked the holy 'women', 'Whom do you seek?' The three canons answered, 'Our Lord, Jesus Christ.' The angel then gave the holy 'women' the message of the Resurrection, and told them to go forth and proclaim it. They then intoned the antiphon, '*Surrexit enim, sicut dixit dominus. Alleluia.*' Finally, the choir, as always, finished matins with the Te Deum.

So the rumour of a play to be performed at Easter could amount to nothing. On the other hand, if it were true, Wilfred had a desire to take part in it. Life at the priory was one of endless, dull repetition. He knew it was a state of existence that he should have realised before he committed himself to God, but when he was a novice it had all seemed so new and exciting. Now, the thought of doing something unusual, like taking part in a pageant, served to lift his spirits. He could not wait until the daily assembly in the chapter house. Perhaps the prior would make an announcement. Easter was only a matter of weeks away, and much would need to be done to prepare the scenes he had heard other priories and abbeys had performed as a way of teaching the lay community some of the key points in the Bible.

It was finally Wilfred's turn to wash. He plunged his hands into the shallow runnel of icy water that trickled down the stone trough in the cloister, and splashed some on his face. He risked darting a quick look behind him to try to identify the novice who had broken the news of the play. From the reddened mark on his forehead, he saw it must have been Alcuin, a ginger-haired youth from Wales with big, ungainly hands and feet. The novice's pock-marked face had a sour look on it that intimated he resented being humiliated by the novice-master. Wilfred wondered if he would last the course, and graduate into the order. He himself had had to contain his prideful anger on more than one occasion, and knew how the new boy felt. He tried a smile of sympathy on him, but Alcuin looked away in embarrassment. Wilfred shrugged and walked through to the refectory. There, the assembled canons ate the usual light breakfast of bread and ale standing up in silence, as was the custom. He groaned inwardly when, all too soon, he heard the 'careful' Brother Paul tolling the inexorable bell calling everyone to Mass.

Once Mass had been celebrated, Brother Paul hurried off to toll the bell calling the canons to the chapter house. His duty was hardly essential at these times, as the routine of the priory – indeed, of every religious house in England – was rigid and regular. Everyone knew to move from the church and into the chapter house at this time of day. The only times the sound of the bell was of use was late morning, when the canons had dispersed to carry out various tasks concerning the business affairs of the priory and needed to be called together for High Mass; and also for vespers. After dinner, the canons had a short rest period, terminated by the office of nones. Then there began the five-hour working day, which the canons spent in the gardens, fields, work-shops, kitchens and storehouses of Oseney Priory. The vesper bell was essential to call them for evensong from their various allotted tasks in the scattered buildings and grounds of the ever-growing priory. But Paul took his task seriously at all times of the day, and even though he knew some canons grumbled about his zeal, that did nothing to dim his enthu-siasm. The marking of the set points of each and every day with the sound of a bell was as important to him as his sevenfold daily praise of God.

As he was ringing the bell to call his brothers to the chap-ter house, he noticed that Brother Wilfred was for once at the head of those entering through the grand doors of the room on the east side of the cloister. This was most unusual. Wilfred was forever dragging his feet from one part of the priory to another, and from one task to another. Paul had tried more than once to rectify this, suggesting that Wilfred should show more enthusiasm as everything the canons did was in praise of the Lord. He had thought that Wilfred would have responded well, as they had been friends from the day they had arrived together as novices at the priory. But on the third occasion that Paul had chastised him – in the friendliest of ways – Wilfred had turned on him, and suggested he mind his own business. Paul preferred to forget the actual words, which had been, 'Go kiss the Devil's arse, Paul. Are you trying for early sainthood or something?' He had put the outburst down to the fact that it had been Lent, and Wilfred, as were some of the other inexperienced canons, was always fractious when hungry. Paul himself relished fasting at Lent as it gave him a curious feeling of flying out of his own skin, and therefore closer to God.

Slipping quietly into the chapter house, Paul waited whilst a few brothers shuffled up along the stone bench that ran around the whole chamber, and then sat in the space made for him. The coldness struck through his vitals, and he silently praised God for his discomfort. He listened as Brother Martin finished the reading of the daily chapter of the Rule, and then the prior stood up.

His seat was set in the rounded apse at the eastern end of the chapter house, and stood at the top of three steps. So when Prior Wigod rose from his chair, he presented an imposing figure appropriate to his position. It had been said in the dormitory that morning that he had an important announcement to make. But Wigod still stuck rigidly to the proper procedure. His first words were to lead the canons in the praise for the saints and martyrs of the day.

'Let us praise St Piran of Padstow, St Caron of Tregaron, and St Kieran of Ossory in Ireland.'

The assembled twenty-five canons and six novices intoned prayers and praise for the saints. It was as if the prior's own words were echoing around the vaulted chamber. Next there came the prayers for the souls of the benefactors.

'Let us pray for the soul of Robert D'Oyly, and his wife, Editha. She it was who saw a group of magpies chattering in the marchlands of Oseney Meadows and realised they symbolised souls in purgatory crying for prayers. In 1129, Sir Robert granted the lands on which our priory now stands. And so this is the twenty-fifth year since our founding.' He paused dramatically. 'And in order to celebrate that founding, and to further our purpose as canons regular, I have decided that a pageant or play will be performed outside the church doors on Easter Sunday.'

A murmur of excited comment rippled around the chamber, which on any other occasion would have been the cause of a severe reprimand from the prior. But on this special day he was pleased beyond measure at its occurrence, and let the lapse pass. He continued to explain his plans, ensuring the canons knew the source of the text.

'The scenes I have written so far include "The Creation of the World", "The Fall of the Angels", "The Fall of Man", "The Story of Cain and Abel", and "The Deluge". I shall complete the central piece of this Easter celebration shortly, with "The Nativity", "The Passion" and "The Resurrection". It will be called *Ordo Representationis Ade – The Play of Adam.'*

The only canon capable of interrupting the prior did so at this moment. He was Brother Sylvanus, and had stood for election as prior against Wigod three years earlier. The previous prior, who had died of a fever, had been quite severe in his sense of duty, and Sylvanus looked to carry on his stern discipline. Unfortunately for him, the twenty-five canons who were in a position to vote on who became prior – the lay brothers being excluded from this process – had expressed a desire for a gentler approach to the praise of God. Wigod had been elected, and the defeated candidate had never let him forget the perceived snub. Sylvanus questioned every proposal and every decision that Wigod came up with. This time it was concerning the language of the pageant. With a sneering tone in his voice, Sylvanus made his position clear.

'I hope that the text to be spoken by the canons will be in Latin, Brother Wigod.' He alone called the prior by his name rather than using his title.

Wigod smiled wearily. 'The liturgy will of course be in Latin, as will the psalms and songs. For example, at the end of "The Fall of the Angels", the choir will sing "*Te deum laudamus: te dominum confitemur*".'

Sylvanus smirked, believing he had cornered the prior. 'I think I hear the sound of "however" hovering over your exposition.'

The prior was undeterred. 'Indeed you do, Brother Sylvanus. The stories will be told in the vernacular. One of the purposes of our order is to preach and teach to the populace. How are we to do that properly unless we speak to them in their language?'

He looked across the sea of nodding tonsured heads, knowing that most of the canons agreed with him. Only Sylvanus' head went from side to side but, seeing he was outnumbered yet again, the disgruntled brother merely satisfied himself with a hiss of disapproval. He seemed to have contented himself with the knowledge that his day would surely come. And almost in the prior's next breath, he saw it had. Wigod, as was his nature, had the inspiration to seek some reconciliation with Sylvanus, and made an offer.

'I would like you, Brother Sylvanus, to select which of our brethren will enact which scenes, and the characters they will portray. I am sure you will be able to match the abilities of each with the person they will represent.'

Sylvanus grinned wolfishly, seeing a way immediately to ruin Wigod's plans.

'I will indeed undertake the task you suggest, Brother

Wigod, if I can also instruct those I select in their roles. And I will allocate the parts according to the zeal and piety of our fellow canons.'

That was not what the prior had intended, having thought more to match each canon's personality with the part as he had written it. He had drafted the words spoken by Noah with Roger the cellarer in mind, because he was vague and uncertain at crucial times. And the spare and sinuous frame of Brother Alfred made him eminently suitable for the part of the Serpent in 'The Fall of Man'. But his decision had been made, and he could not now rescind it. With an inward sigh, he accepted his former rival's plan.

'I am content to leave it all in your capable hands, Sylvanus.'

The prior was so occupied with meeting Sylvanus' cold stare, that he didn't notice the disappointed look on Brother Wilfred's face. With Sylvanus in charge of selecting which brothers were going to take part in the play, Wilfred saw his chances of being involved slipping rapidly away. His standing in the eyes of the strict disciplinarian, who had been novice-master in the days of Wilfred and Paul, was as low as it could be. The pious Paul would be selected first, and then most of the other twenty-three canons well ahead of Wilfred himself. He sighed and slumped in his seat, hardly listening to the rest of the prior's announcements.

He was greatly surprised, therefore, when he felt a restraining hand on his arm as later he shuffled out of the chapter house to his general duties of the morning. He looked round, and saw the beaming face of Sylvanus with a strange look on it.

'I have you in mind for a part in the pageant, Brother Wilfred.'

Wilfred gasped at this unexpected turn of fortune. 'Of

course, Brother Sylvanus. I hardly expected such an honour, but I will be delighted to help in any way I can.'

'Then you shall have the part of Cain. The ... prior ...' Sylvanus managed to squeeze the offending word out somehow, despite his displeasure, '... is even now going to the scriptorium to have the best scribes write out the words for each part in his play. You will have only your words, and the word that will prompt you to say your lines. The whole text is far too long to allow a copy of it all for everyone.'

There was a suggestion in Sylvanus' tone of the play being overlong and wordy, but Wilfred didn't care about the politics of the priory. Let Sylvanus undermine the prior all he wished, he had a part in the Easter play. He thought he understood the principle of the performers' scripts, and hoped he could cope.

'Yes, Brother. I will not let you down.'

It was only after Sylvanus strode away to speak to Brother Paul that Wilfred had a niggling doubt about the part. Was his selection to play the part of Cain some reflection on Sylvanus' opinion of Wilfred's attitude to God? Did he think Wilfred somehow impious? But whatever his fellow canon's opinion, it didn't much matter. He would be in the Easter play.

It was three days before Sylvanus handed Wilfred the single sheet of used and scraped vellum that had his words on it. He peered at it, the minute and ragged script looking as though a spider had stepped in ink and scurried across the page.

'Who wrote this?' he complained. 'It is too small to read, and the lines are not level.'

Sylvanus' mouth turned down in a sneer. 'Wigod has the best scribes making copies of the whole play cycle. Therefore he had the novices trying their skill at writing the actors' pieces. I am afraid Alcuin has proved he is not cut out for the scriptorium. The only merit of his hand is the smallness of his text. At least it has not been wasteful of precious vellum.'

Wilfred was about to point out that the palimpsest he held had been so often scraped that its greyness made the text barely legible. Its worn nature meant it could hardly be said to be precious material. But he kept his mouth shut, fearing that Sylvanus might change his mind and give the part of Cain to someone else. He looked at the line and a half of Abel's first speech that gave him his cue.

Come, brother Cain, I would we went
With hearts full blithe.

He guessed that the last word of this speech was probably rhymed with 'tithe'. Abel's tithe being more acceptable to God was the cause of the fight between the brothers, which had tragic consequences. Reading on, he mouthed his own words.

'What? Where to now? In wastelands gone?
You think I wish this town to leave?'

He looked at the older canon, eager to get it right from the beginning. 'Am I to be argumentative, then? Or do we just read the words solemnly?'

Sylvanus shook his head impatiently. 'You are to put your heart and soul into the part. Don't you understand? You are to *be* Cain, the first murderer on earth, slayer of his brother.'

'And who is to be Abel?'

A sly grin replaced the sneer on Sylvanus' face.

'Why, have you not guessed? Brother Paul, of course.'

*

Sylvanus had selected Paul for Abel almost as quickly as he had settled on Wilfred for Cain. When he had suggested to the prior that he not only select the canons to play each part, but also instruct them in their preparations, he had thought he could ruin Wigod's idea with ineptness. So he had chosen the lazy and feckless Wilfred immediately. Later, he had seen the possibility of being more subtle in his undermining of Wigod's plans. Unwittingly, he had selected a person, in Wilfred, who suited Cain down to the ground. It became clear he should then oppose him as Abel with the most irritatingly pious canon in the form of the 'careful' brother. Paul was Wigod's greatest advocate, and had been rewarded for siding with him in his election as prior by being appointed the toller of the daily warning bells. Sylvanus was therefore Paul's natural enemy, and he sought any way he could to denigrate him. His direction of the pageant of 'The Story of Cain and Abel' would be an exercise in revenge.

As the weeks passed, preparations for the Easter play progressed slowly but surely. Because the weather was cold, the prior agreed for the rehearsals to take place in the warming room, the only chamber in the priory that had a fire other than the kitchen and the prior's own hall. It was a large, low-ceilinged room below the dormitory with vaulted arches curving overhead. On the day he was to begin with Paul and Wilfred, Sylvanus was first tutoring those who were to present 'The Deluge'. Progress had been slow because Brother Roger, the cellarer, was drunk. Sylvanus had been reluctant even to appoint the man as Noah, but the prior, finally poking his nose in Sylvanus' selection of characters despite his promise in the chapter house, had prevailed. One of the novices, a boy with a soft and feminine face, which caused him much embarrassment, was Noah's wife. In recompense for all the

13

ribbing he got about his appearance, he took to the shrewish part, as Prior Wigod had written it, with relish.

Wilfred walked into the warmth of the undercroft just as Noah was being chastised by his wife.

'No; I must go home, I must,
My tasks are numerous.'

Roger, stumbling over the words, replied,

'Woman, why do you thus?
To make us more mischief?'

The novice roared out his response:

'Noah, you might have told me of it!
Morning and evening you were out,
And always at home you let me sit,
Never to know what you were about.'

There was a rustle of parchment as Roger fumbled the sheet that held his words, losing the place momentarily. Sylvanus sighed, and poked a bony finger at the text. Roger hiccuped apologetically.

'Sorry, sorry. My lady, let me be excused for it.
It was God's will, without a doubt.'

The novice, whose name no one seemed able to remember, rushed over to Roger.

'What? You think that you're going just yet?
No, by my faith, you're getting a clout!'

He accompanied the words with an appropriate action, and Roger howled as the blow landed. Sylvanus grinned behind his hand.

'Very well. That is enough for today. I see Wilfred is here, and I must practise "Cain and Abel" next.'

Brother Roger glowered at the fresh-faced novice, and slouched back to his duties as cellarer. It was likely he would sup some more wine through his straw to deaden the blow that had caught him round his ear. The novice blushed, but Sylvanus exchanged an encouraging word with him and he left flushed with pleasure.

Paul entered, apologetic about his lateness, though none had thought him tardy. It was another trait of Paul's that irritated Wilfred no end. His constant regret for minuscule transgressions that no one else would have thought important was further proof of his earnest saintliness. He looked eagerly at Sylvanus.

'Shall we begin, Brother? Only, it will not be long before I must ring the bell for terce.'

Wilfred glowered at the remark, but Paul merely smiled beatifically in return. Sylvanus raised a hand to acknowledge Paul's reminder of his own importance.

'Of course, Brother Paul, we should not delay the passage of the priory routines by one mote of time, should we? Brother Alcuin, who is to play the part of the foolish and lazy Brewbarret – and how appropriate that is – is not free today. So we will concentrate on the quarrel between the two brothers. Where are your scripts?'

Wilfred and Paul each produced the sheet with his lines on it. It was noticeable that, after only a few rehearsals, Wilfred's was already tattered and creased. Paul's parchment was naturally as pristine as the day he had been given it.

Sylvanus guided them quickly through the first section of the short play in which the two brothers paid their tithes to

God. Cain did it with great reluctance, and his tithe burned badly as he offered it up. The prior had written this to reflect the situation in the real world where there was a shortage of wheat due to last year's crop failures in England. It had not affected the wealthy priory at Oseney, but Cain's worries would speak loudly to the peasants and landowners who would come to watch the Easter plays.

As the play progressed, Wilfred became as angry as the character he played. He spoke the lines to the sainted Abel in the form of Paul, with deep feeling.

'Oh, go and kiss the Devil's arse!
It is your fault it burns the worse.
I wish it all were in your throat,
Fire and sheaf and every sprout!'

Sylvanus could not help but encourage him in his anger, pointing at the horse's jawbone he had obtained.

'Very good, Wilfred. I have got Cain's weapon for you. Take it up.'

Paul spoke next, as Abel, giving his lines the very saintliness that drove both Wilfred and Sylvanus mad.

'God's will, I suppose it were,
That mine burned so clear.
If yours smoked, am I to blame?'

Wilfred grabbed the jawbone, and stood close to Paul, his face bright red.

'What? Yeah! And you'll pay for the same!
With this jawbone, as I thrive,
I'll let you no more stay alive!'

Wilfred swung the bony weapon, and in the spirit of the novice playing Mrs Noah before him, struck a heavy blow at Paul, who fell to the ground.

The prior, when informed by Sylvanus about Wilfred's intemperance, was very angry. He stared balefully at his former opponent for the office he now held, who stood contritely before him. He took a deep breath before speaking his mind.

'I cannot blame you for Wilfred's evil action, Sylvanus. It was probably most unexpected. And you tell me that Paul is not seriously hurt.'

'No indeed, Brother Wigod. He ducked just as Wilfred brought the blow down, and it hit him on the shoulder. He is a little sore, but his life is not imperilled.'

Prior Wigod grunted in relief that a more serious matter had not to be given judgement on. Heaven forbid that he would have to deal with a murder. He waved a dismissive hand at Sylvanus.

'You may go. I will decide what to do with Wilfred this afternoon. Let him stew in the meantime.'

It was only after compline, late in the day, that the prior gave Wilfred his penance in the presence of his victim. Paul, for his part, conveyed by the look in his eyes his saintly forgiveness for the sin of his attacker.

It was out of a lifelong habit that Wigod awoke just before midnight.

He sat up in the chair where he had spent an uneasy night, and awaited the bell calling him and fellow canons to matins and lauds. When it did not come as he expected, he at first imagined that somehow he had mistaken the hour. But after a short time, he became convinced that he was correct in his thinking and that somehow the careful Brother Paul had mistaken the time.

Wigod rose from the chair and left his private quarters. He descended the wooden staircase to the cloister, and crossed to the north-west corner where the door to the bell-tower stood ajar. With a sense of foreboding, he peered into the gloom of the tower, where hung the ropes that connected to the church bells. His worst fears were realised when he saw in the dark of one corner a huddled figure lying on the floor. He stepped towards it, his heart pounding with trepidation. He groaned when he saw it was Brother Paul and, on closer examination, that he was lying in a pool of blood. Suppressing an urge to vomit, Wigod realised that Paul's head had been stove in by a heavy object. Next to the body, covered in blood, lay the leering white jawbone of a horse.

The prior heard a gasp from behind him and, turning round, saw that other canons had risen as he had, and been curious about the lack of a peal of bells at the appropriate time. He controlled his own nausea, and waved a hand at the cellarer, who was at the front of the small group of black-robed men.

'Brother Roger, you will close this door and stand guard. Do not let anyone enter until I allow it. Thank goodness the bolt on the other door to the tower, inside the church, is rusted in place.' He approached the cellarer, who was for once sobered by what he had glimpsed, and whispered in his ear. 'This will be resolved internally by myself. No one else will know of the unfortunate circumstances of Paul's demise. Understand?'

Roger nodded and, allowing the prior to slip past him, pulled the door of Paul's temporary tomb firmly closed. Wigod looked severely at the other canons, and pointed to the entrance to the church in the opposite corner of the cloister.

'You will all carry on as normal. Brother William, you will officiate for me.'

The canons turned to obey, but the prior had a word for two of them.

'Sylvanus, Wilfred, you will come with me.'

The two designated canons cast an uneasy glance at each other, and followed the prior towards the chapter house. Once there, Wigod slumped on his elevated seat, his head hung low, while the two canons hovered hesitantly before him. The silence was oppressive, until the comforting sound of the rest of the priory was heard from the church as they began matins. The chant seemed to calm the prior, who raised his head, having come to a decision. He was sure he knew who had murdered Paul, and resolved to deal with the matter in his own way. For the good of the priory. No one else but he knew that his Order had intimated that Oseney was soon to be declared an abbey. Nothing was going to stand in the way of that coming to pass. Not even a murder. He looked hard at Sylvanus and Wilfred. The older man returned his stare brazenly, but the younger looked fearful of what Wigod was about to say. Finally the prior spoke, mustering as much authority as he could.

'I will not allow this ... incident to disrupt the good running of this priory, nor will I let it prevent *The Play of Adam* going ahead on Easter Day.'

He saw that Sylvanus was about to protest, and raised his hand to stop him.

'"The Story of Cain and Abel" will have to be withdrawn, of course, but the rest will go on as if nothing has happened.'

Sylvanus at last managed to get his protest out. 'How can I go ahead directing the canons when one of our number has been murdered?'

The prior smiled chillingly. 'You won't need to. I will take charge of the play. And nothing will be said of murder ever again. Brother Paul died in an unfortunate accident.' His harsh gaze told both canons that this was the way it would be.

'And what of me?' Sylvanus' question was filled with righteous anger.

'You will prepare yourself for a journey. A long journey,' the prior replied.

'To where?'

'There is a solitary cell on an island on Leven Sands close by Low Furness, in the north-west of England. You will spend the rest of your life there pondering on the great sin of murder.'

Sylvanus' face went ashen, but he said not a word on his defence. So the triumphant prior, now convinced of his own rightness, continued his exposition.

'You see, I could tell from the murder weapon that it had to be you or Wilfred who had killed Paul. Only you two, apart from myself, who suggested using a real jawbone, knew of the implement to be used in the play. Only you two harboured resentment at Paul's – shall we say – zealous nature.'

Wigod showed with his own careful selection of words that he was aware how irritating Paul could be. The poor dead fellow had come close to irritating him more than once. But he had not harboured a desire to murder him, as Sylvanus obviously had. His old adversary found some words at last.

'And so, when Paul was murdered, you found it convenient to place the blame on me, who has sought to check your excesses all these years. You could not even consider the possibility that it was Wilfred.'

The young canon in question blurted out a denial, but the prior was unmoved.

'It could not have been Wilfred. I know that for sure. Because my punishment for him hitting Paul in your rehearsal was for him to prostrate himself before the altar all night until the matins bell rang. I watched as he lay face down, his arms forming the cross. He could not have got into the tower from the church because the door bolt that side is rusted in place. Nor could he have come out through the door into the cloister without me seeing him. To make sure he kept to my punishment, I sat up all night in my chamber, from where I can see into the north-east corner of the cloister. Unfortunately, I could not see the part of the cloister directly below me. So I did not see you, Sylvanus, creeping along to the bell-tower in order to kill Paul before midnight.'

'That is that, then.'

Sylvanus was seemingly resigned to his fate. He glanced at Wilfred, who returned his look with one of simple innocence. Turning on his heels he left the chapter house in order to pack his few belongings.

The prior gazed sternly at Wilfred.

'You, brother, must continue to expiate your sins. As it will be an onerous task for your lazy bones, I am appointing you as the bell-ringer in Paul's place. I hope it will prove to be a burden to you.'

Wilfred bowed his head, but found it hard to suppress a grin. He hurried from the prior's presence to begin his new task.

Wigod walked to the outer gate of Oseney Priory to observe a humbled Sylvanus already crossing the water meadow towards Oxford, and his long journey to his exile in the north. Something about Wilfred's grin gave him a cold feeling in his chest, and he returned to the priory church to communicate quietly with God. But first, he walked down the nave to the bell-tower door, which had long been rusted shut. He wiped his hand over the rusty bolt, and it came away with a greasy smear on it. He pulled on the bolt, and it slid easily. The coldness in his chest became a fist squeezing his heart as he thought of Wilfred's grin. He had chosen the wrong man as the murderer in his desire to be rid of Sylvanus. And his old enemy had finally triumphed, knowing that Wigod would be forever mortified by his banishment of an innocent man. But Wigod knew there was nothing to be done now – he had made his decision – and to go back on it would show weakness.

Instead of entering into a colloquy with God, he rushed back to his quarters, and got out his fair copy of *The Play of Adam*. Picking up his quill, and dipping it in ink, he added two lines to the angel's words at the end of 'The Story of Cain and Abel' by way of a warning to others.

Beware the sins of envy and vainglory,
Else foul murder ends your story.

ACT ONE

I

Oseney Abbey, Oxford, September 1199

It was a pretty day, although a nip in the air and the profusion of blackberries in the hedgerows told Canon Wilfred that a hard winter was coming. He settled more comfortably on the camomile bench and turned his face to the sun, breathing in deeply of the sweet scent of herbs, freshly cut corn and scythed grass. He sighed his contentment.

Life had been so much nicer once Prior Wigod had died. The old tyrant had kept Wilfred as 'careful brother' for the best part of fourteen years, a miserable existence for a man who liked his bed – getting up in the middle of the night to call the others to prayer was an onerous, thankless task, and Wilfred had hated it. Then Wigod had died suddenly in his sleep. At least, that was what had appeared to have happened.

That had been more than thirty years ago, and since then Wilfred had been careful not to earn the enmity of another Head of House. The current one was Hugh, a malleable, shy man, who had been only too pleased to accept fatherly advice from one of the foundation's oldest members. Indeed, Hugh considered Wilfred a friend, one of the advantages of which was that Wilfred felt he had the right to lounge in the sun of an afternoon. The other canons resented Wilfred's indolence, but he did not care. Surely, he had earned a little luxury in his evening years, especially after the suffering he had endured under the despotic Wigod.

Of course, Wigod had been a gentler, kinder man before Sylvanus – the canon he had exiled to Leven Sands in an act of poor judgement – had been killed by robbers on his journey north. Wigod had told everyone that he blamed himself for the death, but Wilfred knew it was a lie. Wigod held *him* responsible, which was unfair. It was not *he* who had ordered Sylvanus away. Wigod's sour humour had not even improved when Oseney had been elevated from priory to abbey, with all the privileges that went with a more exalted status.

But three decades was a long time, and no one remembered Wigod now ...

Wilfred closed his eyes and was just slipping into a pleasant doze when footsteps crunched on the path. It was Robert, the young canon Hugh had asked him to mind. Wilfred disliked the task for two reasons: firstly, it was unwelcome work for an indolent man, and secondly, Robert was shockingly impudent. To teach him his place, Wilfred used him like a servant, compelling him to bring wine and treats at specific times in the day – and as Robert considered himself destined for great things, it was proving to be a sore trial for him.

'Two groups of visitors have just arrived,' Robert reported excitedly as he handed his master a cup of wine. 'A bishop elect from the See of St Davids and his retinue; and envoys from the Archbishop of Canterbury.'

'Important men,' mused Wilfred. 'What do they want?'

'Nothing, other than a bed for the night.' Robert smirked. 'They are old enemies, and started quarrelling the moment they set eyes on each other.'

'Then I know how we shall keep them apart,' said Wilfred, pleased. 'With *The Play of Adam*. It is always popular with guests, and we have honed it to perfection over the last thirty years. Prior Wigod took against drama after ... certain events, but I reinstated it after he died, and everyone loves our performances.'

'Yes,' said Robert without enthusiasm. He had been listening to Wilfred's bragging conceit about this particular drama for longer than he could remember, and was heartily sick of it – especially as the old man could never be persuaded to reveal what the 'certain events' entailed. 'I suppose you will play God, as usual?'

Wilfred glanced at him sharply. 'Of course. Why?'

'Because *I* should like to do it, for once. I am tired of being the serpent.'

Wilfred fixed him with an icy glare. 'You will do as you are told, and be grateful you have a role at all. Now go and tell Abbot Hugh my suggestion.'

'Will you include the bit about Cain and Abel this time?' asked Robert chirpily, ignoring the order. 'You always leave it out, but our brethren are bored to tears with the rest of the play after so many years, and a new section may revive their interest.'

'How dare you!' cried Wilfred, outraged. 'They love *The Play of Adam*. Now go and do as you are told before I box your ears.'

Full of resentment, Robert slouched away, while Wilfred struggled to bring his irritation under control. Was the lad right? A number of canons *had* asked recently if he knew any other dramas, and their attendance was not what it had been. But that was too bad. Finding another one would mean work, and that was something Wilfred was unwilling to contemplate.

Still angry, he went to round up his actors.

*

As usual, *The Play of Adam* was scheduled to be performed after the office of nones, in the afternoon when the brethren had free time. Wilfred scowled when he saw how few of them were present. How could they prefer reading in their cells to his production? What was wrong with them?

The visitors were there, though, three standing in one group and four in another. Judging by the way they were glaring at each other, Robert had been right to say they were enemies. Abbot Hugh was between them, his face pale and strained: clearly, keeping them from each other's throats was transpiring to be a trial.

Wilfred turned as someone came to stand next to him. It was Robert who, without being invited, began to tell him which visitors were which. Usually, Wilfred would have berated him for his audacity, but that day he was interested to hear what the boy had learned.

'The tall, proud man is Gerald de Barri, Bishop Elect of St Davids. His companions are Pontius and Foliot, both canons from his cathedral, which voted unanimously to have him as their prelate. Unfortunately for Gerald, the Archbishop of Canterbury does not want him, and refuses to issue the necessary charters.'

Wilfred studied the trio. Gerald was a handsome man with thick grey hair and snapping black eyes; he was certainly elegant and haughty enough to be a bishop. His fellow priests were less imposing: Pontius had sharp, ratty features and wispy fair hair; Foliot was small and dark, but with a kind face and gentle eyes.

'And the others?' asked Wilfred, turning his attention to the four men on Hugh's left.

'Prior Dunstan from our sister house in Canterbury, and his secretary, Hurso. And the two knights who guard them are Roger Norrys and Robert Luci. Luci is the one who looks like a scholar, while the big, loutish brute is Norrys.'

The moment Wilfred saw Dunstan, he was put in mind of a goat. The Prior had a long, thin, white beard, and pale, widely spaced eyes. By contrast, Secretary Hurso possessed a comb of red hair and beady eyes that were redolent of a chicken.

The knights were Hospitallers, recognisable by their black surcoats with white crosses. Luci was cleaner than most warriors, with neatly cut hair and an air of quiet contemplation. Norrys, on the other hand, looked like most of the louts who had forged a bloody trail to the Holy Land a decade earlier: large, brutal, ruthless and stupid.

Time was passing, so Wilfred nodded that the play was to begin. An expectant hush fell over the little audience as the first actor stepped forward and began to tell the story of the Creation. Wilfred was gratified to see the visitors nodding approvingly. He felt vindicated. Guests always liked *The Play of Adam*, even if his brethren were uncouth ingrates. Indeed, he had sold many copies to admiring audiences over the years, keeping the modest profits for himself, of course. The vellum original, beautifully and painstakingly scribed by Wigod, had been purchased by no less a person than the Dean of Ely Cathedral, and put in the library there for posterity.

As usual, the play passed off without a hitch, and when it was over, Wilfred repaired to the kitchen for a cup of congratulatory wine, leaving his actors to dismantle the stage and store away the costumes and props. He had not been relaxing for long when Robert arrived.

'Our visitors are arguing again,' he reported gleefully. 'Bishop Gerald said the Serpent reminded him of Prior Dunstan, and Prior Dunstan took offence. They are yelling loudly enough to be heard in Oxford!'

'Why such vitriol?' asked Wilfred curiously. 'Such spats are hardly seemly.'

'Because Dunstan is the Archbishop of Canterbury's envoy, and he is travelling *west* to tell St Davids that they cannot have Gerald as their prelate. Meanwhile, Gerald is travelling *east* to tell the archbishop to mind his own business. It is the second journey for both of them, and they met on the first one, too. Their hatred is months old.'

'Is that why Dunstan has two knights with him?' asked Wilfred. 'Lest St Davids objects to being told what to do?'

Robert nodded, his eyes gleaming, and Wilfred looked away in distaste. The lad really was disagreeably malevolent.

'Gerald is popular in Wales, so Dunstan's task will not be easy,' Robert said. 'He contrived to meet Gerald here, hoping to convince him to drop his claim and save him a journey, but Gerald refuses. Dunstan is furious, because he did not enjoy his first foray into Wales, and he thinks his second will be even more unpleasant.'

Abbot Hugh arrived at that point to congratulate his friend on the excellence of the performance. The guests, he said, had thoroughly enjoyed it – and so had he, because it had given him a respite from acting as peacemaker.

'Do they really dislike each other so much?' asked Wilfred, a little stiffly after the Abbot's backhanded compliment.

'I am sure they would kill each other, given the chance. For clerics, they are uncommonly vicious. Indeed, Dunstan's servant is ill, and claims that Gerald has poisoned him.'

'And has he?' asked Wilfred uneasily.

'No, the fellow is malingering because he does not want to go to Wales. It is unfortunate, because Dunstan has asked us for a novice to replace him.'

'Not a novice,' said Wilfred immediately. 'Send Robert. I am sure he would love to go.'

'*I* cannot leave Oseney!' cried Robert, horrified. 'I am cultivating friendships and contacts that will stand me in good stead for when I am abbot. A journey would ruin—'

'A journey might teach you some humility,' interrupted Hugh sharply, shocked to learn that his post was coveted by such youthful eyes. 'Wilfred is right to suggest you go.'

Wilfred allowed himself a small smile of satisfaction as the lad stamped away. That would teach him to make disparaging remarks about *The Play of Adam*!

That evening, Abbot Hugh was obliged to entertain the guests in his private hall, although he confessed his reluctance to do so to Wilfred. With the air of a martyr, Wilfred offered to help, waving away Hugh's relieved gratitude. The truth was that Wilfred did not mind at all: fine wine and expensive sweetmeats would be on offer, which would be a lot nicer than a crust in the refectory and compline in the church.

Unfortunately, the guests were disagreeable company, and although Wilfred was not usually averse to being entertained by spats, even he found the constant sparring tedious. Moreover, Robert was there on the grounds that he was now a member of Dunstan's party. The boy's eyes shone with malicious glee as the arguments swayed back and forth.

'You will never be bishop, Gerald,' said Dunstan, for at least the fourth time. His pale goat-eyes were hard. 'So you may as well save yourself a journey and go home to Wales. You are Archdeacon of Brecon, are you not? Why not be content with that?'

'Because I was born to be Bishop of St Davids,' replied

Gerald coldly. 'My father is Norman, but my mother hails from Welsh stock, so my dual heritage will unite an uneasy nation. Moreover, I am familiar with Court, I have three decades of experience in the Church, and I am a scholar of some repute. There is no man better qualified than me.'

'None more modest, either,' murmured Wilfred to himself. Unfortunately, wine made him speak more loudly than he had intended, and the three Welsh priests glowered at him when Dunstan roared with spiteful laughter. Wilfred gulped when he saw he had made enemies of the St Davids men, and was glad they would be leaving in the morning.

'You tried to be bishop twenty years ago, Gerald,' said Dunstan when he had his mirth under control, 'and you were rejected then, too. You should have learned that you are not wanted – not by the Crown, not by Canterbury and not by Rome. You are even less popular with our new King than you were with his father, and should abandon your claims while you can. Only a fool irritates John.'

'I am not afraid of John,' said Gerald contemptuously. 'And I despise anyone who is.'

'Yet sometimes it is wise to be wary,' said kind-eyed Foliot quietly. 'John is not a man to cross, because he bears grudges.'

'I will not sit at a table where treason is spoken,' said Norrys the Hospitaller, standing abruptly. His loutish face was flushed with anger. 'Calling the King vengeful is—'

'Prior Dunstan tells me you were once Constable of Carmarthen, Norrys,' interrupted Abbot Hugh, diplomatically changing the subject while the scholarly Luci grabbed Norrys's arm and tugged him back down. 'That must have been pleasant.'

'It was pleasant,' agreed Norrys, while his scowl suggested

this was not a topic that pleased him either. 'But I was ousted in favour of Symon Cole, a dull-witted youth who had distinguished himself in battle with acts of reckless bravado.'

'It was not just his courage that impressed King Henry,' said Luci quietly. 'He married a Welsh princess, who provided an alliance with powerful native rulers.'

'But the old King is dead,' said Norrys sullenly. 'And the new one has intimated that he would like Cole out of Carmarthen and me in his place. *He* does not care who is related to whom in Wales.'

'That particular Welsh princess is my cousin,' said Gerald icily. 'On my mother's side. So Cole is *my* kin, too. Did I hear you call him a dull-witted youth?'

'He was a dull-witted youth when he took over Carmarthen,' Norrys smirked, and his expression became challenging. 'Now he is a dull-witted man.'

'I take exception to—' began Gerald angrily.

'Enough, please!' cried the abbot. In desperation, he turned to Wilfred. 'Perhaps you will tell our guests about *The Play of Adam*. I am sure they will be interested.'

'Well,' began Wilfred, pleased to be the centre of attention. 'It was—'

'There is a section about Cain and Abel,' interrupted Robert eagerly. 'But it has never been performed at Oseney. It is a pity, because I would make an excellent Cain.'

Wilfred glared at him, glad he had persuaded Hugh to send the boy away. With any luck, he would never return.

'I have a gift for you, Robert,' he said, forcing himself to smile. 'To remember me by when you trudge the long and dangerous road west.'

Robert snatched the proffered package in delight, but his happy expression faded when he saw what he had been given. 'A copy of *The Play of Adam*,' he said flatly. 'How lovely.'

It was the one Wilfred had forced him to make himself, and by giving it back to him, Wilfred was effectively saying that he did not value his work. Abbot Hugh took it from him.

'I see it includes the section about Cain and Abel,' he mused. 'It looks innocuous enough. Why do you always omit it, Wilfred?'

'Because it is dull,' replied Wilfred shortly. 'And I decided long ago that it was not worth an audience's time, although we have rehearsed it on occasion.'

'You have?' pounced Hugh with obvious relief. 'Good! Then summon your actors and put it on for us now. And when it is finished, it should be time for bed.'

'I would rather not,' said Wilfred shortly. 'There is some suggestion that this particular section may bring bad luck, and we—'

'Bad luck?' interrupted Gerald in lofty distaste. 'I would remind you that we are men of God – we put our trust in the Lord, not in heathenish superstition.'

Wilfred opened his mouth to object, but a spitefully glee-ful Robert was already moving tables while the abbot was hastily assuring the company that heresy had no place in Oseney. Wilfred grimaced when he saw he was to have no choice, and itched to wring Robert's neck.

'May I play God?' asked Prior Dunstan, once the preparations were complete. 'I do not know the words, of course, but I can read them, and I have always wanted to act.'

'No,' said Wilfred, more curtly than he had intended. 'That role is mine.'

Dunstan said nothing, but Wilfred was taken aback by the venomous glare he received. Clearly furious, the prior spun round and marched away.

'You should not have annoyed him,' said Secretary Hurso,

watching him go. 'He may look harmless, but he is clever and determined, and will make for a dangerous enemy. Gerald should watch himself, too.'

There was no time to ponder the remarks, because the abbot was signalling to tell him to start. Wilfred shoved his first player onto the makeshift stage, and 'The Story of Cain and Abel' began.

'You are pale,' whispered Robert, appearing at Wilfred's side and making him jump. He held a jug of wine. 'Drink this. It will calm your nerves.'

'My nerves are perfectly calm,' snapped Wilfred, but it was a lie, because his heart thumped and his hands were sweaty. He could not stop himself from thinking about what had happened when this particular section had last been performed at Oseney. It was all very well for Gerald to sniff his disdain at the concept of luck, but Wilfred was less willing to dismiss things he could not begin to understand.

He drank two cups of Robert's claret, but it only served to make him more agitated than ever, and he kept seeing the face of a long-dead canon named Paul in his mind's eye – surprisingly vividly, given that Paul had been in his grave for almost half a century. Wilfred listened to the familiar words, and heartily wished the abbot had found another way to distract his querulous guests.

Beware the sins of envy and vainglory,
Else foul murder ends your story.

For some unaccountable reason, the final couplet struck a cold fear into Wilfred. Was it guilt, gnawing at him in a way that it had never done before? He shook himself impatiently. It was late, he was tired, and he had drunk too much. He would feel better in the morning.

But the room tipped, and he stumbled to his knees. What was happening? He grabbed the table for support, upsetting the wine jug as he did so. He felt terrible – there was a burning pain in his innards and he was struggling to breathe. Was he having a seizure? Or was it divine vengeance for his role in the untimely deaths of Paul, Sylvanus, Wigod and several others who had had the temerity to stand between him and his desire for an easy life?

Then another thought occurred to him, one that made his blood run cold. Had he been poisoned? Prior Dunstan's servant claimed *he* had – by the priests from Wales – and Wilfred was sure the trio had not forgotten his incautious remark about modesty. Or had Dunstan made an end of him because he had wanted to be God? Or was this Robert's parting gift to a master he disliked? Yet surely no one would kill for such petty reasons?

'A seizure,' declared Hugh sadly, when Wilfred had stopped shuddering and lay still. 'He was past three score years and ten, so had reached his allotted time.'

But someone among the onlookers knew different.

II

Carmarthen, December 1199

Gwenllian awoke to a world transformed. There had been a few flurries of snow the previous day, but nothing to prepare her for the fall that had taken place during the night. She opened the window shutters to a blanket of pure white, broken only by the icy black snake of the River Towy meandering towards the sea.

She leaned her elbows on the sill and gazed out at the

town that had been her home for the past thirteen years. She had hated it at first, frightened by its uneasy mix of Welsh, Norman and English residents, while the castle had been an unsavoury conglomeration of ugly palisades, muddy ditches and grubby tents. It was certainly no place for a Welsh princess, who had been raised in an atmosphere of cultured gentility, surrounded by poets and men of learning.

She had not been particularly enamoured of her new husband, either. Her father, Lord Rhys, had arranged the match because it had been politically expedient to ally himself to one of the King's favourite knights, and Gwenllian had been horrified to find herself with a spouse whose mind was considerably less sharp than her own. But she had gradually grown to love Sir Symon Cole, and to love Carmarthen, with its bustling port, hectic market and prettily winding streets.

The castle was improving as well, now that Cole was rebuilding parts of it in stone. He had already raised a fine hall with comfortable living quarters for his household and guests, while his soldiers were housed in dry, clean wooden barracks. He was currently working on the bailey walls, although a spate of silly mishaps meant the project was taking longer than he thought it should.

Yet despite his grumbles, the walls were still ahead of schedule, mostly because he was content to let Gwenllian order supplies and haggle for the best prices, while he oversaw the physical side of the operation. He had no skill at administration, and it was widely thought that he would not have remained constable for as long as he had without his wife's talent for organisation.

It was not long after dawn, and she could hear the usual sounds of early morning – the clank of the winch on the well as water was raised for cooking and cleaning, the chatter of servants laying fires and sweeping floors, and the shrill crow of cockerels. The sharp scent of burning wood was carried on the wind, along with the richer aroma of baking bread.

She could see the builders at the curtain wall already, despite the bitter weather. Cole was there too, shovelling snow off a pile of stones. She smiled. Not many constables would deign to wield a spade themselves, but the labourers liked the fact that Cole was willing to toil by their side. Of course, there was also the fact that he enjoyed it, being a large, strong man who excelled at physical activities.

She watched the mason – a sullen, avaricious man named Cethynoc – climb the wall and walk along the top, kicking off snow as he went. Clearly, he was going to decide if work would have to stop, or if it could continue. Suddenly, there was a yell and the workmen scattered in alarm. Something had fallen off the top of the wall. Gwenllian's stomach lurched in horror – she could not see Cole among the milling labourers!

She turned and raced out of the bedchamber, almost falling in her haste to reach the bailey. Iefan, Cole's faithful sergeant, was also running there, but he stopped and took her arm when he saw her. Gwenllian knew why: her second child would be born in May, and the entire castle had suddenly become solicitous, knowing exactly who was responsible for their regular pay, clean barracks and decent food.

Heart pounding, she approached the wall, then closed her eyes in relief when she saw Cole inspecting a piece of rope. His naturally cheerful face was sombre as he grabbed her hand and pulled her to one side so the workmen would not hear what he was saying.

'You did not believe me when I told you someone was sabotaging our work.' He held out the rope. 'Do you believe me now? This has been deliberately cut, so that a bucket full of rubble would drop from the top of the wall.'

Gwenllian examined it, then shook her head. 'It has frayed, Symon. If it had been cut, the edges would be sharp and . . .'

She faltered into silence when he scraped his dagger back and forth on another part of the rope, eventually producing a break that was identical to the one in her hand. She stared at it, but still could not bring herself to believe what he was suggesting.

'It was an accident,' she insisted. 'Who would interfere with the castle walls? When they are finished, they will benefit everyone – the entire town will be able to take refuge here in times of trouble. There cannot be a saboteur.'

'This is the fifth "accident" in two weeks. The others have been more nuisance than danger – spoiled mortar, lost nails, loosened knots on the scaffolding – but this one might have killed someone. I need to catch the culprit before he claims a life.'

'No,' said Gwenllian firmly. 'It is just a spate of unfortunate coincidences. No one can have anything against your walls. Indeed, they are popular because they are providing employment for the poor at a time when other work is scarce.'

'A stone castle is a symbol of Norman domination,' Cole pointed out, 'and some people are afraid that it might be used for subjugation as well as defence.'

'They know you would never use it for such a purpose,' objected Gwenllian.

'Perhaps, but King John itches to dismiss me and appoint someone else. It is only a matter of time before he finds a way to do it. And people remember my predecessor.'

'Roger Norrys – a vicious, mean-spirited tyrant,' recalled Gwenllian. 'Thank God my father did not force me to marry *him*, or I would have been hanged for murder years ago. Did that falling basket hit you? You are limping.'

'No, the lace on my boot is broken. I will send it to William the corviser to be repaired.'

'Not him,' said Gwenllian quickly. 'He has disliked you ever since you fined him for cheating his customers. I will find another shoemaker. And before you suggest it, William is not your saboteur – he is more likely to wound with words than actions.'

'I will catch the culprit, Gwen,' said Cole with quiet determination. 'I must. None of my labourers will be safe until I do.'

Gwenllian did not bother to argue with him.

As they walked across the bailey, they were intercepted by the visitors who had arrived the previous afternoon. Gwenllian was kin to Gerald de Barri, a fact he had been quick to mention when requesting hospitality. He and his two companions had been to Canterbury, and were travelling home to St Davids. Carmarthen was in St Davids See, but the three priests still had several more days of travel before they reached their cathedral in the far west of the country.

'I am afraid we shall have to impose on you for a while longer,' said Gerald with an apologetic smile. 'All the roads are closed by snow.'

'Are they?' Cole was openly dismayed. He did not enjoy the company of clerics, because they tended to know nothing about horses and warfare, two topics he considered important in a man. The St Davids priests were no exception, and one – Foliot – had compounded the deficiency by admitting to falling off his pony. Cole had been aghast that anyone should have lost his seat on so docile an animal.

Gwenllian felt differently, though. Gerald was witty and amusing, and she had been fascinated by his tales of journeys around Wales. She liked small, dark Foliot, too, with his kindly eyes and gentle manners. Pontius was sharper and more outspoken.

Gerald sighed. 'We have been away for almost four months now, and we are eager to be home. This situation does not please us, I assure you.'

'Nor me,' said Cole bluntly. 'How long do you think it will be before you can leave?'

'A few days,' replied Foliot quickly, when Gerald's eyebrows shot up at the ungracious question. 'No more, God willing.'

'Let us hope not,' said Pontius slyly. 'Your sergeant claims there has been a spate of mishaps here, and *we* do not want to be crushed under plummeting baskets.'

'Then we shall not put you to work on the castle walls,' said Gwenllian, smiling at him. 'Because that is where the accidents have occurred.'

Foliot winced at the notion, putting his hand to the shoulder that had been bruised by his tumble from the horse. 'I shall use the opportunity to rest.'

'So shall I,' said Pontius. 'I have a bad back – too much time in the saddle.'

Cole regarded him wonderingly. 'Is there any such thing?'

Gerald laughed, although Cole had not meant to be amusing. 'It is good to be back in my own See. I was unimpressed with Canterbury – the archbishop is as devious as his master the King. Incidentally, when I am enthroned as bishop, I shall be elevating St Davids to an archbishopric. I do not want to be under Canterbury's sway.'

Cole looked alarmed. He had scant respect for John, whom he considered weak, vacillating and untrustworthy, but as a royally appointed official he was not in the habit of engaging in seditious discussions with strangers. Gwenllian was interested in something that would affect all of Wales, though.

'An archbishopric would make this See the equal of Canterbury and York,' she said.

'Yes,' nodded Gerald. 'And quite rightly so. Why should we be under the authority of Canterbury, a place that knows nothing of us or our customs? And I shall certainly bring it about, because the Pope is a great admirer of mine, and can refuse me nothing. Well, I did recruit hundreds of warriors for his crusade. Did you go, Cole?'

'Yes, I fought in several battles, including the—'

'You are welcome to stay for as long as you like,' interrupted Gwenllian quickly, before Cole could regale them with details. His war stories were not for the delicate ears of priests. 'It will be our pleasure to entertain you.'

'Entertain us,' echoed Pontius, looking around with a smirk. 'That promises to be interesting. How will you do it?'

'We shall go hunting, if the snow is not too thick,' replied Cole pleasantly. 'We have plenty of wild boar, and stags too. Or there is hawking. It is too cold for fishing, but—'

'How about an activity that does *not* involve killing something?' asked Pontius archly.

'My wife can take you shopping,' retorted Cole, unimpressed by the question. 'Or teach you how to embroider a—'

'We shall have some music,' said Gwenllian before he could insult them further. 'Osbert, our archdeacon, plays the crwth, and Symon will sing.'

'Battle songs?' asked Gerald, humour glinting in his black eyes.

'Welsh ballads,' corrected Gwenllian with pride. 'I taught him myself.'

'We shall look forward to it,' said Foliot graciously, although Pontius looked dubious.

'And *I* may honour *you* by reading excerpts from one of my books,' said Gerald. 'I did it in Oxford last autumn, and it was very well received. It took three days, and my audience was spellbound the entire time.'

'You read aloud for *three days*?' Cole was horrified, evidently afraid the same might be attempted in Carmarthen. 'Without stopping?'

'Well, obviously, we went away to sleep,' said Gerald. 'But we started afresh the following dawn. Everyone said they were much edified.'

'God's teeth!' breathed Cole. To Gwenllian's relief, he was prevented from saying more by tripping over his broken lace.

'You should mend that before you hurt yourself,' advised Gerald. 'Do you have a spare to give him, Foliot? Or a piece of twine?'

'I am afraid not,' replied the priest. 'I used it to mend my reins after the ambush.'

'Ambush?' asked Cole immediately. 'Where? Not near here?'

'Once in Brecon and once outside Trecastle,' replied Gerald. 'It was how Foliot came to bruise his shoulder. His pony reared and he slipped off. Do not worry, though: both were well outside your jurisdiction, so we shall not blame you for them.'

Gwenllian laughed at Cole's obvious dismay as their guests walked away, and assured him that she would look after them. He nodded relieved thanks, and she saw he had been worried that playing host would keep him from his walls.

41

'What did Cethynoc say when he made his inspection?'
she asked.

'That we cannot build as long as the weather stays so cold,
but there are other tasks that can be managed – preparing
the rubble infill, cutting stones, moving supplies. The men
are keen to continue.'

Gwenllian was sure they were: they would not be paid for
idle days, and winter was a bad time to be without money.
She followed Cole into the hall, where their baby son toddled
towards them. Meurig squealed his delight when Cole
scooped him up and tossed him high into the air, but
Gwenllian closed her eyes in maternal horror: did he have to
be so rough?

'A person *is* responsible for these mishaps,' Cole said after
a while, handing Meurig to his nurse, and returning to the
subject that so troubled him. 'Five incidents is too many for
coincidence.'

Gwenllian sighed. 'Very well, let us assume you are right.
Who are your suspects?'

He was silent for a long time before replying. 'I do not
have any. Who are yours? You are the one good at solving
mysteries.'

'Only if there is a mystery to solve.'

'There is, Gwen, and I was hoping you would help me
catch the villain.' He grimaced resentfully. 'But now Gerald
and his priests will take up all your time, I suppose I shall
have to unmask him by myself.'

They turned as Sergeant Iefan approached with two other
men. They were Osbert, Archdeacon of Carmarthen, and
a grizzled knight named Sir Robert Burchill. Osbert had a
shiny bald head and was famous for never wearing a hat,
even in the most inclement of weather. Burchill was much
older than Cole, and believed that his age and experience

gave him the right to be condescending. Gwenllian found him irksome and hypercritical.

'Five visitors arrived at my house last night,' Osbert began. 'It was a tight squeeze, but we managed. However, now the snows keep them here, I must make other arrangements – there is simply not enough room for them in my home. Will you take them? They are important men – three Austin canons and two knights. I cannot send them to an inn.'

'If they are Austins, they can stay at the priory,' said Cole.

'Apparently, they did that on their outward journey, and quarrelled so bitterly that the brothers say they are no longer welcome. They are envoys from Canterbury, and have been in St Davids, telling the Cathedral Chapter that it cannot have the prelate it elected, but must have a fellow of the archbishop's choosing instead.'

'Then I cannot help you,' said Cole apologetically. 'Your envoys will quarrel with Gerald, and we shall know no peace. They will have to stay in an inn.'

'You cannot slight them, lad,' warned Burchill. 'Prior Dunstan has the ear of the King.'

'So?' shrugged Cole. 'I do not care whether—'

'John longs for an excuse to oust you,' interrupted Burchill sharply. 'Your marriage gives you powerful allies, so he cannot dismiss you without good reason. However, offending ecclesiastical envoys will certainly give him the pretext he needs.'

Gwenllian had been about to say the same thing, and was irritated that Burchill should have pre-empted her. Cole sighed.

'John will have his way eventually, so perhaps we should go to live on my manor in Normandy – resign before he dismisses me.'

'But I like it here,' objected Gwenllian, dismayed. 'Carmarthen is my home.'

'I like it too, but I am a soldier, not a diplomat, and I do not know how to deal with John. Or with warring clerics, for that matter. And then there is the saboteur . . .'

'There is no saboteur, Sir Symon,' said Iefan, a little irritably, and Gwenllian saw she was not the only one who had tried to disabuse the constable of this particular notion. 'We have just suffered a series of minor mishaps.'

'I will find the culprit – *if* there is one to be found,' said Gwenllian soothingly. 'And I will keep the peace between Gerald and the archbishop's envoys, too. You can work on the walls. They will impress John and may encourage him to keep you.'

'Rather you than me, my lady,' said Archdeacon Osbert wryly. 'Gerald and Dunstan met in Oxford three months ago, and there were ugly scenes, by all accounts. It will not be easy to keep them from each other's throats.'

'Osbert has not told you the worst news yet, Symon,' said Burchill, a little smugly. 'Dunstan has two Knights Hospitaller to protect him, and one is Roger Norrys.'

Cole smiled with genuine pleasure. 'Norrys? It must be more than a decade since we last met. It will be good to see him again.'

'Unfortunately he does not feel the same way about you,' warned Osbert. 'Last night he talked of nothing but how you snatched Carmarthen from him by sly means.'

'But I did not ask to be constable,' objected Cole, stung. 'Indeed, I begged King Henry to let me remain in his household guard, but he would not listen. There was nothing sly about my appointment – not on my part, at least.'

'I am sure of it, but Norrys is bitter and resentful anyway,' said Osbert. 'The first thing he did when he arrived last night was seek out his old cronies – William the corviser and Tancard the brewer—'

'Troublemakers,' said Gwenllian in disgust. 'They *would* be friends!'

'They drank vast quantities of ale and sat muttering together,' said Osbert. 'I tried to draw them into gentler conversation, and so did Prior Dunstan, but to no avail.'

'You will have to watch Norrys, lad,' said Burchill. 'Or he may cause problems.'

'I shall win him round,' said Cole, ever the optimist. 'Fetch these envoys now, Osbert. Gerald is in the chapel, and we might be able to install them without him noticing.'

'He will notice eventually,' said Burchill, startled. 'Our castle is not that big!'

'Do not worry.' Cole gave a happy smile. 'Gwen will keep them from sparring.'

It was not long before a commotion by the gate heralded the arrival of the Canterbury men. Iefan and Burchill glanced uneasily towards the chapel, but Gwenllian had ordered the chaplain to conduct a lengthy Mass, which she hoped would keep them busy while the newcomers settled. First in was Sir Roger Norrys, with his brother Hospitaller at his heels.

It had been thirteen years since Norrys had stormed out of Carmarthen after receiving the news that he had been replaced by a man barely half his age. Gwenllian watched him warily. He was thicker around the middle, and had lost a lot of hair, but he was still an imposing figure in his fine black surcoat. She did not like the way he stalked into the bailey and looked around appraisingly.

'I hope he does not set us alight,' she whispered to Cole, aware that the servants had recognised Norrys and many were looking fearful – they remembered his bullying ways. 'Most of our buildings are wood.'

'Why would he do that?' asked Cole, startled by the remark.

Never thinking ill of anyone was another of Cole's endearing but ill-advised habits, and Gwenllian winced when he strode forward to greet the older knight like a long-lost friend.

'It is a pleasure to welcome you back,' he said sincerely. 'I doubt these Austins will be interested in hunting, but our woods are at your disposal. Yours *and* your companion's.'

'I am Robert de Luci,' said the second knight, speaking before Norrys could tell Cole what to do with his offer. 'And we shall be delighted to accept.'

Osbert introduced the three Austins: the goat-like Prior Dunstan, the hen-like Secretary Hurso and the youngster, Robert, whom Gwenllian distrusted on sight for his scheming eyes and spiteful smile. While Osbert spoke, Burchill and Iefan continued to cast uneasy glances towards the chapel, obviously worried about what would happen when Gerald emerged.

'Did I hear you mention hunting?' asked Dunstan keenly. 'I have not enjoyed a decent chase since I went with the King in the New Forest.'

'John hunts?' asked Cole doubtfully. It did not go with his concept of the monarch as a debauched womaniser with no interest in manly pursuits.

'I meant his father,' explained Dunstan. 'Henry. He knew his way around a bow. So do I, of course, and he once said I was the best archer in Kent.'

Gwenllian had no idea whether it was true, but Cole was impressed, and he and Dunstan were soon deep in discussion about weapons, while Secretary Hurso listened with an indulgent smile. Luci's expression was more difficult to read, although Norrys's was full of open hatred, furious that Cole should have won the prior around with so little effort.

'Cole is a fool to build in stone,' he said to Burchill, looking around in disdain. He ignored Iefan and Gwenllian as of no consequence. Gwenllian bristled, both at his manners and his remark; Cole had done wonders with what he had inherited, and the castle was now larger, stronger and infinitely cleaner than when Norrys had held it. 'The Welsh will only burn it down, and he wastes the King's money with his foolery. I shall tell John so when I see him.'

'It was John who ordered us to do it,' she said coldly. 'And we are proud to report that we are far ahead of the schedule he set. I suggest you tell him that instead.'

'Then it is not surprising that you have suffered so many accidents,' Norrys spat back. Burchill shot Gwenllian a guilty glance, and she supposed the information had come from him. 'You are rushing the work.'

'No,' snapped Iefan. He did not usually speak out of turn, and Gwenllian saw he was offended by the criticism on behalf of Cole and the workforce, many of whom were his friends, family and neighbours. 'We are ahead because we are efficient.'

'It is true,' said Burchill proudly. 'You will not find a better-run castle than this one.'

Norrys released a short bark of laughter. 'That is not what John thinks. He does not trust Cole or his Welsh connections, and it is only a matter of time before he passes Carmarthen back to me. He has virtually promised as much.'

'Perhaps you will show Sir Roger to his quarters,' said Gwenllian to Burchill. She kept her voice level, although she was inwardly seething. Was the claim true, or just hubris?

'I am sorry, my lady,' said Luci when Norrys had gone. 'I managed to avoid Carmarthen on our outward journey, but the weather conspired against me this time. I hope the snow does not last long, because it will be better for everyone when we can leave.'

'Do you anticipate trouble, then?' asked Gwenllian worriedly.

'Yes,' replied Luci simply. 'Norrys hated losing this place, and returning has reopened old wounds. I shall try to keep him contained, but it will not be easy. Meanwhile, our three Austins will certainly quarrel with your three Welsh priests. You will have no peace until we go our separate ways.'

Unhappily, Gwenllian watched him trail after his companion to the hall. Then she became aware that someone was standing close behind her, and whipped around in alarm. It was Secretary Hurso, his birdlike eyes sharp and bright, and young Robert. She had thought they had gone with Burchill, and wondered how long they had been listening.

'Norrys is a vile brute,' said Hurso. 'I cannot imagine why the archbishop chose him to guard us. And he is far worse now he is here, at the scene of an ancient humiliation.'

'Then Luci and Burchill must keep him from brooding,' said Gwenllian. 'And you two must keep your prior away from Gerald. We cannot have our town thinking that the Church is full of men who cannot control their tempers.'

'We shall do our best,' promised the secretary. 'Although we had scant success in Oxford. There, we almost came to blows, especially after that old monk died, and Gerald accused us of poisoning him. What was the fellow's name, Robert?'

'Wilfred,' supplied the youngster with an inappropriately cheerful grin. 'And Prior Dunstan accused Gerald in return. Abbot Hugh had to summon lay brothers to stop them from punching each other.'

'This Wilfred was murdered?' asked Gwenllian uneasily.

'Yes, but he was not very nice, anyway,' said Robert blithely. 'He bullied me, and was incurably lazy. If anyone deserved to be dispatched, it was him.'

'He was not "dispatched",' said Hurso irritably. 'He died of a seizure, brought on by too little exercise and too much fine food.'

'What about the poisoned wine?' demanded Robert, eyes flashing challengingly.

'What poisoned wine?' asked Hurso dismissively. 'Wilfred spilled it in his death throes, so it could not be tested – not that there would have been anything to find if we had. He died of natural causes, and I mentioned him only to warn Lady Gwenllian of the trouble that might arise if we fail to keep Dunstan and Gerald apart.'

'No doubt you will provide two separate bedchambers, my lady,' said Robert, declining to argue. 'But unless you lock them in, they will meet several times a day, and they will certainly fight. However, I have something that will distract them.'

'What?' asked Gwenllian suspiciously.

'*The Play of Adam*,' replied Robert. 'It is a dull thing, full of boring morality and scripture. But I have memorised the role of God, and I shall perform it for you, if you like.'

'Perhaps we can all perform it,' suggested Hurso, suddenly eager. 'We saw it in Oseney Abbey and enjoyed it hugely. A series of rehearsals might serve to keep Gerald and Dunstan from sparring – and Norrys from attacking your husband into the bargain.'

'We shall see,' said Gwenllian, not liking the notion of an activity that would force everyone into such close proximity. 'I will look at it tomorrow.'

The rest of the day passed uneventfully. Cole took Prior Dunstan on an extensive tour of the stables, while Archdeacon Osbert showed the other two Austins his collection of religious manuscripts. Burchill escorted the Hospitallers to a tavern, and Gwenllian listened to Gerald talk about himself.

Meanwhile, Iefan commandeered Cethynoc the mason to help him show Gerald's two priests around the castle. Neither was very interested, and Foliot asked several times to be excused, but Cole had charged Iefan to keep them busy, and the sergeant was not a man to flout orders. The hapless clerics were forced to inspect every last stone, with Cethynoc supplying a detailed technical commentary.

The evening was more problematic. As was the custom on winter nights, everyone gathered in the hall. The cook provided an excellent meal, but the trouble came when the guests left the table and settled around the hearth. One of Cole's dogs was in the way, so Norrys kicked it. It yelped, more from shock than from pain.

'There was no need for that,' snapped Gerald. 'Any man who vents his temper on animals is a brute himself.'

'A brute, am I?' asked Norrys dangerously. He had been drinking all day, and was unsteady on his feet. 'Would you like me to show you just how much? It would be a pleasure to spill *your* guts.'

Gerald regarded him in disdain, then turned to Prior Dunstan. 'The archbishop must hold *you* in very high esteem, to supply such a well-bred warrior for your protection.'

'I agree,' said Pontius, quick to support his bishop elect. 'Of course, if Prior Dunstan was not engaged on such a wicked mission, he would not need guards in the first place. Norrys performs the devil's work.'

'I am not the devil, and neither is my archbishop,' snapped Dunstan. 'How dare you!'

'I shall issue an edict removing you both from office when I am back in my See,' declared Gerald haughtily. 'You stain the good name of the Church with your presence.'

'Osbert, fetch your harp,' said Gwenllian quickly. 'It is time for some music.'

'I do not like music, and it will be banned from Carmarthen when *I* am constable,' said Norrys sullenly. He regarded Cole with contempt. 'It does not surprise me to learn that *you* encourage such nonsense, though. You always were soft in the head.'

'There is nothing "soft" about appreciating culture,' said Gwenllian, gripping Cole's hand under the table to prevent him from responding.

'Your bailey walls are very nice,' said Foliot, in an obvious attempt to change the subject to one that was less contentious. Everyone looked at him, so he flailed around for a way to elaborate. 'Smart stones and lovely mortar.'

'Those defences are far in excess of what is needed,' countered Norrys. 'Who do you think will attack, Cole? Saracens? And you put your workforce at risk with this silly project. I heard you were almost crushed by a falling basket only this morning.'

Cole started to rise, but Burchill grabbed his shoulder. Norrys started to laugh, amused that the constable should let himself be constrained by an old man. Burchill had been right to warn Cole not to react, but Gwenllian wished he had done it more discreetly.

'Do not let him provoke you, sir,' whispered Iefan, who always stood behind Cole's chair at mealtimes. 'No one was in danger. Ignore him.'

'Here is Osbert with his crwth,' said Gwenllian, relieved when the bald archdeacon re-entered the hall. 'It is the custom to listen in silence.'

'Whose custom?' asked Gerald curiously. 'It is not a Welsh one.'

'Carmarthen's,' said Gwenllian firmly, and gestured for Osbert to begin.

At her insistence, he played until the guests were yawning and the fire had burned low in the hearth. All bade their hosts a hasty good night when the archdeacon paused to massage his sore fingers, and escaped while they could. Cole sighed when they had gone.

'Let us hope the snow melts tonight, because I do not think I can stand another evening like that one. They bickered like fractious children!'

They went to bed, and Gwenllian was not sure how long they had been asleep before she became aware that Cole was no longer lying next to her. By the embers of the fire she saw him buckling his sword around his waist.

'What is the matter?' she asked in alarm.

'I heard something,' he whispered. 'Go back to sleep.'

Gwenllian climbed out of bed and tugged her cloak around her. 'What did you hear?'

'I am not sure. A thump, as if something had fallen. It was—'

He stopped when a series of anguished howls tore through the silence of the night. He raced from the room, Gwenllian at his heels. The wails were coming from the chamber that had been allocated to the St Davids priests, and he flung open the door, drawing his sword as he did so. He stopped so abruptly that Gwenllian cannoned into the back of him.

Pontius was lying on a mattress, his head obscured by a stone that had dropped from the wall and crushed him.

The horrified cries of Gerald and Foliot brought the other castle guests running. Prior Dunstan was clad comically in a long white nightshift, although Secretary Hurso and Robert wore their habits. The two knights were on their heels, both holding swords and looking so alert that Gwenllian suspected that neither had been asleep; she wondered what they had been doing.

Iefan and Burchill also arrived. Gwenllian was not surprised to see Iefan, because the sergeant never strayed far from Cole – he hated the idea of not being first to hand if there was trouble – but Burchill owned a house in the town, and never slept inside the castle. He saw Gwenllian looking at him and shrugged.

'I do not trust Norrys,' he whispered. 'Symon is safer with me nearby.'

Cole did not need the protection of an old man, and Burchill knew it, leaving Gwenllian wondering why he had forgone the luxury of his own bed. She forced her attention back to the room. Gerald and Foliot were pressed against the far wall, as if they were afraid more stones might drop, while the Canterbury visitors were clustered in the doorway. Cole was crouching by Pontius, feeling for signs of life. Evidently, there was none, because he stood and addressed Iefan.

'Fetch Cethynoc. Being a mason, he can tell us what happened.'

'I should have thought that was obvious,' sneered Norrys.

'A great lump of rock has dropped out of the wall and landed on Pontius's skull. You do not need a mason to tell—'

'Stones do not fall for no reason,' retorted Cole. 'We need the opinion of a professional man if we are to understand what happened here.'

'You mean someone might have caused it to fall deliberately?' whispered Gerald, while Gwenllian wished Cole had kept his thoughts to himself. 'That Pontius has been *murdered?*'

'We cannot know yet,' she said, stepping forward quickly. 'Perhaps you will tell us what you did after you retired?'

'Yes, of course.' Foliot's voice was unsteady, and his kindly face was white. 'Pontius and Gerald came here directly, while I went to the kitchen for a poultice to put on my injured shoulder. When I returned, they had already doused the candle. I climbed on to my own pallet, and was almost asleep when there was a terrible crash . . . '

'I let Pontius have the best bed, because he has a bad back,' explained Gerald. Anger replaced shock as he glared at the envoys from Canterbury. 'But *they* would have expected *me* to take it, because I am bishop elect. *They* arranged for the rock to drop, because they want me dead. But their villainous plot failed, and poor Pontius is killed in my place.'

'How dare you accuse us!' shouted Dunstan. His goatbeard was stiff with outrage. 'We had nothing to do with it.'

'It is true,' said Secretary Hurso, licking dry lips. 'We did not.'

'We would not sully our hands,' stated Norrys, although there was a glint in his eye that Gwenllian did not like at all. Meanwhile, Luci said nothing, and his face was closed and difficult to read.

'At least it was quick,' said Robert, who had pushed his way into the room and was inspecting Pontius's body with ghoulish relish. Cole inserted himself between them, forcing the young Austin to return to his companions.

'Did you notice anything amiss before you retired?' Cole asked. 'Dust on the bedclothes, for example, which might have suggested the stones were unstable?'

'It did not occur to us to look for such a thing,' said Gerald, troubled.

'Then did you hear anything before it fell?' persisted Cole.

'No, we were asleep,' replied Foliot. He kept glancing uneasily at Gerald, as if he was considering his bishop elect as the culprit. 'The crash woke us.'

'It woke us too,' said Prior Dunstan. 'Along with the screeches that followed.'

'We did not *screech*,' snapped Gerald. 'We raised the alarm. And I doubt *you* were asleep when this happened. I think you were waiting for it, because *you* arranged it to fall. As I said, you want me dead, because you see me as a threat.'

'You are a nuisance,' said Dunstan witheringly. 'Not a threat.'

'It is true, Gerald,' said Secretary Hurso with an apologetic shrug. 'You are not sufficiently important to warrant us staining our souls with the sin of murder.'

'It is another example of shoddy workmanship in Carmarthen Castle,' crowed Norrys. 'Guests will not die under collapsing walls when I am constable.'

Gwenllian studied each of the guests in turn. Norrys had been very quick to blame Cole. Had *he* arranged for the stone to fall, to improve his chances of being made constable? She could not read Luci, so did not know whether he was the kind of man to help a brother knight commit murder.

Meanwhile, Gerald seemed more indignant than dismayed by Pontius's fate. Tears gleamed in Foliot's eyes, but she had seen other killers weep for their victims. Had Gerald or Foliot dropped the stone on the sleeping Pontius, just so they could accuse Dunstan of the act?

She glanced at the three Austins. Or had one of them tried to kill the man who was such a thorn in their side, so they would not have to return to Canterbury and admit failure, and Gerald was right to believe he would be dead if he had taken the best bed? With a sigh, she supposed she would have to find out.

Cole, Burchill and Iefan carried the body to the chapel, leaving Gwenllian to persuade the visitors back to bed. Not surprisingly, Gerald declined to sleep in the chamber where his friend had died, so she helped him and Foliot move into her own. Foliot accompanied Gerald very reluctantly, and once again Gwenllian wondered whether he suspected the bishop elect of foul play. When they were settled – Gerald to sleep, but Foliot announcing that he would spend the rest of the night awake in prayer – she went to the chapel. Cethynoc was there, making his report to Cole.

'There were scratches that suggest the mortar was deliberately prised out,' the mason was saying. 'As you would have seen for yourself had you bothered to look. You did not need to drag me out of bed. Or will you pay me for the inconvenience?'

'No,' said Burchill, before Cole could reply, 'but we will not set you in the stocks for your insolence. How does that sound?'

Cethynoc scowled, and Gwenllian was amazed that Cole was able to tolerate the mason's unpleasantness day after day as they worked together on the walls. Or his greed. She regarded him with distaste, wondering whether he had arranged the petty 'accidents' as a way to earn himself more money. Iefan was also glowering, and she saw he itched to trounce Cethynoc for his disrespectful attitude.

'What else can you tell us, Cethynoc?' asked Cole patiently.

'Nothing,' snapped the mason. 'Except that the bed was moved slightly. I imagine it was to ensure that the stone would land squarely on whoever was lying there.'

'So it was definitely murder,' said Cole unhappily when Cethynoc had gone. 'But who would do such a terrible thing?'

'The three Austins, of course,' replied Burchill. 'They expected Gerald to be in the best bed, and they want him dead. I imagine they have been charged by the archbishop to ensure that he is never consecrated.'

'Lord!' muttered Cole. Gwenllian understood his alarm: the King would not thank him for accusing a Canterbury prior of murder, or for suggesting that the archbishop was complicit in the deed.

'Personally, I suspect Norrys,' argued Iefan. 'He wants the King to accuse you of negligence, so he can be constable in your stead.'

'Or Gerald and Foliot, because they want the world to think Dunstan is responsible,' said Gwenllian, although she spoke reluctantly. She liked both men – far more than she liked the prior and his retinue. 'Why did Gerald let Pontius take the best bed? I doubt he is naturally generous. Moreover, I should have thought that Foliot is more deserving of such compassion. I saw the bruises on his shoulder from his fall, and they look painful.'

'Of course, Cethynoc could be mistaken,' proposed Iefan tentatively. 'It might just be a mishap – like the accidents on the castle walls.'

'Those were not accidents,' said Cole firmly. 'And neither was this. Someone tampered with the stone earlier in the day, intending for it to fall.' He looked at his sergeant. 'You were with Pontius all afternoon. *Did* he have a bad back?'

'He certainly said so – a lot,' replied Iefan.

'So we have seven suspects,' said Cole. 'Can we eliminate any with alibis? I am afraid I left Prior Dunstan to his own devices for an hour while I dealt with a problem on the scaffolding; and Archdeacon Osbert was obliged to abandon Hurso and Robert when it was time to hear his parishioners' confessions.'

'I had business of my own to attend for some of the afternoon,' said Burchill, a little defensively, 'so I left Norrys and Luci in the tavern, but they were sitting at the same table when I got back. I do not believe they left ... but they might have done.'

'Foliot went to the kitchen for wine to dull the ache in his shoulder while I helped Sir Symon with the scaffolding,' said Iefan. 'But I suspect he would have been in too much pain to climb walls and chip out stones. I have no idea where Pontius went.'

'And I left Gerald unattended to spend time with Meurig,' admitted Gwenllian.

Cole sighed. 'So we can eliminate none of them. Damn!'

'Perhaps they are all innocent and our wretched saboteur is responsible,' suggested Burchill. 'He is bored of petty mishaps, so decided to opt for something more dramatic.'

'There is no saboteur,' said Iefan tiredly, 'just a run of bad luck. However, Pontius was not an accident, and I hope Lady Gwenllian catches the culprit before he kills anyone else.'

'Me?' asked Gwenllian in alarm. 'But I—'

'She will,' predicted Cole with touching confidence.

Cole was unrealistically disappointed when dawn broke the following day, and he discovered that there was still too much snow for their guests to leave. Gwenllian's feelings were ambiguous. On the one hand, she was glad there would be time to unmask the killer before her suspects left for good; on the other, she did not relish the thought of a killer in her home, or the prospect of keeping the two factions apart for a second day.

The morning was taken up with burying Pontius. Cole attended the gloomy ceremonies with Gerald and Foliot, while Gwenllian entertained the Austins in the castle. Burchill was allocated the unenviable task of minding the two knights.

The afternoon turned to wind and sleet, forcing the visitors indoors, although Cole and his labourers persisted with their work on the walls. He sent them home when Iefan arrived to report some trouble in the town – the merchants had raised the price of bread on the grounds that their customers could not leave town to find better deals elsewhere. Food was now prohibitively expensive, and the poor objected.

Left to manage the guests with only Archdeacon Osbert to help her – Burchill had sent a message saying that he was unavailable – Gwenllian asked Robert for *The Play of Adam*. A sly expression crossed the young Austin's face.

'You may have it only if you agree to let me play God.'

'I shall decide who plays what,' she retorted with an icy hauteur that reminded him she was a princess of Wales. 'Now fetch the script at once.'

Chastened, Robert slunk away, but not before she had seen the vicious resentment on his face. She recalled what had been said about the monk who had died at Oseney – that he might have been killed with poisoned wine, and that Gerald and Dunstan had accused each other of the crime. Yet Robert had mentioned being bullied by him, so perhaps *he* was the guilty party. And then, flushed with success, he had decided to make an attempt on Gerald, with Pontius paying the price.

'I am not in the mood for drama,' said Secretary Hurso apologetically. 'I slept badly last night, and I would rather sit in our room and read. Do you mind?'

Gwenllian could hardly refuse. The others clustered around Robert eagerly, though, snatching at the scroll as they decided which roles best suited their talents. Gwenllian was not surprised when Gerald and Dunstan were rivals to Robert for the role of God, and there was considerable ill feeling until she had negotiated a series of compromises.

They began by sitting around the fire to read the script aloud, and she was astonished when calm descended. She was a little uncomfortable with Gerald and Dunstan as Cain and Abel, but the scene passed off without incident.

Gerald, Foliot and Dunstan quickly revealed themselves to be competent performers, because they were used to public speaking. Robert was adequate, Luci enthusiastic and Norrys wooden. Unfortunately, there were few sections where all participants were needed at once, so they tended to wander off, and she was unable to monitor them all. Archdeacon Osbert helped, although Gwenllian noticed that he paid particular attention to Gerald, indicating who was *his* prime suspect for Pontius's murder.

Eventually, the light began to fade, so the clerics went to the chapel for evening prayers, while Norrys and Luci disappeared to check their horses. Cole arrived shortly after dark, cold, wet and anxious.

'I have no authority to dictate prices, but I wish I did,' he said, pulling off his sodden clothes and reaching for dry ones. 'What the merchants are doing is shameful – profiteering, no less – and I do not blame the poor for objecting.'

'How did you resolve it?' Gwenllian asked. They were in

the chamber where Pontius had died, because Gerald and Foliot still occupied the one they usually used. Little Meurig was fretful in the unfamiliar surroundings, and she was trying to rock him to sleep.

'I have not resolved it – sleet drove them home. Trouble may break out again later, though, so Burchill will patrol for the first half of the night, and I shall take the second.'

'Oh, Symon! Burchill has been out in the cold with you all afternoon, and he is no longer as young as he was. You cannot expect him to work half the night too.'

'He has not been with me,' said Cole, startled. 'I sent him to help you.'

Gwenllian experienced a surge of unease, although she was careful to conceal it. What had the old knight been doing? Shirking, because neither quelling riots nor minding querulous guests was his idea of fun? It was not the first time he had sloped off on business of his own of late, and although there was no reason to suspect anything untoward, it bothered her none the less.

'I do not suppose you have learned the identity of our saboteur, have you?' asked Cole hopefully. 'I know you have been busy, but it is important.'

'Not as important as preventing influential churchmen from killing each other,' she replied tartly. 'And discovering who murdered Pontius.'

'You have identified the culprit, then?' asked Cole, eagerly. 'Who is it?'

She scowled. 'Of course not! I am not a miracle worker, Symon.'

'You are to me,' he said with a beatific smile.

Hurso did not appear for the meal that night, and when Gwenllian enquired after his wellbeing, she was surprised and then concerned to learn that he had not been seen for some time. Robert was sent to check their room, but returned to say the secretary was not there.

'I saw him in the bailey late afternoon,' the lad said. 'He was yawning and stretching, as though he had been asleep, but had woken and was walking to clear his wits.'

'I saw him then too,' said Luci. 'When I was returning from the latrines. It was sleeting hard, and I suggested he did not linger outside.'

'I am afraid I did not notice much once we started read-ing,' said Foliot apologetically. 'I left the hall for a while – in search of peace, so I could memorise my part in the story of "Jonah and the Whale". You came with me, Osbert, and we found a quiet room by the kitchens. Did *you* see Hurso?'

'No,' replied Osbert. He regarded the bishop elect with open suspicion. 'But I saw Gerald, pacing around in the wet.'

'I was learning my lines,' declared Gerald haughtily. 'It was damp, but free of babble.'

'I will look for Hurso,' said Cole, standing and obviously relieved to pass the duty of entertaining back to Gwenllian again.

When he had gone, the conversation became acerbic, thanks to Norrys, who intimated that Gerald had harmed the secretary in revenge for what had happened to Pontius.

'*In revenge?*' pounced Gerald. 'That suggests *you* murdered Pontius, and so expect Hurso to be dispatched in return.'

'No one has "dispatched" Hurso,' stated Foliot, shocked. 'What a terrible thing to say! He will have found some warm corner to read, and has fallen asleep.'

'Perhaps,' said Dunstan, his pale goat-eyes curiously devoid of emotion. He rounded on Gerald. 'However, no one in *my* party murdered your Pontius.'

'I shall complain to the Pope about you,' threatened Gerald viciously. 'I shall have you *and* your archbishop expelled from the Church. And good riddance!'

'You will never be in a position to excommunicate us,' snarled Dunstan. 'And—'

'I have arranged something special for you this evening,' interrupted Gwenllian loudly. 'Cethynoc the mason has agreed to come and talk to you about castle-building.'

'Castle-building,' echoed Robert in astonishment. 'But I do not know anything about it.'

'Even more reason to listen, then,' said Gwenllian tartly. 'You may learn something.'

Before the young man could argue, she ushered the visitors towards the hearth and began to pour wine, at the same time embarking on a detailed description of a recent journey to Bath.[1] She spoke in a rapid gabble to ensure there were no interruptions, certain there would be a quarrel if she permitted conversation.

Just when she was running out of things to say, Cethynoc slouched in, furious at being ordered to spend his evening 'working', and began a dreary monologue on pulleys and scaffolding that would not hold anyone's attention for long. Gerald was the first to roll his eyes, although Foliot listened with polite attention. Dunstan pretended to be asleep, and Norrys produced a pair of dice. Gwenllian was about to order him to put them away – Cole did not permit gambling in the castle, because it led to fights – when rescue came in the form of Robert, albeit unwittingly.

'I suppose raising fortresses is a lucrative business?' he asked with a bored sigh.

1 See *Hill of Bones*, The Medieval Murderers, 2011.

Cethynoc smiled for the first time since Gwenllian had known him, although it was not a pleasant expression. 'Oh, yes. I am a rich man.'

That secured everyone's attention. 'How rich?' asked Gerald keenly.

Cethynoc's grin was smug. '*Very* rich. Of course, I have other business interests too. Would you like to hear about them? You may learn something to make you wealthy.'

The entire party leaned forward eagerly, and Gwenllian suspected he was about to spin some tale that would allow him to laugh at their gullibility in the tavern later. She did not care, and was just happy for them to be occupied. Then she saw Cole gesturing to her urgently from the door, and excused herself.

'I have found Hurso,' he whispered. 'He is dead.'

'What?' Gwenllian pulled him into the corridor so they could speak without being seen or heard. 'Are you sure?'

Cole nodded. 'He was hanging from a rope on the wall's scaffolding. I cut him down and carried him to the chapel. It was not suicide – he was murdered.'

'Murdered?' echoed Gwenllian, shocked. 'How do you know?'

'Because his fingernails are torn, and there is a cut on the back of his head. Clearly, he was knocked insensible during a fight, after which his opponent tied a rope around his neck and tipped him off the scaffolding.'

Gwenllian was appalled. 'I cannot believe it! The King will not overlook *two* suspicious deaths. He will use them to oust you.'

'Not if we can prove they were none of my doing.'

Gwenllian thought he was being naïve, but said nothing. She considered what they had been told about Hurso's last hours. 'Robert and Luci saw him alive late in the afternoon, and everyone was in the hall eating by dark. That means he must have been killed roughly between four and six o'clock. Unfortunately, all our guests slipped away at some point during that time, when they were not needed for reading.'

'You cannot narrow our suspects down at all?' asked Cole, dismayed.

Gwenllian considered carefully. 'Luci – he was not gone long enough to have reached the walls, killed someone and come back. And Foliot has an alibi in Archdeacon Osbert. But that still leaves Gerald, Prior Dunstan, young Robert and the Hospitallers. I am sorry, Symon! I was so intent on keeping the peace that I did not pay attention to their comings and goings. I should have done.'

'It does not matter.' Cole was thoughtful. 'The sleet turned to rain at roughly four o'clock, which means that anyone out for any length of time would still be wet. Look at me – I am drenched from being out for just a few moments.'

'They all came in sodden at some point, and I made a joke about it, but they said they were glad, because rain melts snow.' Gwenllian felt a surge of panic. 'Then they will leave, and we will never have answers!'

'What about motives?' asked Cole calmly. 'I understand why Gerald would kill Hurso – it is revenge for Pontius. But why would the two Austins or the two knights harm one of their own party?'

'Perhaps it was a sacrifice, to ensure that Gerald or Foliot did not murder *them*. Or maybe there was a quarrel, which led to murderous rage. I shall speak to our servants. Someone must have seen something – the scaffolding is in full view of the castle.'

'Not the part where I found Hurso. I would have missed him were it not for the creak of the rope as he swung in the wind. I investigated the sound, because I thought it might be another "accident" in the offing.'

'This is dreadful!' Gwenllian felt weak with horror for the evil that was unfolding around them. 'We will lose Carmarthen for certain!'

'Then we shall live in Normandy. It is not so terrible.'

'How can you even *think* of leaving our friends at the mercy of one of John's creatures?' cried Gwenllian, distressed. 'Besides, who is to say that he will let you leave the country? He might consider you a traitor and order your execution.'

Cole blew out his cheeks in a sigh. 'He might, I suppose. He certainly prefers his enemies dead to living, and he does not like me. So ask your questions in the servants' quarters, while I try to make sure no one else dies before you have exposed the culprit.'

Unfortunately, Gwenllian learned nothing useful. The foul weather had kept their retainers indoors, while Cole had sent the labourers home long before Hurso had taken his final, fatal stroll. She persisted with the castle's residents regardless, hoping one would remember Hurso walking – and someone watching or following him.

'You cannot have stayed in the entire time.' She felt near to tears, terrified of what would happen if she failed to unmask the killer. 'Some of you must have gone to the latrines, or to fetch water from the well.'

'None of us did,' explained the cook, 'because of Norrys. We remember when he was constable here, see, and when he left . . . well, suffice to say there was great rejoicing and he is a man for grudges. We kept out of the bailey on purpose, in case we met him.'

She returned to the hall to find Gerald and Foliot on one

side of the hearth, and the Canterbury men on the other. Cole, Archdeacon Osbert and Burchill were standing between them, to keep them apart. Norrys's hand twitched over his sword, and Luci's face was pale and drawn. Foliot was gripping Gerald's arm, as if he thought his bishop elect was on the verge of leaping up and launching an attack on their adversaries.

'*You* murdered Hurso,' Robert was snarling to Gerald. 'Because you believe – without cause – that one of us hurt Pontius. But you will pay. I liked Hurso. He was kind to me.'

'I cannot imagine why,' said Gerald disdainfully. 'You are a vile little worm.'

Red with rage, Robert lunged at him. Cole shoved him back. Dunstan objected to an Austin being manhandled, Gerald applauded it, and then a nasty altercation was under-way. Gwenllian took the opportunity to study her suspects. The only dry one among them was Osbert – and the bald archdeacon was not on her list of suspects! She caught his eye and made a desperate sign that he should say something to quell the spat before it turned violent.

'I am going to the chapel to pray for Hurso's soul,' Osbert obliged. It was a clever ploy: Dunstan and Gerald could hardly continue to bicker after such a pious suggestion.

'So will I,' said the prior. 'He was my secretary, after all. Robert, come with me.'

'I would rather do it here,' said the lad, not moving. 'It is still raining, and I do not want to get wet.'

Even Dunstan seemed taken aback at such selfishness, while Gerald and Luci shook their heads in disgust. Norrys only smirked.

'I still cannot believe it,' said Foliot shakily. He looked at Cole. 'Are you sure Hurso is dead? You cannot be mistaken?'

'No,' replied Cole gently. 'I am sorry.'

'You will be,' said Norrys coldly. 'It will mean the end of you. King John will certainly not overlook two murders in as many days.'

There was nothing Cole could say to such a remark, so he turned and led the way to the chapel, where he had set Hurso on a bier and covered him with a blanket. Unceremoniously, Prior Dunstan hauled off the blanket, and did not seem particularly dismayed as he looked at the man who had been his secretary.

Meanwhile, Gwenllian noticed Foliot watching his bishop elect intently. Then Foliot looked at Osbert, who shook his bald head, a stricken expression on his face. She could only assume that Foliot had shared his suspicions with a fellow priest. She clenched her hands to prevent them from shaking. She did not want the culprit to be Gerald – a Welsh candidate for the See of St Davids, and a man – a kinsman – she liked.

She studied the others. Norrys's eyes flashed with vengeful satisfaction, and it occurred to her that he was certainly the kind of man to kill a member of his own party in order to harm Symon. Luci was quiet and shocked, and she thought she saw the glitter of tears.

'We should establish who was where between four and six o'clock,' said Cole. 'It is—'

'Then let us start with you,' interrupted Norrys. 'Did Gerald *pay* you to kill Hurso? Or did Hurso find out that you dispatched Pontius, so had to be silenced? Perhaps that was what Hurso was doing all afternoon – not reading, but investigating murder.'

'I hardly think that Sir Symon—' began Archdeacon Osbert angrily.

'It is Cole's castle.' Norrys rounded on him. 'He will know where to lure a victim, so there will be no witnesses to the foul deed.'

'Symon has an alibi in half the town,' said Gwenllian sharply. 'He was quelling riots when Hurso was killed, and dozens of people can testify to that fact.'

'You are familiar with the castle too, Norrys,' said Gerald when the Hospitaller had nothing to say. 'You were once its constable. And personally, I think it is suspicious that you are so eager for Cole to be blamed. So tell us where *you* were when Hurso died.'

Norrys scowled. 'Learning the role of King Nebuchadnezzar – on my own. I could not concentrate with all that jabbering in the hall, so I came to the chapel.'

'Can anyone vouch for you?' asked Cole.

Norrys regarded him with open hatred. 'No, but I have no reason to kill Hurso. The archbishop hired me to protect him.'

'Which you failed to do,' Gerald pointed out. 'Luci? Do you have a better story?'

Luci nodded. 'I went out briefly – a moment, no more – when I saw Hurso in the bailey. But it was cold and wet, so I hurried back inside and did not leave again. Lady Gwenllian will confirm that I am telling the truth.'

Gwenllian nodded, and Cole turned questioning eyebrows on Dunstan.

'I was in many places,' replied the prior unhelpfully. 'I am an active man, and I dislike being pent up indoors. I walked around both baileys, to stretch my legs.'

Gwenllian was dissatisfied with this explanation, and so was Gerald because his eyes narrowed in suspicion.

'I went out, but Archdeacon Osbert was with me,' said Foliot before Gerald could speak. 'We practised our roles for "Jonah and the Whale" in a room near the kitchens. God help us, but we laughed together while a man was being . . .' He trailed off, unable to continue.

'When we finished, I walked with Foliot to the hall, then came to the chapel to say my offices,' added Osbert. 'I did not see Norrys here, though.'

'You must have missed me in the dark,' said Norrys. Then he realised the chapel was far too small for that, so added, 'Or I left a few moments before you arrived. Regardless, I am not the culprit.'

'I also spent time alone,' said Gerald. 'In my room. I was praying, so my alibi is God. However, no one can possibly suspect me of this crime. *I* am bishop elect.'

It was some time before Gwenllian and Cole were able to steer their guests from the hall to their quarters, because neither party wanted to sleep. Prior Dunstan, Gerald and young Robert were the most vocal, while Norrys watched the efforts of Foliot, Luci and Gwenllian to calm them with spiteful satisfaction.

'It is late,' said Cole, loudly and with finality. 'And time for us all to rest.'

'I agree,' said Dunstan, standing. 'I shall pray for Hurso in the chapel, then retire.'

'I would not walk across that dark bailey if I were you,' said Norrys slyly. 'Not alone.'

'Then come with me,' snapped Dunstan. 'It is what you are being paid for – to protect me from danger.'

'And me,' added Robert. 'Although I hope you do a better job than you did with Hurso.'

'I will go with you, Father Prior,' said Luci quickly. 'Unless you prefer to say your prayers in your room instead. God will not mind, and it will be much more comfortable.'

'Very well,' said Dunstan, capitulating quickly. 'Robert can go in my place.'

'I most certainly shall not,' cried Robert. 'It might be dangerous.'

Dunstan regarded him witheringly. 'Canon Wilfred lied when he told me you were a selfish brat with no sense of propriety. He was being far too charitable.'

Gerald roared with laughter, and Dunstan strode away with his head held high. Robert scurried after him, his face dark with fury, and Luci was hot on their heels, apparently afraid of what might happen once they were alone. Norrys watched expressionlessly, then poured himself more claret. Gerald's amusement faded as he studied Norrys's wine-flushed face and belligerent eyes.

'Who will guard me tonight?' he asked Cole in a low voice. 'I shall be slaughtered in my bed, and Wales will lose the best bishop that God has ever provided.'

'Do not worry,' said Foliot. 'I shall sit by our door, and prevent anyone from entering.'

As Gwenllian had just finished treating Foliot's injured shoulder with a hot poultice, she doubted he would be much use in a scuffle. Then it occurred to her that he might be just as concerned to keep Gerald in, as keeping others out.

'Both of you will sleep,' stated Cole. 'I shall stand guard the first half of the night, and Iefan will take over when I relieve Burchill. No one will harm you, I promise.'

Gerald nodded acquiescence, and Cole accompanied him and Foliot to their chamber. Gwenllian followed, and when the two priests had closed the door, she put her ear to the wood to listen, eager to learn whether Foliot would confront Gerald with his suspicions. But neither man spoke, and after a while the light went out under the door.

'Go to bed, Gwen,' said Cole. 'One of us should be alert tomorrow.'

She nodded, but made no effort to leave. 'Do not forget that Gerald may be the killer, *cariad*,' she whispered. 'He is one of our five suspects. Be careful.'

'If he did kill Hurso, then his motive will have been to avenge Pontius. But if that is the case, then who dispatched Pontius? Or do we have two killers on the loose? We might, I suppose. Both groups hate each other, and emotions are running high.'

'No,' said Gwenllian firmly. 'Murder is a terrible thing, and I do not believe there are two deranged monsters in our castle. There is one, and we must catch him before he leaves, or King John will hold you responsible. And I am not ready to be a widow just yet.'

Cole was silent for a moment, thinking. 'At the risk of sounding petty, I think Norrys is the culprit. Murders in my castle suit him very well, and as a knight, he is no stranger to violent death.'

'No,' agreed Gwenllian. 'And he claims to be close to the King, who is keen to see you ousted. For all we know, John ordered him to make trouble here, with the promise that Norrys will be constable when you are no longer in office.'

'You think John would order priests murdered?' Cole was shocked.

Gwenllian shrugged. 'Not openly – he is far too clever for that. Indeed, he may not have mentioned murder at all, but left Norrys free to do whatever he deemed necessary.'

'Should I arrest Norrys, then?' asked Cole worriedly. 'Lord! John will not like that!'

'Not yet. Norrys is a strong suspect, but not the only one.'

'True. We have eliminated Foliot and Luci, so we are left with him, Gerald, Dunstan and Robert. I suppose Robert is next on my list – he is a horrible lad. No wonder Oseney Abbey lent him to Dunstan: they were desperate to be rid of him.'

'Oseney,' mused Gwenllian. 'We must not forget that other

suspicious death, either –Wilfred. There was talk of poison, and Robert freely admits that Wilfred was a bully.'

'So Robert may have dispatched him? Then realised that murder is an easy way to dispense with people he does not like, so he tried to kill Gerald but got Pontius instead? And he dispatched Hurso when the secretary guessed what had happened?'

'It is certainly possible.'

'Or perhaps the culprit is the same man who has arranged our series of "accidents". A falling stone, a hanging from scaffolding – both are incidents *he* might have organised.'

'If that were true, then our guests cannot be responsible, because none of them were here when those mishaps first started. It would mean that the murderer is from Carmarthen – a soldier, servant or labourer.'

'Christ!' muttered Cole uncomfortably. 'You are right.'

Gwenllian took a deep breath, knowing what she was about to say would be greeted with anger and disbelief. 'Burchill sent me a note to say he was "unavailable" this afternoon, even though he knew I needed his help – and so, I imagine, did you. He also plied Norrys with enough drink to make him aggressive yesterday, and he has been indiscreet with gossip. It was he who told Norrys about the accidents on the wall.'

Cole stared at her. 'You think *Burchill* is the murderer? No! How could you even think such a thing? He is not a killer!'

'He is a knight, Symon – of course he is a killer! And he has been on crusade, one of the bloodiest and most disreputable acts ever committed by one group of men against another.'

'No,' said Cole stubbornly. 'Now go to bed. We shall not discuss this again.'

*

Gwenllian slept poorly that night, wishing she had kept her suspicions about Burchill to herself. Cole was recklessly loyal to his friends, but many did not deserve it. And she knew it must gall Burchill to take orders from a man three decades younger than he.

The hour candle showed it was one o'clock when she heard Iefan arrive and Cole leave to relieve the elderly knight from his patrols in the town. Little Meurig shifted in his sleep, and she wondered whether her discomfiture was transferring itself to him. She rocked the crib gently, then returned to bed, thinking about the murders and the suspects.

She slept deeply shortly before dawn, and was heavy-eyed and sluggish when the maid came to wake her. She washed and dressed quickly, hurrying to reach the hall before her guests. She arrived just in time to prevent Norrys from upsetting a vat of porridge over Gerald, and silenced Robert with a glare when the boy began a speech outlining why the Pope would never raise St Davids to an archbishopric.

The others were in a sombre mood, and she suspected they had slept as badly as she had. When the door clanked open, they all jumped in alarm. It was Burchill, who looked very well rested, and she wondered whether he had worked as hard at peace-keeping the previous night as he should have done.

'The weather is much milder this morning,' he smiled, rubbing his hands together briskly. 'And the snow is melting fast. It will not be long before you can leave.'

'Thank God!' breathed Dunstan, crossing himself. 'When? Today?'

Burchill shook his head. 'Tomorrow perhaps, or the day after, if the thaw continues.'

Gwenllian was torn between wishing them gone before anyone else died, and needing them to stay so she could catch the culprit. She experienced a surge of helplessness. But how was she to find answers when every waking moment was spent trying to prevent quarrels? She fought down her rising panic, and filled her mind with resolve instead. No sly killer was going to give the King an excuse to blame Symon! If the guests argued, then so be it, but that day, she was going to concentrate on asking questions.

'I shall be glad to be home,' Gerald was saying. 'Although I wish Pontius was coming with me. He was my most loyal supporter – and a friend, too.'

'Was he?' asked Prior Dunstan smoothly. 'You cannot be Bishop of St Davids without your most loyal supporter, so perhaps you had better do the decent thing and withdraw.'

'Never!' declared Gerald. 'I have been called by God, and it is not for me to refuse Him. And not for you to thwart Him, either.'

'It will not be pleasant to break the sad news about Pontius to our Cathedral colleagues,' said Foliot quietly. 'He was popular.'

'Not as popular as Hurso,' countered Robert, purely to argue. 'His death is a terrible blow to our Order, because . . .' He struggled to think of a valid reason. '. . . because he had lovely writing.'

Gerald released a bray of derisive laughter, which had Prior Dunstan leaping furiously to his feet and Robert ducking behind him. Luci closed his eyes, as if in despair, while Foliot appeared to be praying under his breath.

'I am sorry you will all leave with a negative impression of Carmarthen,' said Norrys, although there was no sincerity in his voice. He poured himself more breakfast ale. 'So I invite you all to return here when I am constable. I guarantee that no one will be murdered under my governorship. Cole is a—'

'Stop,' ordered Luci sharply. 'It is not polite to denigrate one's hosts, and I want no part in it. Ah, here is Archdeacon Osbert.'

Osbert had come to inform them of the arrangements he had made for burying Hurso, having persuaded the Carmarthen Austins to spare a plot in their cemetery. Gerald decided to accompany the cortège, because he said the priory was in his See, and Foliot offered to go too. Gwenllian was under the distinct impression that he was reluctant to let the bishop elect out of his sight – and not because he felt Gerald needed protection, either.

The little party set out, slithering on the rapidly melting ice. There was still a good deal of white on the surrounding hills, but it was melting quickly and Gwenllian thought Burchill was right to say the visitors would soon be able to leave. She turned to tell him so, but he had vanished. She was alarmed to note that Norrys was nowhere to be seen either.

'Where has Norrys gone?' she asked of Luci, who seemed quiet and preoccupied.

Luci shrugged. 'He has friends here. He has probably gone visiting.'

Gwenllian was distinctly uneasy, but she put Norrys from her mind as they reached the market, and she saw the crowds that had gathered there, mostly people from the poorer part of the settlement. The mood was ugly, and the houses of several wealthy merchants had been pelted with dung. Cole was in the middle with his soldiers, struggling to keep the mob at bay. Gwenllian walked towards him, confident in the knowledge that not even the most reckless rioter would dare harm her.

'Order them home,' she whispered. 'They cannot cause trouble if they are indoors.'

'They all have legitimate reasons for being out,' he replied tiredly. 'Clearing the streets would be tantamount to declaring martial law.'

She gave his arm an encouraging squeeze before hurrying after their guests, glad he was prepared to be tolerant. Carmarthen folk were not naturally rebellious, and an iron fist was likely to be counterproductive. He was wise to be patient.

It did not take long to bury Hurso at the Austin Priory. Osbert raced through the ceremonies at a furious lick, unwilling to linger lest there was another outbreak of hostilities. It started to rain as they walked back to the castle, a drenching that went some way to emptying the streets of resentful paupers too. Gwenllian was glad to reach the warmth of the hall, and was also glad when Osbert offered to stay and help her with the guests.

'Shall we rehearse *The Play of Adam*?' she asked quickly, as Dunstan and Gerald began to fight over a fireside chair. 'Or would it be unseemly after a funeral?'

'It is a religious work,' stated Gerald loftily, 'so I declare it a suitable pastime. Besides, what else can we do? I am not going out again in this weather.'

'He means he is too frightened to wander lest someone repays him for murdering Hurso,' said Robert slyly. 'I suspect the corbel fell on Pontius by accident, but he killed Hurso in revenge, and now he is afraid of being a victim himself.'

'I think we are all afraid,' said Archdeacon Osbert softly before Gerald could reply. 'But I do not believe any of us are killers. I think the culprit is a stranger who—'

'You are right,' nodded Norrys. 'Carmarthen is a pit of insurrection, so of course killers, robbers and other villains stalk its streets. Cole should keep better control.'

'Speaking of riots, I had better relieve Symon,' said Burchill. 'He will be anxious to return here and hunt the murderer.'

'Where were you all day yesterday?' asked Gwenllian, unease and fear prompting her to speak more bluntly than she had intended.

Burchill regarded her thoughtfully. 'About my own business. Why?'

'Because Symon needed your help to quell the trouble in the town, and I would have liked you here, but you were not available for either of us.'

Burchill sighed. 'Yes, but it could not be helped.'

'So where were you?' pressed Gwenllian.

Burchill stared at her for a moment before replying. 'If you do not identify the killer, Norrys will tell the King, and Symon will lose Carmarthen – or worse. I suggest you concentrate on that.'

Seething, Gwenllian watched him go. The pompous ass! How dare he remind her of her duties! And what was he hiding that he felt the need to conceal behind such strictures?

There was a buzz of excitement in the hall: the servants had scraped together an array of costumes and the players were eager to try them on. Their bubbling enthusiasm seemed inappropriate after a burial, and Gwenllian wondered whether they were ruthless or just putting brave faces on matters. Archdeacon Osbert was disinclined for frivolity, though, and asked if he might be excused the dressing-up.

'I am surprised they are so excited over a drama,' he confided. 'To be frank, I would have thought such antics beneath their dignity.'

Foliot overheard and smiled wanly. 'Why? Clerics are used

to dressing up in elaborate garments and holding forth. The stage is their natural home.'

'But not yours?' asked Gwenllian.

Foliot shook his head. 'I have never liked a lot of attention.'

'How is your shoulder?' asked Gwenllian, seeing him raise his hand to it. 'Better?'

'A little.' Foliot smiled ruefully. 'I do not usually tumble off ponies, but it *was* during an ambush.'

'Which ambush?' asked Osbert politely. 'Gerald told me you were attacked twice.

Foliot nodded. 'Once in Brecon and once in Trecastle. I fell in Trecastle, and would have been embarrassed had I not landed so terribly painfully.'

Gwenllian decided it was a good time to speak to Foliot without the others listening. Osbert started to leave, but she gestured for him to stay. There was nothing wrong with having the Archdeacon of Carmarthen as a witness to her interviews.

'Who do you think killed Pontius?' she asked of Foliot.

The priest shook his head slowly. 'I believe it was an accident, and your bad-tempered mason gave a false report to make trouble. As Norrys says, the castle is unstable, and there have been similar incidents on the walls.'

'*Hurso's* death was not an accident, though,' pressed Gwenllian. 'Who killed him?'

Foliot swallowed hard. 'I do not know.'

'Gerald?' asked Gwenllian baldly.

'No,' replied Foliot, but he would not meet her eyes. He glanced at Osbert, though, and the archdeacon looked away quickly. 'Gerald is proud and haughty, but I do not believe ... murder is a terrible sin ... He is bishop elect!' He all but wailed the last words.

'The culprit must be Robert,' said Osbert, although he did not sound convinced. 'He is a spiteful lad. Or perhaps it is Norrys, because he wants Cole disgraced.'

'You believe Dunstan and Luci innocent, then?'

Osbert shrugged, and another glance was exchanged. Gwenllian lost patience.

'What do you two know that you are not telling me?' she demanded. 'It is no time for games, because we shall all suffer if Norrys tells the King that it is Symon's fault.'

'We *know* nothing,' objected Foliot in a strangled voice. 'We just have suspicions and ... I cannot say more. However, I promise I will tell you the moment we have solid proof.'

'Solid proof of what?' snapped Gwenllian, but Foliot would not be budged. He raced away in relief when Gerald shouted for him.

'He is a good man,' said Osbert, rubbing a hand absently over his bald head. 'I have known him for years. It is a pity he is so shy, because the Church needs men of integrity in its upper ranks. Do not press him to speak before he is ready, my lady. He is not a man to besmirch the name of another without incontrovertible evidence.'

Frustrated and angry, Gwenllian hoped it would not be too late.

Although Luci had also been exonerated – from killing Hurso, at least – Gwenllian cornered him next. The scholarly knight seemed observant, and she was hopeful that he might have some intelligent observations to make.

'I have been making enquiries,' he confided. 'Although with scant success. I hope the matter is resolved before we leave, because I dislike the prospect of travelling all the way to Canterbury with three men who suspect each other of a double murder.'

'So you believe the killer is Dunstan, Robert or Norrys?' pounced Gwenllian.

'Or Gerald, but they will forget about him once we are on our way.'

He had no more to add, so she let him go, warning him to be on his guard if he planned to ask questions. He grinned at her, amused that she should think he might not know how to look after himself.

'Luci has changed since we were at Oseney,' said Gerald, coming to stand next to her. 'He was much more light-hearted then. Perhaps being with Dunstan has worn him down. Or Norrys, who is a beast. I pity Carmarthen if *he* ever rules it again.'

'I do not intend to let that happen.'

'You may have no choice. However, I shall write to King John and say that these deaths are not your husband's fault. *Dunstan* is the guilty party – he murdered Pontius out of spite, and then he killed Hurso to disguise the fact.'

'Why would he do such a thing?'

'To harm me, of course. He hates the notion of returning to Canterbury and confessing that he has failed to convince St Davids to choose another candidate. He hopes that these murders will horrify me into withdrawing from the contest.'

'Then he does not know you very well,' said Gwenllian wryly.

'No,' agreed Gerald. 'He tried to bully me in Oseney too – he engineered a meeting for that express purpose, but I soon put him in his place. He is a vile man, and it would not surprise me to learn that he killed that old man – Canon Wilfred – too.'

'I heard about that. *Was* Wilfred dispatched with poisoned wine?'

'He had been guzzling from a jug of his own, but he

knocked it over in his death throes, which meant we could not test it. Dunstan must have been relieved.'

'But why would Dunstan want to kill Wilfred?'

'To blame the murder on me, of course. It did not work, because I left Oseney before accusations could be levelled.'

Gwenllian watched him walk away. It sounded as though Gerald had beat a very hasty retreat from Oseney Abbey. Had he been fleeing the scene of the crime?

Cole returned at noon, cold, wet and tired. He reported that the streets were quiet, but bread was still expensive and the poor were still outraged by the merchants' profiteering. The trouble was far from over.

'Would you like me to tell these greedy tradesmen that they will go to Hell unless they adopt a more reasonable position?' offered Prior Dunstan.

'Osbert has already tried that,' said Cole. 'It did not work.'

'They said they would repent at the next confession, and then all would be well,' explained the archdeacon unhappily, 'because we have a forgiving God.'

'I can disavow them of that notion,' said Dunstan keenly. 'I have had many a congregation quailing in its boots at my descriptions of Satan's Palace.'

'No,' said Cole firmly. 'They do not deserve that.'

'As you wish,' said Dunstan huffily. 'Incidentally, I hope you have not forgotten these vicious murders in all the excitement of the riots. I do not want another of my party to die.'

Cole glanced hopefully at Gwenllian, and she hated having to shake her head to say she was still no further forward. She took the opportunity to question the prior.

'I have been hearing tales about Canon Wilfred this morning,' she began. 'How he was fed poisoned wine.'

'Who has been gossiping?' demanded Dunstan. 'Gerald, I suppose! Well, it is all lies. Wilfred died of natural causes. Robert did *not* conspire to avenge himself on a demanding, critical and harsh master.'

'I see,' she said, thinking it was a curious denial – one that made it sound as though there might be good reason to see young Robert as the culprit. Or was it a sly ruse to detract attention from Dunstan himself? 'So Wilfred was not drinking wine when he died?'

'He was – a large jug of expensive claret intended for the abbot's guests.' Dunstan's frown was thoughtful. 'Yet perhaps I am wrong to say he died a natural death. Perhaps God struck him down for depriving me of a delicious treat.'

'And the Carmarthen murders?' asked Gwenllian. 'Who are your suspects for those?'

'I only have one: Gerald. He killed Pontius because they never really saw eye to eye, no matter what he claims now. And he killed Hurso, because he knew I would be distraught to lose my secretary.'

The prior had not seemed distraught to Gwenllian. She studied him closely, but could read nothing in his face. Uneasy under scrutiny, Dunstan bowed and moved away.

'Is he the culprit?' asked Cole, staring after him. 'He was suspiciously determined to blame someone else.'

'They have all been doing that,' sighed Gwenllian. Then she spoke more urgently. 'Go and do something outside, Symon. Quickly! Norrys is coming, and he has been drinking all morning. He looks set for a fight.'

'Then he shall have one, because I am not running away from him in my own castle.'

Before Gwenllian could explain the difference between running away and a prudent retreat, Norrys was there. His pugilistic face was twisted into a sneer, which looked odd with the stately robes he had donned to play Nebuchadnezzar. Cole regarded him askance, and Norrys's realisation that he looked absurd did nothing to improve his temper.

'So, you have riots in your town, murders in your castle and accidents on your walls,' he began jeeringly. 'Is there anything else wrong with your domain?'

'The presence of surly guests with no manners,' retorted Cole. He was usually slow to anger, and Gwenllian suspected that strain and tiredness had led him to snap.

'We shall soon be gone,' said Norrys. 'And then the King will hear of the chaos here.'

'Hardly chaos,' said Cole coldly. 'And there was no murder before you arrived.'

The blood drained out of Norrys's face. 'Are you accusing me?'

'Why not? You hate the St Davids priests, and you do not seem especially enamoured of your own companions either. Moreover, I have been regaled with tales all day about your excesses when you were constable. Murder is no stranger to you.'

Gwenllian fell back with a cry of alarm when Norrys hauled his sword from his belt. Cole did likewise, and there was a sudden hush in the rest of the hall.

'Put up your weapon,' said Cole in disdain. 'You are no match for me.'

It was hardly the most diplomatic of remarks, and with a yell of fury Norrys attacked. There was a brief clash of steel, and Gwenllian saw Symon was right: Norrys was a poor swordsman, and the fact that he was drunk did not help him. Cole defended himself almost lazily, then began an offensive of his own. Within moments, Norrys was disarmed and pinned against the wall. The Hospitaller showed no fear, only rage.

'Will you skewer him?' asked Gerald carelessly. 'I probably

would, in your position, because he has a poisonous tongue. However, it will make a terrible mess, and these are clean rushes. You had better let him go.'

'Yes, do,' agreed Prior Dunstan, although there was unease in his eyes, and Gwenllian suspected that he was less than impressed with the performance of the man who was supposed to be protecting him. She glanced around for Luci, lest he decided to help his fellow Hospitaller, but he was nowhere to be seen.

Cole stepped back and sheathed his sword. Norrys lunged again, but Cole had anticipated the move, and a punch sent him sprawling. Norrys's face burned with hatred and humiliation. He drew a dagger and lobbed it, but it went well wide of its target.

'Enough!' snapped Cole, grabbing him by the scruff of his neck and hauling him outside, where he deposited him cursing and struggling in a water trough. 'Perhaps that will wash the wine from your wits.'

He strode away. There was a loud cheer from watching servants and soldiers, and Gwenllian closed her eyes in despair. Shame would make Norrys more dangerous than ever! She became aware of sniggering next to her, and saw Robert.

'It is high time someone taught that bastard a lesson. He is a pig, and I bet *he* poisoned Canon Wilfred. He probably killed Pontius and Hurso too.'

'Why would he do that?' asked Gwenllian coolly.

'Because he is a bitter man who hates everyone. Your husband should watch himself from now on, because Norrys will have his revenge.'

The remainder of the rehearsal passed without incident, although Gerald heckled Dunstan's performance, and

85

Dunstan heckled Gerald's. The remarks grew steadily more acerbic as the afternoon wore on, and Gwenllian was relieved when the servants arrived to light lamps and prepare the hall for the evening meal. All smirked at Norrys, who had spent most of the time since his dunking sitting in a corner, seething silently.

'We shall all go to the chapel,' Gwenllian announced, because it was not somewhere Gerald and Dunstan could continue to score points off each other with their witticisms.

Archdeacon Osbert hurried away to prepare, while the guests divested themselves of their costumes and donned normal clothes. The service was quiet and peaceful, and went some way to soothing Gwenllian's ragged nerves. She put murder from her mind, hoping answers would come when it was not so cluttered with questions and worries.

When the service was over, everyone trailed into the bailey, which was lit with pitch torches. Cole was just riding through the gate, Iefan at his heels. He dismounted, saw Burchill and began to brief him. Gwenllian wondered where the older man had been all day – not with Symon, if he needed a report of what had been happening. Iefan began to walk to the kitchens, an uncharacteristic heaviness in his tread. Gwenllian intercepted him.

'What is wrong? The trouble in the town?'

The sergeant nodded, his face unhappier than she had ever seen it. 'People cannot afford bread as it is, and Cethynoc decided this afternoon to stop all work on the walls because of the weather. It is all very well for him – he gets paid whether he works or not – but others have families.'

'Most of the labourers are your kin,' said Gwenllian, understanding his concern. She smiled encouragingly. 'But the snow is melting. Building will start again soon, and folk will be able to leave the town in search of cheaper bread too.'

'Unfortunately, all the merchants in the area have united in greed,' said Iefan bitterly. 'They realise they are a power-ful force when they stand together, and I doubt they can be broken. Sir Symon says he does not have the authority to force them, but I think he should.'

'I will speak to him,' promised Gwenllian. 'And the mer-chants too, if necessary. Do not worry. The wages of Carmarthen's poor will not line the pockets of the rich.'

Iefan smiled at last, and grasped her hand in thanks. Then Gerald and Dunstan began to quarrel in response to some-thing Norrys had said. The Hospitaller's face was vindictive as he watched the results of his handiwork.

'You preside over dinner,' said Cole to Burchill, promptly reaching for the reins of his horse again. 'Quelling insur-rection is infinitely preferable to listening to that all evening.'

Burchill opened his mouth to object, but Cole was in the saddle and riding away before he could speak. Gwenllian beamed sweetly at him. He eyed her warily.

'Have you had a busy day?' she asked innocently.

'Yes,' replied Burchill shortly. He offered her his arm. 'Shall we? Perhaps food will render these querulous clerics more benign.'

Gwenllian was not sure how long she had been asleep before Cole returned that night. He groped his way to the bed and sat next to her.

'I thought I had better come to make sure no one else has been murdered,' he said.

'If they had, I would have sent for you. I am afraid I am no further forward with catching the killer, Symon.' She sat up, worried. 'Our guests might leave tomorrow, and they will have a terrible tale to take to the King.'

'Not tomorrow – the roads are still too icy. But the day after is a strong possibility.'

'You are exhausted,' said Gwenllian, hearing the strain in his voice. 'Sleep a little. Iefan and Burchill can manage without you for an hour.'

'And let Norrys tell the King that I dozed while my town needed me? Still, at least I know who is responsible for the merchants' cabal. It is William the corviser.'

'He has always been a troublemaker, and he has disliked you ever since you fined him for cheating his customers. He will leap at any opportunity to cause you problems.'

'Burchill and I eavesdropped on a speech he made in the Coracle tonight. He told his fellow merchants to raise their prices as high as they liked, saying that as long as they stand united, the townsfolk will have no choice but to pay.'

'I assume you brought him to the castle? The others will crumble without his oily tongue to lead them astray, and I am sure *I* can persuade him to see the error of his ways.'

'It was what I intended, but he escaped. Burchill was guarding the back door, but William managed to slip past him. I have no idea where William might have gone – he is not in his house. Still, I imagine he will reappear tomorrow.'

'Burchill lost him?' asked Gwenllian sharply.

'There was nothing suspicious about it, Gwen.' Cole sounded too tired to be angry. 'Burchill is not as quick-footed as he was, and I should have taken that into account. It was my fault, not his.'

Gwenllian did not argue. 'If you plan to lay hold of William tomorrow, be discreet. The other merchants will be outraged if you do it in front of them, and technically he has done nothing wrong. Profiteering is unethical, but not illegal.'

Cole was silent for a moment. 'I do not suppose you have had time to investigate the saboteur, have you?'

'No, I considered the murders more pressing,' she replied rather shortly.

'Quarrelsome clerics are *not* more important than my workmen,' he said firmly. 'But I shall catch the villain tonight. Obviously, he does not tamper with the walls during the day, when someone might see him, so logic dictates that he must work after dark. I plan to keep watch until dawn.'

'You will be wasting your time,' predicted Gwenllian. 'First, because you cannot know he will strike tonight. And second, even if he does, you may already have missed him.'

'It is a chance I am willing to take.'

'Then I shall come with you,' she determined, climbing off the bed and reaching for her outdoor clothes. 'It will give me a chance to review all I know, and talking is good for clarifying confusion. Besides, it will help you to stay awake.'

'It is too cold, and in your condition—'

'I have a beautifully warm cloak, and my condition is irrelevant. Besides, I am sure you can find me a sheltered spot.'

Cole grumbled all the time she dressed, but fell silent as they left the hall, walking as stealthily and surc-footed as a cat while Gwenllian stumbled along behind him. He found a place where he could watch the entire wall, and arranged a tarpaulin so it would shelter her from the rain. It was a miserable night, but milder than it had been, and she was sure most of the snow would be washed away by dawn.

'We have five suspects,' she began, once they were settled. 'None has an alibi for either death, and all have reasons to want Pontius and Hurso dead. Obviously, Norrys is at the top of the list, for the simple reason that their deaths will harm you. Next is that horrid Robert.'

'Who may have killed Canon Wilfred too,' added Cole. 'A bully whom he hated.'

'Prior Dunstan says it was a natural death, but the more I think about it, the more I believe that Wilfred *was* murdered, and that he is part of whatever is unfolding. Our next suspects are Dunstan and Gerald, both of whom are ruthless, and may well view two deaths as a necessary sacrifice to their ambitions. Although I like Gerald, and he is kin . . . '

'Who is the last suspect? I thought you had eliminated Foliot and Luci.'

'Yes,' said Gwenllian, reluctant to mention Burchill. 'Luci has an alibi in me for Hurso's death, while Foliot has Osbert. And there is the shoulder Foliot injured in his fall; he would have been in too much pain to clamber up a wall and start hacking at the mortar.'

'Do you think so?' asked Cole, surprised. 'Those bruises would not slow *me* down.'

'But Foliot is a priest, not a warrior trained to make light of such matters. You cannot compare him to yourself.'

Frustrated, she realised that talking had clarified nothing. When she said no more Cole began to tell her his ideas regarding the saboteur. He refused to believe that one of his soldiers or labourers was responsible, so his suspicions revolved around a stranger breaking in.

'And what does this mysterious outsider gain from his tampering?' asked Gwenllian.

'We shall ask when we catch him,' replied Cole, thus indicating that his theory had not taken the question of motive into account.

'Then tell me how he gets in?' pressed Gwenllian. 'You run a tight ship, and strangers are not permitted inside the castle after dark.'

Cole could not answer that either, and fell silent. Time

passed slowly. He kept himself awake by standing up, but Gwenllian drowsed, despite the creeping chill. Eventually, the sky began to lighten in the east, and she heaved a sigh of relief that their futile vigil was at an end. She was about to suggest they repair to the kitchens for hot ale when Cole stiffened, and his hand dropped to his sword.

'What?' she whispered softly, straining her eyes in the gloom. Then she saw it: a shadow moving among the supplies.

Cole motioned for her to stay put, and crept towards it. She watched, heart thumping. He was perfectly capable of looking after himself, but she grabbed a piece of wood anyway, ready to race forward and defend him if the skirmish did not go according to plan.

Unfortunately, the wood was tied to something else, which clattered as she picked it up. The shadow whipped round, then made a run for it. Cole followed with a battle cry learned on the crusade, before launching himself forward in a flying tackle. It looked painful, and she was not surprised that his victim made no attempt to escape once pinned to the ground.

Cole peered at his captive in the gloom, then sat back in astonishment. 'Iefan?'

'Sir Symon!' gasped the sergeant. 'You scared the life out of me!'

'What are you doing here?' Cole climbed off him and hauled him to his feet.

'I came to see whether you are right about the saboteur,' Iefan replied. 'If he does exist – and I am not saying he does – he will operate about now, when there is light enough to see by, but before the workmen arrive.'

'He does exist,' said Cole firmly. 'And when I saw you moving through the supplies I thought you were him.'

'And I thought you were a Saracen after my blood.' Iefan

scowled. 'Did you have to wrestle me so roughly? If I had been a weaker man, you might have broken my neck.'

'If you had been the saboteur, I would not have cared,' retorted Cole.

Iefan started to say something else, but footsteps made them turn. It was Cethynoc. The mason stopped dead in his tracks when he saw Cole and Iefan, and had taken several steps away before realising that he had already been seen. He advanced reluctantly, his blunt face sullen and unsmiling.

'You are here early,' said Gwenllian, immediately suspicious. 'Why?'

'Because it will be a fine day, and I wanted to make an inspection of the site before the labourers arrive in the hope that we can resume building,' Cethynoc replied, regarding her with an expression that was difficult to read in the dim light. She had no idea if he was telling the truth. 'And you?'

He smirked when Cole told him about the misunderstanding with Iefan, and then began to prowl. It was not long before he pointed at a pile of stones.

'You both wasted your time,' he growled. 'Look at that.'

'What is wrong with it?' asked Gwenllian, nonplussed.

Cethynoc touched the top one. It teetered ominously. '*I* did not stack it like that, and it was stable when I went home last night. Your saboteur was here sure enough.'

'One stone moved hardly constitutes a—' began Gwenllian.

'You would think it was dangerous if you brushed against it and it fell on you,' snapped Cethynoc. 'It would not kill, but it might break toes – and it would delay us yet again, because Sir Symon would insist on yet another safety inspection before work resumed.'

'You see?' said Cole, looking at Gwen and Iefan in vindication. 'There is your evidence. A saboteur *is* at work, and I will find him if it is the last thing I do. No one puts my men at risk and gets away with it.'

When Cole went to track down the greedy merchant William, Gwenllian had breakfast with the guests. Then, as Osbert was there, she suggested morning prayers in the chapel, charging the hapless archdeacon to make the ceremony as lengthy as possible. As soon as it was underway, she slipped out and hurried to the hall. Iefan was there, warming himself by the fire, so she commandeered his help, and together they explored the guests' chambers and searched their baggage. Unfortunately, their illicit operation brought forth nothing in the way of clues.

'The Mass has finished,' said Iefan, glancing out of the window. He looked around quickly, to ensure all had been left as they had found it. 'We should go.'

She followed him down the stairs. 'I hope Symon did not hurt you with his energetic tackle this morning.'

Iefan shot her a rueful glance. 'There is no saboteur. If there were, he would do something a lot more damaging than arranging a stone so it wobbled, or loosening a few knots. Besides, these things would not happen if he did not insist on working so fast.'

'You think his eagerness to finish is making people careless?'

Iefan shook his head. 'If a labourer is injured in an accident and cannot work, he and his family will starve. They know better than to take needless risks by rushing.'

'Who then?' pressed Gwenllian. 'Cethynoc? Symon?'

'Not Sir Symon.' Iefan sighed. 'And probably not Cethynoc, either, although I cannot bring myself to like the man. He cares for nothing except making money and telling tales to glorify himself in the taverns of an evening.'

He slipped away when they reached the bailey, to avoid the guests who were there, all glancing up at the sky and remarking to each other that the sun was already warm. It would soon melt what was left of the snow, and open the roads again.

Norrys was uncharacteristically silent, though. He was rubbing sleep from his eyes, suggesting he had dozed through the service, and Gwenllian strongly suspected that she and Cole had not been the only ones who had abandoned their bed the previous night. She wondered what Norrys had been doing.

'Your archdeacon needs to learn the art of brevity,' said Prior Dunstan sourly. 'I have never heard such a rambling and inconsequential homily.'

'I was not expecting to give one,' objected Osbert. 'I shall be better tomorrow.'

'Do not bother on my account,' said Gerald haughtily. 'I shall leave this afternoon. The snow is disappearing rapidly, and it is time the bishop elect was home in his cathedral.'

'St Davids is not *your* cathedral, and never will be,' said Robert, his young face full of defiance. 'The archbishop says so. You are dreaming.'

'How dare you!' cried Gerald. He rounded on Dunstan. 'Keep your whelp in order, or I shall box his ears. He is not fit to wear an Austin habit.'

'It is difficult to tell the condition of the roads from here,' said Foliot, speaking quickly to prevent another spat. 'So I suggest we inspect them for ourselves.'

There was a general move towards the gate, leaving Gwenllian uncertain as to whether she should go with them. The St Davids men turned right and began to walk towards the market, while the two Austins took the opposite direction.

94

As his appointed guardian, Norrys should have gone with Prior Dunstan, but he followed Gerald instead.

'I think I know the identity of the killer,' said Luci, speaking urgently in her ear and making her jump. 'I need the answer to one more question, and then I shall be sure.'

'Thank God!' breathed Gwenllian in relief. 'Who is it?'

But Luci shook his head. 'I cannot say until I am absolutely certain, lest I have made a mistake. But I will have my answer by tonight. Tell Cole to meet me by the castle walls at dusk – alone. I do not want our conversation overheard.'

He had gone before Gwenllian could offer to help him find his last answer.

Uneasy that Norrys was trailing Gerald, Gwenllian set off after them, Iefan walking solicitously at her side. She noted with alarm that there was far less snow than there had been the previous day, so that the killer might well leave in a matter of hours.

Carmarthen's streets were oddly deserted, and there was none of the usual morning bustle. She saw why when she arrived at the market. A mass of ordinary folk thronged the middle, while a number of merchants had assembled outside the guildhall, resplendent in robes that flaunted their wealth. They were separated by a very thin line of soldiers.

'Go home,' Cole was shouting. 'All of you. Fighting will solve nothing.'

'We have no intention of fighting,' came the arrogant tones of William the corviser, safely ensconced behind his fellow merchants. 'You will do it for us. It is why we pay taxes, after all.'

'Let me take you home, my lady,' begged Iefan, tugging on Gwenllian's cloak. With alarm, she saw that a number of the townsfolk held cudgels, knives and stones. 'Sir Symon will never forgive me if anything happens to you.'

'We are not going anywhere until we can buy bread at a decent price,' shouted a brewer named Tancard, a man noted for his loud opinions. Gwenllian was not surprised that he was the spokesman for what might soon become a mob.

'William and I will discuss it,' said Cole shortly. 'But not until you leave.'

'Yes, leave,' jeered William. 'Scurry back to your hovels. And tomorrow, you will find that bread costs what *we* decide – not you, and certainly not Cole.'

'One more remark like that, and I am going back to the castle,' said Cole shortly. 'You can defend yourselves against the people you are trying to cheat.'

'Don't you dare side with them!' snarled William. 'We are the ones who count in this town – the ones with power and money, who make things work. The poor are nothing.'

Unfortunately, it was true, although the merchants had never flexed their muscles in so disagreeable a manner before. Then Gwenllian happened to glance to one side, and saw Norrys watching from a doorway. He was smirking maliciously.

With sudden clarity, she recalled Archdeacon Osbert saying that William and Tancard had been Norrys's friends when he was constable. And then she understood exactly why the knight had been so sleepy that morning, and why William had not been at home the previous night. They had spent the time plotting together.

She could see Luci watching too, his scholar's face creased into a frown. Had he identified Norrys as the killer, committing murder as part of his plan to reinstate himself as constable? It seemed likely. She felt anger burn inside her at the enormity of what Norrys had done, and was about to stalk towards him and demand an explanation when there was a commotion nearby. It was Gerald, striding confidently through the crowd with an uneasy Foliot at his heels. The bishop elect looked every inch a prince of the Church with his haughty bearing and elegant robes. People instinctively parted to let him through.

'If the King hears about your ridiculous antics, he will arrange for Norrys to replace Cole as constable,' he said loudly, looking imperiously at merchants and paupers alike. 'Do you *want* Norrys?'

'Yes!' shouted William immediately. 'He will protect honest merchants from mobs.'

'He will protect the poor too,' added Tancard. 'So bring back Norrys!'

'Actually, I would rather have Cole,' countered a merchant named Jung, while his fellows nodded agreement. 'Norrys levied illegal taxes to line his own pockets when he was in power, and threatened to burn down my warehouse if I did not pay.'

'Norrys taxed everyone, even the very poor,' added a ditcher called Kedi. 'He took bread from the mouths of children, and was a brutal tyrant. We do not want him back, thank you.'

There was a growl of agreement from the crowd, and Gwenllian saw Norrys's face turn white with anger and indignation.

'Think about what you wish for,' said William to his fellow merchants. 'Norrys will not side with paupers when we feel compelled to raise our prices. He will take *our* part.'

'No, he will take ours,' said Tancard to the crowd. 'Because he is fair and decent.'

A lot of people laughed at this claim, rich and poor alike, and Norrys's hands clenched into fists of rage at his side. He started to step forward, but then decided against it.

'How much did Norrys pay you to cause trouble, William?' asked Gerald. He swivelled round to include Tancard in his icy glare. 'And you? I know for a fact that you spent an evening drinking together. Luci told me.'

William blanched and Tancard swallowed hard. Both began to deny the charges, but their guilt was so obvious that no one believed them. Meanwhile, Norrys was glowering furiously, and Luci had made himself scarce.

'Norrys told William to persuade the merchants to raise their prices, and Tancard to make sure the poor were vocal in their objections,' Gerald explained to the startled populace. 'And you all reacted exactly as he hoped.'

'No!' cried William. 'He is lying. Norrys never paid us to—'

'But you *did* tell us to increase the cost of bread,' interrupted Jung. 'You said everyone would have to pay, because they would have no choice, and we could all make a quick profit. We knew it was wrong, but you were very persuasive, and we all like money . . .'

'Put the prices back to where they were,' said Cole tiredly. 'William and Tancard, you are coming with me.'

'You cannot arrest me!' yelled William, outraged. 'I am too important to—'

'Do what you like with him, Sir Symon,' said Jung, eyeing the corviser in distaste. 'He no longer has our support.'

The mob surged forward, and it was not easy for Cole to extricate William and Tancard from the resulting mêlée. Both were bloody and bruised by the time he managed, and were glad to be incarcerated in a place where they would be safe from vengeful fists. Norrys was nowhere to be seen.

'Thank you,' said Gwenllian gratefully to Gerald. 'You averted a crisis.'

'All in a day's work for the bishop elect of St Davids,' said

Gerald loftily. 'Besides, I do not want Norrys as constable in my See – not a creature who is in the pay of Canterbury. And Cole will return the favour some day. Please make sure he does not forget it.'

Gwenllian was sure Gerald was quite capable of reminding Symon himself.

It was noon by the time the guests returned from inspecting the roads, and all agreed that it would be unwise to leave that day. However, the sunshine was warm, and more rain was expected that night, so they planned to leave Carmarthen first thing the following morning. It meant that Gwenllian had one afternoon and one evening to prevent more murders – and hope that Luci would be willing to share his conclusions. Or perhaps Foliot would have answers, given that he had intimated that he was exploring the matter too.

'I am surprised you dare show your face here,' she said coldly to Norrys, when the Hospitaller strutted boldly into the hall for the midday meal. 'After what you did.'

Norrys shrugged. 'You cannot prove Gerald's accusations, and the King will not believe them. He will make me constable, and force Cole to answer for failing to keep the peace.'

Gwenllian was so taken aback by his audacity that she could think of nothing to say as he strode to where the food was waiting. She was about to follow him when Foliot approached, the other guests at his heels. Cole was with them after a morning working on the castle walls.

'We must do something to repay you for your hospitality,' he said, smiling shyly. 'Shall we perform *The Play of Adam* for the town? We have been practising, after all.'

'Yes,' said Robert quickly. 'But I shall agree to lending you my manuscript only on condition that I can play God.'

'You play God?' Gerald gave a short bark of laughter that made the youth glower. 'I hardly think you possess the necessary gravitas to depict the Almighty.'

'No, you do not,' said Dunstan, agreeing with him for the first time since they had arrived. 'But why should we not oblige the town with a performance? We have nothing else to do for the rest of the day. We shall stage it in the late afternoon, so that darkness will fall as we finish the final scene. It will be very atmospheric.'

'I suppose the townsfolk will enjoy it,' acknowledged Gerald. 'And it may heal the rifts that Norrys has created with his selfish obsessions. It will also give them an opportunity to see that their bishop elect is a man of the people.'

Norrys regarded him with dislike. 'Do not blame me for Cole's inability to rule. And *I* do not think we should perform that play. We owe Carmarthen nothing, except to report its constable's ineptitude to the King.'

'I shall be making a report, too,' said Gerald coldly. 'One that will inform His Majesty that not only did you plot to see one of his towns in flames, but that you murdered Pontius and Hurso into the bargain.'

'My knights have murdered no one,' snapped Dunstan. 'You did it, so that we—'

'Enough!' roared Cole, and Gwenllian saw their carping had finally penetrated even his genial equanimity. 'What is wrong with you? Do you *want* me to lock you in your rooms like errant children? Because I will, if you persist with your squabbling.'

There was silence, and Gwenllian wondered whether he had gone too far. It was hardly politic to threaten senior churchmen. Norrys was smirking, evidently anticipating anger from Dunstan and Gerald, but Foliot came to the rescue.

'Shall we don our costumes? We have much to do if we are to perform today.'

Once the decision was made, the castle erupted into frenzied activity. The players disappeared to learn their lines; Cethynoc and his labourers were conscripted to build a stage; the servants set about preparing refreshments; and Cole and his soldiers went to announce the event in the town.

The task of overseeing everything fell to Gwenllian, and it was not easy to direct helpers and monitor guests at the same time. Gerald was a nuisance, because he was full of hubris from his victory in the market. His remarks aimed to enrage Norrys and the Austins, and they succeeded. Osbert was helpful in keeping the peace, though, and so was Foliot. She would have liked Burchill's assistance too, but he had gone out, although not with Cole.

During a lull in the preparations, she cornered Luci, and begged him to share what he had learned.

'Not yet,' he said stubbornly. 'What if I am wrong? I would never forgive myself.'

'But time is running out,' she said desperately. 'At least tell me what you still need to know. I may be able to help you find the proof you require.'

'But that would entail me telling you my suspect. Do not worry – I am almost there. I shall speak to Cole when the play is finished. Did you tell him to meet me by the walls?'

Terrified that Luci might continue to be difficult if answers still eluded him, she mulled over the killer's identity in her mind. The germ of a solution glimmered, and she cornered Cethynoc, learning several details that she thought might be important, including the fact that he had known one of the stones in Gerald's room was unstable.

'Then why did you not report it?' she demanded. 'Pontius might be alive if you had.'

The mason shrugged. 'I am paid to build walls, not act as a safety inspector.'

He slouched away, and Gwenllian watched him with dislike. No wonder Cole was keen for the project to be finished as quickly as possible – he wanted to minimise the time he was obliged to spend with his obnoxious master-mason!

The townsfolk began to arrive early, obliging her to oversee the provision of food and ale from the kitchens to keep some semblance of order. Then the play began, heralded by a blare from a trumpet. The 'musician' was Iefan, who was greeted by an enthusiastic cheer from the audience, many of whom were his family and friends. Gwenllian happened to glance at Cethynoc, and saw him scowling jealously, envious of Iefan's popularity.

'The Creation of the World' passed off uneventfully, although Gerald and Dunstan confused their fellow actors when they deviated from the script to give themselves grander roles. Then Norrys stepped onto the stage, but was heckled so violently that he could not make himself heard. Fuming, he flung off his hat and stalked away.

Next was the section about Cain and Abel, and Gwenllian's fears that Gerald and Dunstan might use the opportunity to do each other physical harm were fanned by Robert's whispered suggestion that this particular scene tended to bring bad luck.

'What do you mean?' she demanded uneasily.

'I mean that it has only ever been performed twice, and someone has died afterwards both times,' replied the lad with sly glee. 'Perhaps there will be another murder in Carmarthen Castle before the night is out.'

In alarm, Gwenllian watched him slither away, but her

attention quickly returned to the stage, where the first murder was being so valiantly resisted that she wondered whether the people of Carmarthen might go away believing that Cain had been foiled. But Abel fell eventually, although not without giving his killer a sly kick in his death throes that had the audience roaring its appreciation.

The performance finished with the *Ordo Prophetarum* – a series of scenes containing prophecies about Christ. Gerald inserted a long monologue of his own devising and, not to be outshone, Dunstan did likewise. Robert chanced his hand too, although with considerably less panache, and he was hissed off the stage when the audience grew bored.

It was over eventually, and more refreshments were distributed. Having thoroughly enjoyed themselves, the audience lingered, chatting and laughing. Gwenllian felt the tension rise inside her, and longed to throw them all out so that Cole could speak to Luci – and if the Hospitaller had no answers for them, be about investigating herself. But that would be ungracious in a woman brought up in the tradition of Welsh hospitality, so she forced herself to smile and nod at friends and acquaintances.

Fortunately, the weather came to her rescue. Clouds had rolled in with dusk, and the promised rain arrived. A sharp shower encouraged people home, although it was pitch-black by the time the last of them had trailed away.

'Find Luci,' she instructed Symon, acutely aware of how much faith she was putting in the Hospitaller's skills at detection. 'He should know the killer's identity by now.'

Cole nodded. 'He said I should go alone. Return to the hall and watch our other guests.'

'No,' said Gwenllian firmly. 'I like Luci, but I do not trust him. He is a brother knight to Norrys, for a start. I am coming with you.'

Cole laughed. 'You think you can stop a fight? Go inside, Gwen. You will be safer.'

He should have known better than to issue her with an order she did not like and expect her to follow it. She waited until he was some distance ahead, then trailed him towards the walls, taking care to stay in the shadows.

Suddenly, Cole gave a shout and darted forward. Two shadows emerged from the scaffolding, and Gwenllian's stomach lurched. Had Luci been lying about investigating the murders, and his real plan was to get Cole alone so that he and Norrys could kill him?

She snatched up a spade and ran towards them, but then ducked back into the shadows quickly. It was not the Hospitallers who were there, but Cethynoc and Burchill, both swearing at the fright Cole had given them with his yell. Gwenllian eased forward, aiming to hear what they were saying without being seen herself.

'. . . need a drink,' said Cethynoc sullenly. 'You two can waste your time lurking out here in the rain if you like, but I am off to a dry tavern.'

'And are you sure he is not the saboteur?' asked Cole of Burchill, when the mason had gone. 'It would be a tidy answer, and no one would mind us accusing him. His sullen manners have not made him popular.'

'True,' agreed Burchill. 'But I have watched him very carefully since the first mishap, and I can tell you without the shadow of a doubt that he is innocent.'

'Watched him carefully?' echoed Cole. 'Is that what you have been doing these last few days, so that you were never available when you were needed? I wanted you in the town, and Gwen would have appreciated your help with the guests.'

'These last few *weeks*,' corrected Burchill. 'I have invested a lot of time trying to catch your saboteur, lad. Besides, you did not need me, and neither did she – she is more than capable of managing awkward visitors. Come further into the shadows – I believe the saboteur will strike tonight, but not if he sees us.'

'I am supposed to meet Luci here,' said Cole. 'He knows the identity of the killer.'

'Good,' said Burchill. 'We can watch for him and our saboteur at the same time – two birds with one stone.'

Cole stepped back obligingly, while Gwenllian gripped her spade, ready to race forward and brain Burchill if he showed even the slightest hint of treachery. Both knights were silent, and as still as statues. Gwenllian shivered, more from tension than cold, and the spade grew heavy in her hands. Then she saw Cole stiffen and point. Someone was creeping along the wall, swathed in a cloak.

The person reached a pile of ropes, and there was a flare of light. He was burning them! Cole waited until they were well alight, and there could be no doubt of the culprit's guilt, then surged forward and grabbed him by the hood, spinning him round so he could see his face in the light from the fire.

'Iefan,' he said heavily. 'Damn! I had my suspicions, but I hoped I was wrong.'

'Iefan?' echoed Burchill in shock. 'No! He is your most trusted officer.'

Iefan hung his head, and when he spoke his voice was an agonised whisper. 'I *had* to do it. You are working too fast. We are months ahead of where we should be, thanks to Lady Gwenllian's organisation of supplies and Sir Symon's close supervision.'

'I do not understand,' said Burchill. 'Why should you object to the walls being finished early? Wooden ones burn, and we shall be much safer inside a ring of stone.'

'Yes,' said Iefan wretchedly. 'But the labourers are my kin ...'

'So you arranged "accidents" to slow us down,' said Cole flatly. 'Purely so they will be paid for a longer period of time. But you might have killed someone, man!'

'No! I was always careful.' Iefan winced. 'The frayed rope did not go according to plan – it was meant to break the moment it took the weight of the stones, not when the basket reached the top of the wall. I shouted a warning, and you managed to jump away . . .'

'Yes,' acknowledged Cole ruefully. 'But only just.'

'I knew you were worried,' said Iefan miserably. 'But our people will starve if you finish too soon. All I wanted was for the work to last until it is time to sow the new crops.'

'Did you tamper with the stone that killed Pontius?' asked Cole.

'No!' cried Iefan. 'Of course not! That had nothing to do with me.'

Cole waved his hand to say he could go, although Burchill regarded him sharply, evidently thinking there should be some reckoning for what Iefan had done. Head hanging in misery, the sergeant slunk away into the rain-swept night.

'You can come out now,' said Cole, turning to look at the place where Gwenllian was hiding. 'Burchill and I are quite safe, and there is no need for your spade.'

Somewhat sheepishly, Gwenllian emerged.

'You were not surprised when you recognised Iefan,' said Burchill, ignoring her to study Cole intently in the fading light of the flames. 'You *knew* he was the culprit. How?'

'His dogged insistence that there was no saboteur, when we all knew there was,' replied Cole. 'His assertion that the mishaps were minor, representing no danger to the workmen. His constant objections that the work was proceeding too fast. And I almost caught him in the act yesterday, when he spun a tale about looking for the culprit himself.'

'You did not tell me any of this,' said Burchill reproachfully.

'Or me,' added Gwenllian, sorry for it. If he had confided, she would have found a way to make Iefan desist without the humiliation of being caught red-handed. He had done wrong, but he had been a faithful retainer for years, and she could not find it in her heart to condemn him. Neither would Cole.

Cole shrugged. 'I hoped I was mistaken.'

'Well, I am sorry he transpired to be the villain,' said Burchill. 'You trusted him, and he betrayed you. Thank God we thwarted him, though: he was growing more reckless, and his tricks would have hurt someone eventually. You must dismiss him from your service.'

'No,' said Cole. 'It is over now, and we shall say no more about it.' He turned to Gwenllian. 'We had better find Luci before he has second thoughts about confiding in us. He is not out here – our scuffle must have put him off – so we had better look in the hall.'

The bailey was dark and quiet as they walked across it, although lights gleamed here and there as soldiers and servants settled down for an evening of storytelling around the fire, or perhaps an illicit game of dice. Gwenllian opened the hall door and stepped inside, Cole and Burchill at her heels. Then she stopped in confusion.

Gerald, Foliot, Prior Dunstan, Robert and Archdeacon Osbert stood in a silent semicircle around someone who lay on the floor, leaking blood. It was Luci.

Gwenllian started to move forward, to see whether Luci might be helped, but Burchill jerked her back roughly. Cole started to object, but spun round quickly at the distinctive sound of a sword scything through the air.

It was Norrys, his face twisted with vengeful malice. Cole ducked away, and while he staggered off balance, Norrys struck at Gwenllian. He would have killed her had Burchill not thrown himself in front of her, raising one arm to deflect the blow. The old knight cried out as the blade bit, and fell to his knees. Blood oozed between his fingers.

Cole drew his own weapon, but Norrys snatched up a crossbow. It was wound ready, and he grinned his satisfaction as he pointed it at Cole. Cole faltered. A sword was no match for such a device.

'No!' screamed Gwenllian. She started to step forward, to place herself between them, but Burchill reached up and grabbed her arm with his good hand, yanking her back again.

'Wait,' he murmured softly. 'Assess the situation before acting.'

Gwenllian felt like pushing him away, but she knew he was right. She tore a piece of cloth from her sleeve and tied it around his arm, although almost all her attention was on Norrys. He had indicated that Cole was to drop his sword and stand against the wall. With no choice but to obey, Cole did as he was told.

'Here is our killer,' said Norrys coldly. '*He* stabbed Luci, then went to collect his henchman, to help him dispatch the rest of you. I have just saved your lives.'

'We know everything, Cole,' said Robert gleefully. 'Luci has been conducting his own inquiry into the murders, and was on the verge of exposing you. So you killed him before he could speak. And you intended to slaughter the rest of us so that this miserable tale will never reach the ears of the King.'

'If you believe Norrys's claims, you are a fool,' said Gwenllian coldly. 'You *know* he wants Symon discredited because he longs to be constable.'

'It can be resolved easily enough,' said Gerald. He turned

to Cole. 'Just tell us where you have been since the end of the play. And put that weapon down, Norrys, before it goes off and hurts someone.'

'You will be safer if I keep it trained on Cole,' said Norrys. 'He is ruthless and cunning, and will seize any opportunity to escape.'

Gwenllian felt sick with fear, knowing Norrys was going to kill Symon anyway. She would have run towards him, but there was no strength in her legs.

'I have been with Gwenllian and Burchill,' replied Cole. 'And Iefan.'

'His wife and two henchmen,' sneered Norrys. 'Hardly independent witnesses. He murdered Luci, and has spent the time since washing the blood from his hands and clothes.'

'He is wearing the same tunic as earlier,' said Gerald. 'And it is unstained and certainly not wet. Moreover, your dogged determination to blame him makes me wonder whether *you* are the culprit.'

'I have been with Prior Dunstan from immediately after the play until we came down to the hall together,' said Norrys. 'We were packing, ready for tomorrow. I could not have stabbed Luci – and that means I am innocent of harming Hurso and Pontius too, given that there can only be one murderer. The same is true for Dunstan.'

Dunstan nodded slowly. 'We were together when Norrys says.'

'I have an alibi too,' said Robert gloatingly. 'I was talking to the townsfolk – hearing their accounts of what happened in the market this morning.'

Norrys shot him a look of pure hatred, and Gwenllian suspected that the foolish Robert had just put himself in considerable danger. Norrys would certainly not want *those* tales repeated in Canterbury.

'Well, *I* went to visit William and Tancard in the castle cells,' said Gerald. 'And the guards will testify to that fact, if you ask them. I, too, am innocent.'

'Why would you do such a thing?' demanded Dunstan. 'Or am I to report to the archbishop that you consort with rabble-rousers?'

'You may tell him that I care for the sinners in my See,' said Gerald loftily. 'They are stupid men, but not wicked ones. I went to hear their confessions, and they told me quite a tale. You have a lot to answer for, Norrys.'

'That means Foliot is the culprit,' said Gwenllian quietly, knowing that Burchill would not have taken the blow intended to kill her if *he* had been the guilty party; his act of heroism had exonerated him, too. 'There are no other suspects left.'

There was silence in the hall after Gwenllian had made her announcement, and she saw Norrys's crossbow waver slightly. Her claim had planted a seed of doubt in his mind. Meanwhile, the two Austins nodded to say they had known it all along, Gerald and Osbert gaped, and Foliot himself went white with shock.

'How can you say such a terrible thing?' he asked, once he had found his voice. 'I have an alibi too. I was with Osbert.'

'It is true,' said the archdeacon. 'He was.'

'There is blood on your arm,' said Gwenllian, pointing. 'You washed your hands, but it is messy stuff, and I can see a smear of it on your wrist. There are also spots on your habit.'

'I cut myself,' said Foliot, pulling down the offending sleeve. 'On a nail.'

'Then show us,' she said simply. 'Where is the cut?'

'It is personal,' said Foliot, licking dry lips. 'I will show Osbert, but no one else.'

Gwenllian struggled to tie facts together, easier now she knew the identity of the culprit. She addressed the others. 'Foliot murdered Pontius too. It is obvious now I think about it. Do you remember how he spent his first day here?'

'Being shown around the castle by Iefan and Cethynoc,' supplied Cole promptly. 'Cethynoc is a mason, and knows all about stones and mortar.'

'Precisely!' said Gwenllian. 'Cethynoc told me today that he knew there was an unstable stone in that particular bedchamber, and that he had mentioned it on his tour, as Pontius would have been able to attest, had he still been alive.'

'But stones do not drop out of walls to order,' said Cole. They had everyone's attention now, although Foliot was shaking his head. 'So it stands to reason that Pontius was killed by someone in the same room as him. And I know how Foliot did it.'

'You do?' asked Gwenllian uneasily, hoping he was not about to destroy their case by claiming something ridiculous.

'He chipped the stone loose, and wedged it in place with a pebble. The pebble was tied to a piece of twine. One jerk caused it to fall. The culprit could only be Gerald or Foliot, because they were the only two in that chamber when it fell.'

'But I am injured,' said Foliot, one hand to his shoulder. 'I cannot climb walls!'

'Of course you can,' said Cole scathingly. 'You are long past the stage where your bruises will incapacitate you. Your intended victim was Gerald, of course.'

'No,' cried Foliot. He appealed to the bishop elect, who was regarding him uncertainly. 'This is all a lie – I would never harm you. He wants me blamed so Norrys will let him go.'

'Open your scrip,' suggested Cole. 'I wager anything you like that it will contain twine.'

'Of course it will,' said Foliot, backing away when Robert, his youthful face alight with spiteful glee, tried to take it from him. 'I always carry twine when I travel.'

'But you did not have any when you arrived here,' said Cole. 'You had used it all up by mending broken reins after the ambush in Trecastle. Gerald asked you for some when I broke the lace on my boot, if you recall.'

'I bought some more,' said Foliot desperately. 'It proves nothing.'

'From which merchant?' pressed Cole. 'We shall send for him immediately.'

Foliot looked sick. 'I cannot recall,' he whispered. 'And he may not remember me . . .'

Robert made a lunge for him, and there was a brief tussle, which the youngster won. He took the purse to a table and upended it. Among the items that tumbled out was a length of thin twine that had a loop tied in one end.

'This may well have been knotted around a pebble,' reported Dunstan, inspecting it closely. 'There is grit caught in it that says it has certainly been somewhere dusty, such as hanging from a wall that has had mortar scraped from it.'

'It is not mine,' shouted Foliot, panicky now. 'Someone put it there to see me accused.'

'But you never leave your scrip unattended,' said Gerald, his face full of hurt confusion. 'because it contains money. No one would have had the chance to plant evidence there.'

'And all to ensure that Gerald is not made bishop,' Gwenllian went on. She glanced at Cole, sensing he was readying himself to attack. She shook her head slightly, to tell him to wait. There was doubt in Norrys's face, and she began to hope that the situation could be resolved without Cole risking his life in a wild lunge. 'It was your second attempt, the first being in Oseney, with a jug of poisoned wine.'

'The stuff that killed Canon Wilfred?' asked Robert, wide-eyed. 'Lord! I saw Foliot hovering over it, but then he left, so I filched it for my master. Thank God I did not drink any myself!'

'I did not!' cried Foliot. 'Poison indeed! Is that what you think of me?'

Gerald's hurt had turned to contempt, and he regarded Foliot with such iciness that even Gwenllian winced. 'You were late coming to our room the night Pontius died, and I had doused the candle, so it was dark. You expected me to be in the better bed, but I had given it to Pontius, because he had complained of backache.'

'I would never—' began Foliot.

'It is all clear now,' Gerald went on, cutting across him. 'The stone was the *fourth* time you tried to kill me, not the second. You arranged ambushes in Brecon and Trecastle, too – although they misfired and you were the one who was injured. But God protected me.'

'Is that what you thought, Foliot?' asked Gwenllian. 'That God was with Gerald? So when the ploy with the stone failed, you opted for other tactics – namely to have him accused of murdering Hurso?'

'You certainly made us willing to believe it,' said Dunstan. 'None of us missed the suspicious glances you kept shooting in Gerald's direction. How very clever!'

'This is all nonsense,' cried Foliot. 'Tell them, Osbert!'

'He is right.' Sweat beaded on the archdeacon's hairless pate. 'Because there is only one killer, and if it was Foliot, then it means he killed Hurso, too. But he did not: he has an alibi for Hurso's death, and for Luci's, too, he was with me both times.'

'Yes,' said Gwenllian softly. 'Because *you* are his accomplice.'

'*Osbert* plotted against me too?' asked Gerald, shocked. 'But I barely know him!'

'Of course not!' cried Osbert hoarsely. He fixed Gwenllian with reproachful eyes. 'I have been your archdeacon for years. How can you say such wicked things about me?'

'Because I have proof. Hurso fought his attacker hard enough to break his fingernails. You refused to don your costume for the play yesterday because to undress would have revealed the scratches on your arms.'

Robert made a lunge for Osbert's hand and pushed up the sleeve to reveal marks.

'It was easy for you,' said Gwenllian, disgusted. 'You live here, so you knew exactly where to kill Hurso without being seen. Foliot gave you an alibi—'

'But Osbert was not wet,' said Foliot triumphantly. 'Hurso was killed in the rain, and you said yourself that his killer would have been soaked. I was damp, because I had been to the latrines, but Osbert was dry. And if *he* is innocent of killing Hurso, then so am I.'

'Osbert is bald,' explained Gwenllian. 'His head is easy to wipe dry, unlike one with hair. He divested himself of his sodden cloak and pretended he had been indoors all afternoon. And you stabbed Luci, because he was on the verge of exposing you both.'

'No.' Osbert swallowed hard, and his denial was unconvincing. 'I never did.'

'You planned it from the moment you and Foliot met,' said Gwenllian in disgust. 'Prior Dunstan asked to stay in your house, but you ensured they all came here, knowing trouble would follow. You have been friends for years, and you conspired together like—'

'We did what we thought was right!' cried Osbert suddenly. Foliot closed his eyes, disgusted by the capitulation. 'Gerald should *not* be Bishop of St Davids. He will try to make it an archbishopric, which will earn the wrath of the King, Canterbury *and* Rome. He will be a disaster, inflicting misery and hardship on thousands of people . . .'

'Yes, but murder,' said Dunstan in distaste. 'It—'

Suddenly, Foliot snatched a knife from the table and ran towards Norrys. The knight tensed, but the crossbow bolt trained on Cole did not waver.

'You cannot shoot Cole and leave witnesses, Norrys,' said Foliot urgently. 'Yet you are eager to see him dead. So you, Osbert and I will set this hall alight and lock everyone else inside. We three will be the only survivors.'

Norrys stared at him for a moment, and then his face broke into a slow, savage grin. 'An excellent solution. However, Cole has an uncanny ability to slither out of dangerous situations unharmed, and I should not like him to escape. I need to be certain he is dead.'

He aimed the crossbow and loosed the mechanism. There was a sharp click and Cole slumped to the floor.

Gwenllian stared at Cole in mute horror, and took an unsteady step towards him, but Burchill grabbed her hand, and held her fast.

'The baby,' he whispered. 'Think of the baby.'

But Gwenllian could only think of Cole. She could see he was breathing, but for how long? Norrys had grabbed a second crossbow, already wound, and was toting it in a way that said he would be delighted to claim another victim, so that although Dunstan and Gerald had taken several steps towards the door, both faltered. Young Robert was rooted to the spot in terror.

'I shall set the rushes alight,' said Foliot. 'They are dry and will burn well. Osbert, get ready to open the door – not too soon or servants might see the flames.'

'And I will shoot anyone who tries to escape,' Norrys warned his prisoners. 'So move at your peril.'

'Osbert!' cried Burchill. 'You are not a bad man – you cannot do this evil thing! You know Lady Gwenllian is with child. Do not let Foliot lead you down a dark path.'

'It is good advice,' said Gerald sternly. 'Your immortal soul is in grave danger, because if I die, I shall ensure you *never* join me in heaven. And that is a promise.'

Osbert's expression was agonised, and for a moment, Gwenllian's hopes flared. But Norrys brought the hilt of his dagger down on the archdeacon's head, and he crumpled. Foliot touched a torch to the floor, and there was a crackle as the rushes caught.

Norrys laughed wildly as flames licked towards his victims, but then stopped and stared at his chest in surprise. A knife was embedded in it, and Cole was racing towards him. Cole knocked the astonished Hospitaller from his feet, felled Foliot with a well-aimed punch, and yelled for servants to bring water.

As he held regular fire drills, no one needed instructions to form a line and pass buckets from hand to hand. It was an efficient operation, and the flames were out before any real damage was done. Shutters were thrown open to dispel the smoke, and the singed rushes were hauled out into the bailey. It was not long before the crisis was over.

Iefan, who had worked as hard as anyone, carried Luci to the chapel, but dumped Norrys's body next to the spoiled flooring. Then he escorted Foliot and Osbert, the latter nursing a very sore head, to the castle cells. Gerald, Dunstan and Robert agreed a truce and repaired to the chapel together to give thanks for their deliverance.

'I thought you were dead,' said Gwenllian unsteadily, burying her face in Cole's shoulder. 'Norrys shot you without hesitation.'

'He missed by a mile,' said Cole dismissively. 'He was a wretched warrior. Burchill knew I was unharmed, of course. It was why he warned you to think of the baby.'

'To prevent me from risking myself needlessly,' said Gwenllian in understanding. 'He almost lost his sword arm defending me too. I was wrong to suspect him: he is a good friend – to both of us.'

'The best,' said Cole with a smile.

III

Life soon settled back to normal in Carmarthen. Gerald rode west towards St Davids and Dunstan rode east towards Canterbury. The merchants set their prices at a more reasonable level, and the citizens continued to complain about them anyway. Luci and Norrys were buried in the churchyard, and Cole escorted Osbert and Foliot to the Austin priory, to be incarcerated there until their fates could be decided.

'I do not care what happens to them,' Cole said to Gwenllian when he returned. 'Just as long as they leave my town.'

'They caused all manner of trouble,' agreed Gwenllian. 'They thought their actions were justified, and perhaps they were – Gerald *will* be trouble if he is bishop – but to commit murder to achieve them . . .'

'None of it would have happened if Robert had not filched that poisoned wine for Wilfred,' said Cole with a sigh.

'Gerald would have swallowed it, and that would have been the end of him. Foliot and Pontius would have brought the sad news to St Davids, Dunstan would have gone home to Canterbury, and the entire business would have been over.'

'I disagree,' said Gwenllian. 'Gerald is popular, and his supporters would have asked questions. Besides, I like Gerald. He defended you against Norrys.'

'Yes, he did.' Cole smiled. 'He insisted on reading me some of his book before he left. I tried to dissuade him – I am not a man for sitting idle – but it was actually rather good. Perhaps he should confine himself to writing, and leave the Church to gentler men.'

'Perhaps he should,' said Gwenllian, thinking it must have been compelling indeed if it had secured Cole's approval. He detested literary pursuits.

'Do you think John will use the incident to oust us?' Cole regarded her with a troubled expression. 'There is no Norrys to twist the truth, but four men *were* murdered in my castle, there *was* a saboteur, and the poor *did* stage a riot. A reliable constable would not have let all that happen.'

'I think we can trust Gerald to speak in our favour,' said Gwenllian.

'But that is what worries me. He is not popular with Canterbury or the King, and his support might do more harm than good.'

Gwenllian supposed it might, and there was no answer to his concerns. 'Do you think Robert was right when he said that staging the Cain and Abel section of *The Play of Adam* brings bad luck?' she asked uneasily. 'I know it is wrong to be superstitious, but I cannot shake the conviction that something terrible is going to happen.'

'Nothing will,' said Cole, ever the optimist. Then he reconsidered. 'Well, not unless Gerald is made bishop. His barbed tongue will alienate the King, and there will be trouble. He will claim our support as kinsfolk, and we shall be dragged into murky waters.'

Gwenllian regarded him unhappily. He was right, of course. 'Perhaps the archbishop and the King will prevent his consecration.'

'Perhaps. But I hope they find a kinder way to do it than Osbert and Foliot.'

Robert was pleased to be away from Carmarthen, and even more pleased to be away from Gerald. The man was arrogant and brash, and would do immeasurable harm to the Church if he was allowed to become one of its bishops. Robert had thought so from the moment he had first met him in Oseney Abbey, and he had no regrets about what he had done.

It had been easy to leave documents for Foliot to find outlining Gerald's plans for the future – ones far more outrageous than even Gerald's burning ambition could accommodate. Shocked by what Robert had penned in Gerald's handwriting, Foliot had done his best to ensure that Gerald never reached home, but his failure meant that Robert had had to take matters into his own hands, just as he had done with Canon Wilfred.

Poor Foliot was innocent of poisoning the wine, of course, although no one would ever believe him. That had been Robert's parting gift to Wilfred, payment for the months of misery he had suffered under that lazy, selfish old tyrant. He had intended Gerald to swallow some too, but Wilfred had spilled it in his death throes.

Of course, Wilfred was a killer himself. He talked in his sleep, and as the indolent old rogue had had a penchant for naps, Robert had heard him converse many times with his

hapless victims. Robert knew for a fact that he had smoth-
ered a saintly abbot named Wigod, and there had also been
others, although their names had meant nothing to him.
The villain had deserved to die, and Robert felt he had done
Oseney a great service by relieving it of his malevolent presence.

Robert was not sure why he cared so passionately that
Gerald should not succeed in his ecclesiastical ambitions.
Perhaps it was because such a man would make enemies for
the Church – which Robert intended to rise high within –
and he disliked anyone having the power to make it weak.
Or perhaps it was the man's objectionable character. He fin-
gered the worn pages of *The Play of Adam* in his saddlebag.
And then there was the fact that Gerald had prevented him
from playing God, just as Wilfred had.

He scowled at Prior Dunstan riding beside him. Wilfred
and Gerald were not the only ones who had interfered with
his dreams. Dunstan had too. Would the prior reach
Canterbury alive? Or would he die on this return journey?
Of an accident, of course.

Historical Note

Robert of Oseney succeeded Dunstan to become prior of
the Austin house of St Gregory's, Canterbury in 1213; he
remained for only two years, and resigned to become a
simple monk at Clairvaux, although no reason is given.
Hurso was another Canterbury Austin from the late twelfth
century, and Robert de Luci was a Kentish knight active in
1199. Prior (later Abbot) Wigod ruled Oseney near Oxford
for thirty years until his death in 1168; Hugh was elected
Abbot in 1184 and died in 1205.

Roger Norrys was constable of Carmarthen in the 1170s, and Symon Cole was constable in the 1190s. Osbert was Archdeacon of Carmarthen at this time, while Cethynoc, Tancard, William the corviser, Kedi, Jung and Sir Robert de Burchill are all listed as witnesses to deeds in the diocese in the late 1100s.

Today, Gerald de Barri (Gerald of Wales) is best known for his travels. He was not popular with his contemporaries, who saw him as arrogant, vain and abrasive – and he really did read his books at Oxford over several consecutive days. To them, he was the man desperate to be Bishop of St Davids, and he was elected to the post twice (in 1176 and 1198) by the cathedral's canons. He also wanted to establish the See as an archbishopric, thus placing it on a par with Canterbury. Needless to say, this did not meet with approval in England.

His second attempt to gain the See was blocked by both Canterbury and the King, and the dispute dragged on for four years. He made three journeys to Rome to put his case to the Pope, all with the support of archdeacons Pontius, Osbert and Reginald Foliot. Eventually, though, his followers were persuaded to change their minds, and the See went to another contender.

Furious at what he saw as a betrayal, Gerald wrote about them in his book *De Jure*, noting how they had been rewarded for their treachery: 'Faithless Foliot' was given the church at Llanstephan, while the 'Goitre of Carmarthen' (Osbert) got a manor on the Gower. Gerald remained angry and bitter about his defeat for the rest of his life.

ACT TWO

Wilbertone, Cambridgeshire Fens, Spring 1361

'You cannot ask that of me!' Horrified, the young monk sprang to his feet, backing away from the elderly priest as if he was the devil himself.

'I do ask it, Brother Oswin. More than that, I demand it.' The old man's voice was cracked with age, but his eyes blazed with determination.

'But it is sacrilege,' Oswin protested. 'A sin, a terrible sin. I would cut off my own hand rather than use it to commit such a deed. How could you ask any man to carry out such a wicked act, let alone a man in holy orders?'

'Because only a monk can do this,' the old man growled. 'Come back here and sit down. I said, sit down!'

Brother Oswin, trained like a hound to obey the voice of command, perched on a low wooden stool that had been placed beside the priest's chair, and gnawed at his finger-nails, which were already bitten down to the quick. As soon as he'd entered Father Edmund's tiny cottage he'd noticed the bunch of dried poppy heads hanging from the beam. The syrup made from the white poppies eased the shivers of the marsh fever and soothed the crippling joint pains that tormented those who lived in the dank fenland. It even dulled the gripes of hunger, but sup it too often and it would drive a man's wits from his head for ever. Was that the cause of Father Edmund's madness? For mad he certainly must be, even to contemplate such a dreadful act.

Brother Oswin had known the old priest ever since he was a boy. In fact it was Father Edmund who had helped him to gain admittance as a novice at Ely Priory. So when the priest had sent word to him, asking him to come back to the village, he had sought leave to depart right away, assuming his old confessor was sick or in desperate need of his help. But nothing could have prepared him for what Father Edmund had asked of him.

'Why, Father, why would you ask such a thing?'

'Look around you,' the old man commanded.

The young man's gaze ranged around the dingy cottage. He had not visited Father Edmund for several years and had been shocked to see the misery in which the frail old man was living. Surely it hadn't always been as bad as this. In the blackened hearth, a pitiful fire was struggling for life against the icy blasts whistling through the gaps in the walls, and the ragged blankets strewn across the bed were so threadbare there could be little warmth left in them. A few crumbs of coarse, dry bean-bread still clung to a wooden trencher on the table, the remains of the priest's supper, no doubt, and more than likely the only meal he'd eaten that day.

Spring was always the hungry time, when the winter stores were running low and the new crops were not yet harvested, but the prolonged drought of the previous year had meant that the barns were already three-quarters empty even before the first frosts, and many a man and beast had perished long before the green mist returned to cover tree and field. That this old crow had managed to survive was nothing short of a miracle, but then there were always some villagers willing to sacrifice their last crust to a priest or a monk, in the hope of receiving a whole loaf in the afterlife.

Father Edmund lifted a leather beaker from the table and thrust it under Brother Oswin's nose. It only took one sniff to tell that the ale was sour, not fit even for the hogs.

'Even beggars at the alms gate drink better ale than this,' the old priest said bitterly. 'Is this the way God rewards His faithful servants?'

'But when you're granted your new living—'

'What new living, boy? They've left me here to rot for over twenty years. It's been ten, fifteen years since the Bishop of Ely sent word to me. I doubt he even remembers I'm still alive. I'll stay here until I die. That's my reward for all I accomplished for the Church.' Father Edmund huddled closer to the fire, spreading his mottled hands over the feeble embers. 'When I think of all I did for Bishop de Lisle. If it hadn't been for me, he would be dead and rotting in his grave now.'

'The bishop is fled abroad,' Oswin told him. 'But he's a man of compassion. They say that all through the Great Pestilence he was not afraid to administer the last rites to the dying, though many others refused for fear of the contagion. When he returns, I'm sure—'

'Sure, are you? De Lisle may be many things, but a fool is not one of them. He won't return to Ely again. He daren't. There are still plenty who think him guilty of theft, if not of murder. And now I hear rumours that the Great Pestilence is once more prowling across England. Is this so?'

The young monk bowed his head as he made the sign of the cross. 'It is, Father. But you should not fear it. This time, they say, it's the children and the fit young men that death is snatching first.'

The old man shuddered. 'I have lived through it all before and I prayed I would never do so again – the putrid stench of the bodies, the fires, the mass graves with the corpses thrown in like shoals of rotting fish, then the looting and the murder. Bands of cutthroats roaming through the towns and villages taking whatever they wanted from the living and the dead. They cared nothing for any law, nor for any man. They were worse than savage wolves.'

'But you survived, Father, when all around you perished. Even though you daily ministered to the dying and buried the dead with your own hands, yet you did not fall sick. You knew how to defend yourself, and Bishop de Lisle too. They say you conjured the angels and demons to protect him. You will survive the pestilence again, Father.'

'What is the use of surviving?' the old man asked savagely. 'When the villagers die and there is no one left to bring tithes to my crumbling church, no neighbours to share their pottage with me, no boys to fetch fuel for my fire, how will I keep from freezing? How will I cook? Where will I buy food when a single loaf costs a king's ransom?'

Oswin laid his hand comfortingly on the aged knee. He could feel the sharp bones even through the patched robe. 'I will try to persuade the prior that you should be granted a place in our hall or infirmary. I know you cannot pay a corrody for lodging and food, but they will surely take you in out of charity. After all, as you said, you did great service for Bishop de Lisle.'

Father Edmund flapped his hand impatiently. 'You'd be wasting your time. They don't want me back. I know too much. I'm an embarrassment to them.'

He closed his own cold fingers over Oswin's, gripping his hand with a surprising strength. 'Just bring me what I have asked of you, Brother Oswin. If I possess that I will have people flocking to my door, for I will have the certain cure. They will sell everything they own to save themselves and their children from the Great Pestilence, and if they don't ...'

he laughed bitterly, '. . . then I'll put it to another use. They say it will open any lock and it puts a household into such a deep sleep that a thief may steal the bed they are lying on without waking them.'

'No, Father, no . . .' the young monk protested, tears of anguish welling up in his eyes. 'This is not you speaking. The poppy juice has turned your wits, or an evil spirit has entered into you. The godly man I knew as a boy, the man who guided me into the priory, would never have entertained such wicked thoughts.'

'I am the man that the Bishop of Ely has turned me into and it is Ely who will suffer for it. They owe me this, and you will bring it to me. Don't you dare shake your head at me, boy. Do you think I've forgotten what you confessed to me before you entered the priory, the reason you became a monk? The fool of a blacksmith still believes to this day his daughter ran away, but you and I both know she did not. No, that poor girl lies at the bottom of the sucking marsh where you dumped her, after you and your brother raped and murdered her.'

Oswin's face drained of colour. 'But . . . we were scarcely more than boys . . . we were drunk . . . it was just high spirits . . . Her death was an accident. We never intended her any harm. And I made a full and contrite confession to you as my priest. You absolved me . . . No priest may reveal what is told to him in confession. The Church forbids—'

'I told you, boy, the Church has betrayed me. I no longer care what it forbids. And I still have the necklace you took from her body. If her father should be shown that . . .'

The young monk looked as if he was going to vomit, but he swallowed hard and took a deep breath, thrusting out his chin defiantly. 'I will confess my crime before the whole priory and accept whatever penance they lay upon me even if it should last my whole life, but I will not add to my sins by doing what you ask. I will not!'

Father Edmund leaned back in his chair. 'Brave words, boy, for you know that whatever you confess you will be safe. As a monk, you cannot be executed for your crime. But your brother is not in holy orders. He has a wife and three little children. Will you watch him as he dances on the end of a rope? Will you listen to the sobs of his wife and children as they starve?'

He leaned forward again, grasping Oswin's sleeve. 'Make no mistake, I care not one wit for man or Church now. Do as I ask, boy, or I swear your brother will be dangling from the hangman's noose before the month is out.'

Ely, Cambridgeshire

'It'll never work,' Henry said, staring in dismay at the huge throng of people swarming around the door of the cathedral.

'Course it will,' Martin said cheerfully, giving his cousin a bracing punch on the arm. 'Besides, you got a better idea? I don't think we'd exactly get a warm welcome if we went back to Cambridge. With the pestilence spreading it won't be long before the towns start shutting their gates and I've no mind to be stuck out on the road when they do. This way we get money enough for food and wine, and with a bit of luck, snug lodgings in the priory guest hall too.'

'But you heard those jugglers: they nearly got their heads broken by the lay brothers when they threw them off the priory's land.'

'They had a half-dressed girl with them. It's hardly surprising they were chased off if the prior saw her turning cartwheels and displaying all her wares in front of a gaggle of pimple-faced novice monks. But we will offer something quite different, something –' Martin groped about for the word, which wasn't one he often had cause to use – 'something *holy*. The lay brothers can't control the rabble. If the pilgrims keep pouring in at this rate, sooner or later there's going to be a riot. The crowds need something to distract them and that, dear cos, is where we step in, like angels of mercy, to deliver them from evil.'

Henry had to admit his cousin was right about one thing: the lay brothers were losing control of the crowd. People had been flocking to the cathedral for weeks in far greater numbers than usual, not just seeking alms to feed their starving families, but to pray at the shrines of St Etheldreda and her sister St Withburga for an end to the droughts and for a good harvest. But since the rumours of the pestilence had begun to spread, the crowds streaming to the shrines had more than doubled, with men, women and children desperate to seek protection from the sickness and prepare their souls for death should they fall to the Great Mortality.

The queues were now so long that the great doors of the cathedral had to be slammed shut in the evening before some of those who had been waiting all day had a chance to get inside, never mind come near enough to touch the shrines. Forced to spend another night in the overpriced and overcrowded inns if they could afford it, or camping out in the cold, the pilgrims found their tempers were fraying badly. Those who had been trying to get in for days screamed abuse at the newly arrived who pushed ahead of them. Fights erupted as people attempted to wriggle their way to the front of the queue, with the old, the weak and the lame being shoved aside.

Even when they gained admission to the cathedral, violent

arguments broke out between the lay brothers trying to collect the fee for visiting the shrines and the pilgrims who
argued that, having been forced to wait for days, they now
had no money left to pay. Although the lay brothers were, on
the whole, burly men, well armed with thick staves, they
were having a hard time trying to prevent the crowds from
simply storming their way in and smashing off fragments of
the shrines to carry home with them. Something had to be
done to distract the mob before someone got a knife between
his ribs or was trampled to death.

'Come on.' Martin tugged at his cousin's arm. 'No use
trying to talk to the lay brothers. We need to talk to the prior
himself.'

Pushing his way through the tide of people flowing
towards the cathedral, Martin led the way down the Heyrow,
towards Steeple Gate, close to Goldsmith's Tower where the
gold and silver vessels and ornaments were wrought for the
cathedral under the gimlet eye of the sacrist, who had his
office on the floor above.

Henry trailed after Martin, as he had done ever since he
could toddle. Martin, two years older than Henry, was still a
head taller than he, even though they were both now in their
twenties. Henry was also painfully aware that Martin was
the more handsome of the two, with speedwell-blue eyes of
disarming innocence, which could entice maids and matrons
alike to climb into his bed, and made men foolishly trust
him in spite of their own good sense. Henry had only ever
been the insipid shadow following on his cousin's heels, the
one who women ignored and men overlooked.

Sometimes he tried to convince himself that women
would find him desirable if his handsome cousin wasn't
around to make him look dull and plain by comparison. But
he never had the courage to put it to the test and face the

world alone. His cousin had always looked out for him, and as Martin reminded him at least once a day, Henry simply didn't have the wit to fend for himself.

A man squatted in front of Steeple Gate, his arms bound in filthy bandages through which greenish-yellow stains were oozing. Half a dozen more beggars sat around in a state of near stupor, hunched against the cold wind from the river. But as soon as Martin tugged at the bell rope hanging above the gate they sprang to life and clustered round, pushing wooden bowls at Henry and Martin, whining for coins.

A young monk dragged open the gate and took a step forward. The beggar with the bandaged arms almost hit him in the face with his bowl as he thrust it towards him. The monk shoved the beggar hard in the chest, so that he stumbled over the crutches of another and fell sprawling on the stones.

'I've told you before,' the monk snapped, 'not another loaf will you get from us, so it's no use your waiting.' Seeing the shocked expression on Henry's face the monk flushed slightly. 'He's avering, an old trick. He's only pretending to be sick, but I reckon he takes the meats we give him and sells them, then spends the money in the local tavern.'

The beggar let forth a stream of vehement denials and curses, and the others joined in, but the young monk was evidently well used to ignoring them.

'What's your business here?' he shouted over the din.

Martin raised his voice to match him. 'We've a proposition to put to the prior.'

The monk raised his eyebrows scathingly. 'And what might you be wanting to propose that would be of any interest to an important man like the prior?'

'Those crowds outside the cathedral are on the verge of a riot. We have a plan to keep them calm and quiet.'

130

'I've a plan to do that myself, but I don't think the prior will sanction firing arrows down on them from the towers,' the monk said sourly. Then, as the beggars' demands grew ever more insistent, he retreated back into the gateway and began pushing the gate closed behind him.

Just before slamming it shut, he peered at Martin through the gap. 'Look, even if you could perform the miracle of the loaves and fishes, Prior Alan wouldn't see you. Why don't you try Subprior Stephen? He went out of here a little while ago making for the quayside. If you hurry you'll catch him.'

Without looking to see if Henry was following, Martin raced off down the hill, dodging round the pilgrims and traders, the boys hefting great stacks of dried peat on their backs and the women hurrying home with fat eels for their husband's dinner. Henry didn't trouble to follow. If there was wheedling and persuading to be done, he could add nothing. He would simply be expected to stand and listen to one of his cousin's eloquent speeches as he convinced yet another fool to part with his money. Henry might occasionally be called upon to back up some wild claim or other, but he couldn't even do that without blushing. He sighed. If Martin put half as much effort into finding work as he did into dreaming up schemes for making money, they could both have settled down long ago.

Henry peered down the hill to see if Martin had caught up with the subprior, and noticed a man walking up towards him, threading his way through the crowds. He was taller than most of the men around him. From this distance it was hard to make out his features, but his crow-black hair stood out clearly and there was something about that uneven gait that was vaguely familiar. Then in a sudden flash of recognition Henry realised who he was. He felt as if someone had

thrown a pail of ice over him, for he was the last man he
wanted to see in Ely. Henry fled across the market square
and dived into the nearest inn. He scuttled into the corner,
trying to peer out through one of the open casements without being seen.

'Ale, is it? We've a stew of eels, if you're hungry.' A
disheveled-looking girl, balancing a flagon on each hip, wriggled up beside him and peered curiously out of the window.
'What's so interesting out there? A fight, is it?'

'I was waiting for someone.'

She snorted and moved away from the window. 'You can
drink while you wait, can't you? What'll I bring you?'

But Henry had already crept back to the door. He anxiously scanned the crowd, but there was no sign of the face
he was searching for. Maybe he had turned off down one of
the lanes. Then he saw Martin sauntering up the street with
all the arrogance of a cat with a sparrow in its mouth. Even
before he was near enough to speak, Henry knew that
Martin had managed to persuade the subprior.

'He says he will have to consult the other obedientiaries
who have the running of the cathedral grounds, but he is
sure they will be persuaded. And he says they have a wagon
long enough for us to perform on. He will even ask the sacrist to loan us a couple of carpenters to build the mouth of
hell and the celestial heaven. So, young cos, we are in business! *The Play of Adam* will be performed to the adulation of
the crowd, well, as much of it as we have time to prepare.
Subprior Stephen says that they have the whole manuscript
in their library, and he'll assign some of the younger scribes
to copy out the parts for each actor when we've decided
what we will perform. I tried to persuade him to let me
borrow the manuscript so that I could find the best sections,
but he says the scroll is over two hundred years old and far

too valuable.' Martin scowled. 'I don't know why he wouldn't trust me with it.'

If he had, Henry thought to himself, it would certainly have been the last the subprior ever saw of it.

Martin brightened again. 'No matter. At least we'll make good money from the crowd. You wait, they'll be showering us with silver.'

When he finally paused for breath, Henry managed to deliver his own news. 'The alchemist is here ... from Cambridge ... I saw him walking up the hill. He could only have been a few yards in front of you. Saints be praised that I recognised him in time and managed to hide before he saw me, but we have to get out of here. We must leave Ely today.'

'Haven't you been listening, young cos? It's all settled. We are going to perform *The Play of Adam* and I've no intention of leaving until we've milked this pretty little goat completely dry.'

Henry stared at his cousin as if he was insane. 'Don't you understand what I said – the alchemist is here! We can't possibly perform in front of a crowd now. That would be the quickest way of drawing attention to ourselves. If he recognises us we'll be arrested and hanged.'

Martin laughed. 'And the stars might fall out of the sky tonight. Why do you always have to imagine the worst? Even if he is here, what does it matter? He'll have come on business. He's no reason to suspect us of anything. I covered our tracks carefully. So if you do bump into him just act as if you're delighted to see an old friend. And whatever you do, don't start stammering and turning red like a naughty schoolboy expecting a birching.' He flicked Henry's chest hard with his finger. 'How often do I have to tell you, young cos, I have brains enough for the both of us, so stop worrying. Now what we need to do is round up a few more actors, and there's only one place to find actors – in any tavern that sells good cheap ale.'

The Mermaid Inn on the bank of the great river was empty of drinkers save for eight men clustered around the fire. It was barely an hour after sunrise, as the yawns and scowls of the serving maid testified, and the boatmen still had many hours of work ahead of them before they could stop for a flagon of ale and some slices of brawn fried in lard. But Martin had insisted that the players must make an early start.

Cudbert, known to his friends as Cuddy, was a coarse-featured man with a neck as thick and corded as a plough ox. He took a large swig of ale from his leather tankard, and wiped his mouth with the back of a grimy hand.

'So are we doing *The Shepherds' Play*, or what? I always play Gib, him with the sour wife.

"As sharp as a thistle, as rough as a briar
She is browed like a bristle, with eyes full of ire
When she once wets her whistle she can outsing the choir."'

Cuddy roared out the words as if declaiming in front of a raucous crowd.

'But that's the play we do for the Christmas feast, Uncle,' a graceful, fresh-faced lad protested. 'It isn't fitting for this season.'

Cuddy curled one massive paw into a fist. 'Anyone ask for your opinion, whelp?' He turned to Martin, rolling his eyes. 'My nephew, Luke, or so his mother swore afore she died. My brother ran off and abandoned him, not that I can blame him when he saw what he'd been cursed with as a son. I mean, does he look like he's got our family's blood running in his veins? Ditchwater, more like. But my old woman insisted we took the brat in. Seventeen, he is now, and still useless. But I say this for him, he makes a comely maid when you dress him in skirts. Course, he doesn't need to do any acting to play a virgin.'

The other men, including Martin, roared with laughter as Luke flushed scarlet and glowered at the rushes on the floor, trying to hide his humiliation behind an unruly tangle of dark hair. Henry alone didn't smile, wincing as if he felt the lash of the words on his own back.

'*The Shepherds' Play* it is,' Martin said. 'And, from *The Play of Adam*, "The Sacrifice of Isaac". Always makes the women cry, that one. The crowds won't care what we give them so long as it's bawdy and bloody.'

'John's eldest son can play Isaac,' Cuddy said. 'He's small for his age, but he's as sharp as a whetted scythe.' Catching sight of Martin's alarmed expression, he added, 'Don't fret, young Ben looks nothing like his old man.'

It was just as well, Henry thought, for John was a stocky, pugnacious-looking man, with a broken nose and fists as big as turnips, hardly the type to meekly lie down and prepare to be slaughtered.

'Then young Ben shall indeed play Isaac,' Martin beamed round at the assembled company. 'But we'll start with "Cain and Abel", a play that Henry and I know well.'

A murmur of consternation rippled around the other men.

Cuddy shook his grizzled head. 'No, we won't be doing that one. That's the play of the Glovers' Guild. They'll not take kindly to us performing that.'

Martin flicked his fingers dismissively. 'It's to be performed on cathedral grounds and it's the Priory who has to right to say what will be performed and by whom. Besides, I'm told the guild haven't performed "Cain and Abel" for three years now.'

'Aye, and there's good reason for that,' another man piped up. '"Cain and Abel" brings bad luck, everyone knows that. I've heard tell that the very first time the words of that play were said aloud one of the actors was murdered, and he a holy monk. Glovers swear the spilling of his blood must have sealed the curse that Cain utters in the play and made it come to pass in truth, 'cause any man who acts in that play has nothing but ill fortune for the rest of the year.'

Cuddy nodded vigorously. 'One poor bastard had his workshop burned down and him with a new stock of leather just bought in.'

'Remember the man who played Abel?' another said. 'His son drowned in the river the very next day and he could swim like an eel.'

A couple of the men crossed themselves as they recalled other misfortunes that had overtaken members of the guild – mysterious fevers, a man struck down with apoplexy, not to mention a wife running off with her lover. It was as plain as the balls on a bull, they said, that the play of 'Cain and Abel' was cursed.

John reached across the table and poured himself another generous measure of ale from the flagon. 'You're talking out of your backsides as usual. Hugh's wife running off had nothing to do with the play. The whole town knew her for a brazen strumpet long afore the glover married her. She was bound to be up to her old tricks sooner or later. Anyhow, I don't hold with this curse nonsense. They've been playing "Cain and Abel" since I was in clouts. It stands to reason, if it was cursed they'd have stopped it years ago.'

Martin laughed. 'And I've played in "Cain and Abel" for

years and not one drop of ill fortune has fallen on me, nor on any others who acted in it. Isn't that right, Henry?'

Henry nodded, not trusting himself to speak. There was plenty of ill fortune he could have named, not least that business in Cambridge, but he knew from bitter experience not to contradict Martin, especially not in front of others.

'See,' Martin beamed. 'And just to prove it, Henry and I will act in the play ourselves. Nothing like a good murder to keep the crowds entertained. I told Subprior Stephen as much and he agrees. Besides, he says it will remind the people not to hold back their tithes even when the harvest is poor, for fear of being cursed like Cain.'

'I'll take a part in it too,' Luke said eagerly, obviously desperate to play someone other than a girl. 'I could play the angel.'

'*I* will play the angel,' Martin announced firmly. 'The part calls for a man who has a commanding presence.' He struck a pose, his eyes turned beatifically up to heaven, his right hand lifted in blessing.

'Hear that, boy?' Cuddy said. 'It takes a man to play an angel, so you'll still be playing simpering wenches when you're in your dotage.'

The men all laughed, and the muscles of Luke's jaw tightened so hard, Henry was sure he was going to break a tooth.

'Besides,' Martin said, 'I have the robe and the sword of justice, and I shall wear a gold coronet.'

A look of alarm flashed across Henry's face. 'No . . . you wouldn't. Don't be a fool.'

Martin wrapped an arm about Henry's shoulder, and tousled his hair with his other hand as if he was a silly child. 'Stop fretting, little cos, or everyone will think you are as much of a girl as young Luke here. Now I think Luke should play the role of the timid and lazy servant Brewbarrel.'

His uncle roared with laughter, slapping his thigh. 'Aye, he's suited to that role, right enough.'

'And what should your part be, little cos? Yes, the pious Abel, I think. You fit that role.'

Blushing nearly as hard as Luke, Henry jerked himself out of Martin's grasp. 'I will play Cain.'

His cousin laughed. 'You'd never make a convincing Cain. You couldn't kill a mouse, never mind a man. You,' he gestured towards the man with the broken nose, 'John, isn't it? Could you learn the part of Cain if I teach you?'

'Heard it often enough. Used to be my favourite. I reckon most of it would come back to me with a bit of prompting.'

'Settled then,' Martin declared, beaming. 'There's a barn the subprior said we could use to practise in. It's big enough for us to rehearse all three plays at the same time. Then if one of us is needed in another play he can just walk across and say his lines.'

He looped his arm through Henry's and grinned at him. 'So in the words of that saintly little Abel:

"Let us both go forth together.
Blessed be God, we have good weather."'

Come the morning of the first performance, the weather had indeed turned to the good. Although it had been windy and cold for weeks, now the sun sparkled down out of a cloudless sky, tempered only by the pleasingly refreshing breeze from the river. The mood of the queuing throng lifted in the sunshine and they settled themselves on the grass, more than willing to be entertained now that they were no longer shivering in the biting wind.

The carpenters had done their work well. The entrance to hell, in the form of the gigantic gaping jaws of a great sea monster, was lined with sharp white teeth and real smoke belched from its scarlet maw. On the opposite side of the long cart the throne of heaven mounted on a high dais glittered with tiny glass jewels, and a painted rainbow arched triumphantly over it. Between the two was a pyre of wooden twigs, which would serve as the altar upon which Abel would make his sacrifice, then the place where Isaac was to be slain, and finally the fire around which the shepherds would watch their flocks. It too could be made to pour with smoke.

The whole cart had been covered with sailcloth lashed to the sides to protect the scenery as the carpenters worked, and to keep out the more inquisitive of the local brats. When it was finally rolled up to reveal the stage, to the accompaniment of a lively tune played on frestelles and drums, appreciative murmurs broke out among the waiting crowd.

But it was nothing to the gasps of admiration that arose as Martin strode onto the stage. He had decided that it was only natural for him to play the angel in each of the three plays and blithely ignored the angry muttering of the Ely man who always took that role in *The Shepherds' Play*. But even the Ely man was forced to admit his appearance in the third play would only have been an anticlimax after Martin's. For Martin was clad in white, with a pair of wings covered in swans' feathers fastened to a concealed harness on his back. His luxuriant blond curls were freshly washed and crowned with a circlet of gold that dazzled in the sun. In his right hand he carried a gleaming silver sword, which he thrust high into the blue sky.

'His angel, clear as crystals bright
Here unto you thus I am sent this day.'

Of course, the adults in the crowd knew the sword and the coronet were nothing more than wood, the jewels on the

139

throne were glass and the mouth of hell was not really ablaze, but they were more than willing to allow themselves to believe, for the space of the play, that Abraham really would slaughter his son, and the beautiful creature before them was indeed an angel descended from heaven itself.

As Martin had predicted, though most of the pilgrims had little to give, they were far more willing to pay the players who had entertained them than the keepers of the shrines who would barely allow them time to say a paternoster before the tombs of the saints, despite the many hours they'd waited to get in. So when Ben, John's doe-eyed little son, went round with the collecting bag, he brought it back bulging to Martin. Even Cuddy was grudgingly forced to admit that if there was a curse on the 'Cain and Abel' play, Martin had managed to reverse its fortunes.

Henry, however, was beginning to believe that the Ely men had been right all along when they said the play was ill-omened, at least for him if not for the others. The highlight of 'Cain and Abel', at least for the pilgrims, was the moment when Cain bludgeoned Abel to death with a jawbone. Urged on first by Martin when they rehearsed, and then by the crowd thirsting for a good fight, John's blows were becoming evermore vicious.

By the third performance, Henry, already stiff and aching from the bruises on his arms and shoulders, could not force his shrinking flesh to submit to another battering. As John walked towards him brandishing the jawbone, Henry ran to take shelter behind the throne of God. The crowd jeered, calling Abel to come out and face Cain. But when he showed no signs of moving, Martin, resplendent in his angel's robes, marched round the other side of the dais and, coming up behind Henry, kicked him hard on his backside so that he sprawled forward across the centre of the stage.

The mob screamed with laughter and as John again advanced on Henry, he scrambled to his feet and the two of them began dodging and weaving round hell and the pyre, to the whooping delight of the crowd. Egged on by the spectators, John assailed his victim with reckless and violent blows until Henry realised there was a very real chance of receiving a fatal crack to the head. The only way he could think of bringing it to an end was to lie down and pretend to be slain. But even that did not prevent John whacking him several more times on the back just to please the pilgrims.

'"Yeah, lie there, villain! Lie there! Lie!"' John shouted triumphantly, striking Henry with each cry of 'lie'!

The mob gleefully joined in, bellowing the line with John.

The takings were greater than ever after that performance, and as Martin stuffed the cloth bag bulging with coins into his leather scrip, he slapped Henry enthusiastically on his throbbing back.

'Did you hear how that crowd roared when I kicked you up the arse? We'll have to keep that in tomorrow, and that chase with John. They loved it.'

John grinned. 'And they paid for it too.' He held out a meat-slab of a hand. 'That looks like a weighty purse. Let's see it.'

Martin glanced around at the crowd. 'Not here. Too many thieves and cutpurses about, never know who's watching. I'll divide up the takings in the barn at the vespers bell this evening, like always. Meantime, my throat's drier than a bishop roasting in hell. What about you, lads? Who's for a flagon?'

Henry hunched morosely in the corner of the barn. His back was so sore and stiff he wondered how he was going to lie down to sleep, and his resentment had not been one whit tempered by the ale. Indeed, if anything, he felt himself growing more sober as the others became merrier. The only other one who looked as sullen as he felt was poor Luke, who was as ever the butt of his uncle's jokes and temper in equal measure.

The men gathered round as Martin drew the sack of coins from his scrip and tipped them onto the top of an upturned barrel. He began counting them out into eight piles with another half-pile for John's son. Ben was just a boy and even though he had a good many words to declaim, he certainly wasn't entitled to a grown man's share.

The coins were of small value: mostly farthings or half-pennies. The men watched intently, making sure the same value was deposited on each pile.

Cuddy's eyes narrowed. 'Doesn't look as much there as I thought there was. Sack looked fuller than that. You sure some of it hasn't dropped out in that scrip of yours?'

Martin obligingly held his scrip upside down and shook it, but nothing more fell out.

The men glanced unhappily at one another, then shrugged. Life had long ago taught them there was no use wishing for roast venison when you only had eel in your pot.

Cuddy's great fist hovered over one of the piles, preparing to take his share.

'Which pile has the half-noble in it?' little Ben suddenly piped up.

Everyone turned to look at the boy.

'I didn't see any gold on the barrel,' Cuddy said.

Martin smiled and ruffled Ben's hair indulgently. 'There's no half-noble, lad.'

'But there was,' Ben said indignantly, jerking his head away. 'A merchant's wife put it in the bag. She held it up in her fingers and asked me if I'd ever seen one afore. Her husband chided her for giving so much, but she said . . .' He hesitated, suddenly looking abashed.

'Said what, Ben? Speak up, his father encouraged him with a prod.

'That I had eyes that put her in mind of her . . . her lapdog,' he mumbled to the earth floor, 'and she was sure I wasn't getting enough to eat.'

'Was she indeed,' John bridled. 'As if I'd let any son of mine go hungry. Who does she think—'

'Never mind that,' Cuddy said impatiently. 'The boy said she put a half-noble in the bag, so where is it now?'

He took a menacing step towards Martin, who stumbled backwards, spreading his hands wide. 'I swear by the Holy Virgin, I've haven't seen it. The boy must have imagined it. As if anyone in that crowd would give players a half-noble. The boy said the woman held the coin up. In that bright sunshine it must have looked like gold, an easy mistake to make.'

'It was gold!' Ben said stubbornly.

'Aye, and it's not just that coin that's missing either,' Cuddy growled. 'I reckon that money sack was considerably more weighty this afternoon.'

'Doubtless you wish it so, my friend. But I've just counted the coins out in front of you all and the bag was not opened before. I've been in your company ever since the play ended. I'm sorry that the crowd hasn't paid us as much as you would like, but I warrant it is a sight more than you would earn hanging around the quayside hoping for a cargo to unload. But perhaps you think my performance isn't pleasing enough to the crowd. Perhaps you think that's why they haven't paid us more.' Martin snatched up one of the piles of coins and thrust it at Cuddy. 'Here, take my share and divide it among yourselves, if you think I haven't earned you enough. Go on, take it!'

So saying, he seized Cuddy's wrist and slammed the coins into his massive palm. Then, his face a mask of hurt, he swept out of the barn. Cuddy and the other men stared after him in silence. With grim faces they collected their shares from the top of the barrel, glaring at Henry as they filed out and leaving him in no doubt they thought the two of them were in this together.

Henry dragged his aching body over to the barrel and scooped up the one remaining pile of coins, but decided to wait in the barn until he was quite sure the others had returned to their homes. He couldn't face walking past them. He was as sure as Cuddy was that the bag had been much better stuffed when Ben had brought it back to Martin that afternoon. But if Martin had removed the coins, the question was when? He'd gone out to the back of the inn to piss a couple of times, but the yard was no more private than the inn itself, with men and serving maids crossing to and fro all the time. Besides, he hadn't been gone long enough to sort through the bag and remove all the coins of greater value, though Henry was pretty sure that's exactly what he had done.

Henry savagely kicked the barrel. After he'd so nearly got caught in Cambridge, Martin promised – no, not just promised, swore on his own life – that he'd never steal again. And now, just when he'd started to believe that for once his cousin had learned his lesson, Martin's greed had got the better of him once more. But not this time! Martin wasn't going to drag him through one of his stinking dung heaps again.

'No more, Martin, do you hear me? No more,' Henry shouted into the empty cavern of the barn. 'You are not going to use me again. I'm going to make quite certain of that!'

Wilbertone, Cambridgeshire Fens

'Have you brought it?' Father Edmund wheezed, as soon as the young monk managed to wedge the warped door back in its frame.

Brother Oswin studiously avoided the old man's intense gaze. 'I swear I've tried, Father. But the cathedral is swarming with pilgrims. The crowds are so great that the lay brothers have had to double their watches in case thieves should use the distraction of the throng to steal anything of value. I cannot get near it, much less take it.'

He stumbled the few steps to the priest's chair, and fell on his knees, grasping at the old man's tattered robe. 'Don't you see, Father, God is preventing me from taking it. His angels are blocking my path at every turn, just as the angel stood in the road in front of Balaam's ass and refused to let Balaam pass to sin against God. The angels are keeping us both from sin.' He bowed his head, crossing himself.

'And you must have the brains of an ass if you think such feeble excuses will turn me from my purpose,' Father Edmund growled. 'You will find a way to get it, boy, unless you want to see your brother hanged.'

Oswin raised his head, his face contorted in anguish. 'I beg you, Father, don't force me to do this. You wouldn't break the sanctity of the confessional, you couldn't do that. You're bitter, I know that, and you have every right to be, but you would not damn your own soul with such a sin—'

He broke off with a squeal as Father Edmund grabbed the short fringe of hair around his tonsure and forced his head painfully backwards.

'Don't tell me what I would not do, boy! And don't think for one moment I would not expose you and your brother for the murderers you are. If you care so little for your brother's life, think of this, boy. You know I once conjured demons to shield de Lisle from the pestilence. Do you imagine I'm so feeble-witted that I couldn't do it again? Just because my legs don't bear me up as once they did, doesn't mean my memory has also deserted me. I still know the signs and symbols, the incantations and the secret names. But if I summon a demon again, boy, it will not be to protect you, of that you can be sure. Get me what I ask, for if you fail me, I promise you will know such torment that before the month is out you will be screaming for the mercy of the hangman's rope yourself just to bring an end to your suffering.'

He let his hand fall from Oswin's hair, overcome by a fit of coughing, then hugging his ribs, turned to stare into the embers of the dying fire.

'You have three days, Brother Oswin,' he said softly. 'Just three days left.'

Ely

As soon as he was out of sight of the barn, Martin broke into a run, glancing round several times to make sure he was not being followed. If Cuddy and John caught him out on the street they might take it into their heads to search him by force, and it wouldn't take them long to find the coins folded into a strip of cloth and tied around his chest. They were the sort of men who would choose to settle a score with their own fists rather than through the justices, and with fists like theirs, he'd be lucky if he could remember his own name by the time they'd finished with him.

Still it had been worth it. That serving girl in the Mermaid Inn on the quayside was good, so good he was sure she'd done it before. She'd waited in the yard for him to slip her the bag of coins on his way to the midden to pass water, giving her the chance to separate the coins at her leisure before handing them back the next time he came out to relieve himself. Of course, he was certain that in addition to what he paid her for her trouble, she'd pocketed a few extra coins herself – it's what he would have done – but he didn't begrudge her that so long as she didn't get too greedy. They could have kept this scam going for days, weeks even. His only regret was there hadn't been an accident with the knife when young Ben was being sacrificed as Isaac. If he'd known the trouble the boy was going to cause he might have arranged one.

With one further glance up and down the street Martin slipped into the Lamb Inn at the top of the hill and wove his way to the most dimly lit corner. He'd have to be ready to leave as soon as Ely's gates were opened at dawn, but certainly he wasn't going to flee empty-handed. There was something he had to retrieve from the wagon first. He had no intention of leaving it behind, not after all the risks he'd taken to acquire it.

Martin had consumed several tankards of good ale before he deemed it late enough to return to the wagon without risk of being seen. Yawning, the innkeeper hustled his last remaining customers out into the cold chill of the night. Martin huddled in the darkness of a doorway, watching them reeling up the street, and remained there until the last drunken calls had faded. Then he cautiously made his way back to the wagon.

A scattering of shards of yellow light marked where candles and rush lights flickered through holes in the shutters of the dozing buildings, otherwise the night was as black as the devil's armpit. Doors rattled in the wind and somewhere a cat yowled unseen. Martin edged around the back of the wagon.

The props and costumes were kept in a long chest beneath the wagon and securely chained to one of the wheels. Martin reached inside his scrip for the two keys. He slid his hand along the chain to the lock, and by touch alone wriggled the key until it slipped inside. But however carefully he lowered the chain to the ground, he could not avoid the heavy metallic clunk, which echoed through the darkness. He froze, holding his breath, then shook himself impatiently. The chest contained his clothes – why should he not open it anytime he pleased? But all the same he did not want to have to explain his presence on the streets to the night watch.

He groped for the lock on the chest itself and had just turned the key when he heard the sound of shoes scuffing over the grass and the scrape of clothing against sailcloth. Someone was moving down the side of the wagon. Cuddy? John? Had one of them returned to search for the missing coins?

Scarcely daring to breathe, Martin crawled away into the darkness and threw himself flat on the grass, as the figure held up a lantern, shielding the light with the edge of his cloak. The man ran his fingers down the ropes, feeling for the point where he could unhook them and pull aside the stout canvas. Martin cautiously raised his head, trying to make out who he was, but his face was concealed deep within his hood, and the shape of his body was masked by the heavy cloak.

There was a clunk as the man's shoe knocked against the chain on the ground. The figure glanced down. Martin instinctively scrabbled in his scrip, searching for the keys and cursed himself as he realised they were still in the lock of the chest. Perhaps the man wouldn't notice them. But his curiosity had evidently been aroused, for he crouched down, holding out the lantern. As he bent over, his face dipped into the pool of light. It was only for a moment, but Martin recognised him at once.

Brother Oswin glanced up at the cathedral as he hurried towards it. Candles shone out from the top of the octagon tower, turning it into a great lantern that could be seen for miles across the dark water of the fens. Always before he had been comforted by the sight of it, a beacon of hope to guide the lost. Its holy light warded off the evil spirits that stalked the causeway, and the dead souls that haunted the marshes waiting to lure men to their deaths in the treacherous bogs. Yet now he saw only accusation and judgement in that light, as if heaven was staring down at him, stripping him naked for all the world to see his vile sin.

Though the watchman at the bridge gate entrance to Ely would normally have refused admittance at this hour, even he could see the young monk was in great distress.

'What is it, Brother? Why are you out so late?' He raised the blazing torch, peering closer. 'You're as pale as the dead, and shaking. Were you attacked?'

Oswin shook his head, struggling to speak. 'A sick man . . . I had to . . . sit with him.'

The watchman stepped hastily backwards. 'Holy Virgin, he's not been stricken with the Great Pestilence, has he?'

Oswin shook his head, drawing his cloak more tightly around him as he tried to stop his teeth chattering. The watchman held open the gate, taking pains to keep at arm's length in case the monk should brush him as he passed through.

Oswin staggered up the street towards the priory, glancing

fearfully upwards at the great looming mass of the cathedral. The monstrous grotesques and gargoyles leered down at him from the shifting shadows as if the walls and turrets of the cathedral were swarming with demons, massing like some great flock of malevolent birds, all watching him, waiting for him.

He could not do it. He would not! Yet he could think of no means of avoiding it. He was certain now that the old priest would carry out his threat and denounce his brother, and if what they said was true, if Father Edmund really could conjure evil spirits, maybe even the devil himself, then ... *Blessed Virgin, help me! Show me what to do, how to escape!* As he stumbled on towards the cathedral, he stretched out his arms in supplication, mumbling frantic prayers in a fever of delirium. Then, without warning, he tripped and found himself sprawling face down on the grass.

He lay where he fell, shaken by the tumble and unable to gather his mind to comprehend where he was. Finally he pushed himself to his knees and felt for what he had tripped over. He knew at once it was a man.

Most of the body lay in darkness, only the feet were caught in the edge of the pool of light spilling from the tower. Oswin shook the man's leg, but he did not stir. The young monk shuffled forward, still on his knees, and felt the man's chest. The flesh was still warm, but the ribs were not rising and falling, and as he drew his hand away he felt the warm, sticky fluid on his fingers.

Oswin crossed himself and his lips began to mumble the prayers for the newly dead. But the words ceased abruptly as a thought exploded into his head. His prayers had been answered! The Blessed Virgin had heard him. This was his escape from his tormenter. It was as if the Virgin Mary herself had cast this corpse at his feet. Whispering fervent prayers of gratitude and with hands trembling now, not from fear, but excitement, Brother Oswin fumbled for his knife.

It was after the noon bell when Henry and the Ely men once again assembled behind the wagon, ready to begin the first of the plays. It had rained heavily before dawn and the sky was still grey and swollen with cloud. The corners of the heavy sailcloth lashed over the wagon flapped in the strengthening wind and the ropes creaked with the strain of holding it down. The players prodded the canvas with poles, trying to shake off the puddles of water that had accumulated on the top. The men's mood was as gloomy as the day. Their pride had been wounded as well as their purses, but they were determined no trickster would make fools of them for a second time.

'You bring the money straight to me, young Ben,' Cuddy said. 'Don't you let Martin or that cousin of his lay a finger on that bag till we've counted the coins.'

He didn't trouble to lower his great booming voice, and Henry was certain he was meant to hear. John came ambling over, the jawbone already tucked into his leather belt. Henry felt his bruises throb at the mere sight of it.

'Where is this thieving cousin of yours?' John demanded. 'Crowd's calling for us to start, but he speaks first as the angel so we can't begin until he takes his place. Too ashamed to show his face to us, is he?' Then a thought struck him and he grabbed the front of Henry's robe in his great fist. 'Has he run off with our money?'

'Course not!' Henry protested.

'Well, where is he, then?' Cuddy demanded.

'I haven't seen him since he left the barn last night,' Henry said. 'Look he . . . he must be around here somewhere. The costume box is unlocked, so most likely he's taken his robes to dress for his part and has gone for a mug of ale. He'll want to soothe his throat before the play begins.'

'He'll need more than ale to soothe his throat when I get hold of him,' John said sourly. 'But never mind that, the crowd is going to start chucking things if we don't give them something soon. I've already seen some lads creeping to the front with rotten fruit in their hands. We'll just have to start with your first speech. And hope our angel turns up in time to say his "Cursed Cain" part at the end.'

Henry's stomach lurched. If John had played up to the crowd with that jawbone before, it was nothing to how he might wield it if he thought that Henry had been party to cheating the Ely men of the money.

'Look,' he said desperately, 'why don't we forget all about "Cain and Abel" and just give them "The Sacrifice of Isaac" and *The Shepherds' Play*? That'll give me a chance to go and look for Martin.'

'Wouldn't work,' John said. 'The angel's the first to speak in the "Isaac" too, and if he doesn't say the line. "Now show he may, if he loveth God more than his child", the rest of the story makes no sense.'

'Besides,' Cuddy said, 'we're not such fools as to let you go running off with your cousin and our money. You're staying here, until your cousin brings us what he stole. And you'd better hope he turns up soon or you'll soon realise a blow from that jawbone is nothing more than a smack with a feather compared to what we'll do to you.'

Henry, his stomach churning, took up his place on the darkened wagon. He heard the players strike up a tune on drums and frestelles to draw the attention of the crowd. Then Cuddy gave the orders to start the smoke belching from hell, while the others loosened the last of the ties holding down the sailcloth. Light flooded in as the cloth was pulled aside. Henry swallowed hard and cleared his throat. Painfully he kneeled with his back to hell, facing the throne of God. It seemed to make more sense to address his lines to that rather than empty air where the angel should have been standing.

"'I thank you, Lord, for Your goodness,
That has made me, on Earth, Your man.
I worship . . . '"

He became aware of a loud murmuring in the audience. He glanced sideways, trying to see what was amiss without turning his head. Were they disappointed because there was no angel?

Henry raised his voice over the buzzing of the crowd. "'I worship you with—'"

A woman started to scream. Others joined in. Some were backing away, desperately trying to extricate themselves from the throng, but they were trapped by the rest of the crowd, who were trying to wriggle nearer to the wagon.

Still on his knees, and unable to move swiftly because of the stiffness of his back, Henry turned his head in bewilderment, as John stumbled past him and halted abruptly in front of the great gaping mouth of hell.

'Stop that smoke,' he roared, flapping his arms vigorously to disperse it.

He peered into the open jaws, then staggered backwards as if he'd been punched.

'Holy Virgin, defend us!' John crossed himself several times in rapid succession and stood rocking on his heels.

Henry clambered stiffly to his feet and tried to peer round John's broad frame, but John caught hold of Henry's arm and pulled him away.

'Don't look, lad. Trust me, you don't want to see.'

But his warning came too late, Henry had already seen.

A faint trickle of smoke still swirled in hell's mouth, but it was not enough to obscure the figure that was lying inside. The man, dressed in white angel robes and feathered wings, was lying on his belly. His arms were stretched out on either side in a cruciform, like a monk doing penance before an altar. But where his head should have been there was nothing but the bloody stump of a neck. The pool of blood had seeped into the pure white robes, and stained the tips of the swan's feathers scarlet. And the man's head wasn't the only part of him that was missing. His right arm now ended at his wrist from which the splintered bone glistened white against the red.

For a moment Henry stood and stared as if the corpse was just another of the carpenter's painted props. Then with a shriek of horror, he knocked John aside and fled.

If it hadn't been for the river at the bottom of the hill, Henry might never have stopped running. He ran as if that mutilated angel was swooping after him like a falcon and he was the quarry. He charged blindly towards the water and would have tumbled in had not a river-man caught him and dragged him back.

'Steady, lad! You don't want to go falling in there. River's thick with boats, you'll get your head staved in by a bow or an oar. Here, are you sick?' he added, as Henry sank to his knees. 'It's not the pestilence, is it?' he said, backing away in alarm as Henry vomited copiously.

By now Henry had attracted a small crowd of curious onlookers, staring at him intently to see if his face and arms bore any sign of the telltale blue-black marks, though they were all careful to keep their distance. Henry staggered to his feet and stumbled along the bank, though his legs were trembling so much he could barely manage to walk never mind run.

'There he is!' someone yelled. 'Seize that man! Don't just stand there, grab him! Don't let him get away.'

Without thinking Henry glanced back to see who they were shouting about. Several lay brothers were racing down towards the river, their sandalled feet slapping loudly on the stones. Henry's mind was so dazed that it took several moments to register that they were pointing at him. By the time he realised, it was too late. Two of the rivermen had grabbed his arms and he found himself being dragged back along the bank.

'This the man you're after?' one of the river-men said, thrusting Henry towards the first of the lay brothers, who was panting so hard he could only reply with a nod.

'What's he done?' the other river-man asked curiously.

'K . . . killed a man, that's what . . . Not just murdered him, but mutilated the body too. And if that weren't bad enough, he did it on priory land, right in front of the cathedral door, with the holy statues of Christ and the saints looking down on the bloody deed.'

The river-men and bystanders growled their outrage. The lay brother nodded with satisfaction, gratified by the reaction he was getting.

'And you haven't heard the worst of it. It wasn't a stranger he murdered. It was his own kin, his poor cousin, wickedly done to death.'

The river-man gripped Henry's arm as if he was trying to snap the bone in two. 'God's blood, you'll hang for sure, boy, that's if you survive the flogging they'll give you first. And, trust me, there won't be a man or woman in Ely who'll beg mercy for you.'

*

It wasn't for nothing that the priory's gaol was known as 'hell'. It lay beneath the infirmary, its walls stout and windowless, and it was as well they were, for once news of the heinous crime spread through the town, not even the lay brothers could prevent the mob gathering to hurl insults and missiles at the priory gate. The women were the worst, for hadn't Martin been the very image of Gabriel himself with his golden curls and blue eyes, and by the end of that day they had convinced themselves Henry wasn't just guilty of slaying a man, but of murdering a holy angel.

Henry, dragged past the gate on his way to the gaol, heard the shrieks of abuse and cringed as the stones thudded against the thick oak door. He was almost relieved when they threw him down inside the safety of the dark, stinking pit. The great stone walls were green with slime and as dank as a village well. But Henry was not left to suffer the misery of hell alone. Cuddy and John were already sitting with their backs against the wall, their necks encircled with heavy hoops of iron chaining them to the rough stones. Henry did not resist when he was chained to the opposite wall, though the metal cut painfully into his neck and the chains were too short to allow him to either lie down or stand. He knew if Cuddy and John had not been similarly chained, he'd be dead long before the hangman could do his work.

Henry had sworn before Prior Alan de Walsingham that he was innocent. It was John and Cuddy who had quarrelled with Martin. It was their money he had stolen. It was they who had killed him in revenge, or else it was a member of the Glovers' Guild. Hadn't the Ely men said the Glovers always performed 'Cain and Abel'? Maybe they'd done it to prove they were right about the curse and to frighten off anyone else who had the audacity to dare to perform their play.

Cuddy and John, in turn, insisted that the culprit was

Henry for, unlike him, they had been in the company of the other players drowning their sorrows half the night and had then walked home in each other's company to their families, never leaving their hearths again until it was time to perform the play. Besides, they were God-fearing, honest Ely men, which all the neighbours would swear to, while for all anyone knew, Henry might have murdered a dozen men before he arrived in Ely.

Prior Alan had long held the belief that any man in Ely would murder his own grandmother and sell her hide for leather if he thought he could get away with it. And the more he listened to the tale of the stolen money, the more certain he became that since all of the actors had been cheated of their money they had all colluded in the murder, for had they not already admitted they had spent the night drinking together?

But when the prior sent men to the houses of the other players, they discovered the rest of the actors had taken full advantage of the delay and had already slipped out of Ely, assisted no doubt by the local boatmen, who were firmly convinced, as were all the locals, that Henry was the killer, and certainly not one of their own.

On hearing the news Prior Alan uttered an oath that would have made a whore blush, for if the fugitives were hiding out in the marshes or were in a boat halfway down the river concealed under empty sacks, it would take weeks to round them all up and a good number of men too, men he could ill afford to spare with the crowds of pilgrims pouring daily into Ely. But at least he'd had three of the murdering wretches safely under lock and key, and if the crowd no longer had *The Play of Adam* to divert them, they would soon have a hanging to entertain them instead.

*

'Father Prior, the stench is definitely getting stronger,' Will de Copham said anxiously. 'We can't continue to ignore it. Even old Brother Godwin remarked on it and you know he sat on some dog dung the other week and didn't even notice the stink of that.'

Strictly speaking, of course, it was the sacrist's job to maintain the fabric of the cathedral, but as custodian of the cathedral, Will was not only responsible for security but also for maintaining good order. He already had enough problems on that score without the lay brothers refusing to keep watch near the shrine because the stench was making them sick.

'But the smell cannot be emanating from the tomb of St Withburga,' Prior Alan protested. 'She's a holy saint and saints' bodies emit the sweet perfume of the rose of heaven, not the stench of corruption. Are you sure it's not simply the odour of the pilgrims themselves? I saw one with such a stinking sore on his leg even his fellow pilgrims were gagging. Perhaps the smell lingered.'

Will shook his head. 'Most pilgrims stay longest at St Etheldreda's shrine, for she's the one they most favour. If it was the pilgrims themselves, the smell should be worse there. Even the perfume of incense is no longer masking the stench. If we don't do something soon, rumours may begin to spread that St Withburga is no longer at ease in her tomb and wishes to return to Dereham.'

The prior winced. St Withburga's body had been taken from her grave in Dereham almost four centuries ago and brought to join her sisters in their tombs at Ely, but even after all these years the Dereham folk still regarded this act of piety as theft and regularly sent demands for her return, not least because of the valuable income this would bring from the pilgrims.

Having been sacrist himself for many years, Prior Alan was nothing if not a pragmatic man, and distasteful though it might be to disturb the resting place of a saint, he knew the pilgrims would soon cease to come if the shrine to which they came for cures made them want to vomit.

He sighed, pressing the tips of his fingers together, then finally nodded. 'I dare say it's nothing more than a family of mice that have crawled inside and died, or even a rotting eel that some wicked little brat has managed to push through a hole just to annoy his elders. But you and I will investigate tonight after the cathedral is closed. None of the monks or lay brothers must be present. The slightest hint of anything amiss and gossip will be all round the town before dawn, most of it wilder than a rabid wolf. The townspeople are already so anxious about the pestilence they will take any-thing as a sign of ill omen. There's been quite enough upset with the murder of that player Martin; I want nothing more to agitate the people or the priory.'

The cathedral was in darkness save for the candles on the altars and those flickering around the tombs of the saints. Will had placed a few lanterns on the floor to illuminate the shrine, but in a position where they would not shine out through the windows. It was vital that the townspeople did not notice any unusual activity in the building. The gold, silver and jewelled offerings that normally adorned the tomb had been carefully collected and now lay in a heap on a piece of cloth, glittering in the flickering candlelight like a pirates' hoard.

Working in silence, the prior and custodian together pulled away the back panel of the shrine, which allowed access to the inside, so that coins pushed through the holes could be removed. Prior Alan pressed a cloth to his nose. There was

159

no mistaking it now that they were so close, the stench was coming from somewhere inside. He kneeled down, moving the lantern so that the light fell in turn into each corner of the tomb as he searched for rodent corpses or anything else that might account for the smell, but he saw only candle wax, the glint of a few coins and eons of dust scuffed by the sandal prints of the monks who had over the years squeezed in to retrieve the offerings.

He was just struggling to his feet again when Will tugged on his sleeve. 'Look, Father Prior,' he breathed, 'the coffin's been disturbed.'

Alan raised his lantern so that the light fell on the top of the stone coffin. The lid was still in place, but it had been twisted slightly at an angle so that the top corner lay open just a couple of inches. As soon as he bent over the gap Prior Alan was left in little doubt that the stench was coming from inside.

He crossed himself, and muttered a prayer for forgiveness to St Withburga for the offence he was about to offer. Then placing both hands against the stone lid, he pushed it. The rasp of stone on stone seemed to echo off the dark walls and for a moment he hesitated, unnerved by the ominous sound.

Then he gestured impatiently to Will, who had taken a few paces back.

'Bring your candle, I need more light. Stop looking so fearful. It's a saint not a revenant buried in this coffin.'

Reluctantly Will stood behind him and raised his lantern so that the light from the candle glowed yellow inside the hollow stone. The saint's bones were wrapped in a cloth that had turned brown with age. Carefully, Prior Alan eased the rotting fabric aside. The bones and skull were still covered in strips of parchment-like skin and strands of grey hair. But there was something else in the coffin, something lying where St Withburga's desiccated hand should have been. It was a human hand, a right hand, but it was not the hand of a saint. This hand had been severed at the wrist, and the rotting flesh was covered in a stinking mass of writhing maggots.

Prior Alan sat in the great carved chair in his solar, and pressed his fingers to his throbbing temples. Subprior Stephen and Custodian Will de Copham slumped opposite him, gazing equally morosely into mid-space. The bells for prime and for the early Mass for the servants had long since rung, but none of the three of them had moved.

'You're sure that is the hand of the dead actor, Father Prior?' Will asked.

He glanced uneasily at the small lead-lined casket, which had been hastily emptied of its scrolls of parchment to provide a temporary resting place for the offending appendage. Fortunately the seal on the box was tight enough to stop the smell from escaping, but his stomach still heaved every time he remembered picking it up.

Alan grimaced. 'Unless we dig up the body and match the bones to the arm we can't be certain, but it seems most likely. I could ask the infirmarer if he's heard of anyone in Ely who has recently lost his hand in an accident, but even so, men don't normally leave such things lying around in the street.'

'Then whoever put the hand in St Withburga's coffin murdered Martin,' Stephen said, 'and that means those three actors must be innocent, for they've been in gaol ever since the body was discovered.'

'I don't see how that proves their innocence,' Prior Alan snapped. 'They could have placed the hand in the coffin before the body was discovered and that wasn't until well past midday. Men who are capable of the heinous murder and mutilation of one of their own would think nothing of desecrating the body of a blessed saint, which is why we must redouble our efforts to capture the rest of the actors. Since the three felons in gaol didn't have the hand of St Withburga in their possession when they were searched, then one of their fellow conspirators must have it.'

Will rolled his tongue around his mouth in disgust. He could still taste that stench. He rose and poured himself another goblet of wine in the vain attempt to settle his stomach.

'But what I don't understand,' he said, 'is if they intended stealing the saint's relic, why draw attention to the theft by placing the severed hand in the coffin to stink. If they hadn't done so the theft would have gone unnoticed for years.'

Prior Alan shrugged. 'Perhaps they thought the hand would mummify and, in time, become indistinguishable from the other remains. As indeed it might well have done had the coffin lid not accidentally been left slightly ajar, allowing the flies to get in.'

'But why replace it at all? Why not just take the relic?' Will persisted stubbornly.

'To mock us,' Stephen said firmly. 'It's the Dereham men who have done this, not the actors. This is their way of thumbing their noses at us. I'm sure their plan was to display her hand in the church in Dereham, knowing we'd be forced to open the coffin before witnesses to prove we still have the body intact. Then the rotting hand would be revealed and we'd be a laughing stock.' He turned eagerly to the prior. 'We should send men at once to Dereham and—'

Alan held up his hand to silence him. 'Have you forgotten half the men are out combing the fens for the other actors

162

and the rest are trying the keep the townsmen and pilgrims from killing one another? Besides, we've no proof that Dereham men did this, and I certainly don't intend letting them know the hand is missing. You said yourself, Brother Stephen, whoever put the hand in the coffin murdered Martin. What cause would anyone from Dereham have to do that? Unless you're suggesting that they murdered the first stranger they came upon just to obtain his hand, and if that's so, why cut off his head and remove it? No, only his fellow actors had sufficient grudge against him to do that.

"Beware the sins of envy and vainglory,
Else foul murder ends your story."

Isn't that what is written at the end of that wretched "Cain and Abel" play? And when a man such as Prior Wigod of Oseney writes such words it is never for his own amusement. He wrote it as a warning, a warning you should have heeded before engaging those players, Brother Stephen, for I can think of no breed of men more steeped in the sins of envy and vainglory than base actors.'

Stephen's mouth fell open, but before he could speak Will leaned forward frowning.

'But even if it was the actors, Father Prior, what I don't understand is, how could they have accomplished it? All the time the cathedral is open to the pilgrims, I insist on there being a monk on duty up in the watching loft, in addition to the lay brothers keeping guard at ground level. A skilled thief might manage to snatch one of the offerings, or even a precious stone from the outside of the shrine if he was working in league with others who could set up a distraction for him, but to get inside the shrine and open the coffin unseen, that's beyond the powers of any mortal man.'

'Are you suggesting that this was the devil's work, Brother Will, witchcraft?' Stephen said, his eyes widening in alarm.

Prior Alan leaped from his chair. 'No!' he said firmly. 'There is to be no talk of that. I forbid you even to think of it. If rumours should start to circulate in the town that the cathedral can't even protect one of its own saints from the forces of darkness, then—'

But whatever warning Alan intended to issue was severed by a scream that rang out over the priory, a shriek that continued so long, it seemed that whoever was screaming had forgotten how to stop.

The stonemason's apprentice was still howling when Prior Alan, Stephen and Will, all panting, emerged from the narrow spiral staircase onto the roof of the octagon tower. He was several feet higher up and further out, clinging to one of the little stone pinnacles. A narrow, rickety wooden scaffolding bridged the gap between the pinnacle and the roof's parapet, behind which the stone mason and two anguished-looking monks were gathered.

'What ails the lad?' Prior Alan asked. 'Has he suddenly grown afraid of heights?'

It would hardly be surprising if he had, it was a dizzyingly long way down.

'Can't get any sense out of him, Father Prior,' the stonemason yelled above the boy's shrieks. 'He bounded up there like a squirrel, same as always, next thing I know he was screaming like a girl.' He raised his voice still louder, fingering the stout leather belt squeezed around his corpulent belly. 'I'll give you something to yell about, my lad, when I get hold of you.'

'Threatening the boy isn't going to make him come down,'

Stephen said. 'Are you stuck, lad? Don't look down. Just try to climb back slowly.'

But the boy's arms seemed have become part of the turret they were clinging to, and he would neither loose his grip nor stop shrieking. Prior Alan glanced down at the swelling crowd of pilgrims and townspeople who were gathering below, all craning up to see what was amiss.

'Someone will have to climb up and fetch the boy down.'

The stonemason was clearly too stout and aged to climb the narrow scaffolding to retrieve his apprentice. Alan glanced around him and selected the lighter and more nimble-looking of the two young monks for the task.

But even when he climbed up and grabbed the boy around the waist, the lad would not budge and the monk came perilously close to toppling from the scaffolding himself as he wrestled with the boy. Finally he was forced to deliver a few sharp slaps to make the lad let go. But as the boy, sobbing, dropped down from his perch, it was the monk's turn to cry out in horror as he glimpsed what had been hidden behind the boy. It was too far round the turret to be visible from the parapet, but up on the scaffolding it was all too evident what had scared the wits out of the lad. For there, among the grimacing grotesques and carved saints, was a human head, not made of stone but of rotting flesh and blackened blood.

Prior Alan stared dismally out of the casement of his solar. Masses of delicate pink and white apple blossom covered the trees below like a fall of new snow, but that sight, which normally lifted his spirits, did nothing to raise them now. The blossom was abnormally late this year, yet another sign, if one were needed, that chaos was once more descending upon the fragile world.

'At least now we have the whole corpse,' Stephen said, desperate to break the icy silence. 'We can bury the head with the rest of Martin's remains and his spirit will surely rest easier for it.'

Prior Alan turned and glowered at his subprior. 'His spirit will not rest easy until his murderer has been punished, and nor will mine. We may have been able to keep the theft of St Withburga's hand between ourselves, but thanks to that wretched boy screaming from the rooftops, news of what he found will be across Ely before nightfall and what the towns-people lack in facts they will surely make up.'

'They already have,' Will said grimly, striding through the door and closing it firmly behind him. 'I've just come from Steeple Gate. The crowds are as thick as flies on . . . '

He closed his eyes briefly and swallowed hard. He'd never thought of himself as a squeamish man, but being forced retrieve two maggot-infested body parts in one day was enough to sicken any man's stomach.

'The rumours have already started, Father Prior. They say a demon must have placed the head where no mortal man could.'

'Utter nonsense!' The words exploded from Alan's lips. 'Any man who was reasonably agile could have climbed that scaffold and put it there. After all, you climbed up and you're certainly mortal.'

'I certainly felt my mortality up there,' Will said with a shudder. 'But the trouble is, Father Prior, the crowd can't see the scaffolding from the ground and they're not in a mood to listen to reason. They're claiming a demon flew down from the octagon tower, slew Martin, then carried his head back up to the tower to devour at its leisure.'

Prior Alan shook his head in utter disbelief at the notions that filled the heads of men. As sacrist, he had designed the octagon himself, after the original tower collapsed, and he always took any slight directed at his beloved creation as a personal affront.

'And that's not the worst of the rumours, Father Prior . . .' Will saw his superior's jaw clench in anger and hesitated, but Alan had to be told. 'The townspeople may not know we found Martin's hand in the shrine, but they do know there was a stench as foul as hell coming from St Withburga's tomb. Now they're saying that a great evil has come upon the whole priory and cathedral, because of that play. The Glovers have wasted no time in telling everyone the play of "Cain and Abel" is cursed and that by performing it on cathedral grounds we've raised a demon of death, which is hunting human prey. Apparently not a man, woman or child in Ely is safe. It will slay them all just as surely as Cain slew Abel.'

'This has gone far enough!' Prior Alan slammed his fist down onto the wooden table so hard that both Will and Stephen flinched. 'I hold you entirely responsible for this, Brother Stephen. If you hadn't given them leave to perform that wretched play, there'd never have been a murder, never mind these bits of rotting corpse popping up all over the cathedral.'

Subprior Stephen open his mouth to protest, but Alan hadn't finished.

'We have to do something to bring these rumours to an end before the townspeople take it into their heads to storm the cathedral and tear down my tower, stone by stone. Fetch those murderers from the hell-pit at once. I intend to confront them with that head and force them to admit they killed Martin. I swear on God's bones I will wrench a confession out of those actors even if I have to make them eat that head to do it.'

*

Henry, Cuddy and John stood unsteadily in the prior's hall, blinking painfully in the light. It had been two weeks since they had been able to stand up and now their legs trembled beneath them, not helped by the weight of the chains shackling their wrists and ankles. Henry glanced at the other two actors. They were filthy, covered in bits of mouldy straw and excrement. He noticed the monks wrinkling their noses and discreetly taking a few steps back and he was suddenly aware of how much he himself must stink.

But it was nothing to the stench that filled the hall when the lead-lined box was opened and the rotting head and hand were laid out on the great long wooden table. One glimpse of the empty blackened eye sockets, where the ravens had been at work, was enough to make Henry collapse to his knees and start retching.

The prior gestured to one of the muscular lay brothers, who reached down and hauled Henry back to his feet by his hair, dragging him closer to the foul remains.

'Too cowardly to face the sight of your own crime, are you?' Alan thundered. 'Gaze upon the ravaged countenance of your cousin, and weep in shame for what you have done.'

The lay brother pulled Henry's head up, forcing him to look. At first Henry was too appalled to take in what he was seeing, but something finally worked its way up through the fog of his dazed mind.

'That . . . isn't Martin. It can't be Martin.'

'Even his poor mother would not know him now that the maggots and birds have been to work on him,' Alan said sternly.

'No, not the face . . . ' Henry swallowed hard, trying to bite back the bile that had risen in his throat. 'His hair . . . Martin was blond. That hair is dark.'

At once everyone else in the room who had been studiously avoiding looking at the head now stared at it.

'He's right!' Stephen said. 'I spoke to Martin several times. His hair was the colour of ripe corn, and even allowing for the dried blood—'

Prior Alan rounded on him. 'Then why didn't you say that as soon as Brother Will retrieved the head?'

Stephen gulped. 'I could only bear to look at it once and that briefly. I didn't even notice the hair. I just assumed— '

'Then if it's not Martin, who is it?' Prior Alan demanded.

There was a loud groan from Cuddy. He was swaying so alarmingly that two of the lay brothers made a grab for him, certain he was going to fall.

'God in heaven, that's Luke, that is,' he whispered. 'That's my poor nephew, Luke.'

Shaking off the lay brothers Cuddy suddenly launched himself at Henry, but his chains brought him crashing to the ground before he could reach him.

'You murdering bastard, you've butchered my Luke. I'm going to kill you. I'm going to rip you apart with my bare hands.'

Once again, Alan, Stephen and Will found themselves sitting in the prior's solar in morose silence. None of them had been willing to eat at the common table, knowing that the wild speculations of their brothers would be even more lurid than those circulating in the marketplace. But they had hardly touched the meal of roast duck and stuffed eel that had been brought to them in the solar, for the day's events had considerably blunted their appetites.

It had taken some time to clear the hall and return the prisoners to the hell-pit beneath the infirmary. Cuddy, for all that he had been kept chained and on meagre rations for

the last two weeks, had surprising reserves of strength and in
his rage kept trying to throw his chained wrists round the
terrified Henry's neck and throttle him. And Cuddy's fury
had only increased when he heard the order to return him
to the gaol. But Prior Alan was in no mood to release
anyone, not until he got to the bottom of this whole sordid
mess.

Now Stephen glanced anxiously towards his superior.
Stephen hadn't become subprior by being timid, but all
the same he was well aware that not only did his prior hold
him responsible for staging the accursed play, but he was
now also blaming him for failing to recognise the head.
And when a man like Prior Alan was already in a black
humour, adding to his fury was as wise as prodding a
wounded boar with a sharp stick. Nevertheless, Stephen
felt it his duty to speak.

'Father Prior, now that we know the victim is his own
nephew, this must prove the man Cudbert innocent. Surely
he at least should be released. He has a wife and children to
support.'

'I see no proof of innocence,' Prior Alan said sourly. 'It's
been my experience that men are far more disposed to
murder members of their own family than outsiders.'

'But he seemed genuinely shocked to discover the dead
man was Luke and not Martin. All three of the players did.
Surely that shows they had no hand in the killing.'

'Unless there were two murders,' Will said. 'We have a
body, a head and a hand, but short of digging up the corpse,
we can't tell if they all belong to the same man, and even if
we do, if the corpse is in the same state of decay as the other
remains, it might be hard to be certain. Cuddy is just the
sort of fellow who would've taken the law into his own hands
and killed Martin in a fit of rage, if he learned that Martin

had decapitated his nephew. You heard the threats that he made to Henry.'

'Exactly so,' Stephen said. 'He accused Henry of killing Luke. He wouldn't have done that if he knew Martin had committed the murder. Besides, he plainly didn't know that his nephew was dead. He must have thought him fled with the rest.'

Prior Alan stabbed a piece of roasted duck with his knife and brought it to his mouth, then tossed knife and meat together back on the platter, clearly unable to bring himself to eat it. 'So we now have two possible murders – Luke and Martin. But if the head does belong to our corpse, then Martin is not a victim but one of the murderers, fled with the other actors.'

He rose to his feet, wiping his hands on a linen cloth. 'It seems to me the only thing we can be certain of is that the missing actors are in possession of the hand of St Withburga and they are hiding somewhere out there in the fens.'

He strode to the casement and stared out as if he could see right into the dark heart of the marshes. 'I want every village and island out there turned upside down. Take the dogs skilled at tracking quarry. Recruit hunters from the fenland villages who know the marshes and the waterways. The fen-landers have no love for townsfolk or outlanders. They won't hesitate to turn the actors in if the reward for their capture is big enough. Do whatever you have to, but I want those men found, and quickly.'

'I'm not going begging,' little Ben said furiously, blinking back the tears. 'Father'd be as angry as a nest of wasps if he knew you were trying to make me.'

'Well, your father isn't here,' his mother retorted. 'He's sitting around in gaol, and he hasn't got to worry about where his next meal's coming from. I dare say he won't have been dining on roast goose, but at least the Priory gives their prisoners something to fill their bellies, which is more than we will have today if you don't get out to that alms gate. If the monks are going to go around arresting innocent men and keep them from earning an honest living, the least they can do is provide their starving families with food. Why your father didn't stick to pagging and loading for the boatmen down on the quay, I'll never know. I warned him that play was cursed, but would he listen?'

'But, Mam,' Ben wailed, 'my friends'll see me there among all the cripples and gammers. They'll torment the life out of me.'

'A bit of teasing won't do you any harm. You and that father of yours were getting far too high and mighty, lording around in that play as if you were the King's minstrels. And it's no use you sulking. If you hadn't made up one of your stories about gold coins and set the men against each other none of this would have happened. Now you see you get to the front and don't let the others push you aside. Be sure to tell the monk you've three little brothers and sisters at home all going hungry.'

She grabbed Ben's shoulder and marched him out of the door, and with a light cuff around his head she sent him off in the direction of the hill that led up to Heyrow. Ben knew, without turning round, that she was standing in the doorway of the tiny cottage, her arms folded, watching him.

In the past, when his mother had sent him on a errand he didn't want to perform, he'd run off to play instead, refusing to think about his mother's wrath until he was finally forced to return home, but no such temptation entered his head now. Ben didn't need his mother to remind him that it was his fault his father had been arrested. He'd been blaming himself ever since it had happened. He hadn't made up that story about the half-noble. He had seen it, he had! But if he'd only kept quiet, the men would never have argued, he would still be performing the play and his little brothers would not be whining with hunger. Of course, he didn't for one moment believe that his father had killed Martin. He couldn't have. But suppose no one believed him? Suppose they hanged him anyway? That too would be all Ben's fault. He swallowed the hard lump in his throat and tried desperately to think of something else.

By the time he had reached Steeple Gate, a large crowd of beggars were squatting on the ground before the thick wooden door. They were mostly cripples and the old and frail whose faces were as wrinkled as last year's apples. One man, whose face was half covered in filthy bandages, gripped his crutches tightly as if he feared even these poor things might be snatched from him, while a young hollow-cheeked woman, with a grizzling baby, continually batted at the hands of a small girl to stop her picking at the yellow-crusted sores on her scalp. Ben attempted to step round the prone figures and edge his way to the front, but a hand shot out and caught his leg in a painful grip, dragging him back.

'Here, where do think you're going, brat?'

The man was crouching on a low wooden cart. He'd lost both his legs and the knuckles of his hand were covered with thick pads of brown skin where for years he had used them to propel himself along the ground. He might not be able to walk, but the muscles on his arms were harder than those of the paggers who humped loads down at the quayside. Ben wasn't going to argue with him. He obediently crouched down where the man thrust him.

'That demon will be hunting again tonight,' the cripple on the cart said to the old man beside him. 'You want to make sure you're back inside your shelter long afore dark. Killed two already, but he must be getting hungry for some more by now.'

All the heads lifted as one, glancing apprehensively up towards the cathedral tower.

'Two, is it now?' The old man chewed on the news.

'Aye, first was that fellow who played the angel, then that Ely boy, Luke. It's his head they found up on top of the tower.'

'So we've nothing to be afeared of then,' an old woman cackled. 'The monster's only going for the tender, pretty ones.'

The beggars grinned, but their smiles quickly faded and their eyes kept swivelling back up at the grey skies as if they expected any minute to see the creature swoop down.

'Luke,' the old man said. 'His uncle's one of those they locked up. I knew his brother once, the one that ran off. He—'

'Shouldn't be keeping them locked up,' a woman with a withered arm interrupted. 'Speaking that cursed play. It's them who's to blame for calling up the demon. What they want to do is to hang them from the top of the tower and leave them there for the demon to eat.'

'No!' Ben yelled. 'It's not their fault. It was the monks that give them the cursed words. They're written down, they are, on a scroll. The monks keep it hidden in the priory.'

'Aye,' said the women, 'but a curse doesn't work until it's spoken aloud for all the imps of hell to hear.'

'Well, there wouldn't be any curse to speak if monks didn't have that scroll,' Ben retorted, scarlet with indignation.

'Lad's right,' the old man said. 'Who knows what other curses they've got written down on their bits of parchment. Someone should go in there and burn the whole lot of it,

every last scrap, just to make sure they can't call up something worse.'

'And who do you think is going to do that?' the man on the
cart sneered. 'You going to volunteer, you old fart?'

'Whole town will,' the woman said sourly, 'and they'll burn
the cathedral down too if the demon that haunts that tower
snatches another soul.' She swivelled to face Ben. 'Here . . .
I've seen you before, haven't I? You're that brat played Isaac,
aren't you?'

An angry rumble ran through the beggars. The woman
started towards Ben, clambering awkwardly over the beggars sitting between them. Several of the other beggars were
also trying to heave themselves up. Ben scrambled to his feet
and fled.

He was already several yards away when he heard the
creak of the wooden gate opening behind him and the
sudden clamour for alms. He stopped and cautiously turned
around. The beggars had forgotten him in their desperation
to attract the attention of the two monks in the open gateway. The brothers were handing out loaves of bread from
one basket and kitchen scraps from the other, a random
assortment of whatever the almoner had cajoled from the
cook or gardener. An onion was dropped into one begging
bowl, a small measure of withered beans into another, a
lump of cheese into the next. The favoured ones were given
pork bones, albeit with much of the meat cut from them,
but still with enough remaining to make a coveted addition
to the cooking pot. Those who had received only beans
howled with envy.

Ben jiggled anxiously from foot to foot as the beggars
stowed the food in sacks or under threadbare cloaks and
shuffled off, glancing warily around them as if they feared
cutpurses might be lurking to snatch their loaves from them.

Even the man on the little cart had managed to claim his share by dint of ramming his cart hard and repeatedly against the ankles of those in front. The monks' baskets were emptying fast.

Ben made up his mind and rushed forward, trying to wriggle his way to the gate. But the beggars, even the old ones, were well practised in the art of blocking those behind them, while thrusting forward their own bowls. When Ben finally reached the front he was dismayed to see the monk preparing to close the gate. He clutched at the monk's basket.

'Please, I need a loaf and some beans. I've a sister and two little brothers at home – my mother too. We've no food left and my father . . .' he hesitated.

He wasn't convinced that the monks would share his mother's view that if they'd imprisoned his father, they should be feeding his family. Besides, there were still a few beggars remaining, pressing forward like him, their ears wagging.

'My father's dead,' he finished in a rush and was immediately seized with a terrible panic, as if now that he had said the words they would come to pass.

'Too late, it's all gone, lad,' the monk said, tipping the bread basket to prove to them all not a crumb remained. 'He had the last loaf,' he said, indicating with a jerk of his chin the man on crutches with the bandages over his eye hopping away from the gate. 'Give thanks to the Blessed Virgin you're sound in limb, boy. At least you've a chance of finding work to help your mother. Poor wretches like him haven't.'

Ben stared resentfully at the back of the man. 'But it isn't fair, he isn't even a cripple,' he yelled.

The monk, already with his mind on other things, would scarcely have registered this remark had it not been for the howl of protest that rose from the half-dozen beggars who were still milling around the gate, as frustrated and angry as Ben at having been denied their alms.

One of them roughly grasped Ben's arm. 'How do you know he's no cripple?'

Ben had blurted it out even before he'd realised how he knew, but now he thought about it. 'That leg he's dragging – it's as thick as the good leg. Not like his,' Ben pointed to one of the other beggars in the little group, who also supported his weight on a crutch. 'His crippled leg's no more than a stick next to his good leg.'

'The lad's right!' the beggar said. 'That leg should be wasted if he can't use it.'

The man was still hopping away up the road, oblivious to the growing commotion behind him at the gate. The monks threw down their baskets, and with a surprising turn of speed raced up the road. Before the beggar even knew what was happening they had seized him, one on either side, and were dragging him back towards the gate. The man's crutches clattered down onto the stones as the beggar struggled to break free, but the monks managed to keep their grip on him.

They had almost dragged him back as far as Steeple Gate when the almoner appeared, bristling with anger.

'Who left the gate wide open and unattended?' he began, then seeing the beggar struggling between the two sweating monks, he took a step forward, frowning.

'What's all this? Why have you laid hands on this man?'

'He's an averer,' one of the monks spat. 'Pretending to be crippled to get alms, and taking food from the mouths of those who are in genuine want.'

A growl of fury went up from the other beggars.

'Is that so?' the almoner said grimly. He seized the beggar

by the front of his filthy shirt, almost pushing his face into his. 'It's wicked enough to steal from the needy when food is plentiful, but with harvests as bad as they were last year, we certainly haven't any to waste on scoundrels like you. I'm going to ensure you're made an example of, my lad. I'll see to it that you're whipped bloody for this.'

The other beggars grinned their approval, all except one who was quietly slinking away, no doubt thinking he had come perilously near the same punishment.

The averer was fighting to free himself, while at the same time begging for mercy.

'I didn't take the food for myself, it was for my poor bedridden mother, I swear.'

The almoner was unmoved. He reached up and tugged at the end of the filthy bandage covering half the man's face.

'I warrant this is false too and we'll find a good eye beneath here.'

The man desperately tried to extricate himself from the monk's grasp. 'No, I beg you. The pain! I can't bear the pain of the light in that eye. It's agony. Don't!'

But it was too late. The last twist of bandages was torn away to reveal a somewhat crumpled but unblemished face and a second eye as bright and blue as its twin.

For a moment Ben gaped up at the figure in disbelief. 'But you're dead!'

'You recognise this man?' the almoner said.

Ben, his eyes bulging like a frog in fear and bewilderment, could only nod his head.

'Well, who is it, boy?' the almoner demanded in exasperation.

'He's the angel. He's Martin.'

The almoner didn't trouble to disguise his glee when he bustled into the prior's hall at the head of the small procession comprising the two monks, Martin struggling between two lay brothers and, nervously bringing up the rear, the small figure of Ben. There was always a certain amount of rivalry and squabbling between the obedientiaries who held posts of responsibility in the priory. And it was no secret among the brothers that Prior Alan blamed his subprior for all the misfortunes of the last few weeks. Now here was another humiliation. Stephen had men combing the fens for Martin's murderer, and all the time the victim had been very much alive and sitting at the priory gate.

The almoner could barely keep from smirking when he announced that he had personally apprehended the murderer of the poor Ely lad, Luke. The two monks who had in fact caught Martin exchanged sour looks, but they were resigned to their superiors taking credit for anything that had gone well, though they were never so eager to take the blame when things went amiss.

Prior Alan lowered himself into the chair at the far end of the long table.

'Come closer.'

The two lay brothers shoved Martin forward with such force that, with his wrists bound behind him, he almost fell sprawling across the table, but he pulled himself upright.

'There's been a mistake . . . I confessed that I begged a little food at the alms gate, but my poor mother is dying—'

'Dying now, is she?' the almoner said. 'She's suffered a remarkably sudden decline in her health. Just now you told us she was merely bedridden.'

'She's bedridden because she's dying,' Martin said, glowering at him. 'Please, Father Prior, I have to get back to her. Suppose she should die alone, thinking her only son has abandoned her? I swear I will return and undertake any penance you wish. But you would surely not deny an old woman the comfort of her son's hand in her final hours.'

The almoner opened his mouth to protest but the prior held up his hand to silence him. 'You say this is the man we thought was dead. How do you know it's him?'

The almoner looked round for Ben, who had retreated to the furthest corner and was gazing round the long panelled room in wide-eyed astonishment.

'The boy identified him. He's the lad who acted the part of Isaac in *The Play of Adam*. And I understand the lad's father is one of the men you arrested, Father Prior. You, boy, come here.'

Ben was so busy staring at the brightly stitched wall hangings that he didn't even seem to be aware he was being talked about, never mind addressed. Impatiently the almoner strode over and grabbed him, propelling him towards where the prior sat.

Prior Alan adopted what he clearly thought was a kindly expression, but it did nothing to reassure the boy, who stared at him like a rabbit bewitched by a stoat.

'Do you see the man with his hands bound?'

Ben's gaze flicked to Martin and back to the prior. He nodded, uncertain why the prior should be asking him if he could see someone who was standing only feet away, unless Martin really was a ghost.

'Do you know who he is?'

'M . . . Martin.'

'No, I swear I'm not. I know no one of that name. I live out in the fens. I came to Ely to find food for my poor dying mother. I've never seen this boy before. The child is mistaken.'

I'm not,' Ben said indignantly. 'You are Martin and there *was* a half-noble in the bag. You stole it.'

'You see the boy is clearly making all this up. No doubt he hopes for a reward.'

Prior Alan gestured to the two lay brothers. 'Be so good as to find Subprior Stephen and ask him to come here. He's spoken to the actor on several occasions; if this is the fellow Stephen will know. And please fetch Custodian Will too. You need not return here yourselves. When we have done with the prisoner, I shall send for you again to conduct him to the hell-pit. Whoever he may prove to be, one thing is clear, he is guilty of posing as a cripple to beg for alms and he will be punished for that, though I suspect that will prove to be the very least of his crimes.'

When Stephen came hurrying into the prior's hall, no one could be left in any doubt as to the identity of the man.

'That's him, that's Martin,' Stephen said the moment he caught sight of him. 'So he *is* alive. Where did you find him?'

The almoner had been anticipating this question and had been rehearsing the words of his gloating reply in his head while they had been waiting, but he never got a chance to utter them.

Prior Alan at once dismissed him from the hall, together with the two monks, ordering that the boy should be taken to the kitchens there to be given a generous basket of food and a few coins by way of a reward. Scowling, the almoner marched Ben from the room, gripping his shoulder so tightly in his indignation at being excluded that the lad would have protested had he not been so delighted at the prospect of taking home not just a loaf but a whole feast.

When the heavy door had closed behind them, Prior Alan turned his attention back to his prisoner. 'You look remarkably well for a man who's been dead for over two weeks.'

Martin said nothing. Even he realised that there was little point in continuing to deny who he was. They had only to bring his cousin, Henry, here, or Cuddy or John. They would take the greatest pleasure in identifying him.

Prior Alan rose and paced the length of the room. Only when he reached the far end did he turn and address Martin.

'So, you murdered your fellow player Luke. You cut the head from the corpse and hid it, and you dressed him in your robes. The question is why? Was it to make everyone believe you were dead, so that you could escape with the relic?'

Martin gaped at him. Only a few of the words had filtered through the panic fogging his mind. '*Murder?* No! No! I swear it on the bones of every saint in Ely, I did not kill Luke. He was already dead when I found him.'

'I seem to recall just moments ago you swearing you were not Martin,' Alan said coldly. 'It would appear little value can be placed upon your oaths.'

'But it's true. I came across his corpse ... by accident. There was no mistaking he was dead – a sword cut to the neck. His head was almost severed.'

'How do you know it was a sword cut, if you did not kill him?'

'Because ... I realised who must have done it, and the sword ... I ...'

Alan resumed his pacing. 'If a man finds a corpse he is by law required to raise the hue and cry, but you did not. Why would you not report it, if you are as innocent of the death as you claim, especially if you knew who had murdered him?'

Martin stared wildly round the room, looking for someone who might take pity on him, but the faces of all three men were equally impassive.

'I ... suspected that his killer was really after me. It was dark, Luke was wearing a hood. He must have returned to the wagon to search for the money his uncle accused me, quite falsely, of taking. The man who killed him obviously mistook him for me. We're much the same height. When I saw Luke's body I realised that could have been me lying there, and if the man who killed him learned he had made a mistake, then he'd continue looking for me. So I thought if everyone believed I was dead . . .'

'Including the players you robbed, then you could escape with your life and their money, was that it?' Stephen said.

'I was merely trying to prevent another murder being committed,' Martin said resentfully.

'Continue,' said the prior sternly. 'What did you do after you *found* Luke's body?

'I didn't want the corpse to be discovered by the watch before I had time to get out of Ely when the gates were opened the next morning. I tried to drag the corpse into the wagon, but the head was lolling about too much, so in the end I took my knife and sawed through the last bit of the neck, then I heaved the corpse in. I dressed Luke in my angel costume.

'I realised I had to dispose of the head where no one would find it. My clothes were soaked in blood from moving the body. So I changed into some old clothes from the props box, wrapped the head in my bloodstained clothes, put it all in a sack along with Luke's clothes and set off for the river. But when I was halfway down the hill I saw the flames of a torch moving towards me. I thought it might be the watch making their rounds, so I fled back to the wagon and hid beneath it until morning. I couldn't go to the river then, all the players live down there and besides it would be swarming with boatmen and paggers. And I daren't risk carrying the head out of the town gates in the sack, in case I was stopped and searched.

'It was looking up at the roof of the cathedral, at all those carved heads, that gave me the idea. I managed to mingle with the crowd going in for the servants' Mass. I couldn't believe my luck when I found the door to the tower open. With all those people milling about, no one noticed me slip inside. I stuffed the sack and clothing under one of the beams in the dark corner inside the tower, then put the head on the turret where the birds could pick it clean. I thought when it was eventually found, people would think they'd found my head.'

'As indeed some did,' Alan said, glaring at Stephen.

'But when I came down the tower, someone had locked the door at the bottom. I couldn't get back out. I had to hide and wait for someone to open it again, but no one came until long after the noon bell. I made straight for the town gate, but even before I got there I saw the long queues waiting in front of it and I realised the guards were stopping and questioning everyone. I couldn't leave Ely.'

'So you decided to hide in plain view,' Alan said.

'No one looks at beggars,' Martin said, with something of his old swagger at his own cleverness.

'But what I don't understand,' Will said, 'is how you broke into St Withburga's tomb. You said yourself there was a crowd of people, and the cathedral is searched thoroughly each evening to ensure no thief is hiding.'

'But I didn't go near any of the saints' tombs. I didn't want to risk being seen.'

'Then how did you steal the saint's hand and replace it with Luke's?' Will demanded.

'How he did it is irrelevant,' Prior Alan snapped.

'But, Father Prior, if there has been some breach in the security of the cathedral, others may use it to steal, and as custodian—'

'That can wait. The only thing that matters at this moment is recovering that relic.'

Alan strode across to Martin and seized his shoulders, shaking him as if that would make the words drop out of his mouth. 'We know you placed the hand of the murdered boy in the shrine and stole the saint's hand. Tell us what you've done with it. Where have you hidden it?'

'But I didn't take anything from the shrine. I told you, I couldn't get near it.'

Martin tried desperately to pull himself out of the prior's grasp, but his hands were bound fast and, for a man in his sixties, Alan was surprisingly strong.

'Then what did you do with Luke's hand,' Alan demanded, 'the hand you so brutally sliced from his corpse?'

'Nothing! I did nothing. Luke's hand was already missing when I found him.'

'You didn't mention that before,' Stephen said.

Martin hesitated. 'I . . . I guessed the man who took it had cut it off . . . because he thought Luke was a . . . thief.'

Prior Alan pounced. 'But you told us this mysterious man believed he was killing you, that means that you are the thief. So what did you steal from him? It must have been something of great value to warrant murder. Well?' He shook Martin again.

'All right, if you must know it was a sword . . . a silver sword.'

'Valuable indeed,' Alan said grimly. 'But why did he not simply have you arrested? He would have had the satisfaction of seeing you hanged without risk to himself.'

'He didn't dare,' Martin said sullenly. 'It's no ordinary blade. The sword is inscribed with the secret names of God, *Agla* and *On*. And this man is an alchemist . . . from Cambridge.'

185

Prior Alan sank down into the nearest chair. 'This gets worse by the hour,' he groaned.

Stephen and Will looked bewildered.

'Only twelve such swords were ever made,' Alan explained wearily, 'to be used by consecrated priests who were specially trained in the art of conjuring spirits and angels. The Mass of the Holy Spirit was said over those blades. They're all supposed to be safely under lock and key. So how on earth did a layman get hold of one? It's obvious why this alchemist did not report the theft. He must have stolen the sword himself or bought it knowing it was stolen.'

The colour drained from Stephen's face. 'You used a sword in the play of "Cain and Abel" . . . surely it was not that one.'

Martin's silence told him it was.

'What evil demon have you conjured!' Stephen cried.

Prior Alan thumped the table. 'He has conjured nothing! Whatever mischief has gone on in Ely has been the work of human sin, as the very play itself warns. The townspeople may believe in demons flying down from towers, but we know it is not so.'

Will and Stephen exchanged glances that plainly said they knew no such thing.

'But Father Prior,' Will said, 'what about the theft of St Withburga's hand? I still don't see how Martin could have accomplished it.'

Martin looked positively triumphant as if he'd just been proved innocent.

'*If* what this man says is true,' Alan said icily, 'then we have found our thief and he is most definitely human. If the alchemist cut off Luke's hand, then he must have placed it in the shrine and stolen the saint's hand, no doubt to use in some evil charm or sorcery. Find the alchemist and we will find the hand.

'You,' he turned to Martin, 'tell Brother Will all you know about this man and the places he is likely to go. Will and Stephen, you must prepare to set out at once for Cambridge, but you'll have to travel alone. No one outside this room is to learn St Withburga's hand is missing. If you have to enlist help when you are there to apprehend this alchemist, then tell them only that he is wanted for murder in the cathedral precincts, but make sure you search his lodging and work-shop thoroughly. I want that hand found.

'As for you, Martin, you will be reunited with your cousin in the hell-pit. He will doubtless be overjoyed to discover you're alive, but I suspect Luke's uncle will be somewhat less welcoming, especially when he learns it was you who placed his nephew's head on the tower.'

Cambridge

It took Stephen and Will three days to locate the alchemist's house. On the first morning after they arrived in Cambridge they sought an audience with the sheriff and explained they were in pursuit of a man who had committed murder in the grounds of Ely Priory, though they were careful to make no mention of either the relic or the sword. The sheriff showed little interest. Scowling, he told them that he had his hands full trying to keep the townspeople, the students and the various orders of monks from killing one another, without solving Ely's murders as well, and demanded to know why they hadn't brought more men with them. Finally, but only after he had been reminded in no uncertain terms by Will that he had a sworn duty to root out fugitives from justice hiding in his city, he grudgingly assigned two of his men to go with them and arrest the man, if he could be found.

Martin, realising his only hope of escaping the gallows was the arrest of the alchemist, had told Will exactly how to find the undercroft of a house where the alchemist had his workshop. But when Stephen and Will arrived and hammered on the door, they were met only with silence. Finally, after they had knocked a good many times, a woman leaned out of a casement on the upper storey.

'We were told that we might find a man called Nicholas working here,' Will called up.

'Used to. Left in the middle of the night, he did, and the bastard still owes me rent.'

'Do you know where he went?'

'Do you think he'd still owe me rent if I did?' the woman retorted, and promptly withdrew her head.

But even in Cambridge the smells and noises of an alchemist's workshop couldn't remain unnoticed for ever. Stephen and Will were eventually led to a house backing on to the stinking waters of King's Ditch by a grubby street urchin who seemed to know the business of every household in Cambridge, information that he was eager to sell, though only after negotiating his fee as ruthlessly as any lawyer.

Without apparently any understanding of the word *stealth*, the two sheriff's men thundered up the rickety staircase to a room tucked under the eaves of a house. Not even a deaf man could have failed to hear their coming and when they burst in, the alchemist was frantically trying to squeeze himself out through the impossibly small window. Where he imagined he could go next was anyone's guess, since only a bird could have escaped that way, but the soldiers didn't waste time asking questions. Their instructions were to take the prisoner back to the sheriff at the castle, what happened to him after was not their concern.

'Go with them,' Will whispered to Stephen. 'Find out what he says to the sheriff. It'll give me time to search this room.'

He glanced round at the vast array of boxes, jars, charts and scrolls that were crammed onto every shelf, and the many more lurking between the curiously shaped flasks that steamed and bubbled over candle flames and small braziers.

'The hand must be in here somewhere,' Will said. 'He's evidently a man who likes to keep his possessions close, but it could take me a month to search through this lot.'

'I should douse those flames first,' Stephen warned. 'That pot looks near to bursting open.' He hastily backed away from a vessel that was wobbling alarmingly as clouds of greenish steam belched out of it.

But after several hours of methodical searching, even examining the walls for any concealed hiding place as well as the mysterious contents of the flasks, Will was reluctantly compelled to admit the bones of St Withburga were not in the room. He had discovered the silver sword concealed in a roll of bedding, and a desiccated mouse squashed behind a chest, but otherwise nothing. He was forced to conclude that if the alchemist had indeed stolen the hand, it was no longer in his possession.

Subprior Stephen confirmed this as soon as they met up again. 'Nicholas confessed to the murder, in fact he seemed quite proud of it. Even the news that he killed the wrong man didn't disturb him. He showed no remorse at all. It was as if the killing of Luke meant no more to him than the squashing of a beetle compared to the importance of his work. I'm certain he believes that no one would dare to exe- cute a great alchemist like him over something so insignificant.'

'But did our alchemist mention the hand?' Will asked.

Stephen grimaced. 'I managed to persuade the sheriff to leave us alone for a few minutes and questioned him, but he was adamant he didn't steal St Withburga's hand. In fact he was scornful of the very idea he should need it. He also claimed that Luke's corpse still had both hands when he left. I'm inclined to believe him. He's so arrogant; he would certainly have boasted about the cleverness of the theft if he had committed it.'

'Then that brings us back to Martin again,' Will said grimly. 'Though I still can't see how he could have done it. I'm beginning to think the townspeople might be right and thanks to that wretched play there is a demon at work.'

The two monks left Cambridge without the alchemist. Having decided that Nicholas was a dangerous lunatic, the sheriff was not going to risk having him escape from the two monks, or being rescued by his friends, if indeed a man like that had any. But the sheriff refused to spare men to accompany them to guard the prisoner, saying that if the prior wanted the alchemist returned to Ely he should send an adequate number of men to fetch him, otherwise he would remain safely locked up in the castle to await the next assizes.

Stephen and Will broke their journey at Denny Abbey, knowing they would not reach Ely by dark. The ancient causeway track across the waterways and sucking mires was dangerous enough by day, but only a man who longed for death would venture upon it at night. When they set off shortly after dawn the following morning, to their great relief a brisk wind was whipping across the bleak wetlands. It cut through their robes, but at least it blew away the thick mists that so often curled over the marshes.

The track was an ancient way constructed to take man

and beast dry-shod across the sucking marshes and black expanses of water. But over the centuries the causeway had sunk in places, so that mud and water oozed back over it, and the last hot dry summer had cracked the bridges, making some of them so perilous that Stephen and Will were forced to dismount and gingerly lead their horses across on a long rein, as the wood creaked ominously beneath them. But the state of the track wasn't the only thing that made them nervous. The tall reed beds, and the patches of willow and birch scrub, made the perfect cover for cutpurses and robbers. The monks' cowls and tonsures would not protect them. Everyone knew that Ely Priory was wealthy, and monks travelling that road might well be carrying heavy purses or other treasures.

Stephen kept looking ahead of him to catch his first glimpse of the cathedral rising above the fenland. At any other time he would have been eager to see it, knowing he was in sight of a good meal and bed to rest his aching backside. But on this occasion, he found himself dreading his return and the inevitable interview with his superior. As Prior Alan had reminded him before they left, this whole sorry business had been his fault and he did not look forward to having to report yet another failure. But at least they had recovered the sword. Prior Alan must surely be a little cheered that such a sacred object was once more back in the hands of the Church.

It had begun to rain, and the wind was lashing it so hard against them that even their oily woollen cloaks were becoming sodden. However low a man's spirits are, being cold and wet are certain to drive them still lower. Ahead of him Stephen saw Will dismount and start to lead his horse over another of the rickety bridges. With a sigh, he prepared to do likewise.

Will was halfway across the bridge when both monks heard the cry. The words were so faint that neither of them could make them out, but the voice was unquestionably human.

They stared around, but saw nothing except the reeds, which towered high above them and the sluggish black water in the ditch. This was just the kind of place an ambush might be set.

Will hesitated, uncertain whether to cross or go back. But it was plain he'd have to continue, for if he tried to turn his horse on the creaking bridge they would probably both end up in the water. As quickly as he dared he pulled the horse forward and Stephen prepared to follow him the moment Will's horse was on solid ground, for it was well known that outlaws would try to separate travellers, making attack easier.

Just as Will's horse cleared the bridge they heard the cry again.

'Help me! Of your mercy, help me.'

'I think it's coming from under the bridge,' Will called.

He hastily tethered his mount to a birch tree before stepping back onto the bridge. He peered down through the gaps in the warped planks.

'There's someone under there. I'm sure I can see something moving. Who's there? Are you hurt?'

'Mud, can't pull my leg out . . . so cold.'

'It might be a trap,' Stephen warned. He stared round wildly, trying to peer into the reeds to see if anyone was lurking, waiting to rush out at them. His heart almost stopped as he heard something rustling, but it was only a moorhen.

Will leaned as far over the side of the bridge as he dared. 'I see him! He's just under this side . . . God's blood, I think it's one of our own brothers.' He straightened up. 'He's up to the armpits in water. God knows how long the poor fellow has been struggling in there, but he must be numb with cold. If we knot the cords from our habits together, I can try to loop them around him and get one of the horses to pull him out.'

'But suppose you fall in and get stuck,' Stephen said. 'Shouldn't we go for help?'

'No time. He's exhausted. If he faints, he'll go under and drown. See if you can find a pole or branch or something I can hang on to.'

It was not an easy matter pulling the poor monk out. Stephen locked his arm round the strut of the bridge and gripped the end of an all-too-slender birch branch. Will, grasping the lower end to steady himself, inched as far down the steep, slippery bank as he dared. Blinking the rain out of his eyes, he made several attempts to toss the loop of the knotted cord to the monk. At first, the monk couldn't seem to summon the strength to grasp it, but finally, with Will shouting encouragement and threats in equal measure, he roused himself and managed to grasp the rope and eventually hooked one arm through it.

With Will safely back on the bank, they tied the end of the cord to the long leading rein of his horse and urged it forward. The cord straightened and groaned, then with a great splash the monk shot forward in the water and went under. For a sickening moment they thought they had lost him, but he reappeared coughing and choking, still holding onto the cord. Urging the horse another few paces forward, they hauled him out of the water, before finally managing to grasp his arms and drag him up the bank.

He lay on the track, his eyes closed, as black water streamed from his robes and mouth. It was only then, when they saw his face free from the deep cowl, that Stephen recognised him.

'Brother Oswin! But what are you doing out here and how did you end up in the ditch?'

It was a long time before the young monk could manage to speak, never mind answer that question. Covering him as best they could with their own damp cloaks, Stephen and Will rubbed warmth back into his deathly cold limbs, and urged him to take a few sips of the wine from the leather bottle Will had in his pack. Finally, Oswin managed to sit up and his teeth began to chatter, which both men knew to be a good sign. When he did speak, however, his words made little sense.

'Slipped off the br-bridge in the dark. Tried to stand up . . . wade back to the bank . . . sank into the mud.'

'But what on earth possessed you to travel on this cause-way in the dark, Brother?' Stephen said. 'No one from the priory would have sent you out on an errand alone at night.'

'Have to get it back . . . Prior Alan called off the search. I thought they'd find it when they were searching for the actors, but they're not even looking any more.'

'Find what?' Stephen asked.

'Hand . . . hand of St Withburga.'

Will and Stephen gaped at each other.

'Prior Alan told you it was missing?' Stephen asked incredulously. After all the steps he had taken to conceal the theft, surely he would never have confided in a monk as young and inexperienced as Brother Oswin.

'Prior Alan, no . . . I took the hand. It was me. I refused at first. I told him it was sacrilege, but my brother . . . Father Edmund threatened that if I did not bring him the hand he would betray a secret told to him in confession and my brother would be hanged . . . I had no choice.'

'So you broke into the shrine and stole a holy relic, a relic from your own priory,' Will yelled at him. 'And then you desecrated the sacred body of the saint with that piece of rotting flesh. Did this Father Edmund also force you to do that?'

Will looked so angry, Stephen thought for one moment he was going to hurl the young monk straight back into the water.

'Desecrate? No . . . No! I would never desecrate the shrine of the blessed saint. I prayed to the Blessed Virgin to help me and she showed me what to do. She threw the corpse at my feet. It was an answer to my prayers, don't you see? At . . . at first I thought she wanted me to cut off the hand and give that to Father Edmund instead, but I realised he wouldn't believe it was the saint's hand . . . So after the midnight service, I lingered behind and hid in the shadows until the gate was locked and all the brothers were gone.'

'That's how it was done!' Will said savagely. 'I should have known. When the pilgrims leave after vespers, we search the cathedral thoroughly to ensure no one is hiding, but once the great door is locked, it isn't searched again, because only the monks attend matins and lauds at midnight and no monk would ever dream of stealing from his own cathedral, would he?'

He glowered at Oswin. 'So you had nearly four hours to steal the saint's hand before the gates were opened again to admit the monks for prime at daybreak, and then all you had to do was slip back into your place among the brothers. But you still haven't told us why you left that foul abomination in that holy place.'

Oswin shrank from Will's fury. 'I . . . I put that corpse's hand in the coffin and left the coffin lid a little ajar so that the smell would force you to open the shrine and discover the saint's hand was missing. I thought you would understand it was a message.' He clutched at Will's sleeve. 'I wanted you to search and find the bones. But they've stopped searching. So I must go to Father Edmund now. I must put right what I did wrong.'

He struggled to rise and collapsed again almost at once. Beads of sweat broke out on his forehead. Stephen pressed his hand to the young monk's face. It was burning.

'He has a fever. We should get him back to the priory at once.'

'What about the relic?' Will protested.

'Promise . . . promise you will find it. I must . . .' Oswin suddenly screamed and doubled up in pain.

'That's it,' Stephen said. 'The relic will have to wait. We must take Oswin to the infirmary now.'

Ely

There was silence in Prior Alan's solar, broken only by the crackling of the fire in the hearth. Candles burned steadily on their spikes, and outside the shuttered casements the world slept on in darkness. Prior Alan stared miserably at the jar before him on the table. There was nothing in it save sodden ashes and fragments of charred bones.

'You are sure this is all that remains.'

Will nodded. 'Father Edmund was so close to death when we arrived that I'm certain it was only malice that kept him breathing. He laughed when he saw us. "You're too late," he said, pointing to the fire. "She betrayed me, just like de Lisle, so now her bones can warm mine."'

'Those were his very last words,' Stephen added. 'A great spasm seized him. He choked and clutched at his throat as if someone was strangling him, blood gushed from his mouth, then he fell back dead. Will quickly threw the remains of the priest's ale into the fire to douse the flames, but the hand was already burned away.'

'At least we recovered something,' Alan said. 'We three will inter what remains in her shrine tonight and hold a vigil until prime. We have much to pray about.'

He lifted the silver sword, which lay next to the ashes on his table, turning the blade over in the candlelight, tracing with his finger the secret names of God – *Agla* on one side of the blade and on the other side, *On*. The intricate engraving of mystic signs and scrolls was so delicate, the angels themselves could have fashioned it.

The alchemist had evidently cleaned the sword, but not well enough, for when Alan held it close to the ball of glass that intensified the candlelight he could just make out dark threads of blood trapped in the fine line of tracery. It was a sword of exquisite beauty, intended only for holy work, but now it was tainted by murder. For this sword had never been honed for battle, though it was sharp enough to bisect a single hair. It had been made to conjure spirits and angels. And such a sword was worth ... ah, yes, that was the question. What would a man with knowledge of how to use it be prepared to pay for such a sword?

Alan laid it down with a sigh. 'This must be locked away in our own vaults, at least until we can discover which cathedral or abbey it was stolen from.'

'Father Prior,' Stephen said, 'what do you intend to do with Martin now, and the other players? For it seems they were telling the truth after all.'

There was more than a hint of 'I told you so' in his tone, but if Prior Alan noticed, he was choosing to ignore it.

'I'll release them in the morning – all except Martin, of course. I think he would find himself a murder victim in truth if we left him to the mercy of the other actors. Besides, he may be innocent of murder, but there's still a long list of other crimes for which he is assuredly guilty. But I don't intend to keep him lying around in the hell-pit. He can spend his nights chained up in there, but I'm sure we can find work to keep him occupied during the day, until the alchemist's trial. I think cleaning out the latrines might be a good start, then the stables, that way he can start earning the bread he received in alms.'

There was a knock on the heavy oak door and the infirmarer entered.

Alan motioned to him to join them round the fire, but he shook his head and remained standing just inside the door.

'I have bad news, Father Prior. It's Brother Oswin.'

'Has his fever worsened?'

'It has, but I am afraid it's no common fever.' He sighed and wearily massaged his eyes. 'He is coughing blood and the black marks have appeared on his skin. There can be no doubt, it is the Great Pestilence.'

Prior Alan groaned. 'God have mercy on us all.'

Will and Stephen stared aghast at each other. They had both touched Oswin, held him up on Will's horse as they brought him home and carried him to the infirmary.

'You changed your robes, did you not?' the infirmarer asked, in answer to their unspoken question.

'They were wet and muddy.'

'They should be burned. But if it's any consolation, by all accounts it's mostly the young men like Brother Oswin the pestilence is claiming this time.'

Will had turned very pale and his hands were trembling. 'Father Edmund coughed blood at the last. Do you think . . .?'

The infirmarer grimaced, refusing to meet his frightened gaze. 'I will prepare some draughts for you that are thought to be efficacious, and, Father Prior, with your permission I will have fumigants burning in every part of the priory by morning. But I think that you should order a grave to be dug in the monks' cemetery as soon as it's light. There is no physic that will help Brother Oswin now.'

'I pray it's the only grave we will need to dig, but I suspect there will be many more,' Prior Alan said.

Stephen shuddered. He knew he should not fear death. His life was in God's hands and it was His to take it, whenever it pleased Him to do so. Nevertheless, Stephen could not help but be comforted that they would be spending the night in vigil at St Withburga's shrine. He felt the need for her protection more tonight than he had ever done in his life before.

The infirmarer made to leave, then turned back. 'There is something else you should know, Father Prior. Some of the brothers are saying *The Play of Adam* is the cause of this misfortune and when the people of Ely learn of Brother Oswin's condition they will surely blame the curse of the play as well. They may even try to storm the priory.'

'I'm not a man to believe in curses,' Alan said, 'and I've always tried to ignore the legend that the very first time the play was performed in Oseney Abbey, a monk was cruelly murdered. But I am beginning to believe that play has a strange way of bringing forth the evil in man.'

He sat in silence for a few minutes as if he was trying to make up his mind about something. Then he gave a great sigh. 'Brother Stephen, would you be so good as to fetch *The Play of Adam* from the library for me?'

Stephen bowed his head and left the room. He returned a while later with a long wooden case and laid it on the table in front of Prior Alan. Alan opened it carefully and slid out a roll of vellum and unrolled the first few inches.

'This is over two hundred years old and see, the writing is as bold and clear as the day it was scratched upon this scroll. The author used the finest quality ink and vellum. Perhaps he was once a sacrist himself, like me, and knew how to buy the best. A pity, such a pity that what was written in faith should be used for such foul ends, yet that is ever the way of man. But we must put a stop to this and let it be known in the town that *The Play of Adam* is gone and will never again be performed.'

'You surely don't mean to burn it,' Will said. Although he, unlike Prior Alan, was convinced the scene of "Cain and Abel" was cursed, still he could not bear to think of anything so old and beautiful being wholly consigned to the flames.

'No, I would not destroy it, but like the sword it must be placed where it cannot be used for evil.'

Alan turned over the scroll and dipped his quill in his ink pot. He carefully wrote a few lines on the back of the vellum at the top, then he rolled it up again. Melting the end of the stick of wax in the candle flame, he allowed a glob of it to fall precisely on the edge of the scroll, before swiftly pressing his seal to it. The wax hardened almost as once, sealing the scroll shut.

'Brother Stephen, choose two of our younger brethren. Tell them they must be ready to leave Ely at dawn. They must take this scroll straight to the Benedictine House at Westminster, and give it into the hand of the abbot. He's an old friend of mine. He will understand my warning. And it might be wise to instruct the brothers to disguise themselves as lay folk just until they are well beyond Ely. As soon as the news of the pestilence breaks, there will be a great throng scrabbling to leave the town and I don't want the monks to be at the mercy of their wrath. Tell the brothers not to return until they know Ely is free from the contagion. If God wills it, this *Play of Adam* might for once save two young lives instead of taking them.'

He handed the scroll to Stephen, who looked down at the words his superior had written.

> *In that this scroll contains Holy Writ, you shall not suffer it to be destroyed. Yet neither shall you break the seal upon it, lest fools and knaves make of it swords to slay the innocent and infect man's reason with the worm of madness.*
> *Alan of Walsingham, Prior of Ely.*

Outside in the darkness a single bell began to toll. Brother Oswin was dead. How many more times would that bell ring over the coming weeks? Whatever Prior Alan chose to believe, Stephen felt a shadow hovering over Ely, darker and more terrifying than any demon. And he knew then with a dreadful certainty that the scroll had been sealed too late – far too late to save them now.

Historical Notes

In the seventh century St Eltheldreda, daughter of Anna, King of East Anglia, founded the monastery of Ely and her youngest sister, Withburga, founded a nunnery at Dereham. Many miracles were attributed to Withburga, including that a wild doe came to her to be milked twice a day to provide food for the workmen who were building the church at Dereham. When she died in around AD 743, she was buried at Dereham, which became a place of pilgrimage.

In 974, Brithnoth, Abbot of Ely, decided that Withburga should be interred in the cathedral along with her sister

Etheldreda. The abbot and his monks broke into the shrine at Dereham and stole the saint's body. In the morning the men of Dereham gave chase, but the body was already on a boat sailing up the river towards Ely. When the Dereham men returned home they found a miraculous spring had welled up in the empty grave. The shrines of the two princesses, together with the shrines of their sister Sexburga and her daughter, Ermengild, made Ely Cathedral an important medieval pilgrimage site, but, sadly, the shrines were destroyed in 1541 during the Reformation.

Relics of saints were widely used to heal the sick, and also in rituals to raise spirits, angels and demons. The sword described in the story was used by priests who had been trained in the art of necromancy and in summoning spirits. Priests would undertake these rituals in the service of the Church, just as others would perform exorcisms. Today such rites would be condemned by most bishops, but in the Middle Ages they were regarded as part of Christian belief and practice, and a number of learned medieval scholars and theologians wrote detailed treatises on these rituals.

The widely held superstition that a dead man's hand, or 'hand of glory', could be used to open any lock, render a thief invisible and put the occupants of the house to be burgled into a deep sleep was still believed as late as the nineteenth century. Indeed, the *Observer* newspaper of 1831 reports the arrest of a burglar caught using a hand of glory. These hands were normally cut from the corpse of a hanged man, but since they were also believed to have great curative powers, Father Edmund, in his crazed mind, might well have believed he could use the saint's hand for this purpose, if she failed to cure the plague.

The return of the plague in 1361 affected Cambridgeshire

particularly badly, striking many villages and towns that had escaped the first wave in 1348, with devastating results. Although young men and women were the major casualties of the 1361 outbreak, it did claim the lives of many others, especially those already weakened by the famine.

ACT THREE

I

The events that led to the death of Christopher Dole, playwright and player, began one autumn evening when he put down his pen with a sigh. He rubbed his eyes and, by the light of the guttering candle, looked again at the last word he had written. *Finis*. The End. The conclusion of two days and nights of frantic scribbling. He had scarcely stopped to eat or drink. He had taken no more than a mouthful of bread and cheese or a gulp of small beer. If there were moments when he slept, he did not remember them.

Christopher shuffled the loose, folio-sized pages into order on his desk-top. He noted, almost with indifference, the way his handwriting grew worse as side after side of the ruled sheets was filled. The first few pages were neat enough but after that came the blotches, the crossings-out and inserted words. 'Foul papers' was the name for this, the first draft of a play. Well, these were very foul papers indeed.

Usually, the draft would be passed to a professional scrivener to make a fair copy. Then it would be transcribed once more into separate rolls containing the parts for the various players. But this play by Christopher Dole would never be seen and heard by an audience. A pity, thought Christopher, blinking and looking through the casement window, which was so small that, if he wished to read or write, he required a candle even on midsummer's day. Yes, it was a pity this play he'd just completed would never be staged. There were some good things in it. Good things beginning with the title, which was *The English Brothers*. It contained a scattering of neat verses. A few good jokes. But there were also some dangerous items in *The English Brothers*. Items meant to bring down trouble on the head of the playwright. Not Christopher Dole but Mr William Shakespeare.

As Christopher thought of Shakespeare, his hands clenched and he felt the familiar knot in his stomach. The rest of the world considered the man from Stratford to be one of nature's gentlemen, a generous and mild-mannered individual. But Christopher had particular reasons to hate the more successful playwright. One of them was to do with Shakespeare's opportunism. Years before, Christopher had devised a play based on an old poem entitled *The Tragical History of Romeus and Juliet*. Perhaps he was unwise enough to speak about his intentions, and word got back to WS. Or perhaps the Stratford man stumbled, by coincidence, across the same source. Certainly he worked much more quickly than Christopher. And, as Dole was bound to acknowledge when he finally saw Shakespeare's love tragedy, WS had done a better job than he, Christopher, would have been capable of. A much better job.

This was the beginning of their rivalry, even if it was a rivalry mostly apparent on Dole's side. Now he was determined to revenge himself on the individual who'd wronged him, using the playwright's own medium of words. It was his last chance for revenge since Christopher Dole did not think he would be alive for much longer.

So he cobbled together, during forty-eight hours of frantic scribbling, a piece guaranteed to cause WS a few problems. And it was all his – Christopher Dole's – own work. Or very nearly all. Lying on the desk-top was an ancient vellum manuscript, some of which Christopher had put to use in *The English Brothers*. This was an old drama known as *The Play of Adam*. To bulk out his own play, Christopher had copied a couple of pages from this piece, ones telling of the rivalry between Cain and Abel and the first murder, and presented them as a play-within-a-play. The manuscript was worn and, in places, the writing so faded that Christopher was forced to peer closely in order to copy it out. The play-within-a-play was a fashionable device. Shakespeare himself had done the very same thing in *Hamlet*.

A few months earlier Christopher had discovered the vellum manuscript in a chest in a neglected corner of the shop belonging to his brother, Alan, a bookseller. Alan had just turned down Christopher's request for a loan and disappeared upstairs, above the shop. Christopher, feeling aggrieved at his brother's refusal, had poked around among Alan's stock of books. He'd unfastened the chest in the corner and, straight away, his curiosity was sparked by a wax seal securing one of several rolls bundled inside. The elaborate seal suggested the contents might be valuable.

Unthinkingly, Christopher broke the disc of wax. Casting his eyes over the text inside, he soon saw that it was from the earliest days of drama, a period when plays were scarcely to be distinguished from religious celebrations and festivals. He secreted the scroll inside his doublet, believing it might come in useful. And so it proved when he had transcribed a few dozen lines from the old text into his own hastily composed piece. Since Christopher Dole did not get on with his brother, he liked the fact that the section he'd copied out was to do with Cain and Abel. It had given him the idea of titling his work *The English Brothers*.

206

The material for the play itself he had discovered in a collection of antique tales. It was a narrative about the rivalry between a pair of English siblings who should have been fighting the Norse invaders but were instead more interested in fighting each other over the same noble lady. Christopher versified this story and dashed it down any old how, hardly caring how it came out.

The English Brothers was never going to be performed.

It would be printed, however. Printed without the approval of the authorities and without a licence. And it would bear Shakespeare's name on the title page or, if not his name in full, then a hint of it. Let the man from Stratford explain himself to the Privy Council. They would definitely be interested in some of the coded comments in *The English Brothers*.

It was a late afternoon in autumn and growing dark. Christopher Dole might have slept now his work was complete but he was seized with the desire for action. He took the old vellum manuscript and hid it away inside his own chest, which contained nothing more than his shirts and other faded garments. Then he folded up the foul papers and tucked them inside his doublet. He snuffed out the dying candle and made his way out of the little top-floor room and down the rickety stairs of his lodgings.

In the small dark lobby he almost collided with a figure who was leaning against the jamb of the front door and blocking the exit.

'Ah,' said the figure, 'it's Christopher, isn't it?'

'You are in my way.'

'I knew it was you. I can identify every member of this household by their tread, even when they're hurrying, as you are.'

'I am going out.'

The figure pushed itself away from the door-jamb and

moved slightly to one side so that Dole was forced to brush past him. He smelled meat and liquor on the other's breath. It reminded him that he had not eaten properly for at least forty-eight hours.

The lounger in the lobby was Stephen. He was the land-lady's son. Stephen did not seem to do anything in his mother's house other than pad softly around, like a cat, and push his nose into other people's business, like a dog.

'You are surely on your way somewhere important, Christopher,' he said in his usual familiar style. 'Judging by the way you came downstairs almost running – for a man of your age, that is.'

'Shog off, Stephen,' said Christopher, opening the door and stepping into the street. He heard the other say, 'My pleasure', as the door closed behind him.

It was damp and cold in the streets outside but no damper or colder than it was in Dole's garret room. The playwright walked briskly so as to keep out the weather and because he was eager to reach his destination, a tavern called The Ram. The tavern was in Moor Street in Clerkenwell. Dole knew that he would find the man he wanted there. Old George preferred The Ram to his home. It was quieter in The Ram. It was too distant for any member of his household to come hunting for him. Ensconced in the tavern, he would not be bothered by wife and children.

Sure enough, George Bruton was sitting in front of a pint pot in a corner. The interior of the tavern was smoky and no better lit than Dole's own quarters. But George always sat on the same bench in the same corner, and a blind man might have found him. There was a knot of men in another corner of the room. Christopher could see nothing of them except the flash of an arm, the turn of a jaw.

George Bruton observed Christopher coming in his direction. Before the playwright could reach him he pinged his fingers against the side of his pot, and Dole took the hint to order two more pints from the passing drawer. Then he sat down next to Bruton. He waited until the drinks arrived and his companion had taken several gulps, almost draining the pot. Bruton was a large man who occupied more than his share of the bench. Dole remembered the days when he'd been slender. Their association was through Christopher's brother, Alan, the bookseller and publisher. George Bruton was a printer who sometimes worked for Alan.

'A damp evening, George,' said Christopher.

George humphed. He was not a great one for talk. Neither was Christopher Dole, for all that his business was to do with words. So Dole decided to get straight to the point.

'You recall that commission, a private one, that I mentioned to you a few days ago?'

'My memory is not so good these days,' said the printer. 'It will take another one of these to stir it into life.'

Christopher had hardly drunk anything from his own pint but he snapped his fingers for the drawer, a pimply lad, and placed a fresh order. There was a bark of laughter from the shadowed group in the opposite corner. The very sound of the laughter, and a disjointed sentence or two, was enough to tell Christopher that these were gentlemen. The Ram was rather a down-at-heel place but perhaps the group liked it for that reason. He turned his attention back to George Bruton.

'I require something to be printed – printed privately.'

For the first time George swivelled his block-like head to stare at Christopher.

'Printed in small quantities – and then distributed discreetly.'

'Some filth, is it?'

'Not filth, not exactly.'

'A pity.'

'It is a play.'

'One of your plays, Christopher?'

The boy returned with Bruton's fresh pint. Christopher took advantage to delay replying to Bruton's question. Then he said: 'No, not mine. I am merely an intermediary, acting for someone who wishes to see it published.'

'That's strange,' said Bruton, 'because from your silence I'd been assuming it was one of your things. Like your tragedy about the Emperor Nero? What was that called? *The Mother Killer? The Matricide?* It was put on by Lord Faulkes's company for a single performance, wasn't it?'

Christopher Dole might have replied that plenty of plays were only put on for a single performance but he said nothing. There was another bark of laughter from the shadowy group of gents in the other corner and, if Dole had not been so fixed on what he was saying to Bruton, his sensitive spirit might have interpreted the sound as a judgement on that disastrous play about Nero and his mother.

George Bruton took another great swig from his pint before saying, 'But then I am forgetting that *The Matricide* is something you'd rather not talk about, my friend. I told you my memory is not so good.'

'Then let us agree not to speak another word of that play, Mr Bruton. I have in my possession the foul version of a drama entitled *The English Brothers.* Who the author is doesn't matter. It has not been performed. In fact, I do not think it will ever be staged anywhere. But I want it printed . . . no, *he,* the author, wants it printed on the quiet.'

'Without a licence?'

'Yes, without a licence,' said Christopher. 'Come on, George, don't act surprised. We both know that books are issued from time to time that are not licensed or registered with the Stationers' Company, whether by oversight or intention.'

'Are you well, Christopher?'

'Yes,' said Dole, wondering whether Bruton meant well in his head or his body. 'Why, don't I look well?'

'As a matter of fact, you do not. Even in this light, you appear white and thin, and there are bags under your eyes like sacks of coal.'

'I've been too busy to sleep.'

'Ah, yes. You say you've got the play with you. Let's see it.'

Christopher Dole dug inside his doublet, retrieved the script that he had so recently finished in his little room, and gave it to George Bruton. For all that the light was poor in The Ram tavern, Bruton riffled through the pages, stopping every now and then as if he was actually able to read the thing. Perhaps he could. Christopher knew from his dealings with printers and publishers that they had an instinctive feel for a handwritten script. It was almost as if they were capable of reading with their fingertips.

'It's messy,' said George.

'It must have been composed at speed.'

'Your author friend was obviously inspired. Even so, it would be easier to work from a fair copy.'

'He doesn't want it to be seen by more eyes than necessary. I can be on hand in your printing-house to help ... interpret it.'

'Your friend is prepared to pay well for this to be printed, Christopher Dole? Even to pay over the odds, seeing it has to be done *on the quiet*.'

'Yes.'

'Quarto size?'

'Quarto size, and not bound in vellum either, but merely sewn together.'

'We call it "stabbed" in the trade. But I gather your friend wants to keep the cost down.'

'He is not concerned with appearances.'

'I was concerned with appearances, once,' said Bruton, handing back the sheaf of papers containing *The English Brothers* and staring mournfully into his newly empty pot. 'Once I had ambitions to follow in the steps of John Day ... of Christopher Barker ...'

These were the names of well-known printers, distinguished and successful ones. Christopher Dole cut across what threatened to turn into a bout of self-pity from Bruton. He said, 'You'll do it then, you'll print the play?'

Bruton paused. There was a further outbreak of laughter from the men in the opposite corner. The printer said, 'On one condition. Tell me now the author of *The English Brothers*. If you do not, I shall be forced to the conclusion that it must be you after all.'

William Shakespeare was the supposed author, of course, but Christopher did not name him. Even George Bruton, however negligent, would never have accepted that this bundle of untidy, blotched papers was by the man from Stratford. So he invented an imaginary author.

'It is by a gentleman called Henry Ashe. He is a friend of mine. He has asked me to be his agent in this matter.'

Christopher Dole spoke so promptly and confidently that he almost believed himself. Henry Ashe? Where had that name come from? It seemed to have dropped out of the dark, smoky air of the tavern. Yet Bruton must have been convinced for he nodded and went on: 'This play by Henry Ashe, which you say is not for performance, contains nothing seditious or blasphemous?'

'I guarantee it,' said the playwright. 'One more thing. I don't want my brother, Alan, knowing anything about this.'

'As it happens,' said Bruton, 'I saw your brother the other day. Or rather he saw me. Demanded to know if I knew the whereabouts of a scroll called the Oseney text. Apparently it's disappeared from his shop.'

'I've no idea what he was on about,' said Christopher Dole, but guessing that this might be a reference to the manuscript he'd uncovered at Alan's place. Quickly, he changed the subject.

'Time for another?'

'Always time for another, in my opinion,' said Bruton, clinking his plump fingers against the pot.

So Christopher Dole summoned the drawer again and bought George Bruton yet another drink. His own was scarcely touched. They shook hands on the arrangement. *The English Brothers* would be printed and published.

George Bruton's printing establishment was in Bride Lane on the city side of the Fleet Bridge. Downstairs was where the work was carried on. Upstairs was where the family – Martha Bruton and her many children – lived. Bruton employed two men. One was Hans de Worde, a long-time apprentice and then assistant to Bruton. Hans was second-generation Dutch, one of two brothers, and the respectable one. The other brother, Antony, had somehow shouldered his way into the rough but closed world of the ferrymen and he transported passengers across the Thames for a living. As for Hans de Worde, the joke was that George Bruton had taken him on originally because of his surname. Hans wore spectacles and had a nose on whose very tip was a large black mole as though he had dipped it in a pot of ink.

George Bruton's apprentice was called John. He was a wiry figure, and adaptable, which was just as well since he slept in a space hardly bigger than a cupboard in the press room. Hans de Worde, as befitted his higher standing in the household, occupied a little room at the top of the house.

These young men had not met Christopher Dole before but the playwright became a familiar figure at Bride Lane when he called in from time to time to check on the progress of *The English Brothers* and to help clarify the blotches and crossings-out in the foul papers. If it occurred to Hans or John that it was odd to be printing a play that had never been performed, they did not mention it. Probably they were not even aware of the fact. Hans was a serious individual and a devout attender at Austinfriars, the Dutch church in the city. His spare time was spent poring over religious pamphlets and tracts in his top-floor eyrie, undisturbed by the racket of the family coming up from the floor below. John was supposed to be bound by the terms of his apprenticeship and to avoid taverns, play-houses, brothels and the like, but George Bruton tended to turn a blind eye so it's likely that he went to at least one or two of those places.

During one of the playwright's visits, George Bruton had a question for Christopher Dole. Using the same gesture as when he signalled for another pint pot in The Ram, the printer tapped with his fingernails at a bit of verse on the page in front of him. They were standing to one side of the press room. From overhead came the thump of children running around. Christopher wasn't sure how many there were up there. Perhaps Bruton himself did not know.

'Where did this come from?' said Bruton. 'This Cain and Abel stuff. "Oh, go and kiss the Devil's arse! It is your fault it burns the worse." Or "With this jawbone, as I thrive, I'll let you no more stay alive!"'

'I believe that Henry Ashe copied it from an old manu-script that he found . . . somewhere,' said Christopher, suddenly remembering that Bruton had heard of the Oseney text from his brother.

'It is cleverly worked in,' said Bruton. 'There is a troupe of mummers performing a fragment of an old play that reflects the action of the main piece. Ingenious.'

'I'll tell Mr Ashe,' said Dole.

'You haven't said yet what you want on the title page. No author's name, I assume?'

'No, no. Not even initials.'

Bruton did not look surprised. It was usual for plays to be printed anonymously.

'But I am asking you to include this device,' said Dole, taking a scrap of paper from his pocket. On it was a simple drawing of a shield with a bird perched on the top. It appeared to be a coat of arms but when one looked closely it was more of a mockery than anything else since the bird was a ragged black thing and clutching a drooping lance in one of its claws.

'I'm not so sure about this,' said George Bruton. 'It is a serious matter, the right to bear arms. I don't want to find myself in trouble with the law. Your own name may not be appearing on the title page, Mr Dole, but mine will be as printer.'

'It is not anybody's coat of arms, I promise you. I'll pay you extra for this. Mr Ashe is very insistent on it.'

'Very well.'

George Bruton agreed because he did not have much pride remaining in what his workshop produced and because he needed the money. There were dozens of printers in London – more than the city required – and he knew now that he would never achieve the reputation of a Day or a Barker, those names he'd mentioned to Christopher. Besides, there was always the insistent beat of little feet overhead, reminding him of the many mouths gaping to be fed. Although Bruton preserved what money he could to spend on himself in The Ram, sitting snug and alone in his corner-place, he was still a responsible family man. As regularly as the turning of the seasons, Martha produced another little mouth to add to those responsibilities. So when someone like Dole was willing to pay more than the going rate for printing an odd piece of work, Bruton wasn't going to protest or look too closely at it.

As for Christopher Dole, he wasn't concerned about the money which he was paying out. It amounted to everything he had, but since he did not think he was much longer for this world, he reasoned he would not have any further need of money. He had no wife to think of, nor any children. Death was on its way. He'd dreamed recently of a figure lying flat out on a bed, with a couple of others standing round in attitudes of mourning. Squeezing past them to see who was lying there, he'd been astounded to see that it was himself. When he'd turned round to identify the onlookers, they had disappeared. He had woken chilled and sweaty at the same time.

It was more than a matter of simple dreams and premonitions. The thinness and pallor that George Bruton had commented on during their meeting in the tavern were not only the result of a sleepless night or two. For several months Christopher had observed himself growing more scrawny. His appetite was diminished. He was subject to inexplicable pains everywhere, and bouts of nausea and dizziness.

His last resources would be spent on seeing *The English Brothers* into the world. He would not be like Master Shakespeare, buying properties in Stratford and playing the part of a gentleman, and dying when his time came, in a four-poster bed with priests and lawyers at his beck and call.

216

No, Christopher Dole would make his exit like those true men of theatre, Robert Greene or Will Kemp. He might be neglected and poor but he still had integrity.

II

William Shakespeare and Nicholas Revill were talking in a little room behind the stage of the Globe playhouse in Southwark. It was the end of a December afternoon. The play for the day was finished and everyone – players and the paying public – was glad to get back indoors because of the cold. Snow was falling, not steadily but in occasional flurries.

WS and Nick were sitting on stools on either side of a small table whose surface was occupied with neat stacks of documents. This room was set aside for the business of the partners who owned the Globe, of whom Shakespeare was one. The principal shareholders were the Burbage brothers. Cuthbert Burbage attended to the account books and other business matters while Richard Burbage was their chief actor, known for his skill in playing tragedy parts. Nick Revill had been with the King's Men for a good few years now. Although not a senior in the company, nor one of those whose name alone was sufficient to draw in the public, he had built up a reputation as an adept and reliable player, with a particular skill in the darker parts (lust-maddened dukes, vengeful brothers).

At that moment Nick was about to look at a book that WS passed across to him. It was already dark outside and Nick drew closer one of the pair of candlesticks on the table. He cast his eyes across the pages, crudely sewn together. He read a few fragments and would have read more had he not been interrupted.

'What do you make of it?' said WS. He sounded impatient, unusually for him. 'Start at the beginning.'

'It is a play entitled *The English Brothers*. No author is given, of course, but it is printed by George Bruton—'

'Of Bride Lane near Fleet Bridge.'

'Yes,' said Nick. 'And there's also a little heraldic image here of a bird on top of a shield.'

'And the contents?'

'It's about some knights, isn't it, and there seems to be a rivalry between them?'

'The knights are brothers,' said Shakespeare, ticking off the points on his fingers. 'They should be fighting together under the king against the hordes from Norway and Denmark. Instead they fall in love at the same instant with the same woman, after glimpsing her in a garden. Then the two of them fall out – quarrelling over who saw her first and so on – and the jest is that she isn't even aware of their existence.'

'Sounds like a good subject,' said Nick.

'It is a good subject,' said Shakespeare. 'Not new, of course. The best subjects never are. The knightly brothers are caught fighting each other by the English king, they're banished, they go wandering off, they come back together in time to vanquish the horde of Norsemen, they are reconciled, one dies in battle, the other gets the woman.'

'I might pay to see that.'

'So might I,' said WS, 'but this piece is put together in a very slapdash style. At one point there is a portion of an old play about Cain and Abel, supposedly seen by one of the knights on his travels. The other knight finds himself in Scotland for some reason. It is absurd enough. And there are opportunities that have been missed in telling the story, obvious opportunities.'

Nick wondered why Shakespeare was bothering to ask for

his views since he'd obviously examined the drama for himself and come to his own conclusions. He also wondered
whether Shakespeare was irritated because he hadn't come
up with the idea for the play himself. But it turned out that
WS was concerned because it might be believed that he was
the author of *The English Brothers.*

'The image at the front is a crude version of my own
family's coat of arms,' he said. He spoke in a matter-of-fact
way but Nick sensed a touch of pride as the playwright continued: 'Our coat of arms depicts a falcon, his wings
displayed argent, supporting a spear of gold . . . I don't suppose you want to hear these heraldic details, do you?'

Nick was aware of Shakespeare's gentlemanly standing.
By the candlelight, he took a closer look at the shield on
the title page of *The English Brothers.* He noticed the bird
was holding a lance or spear with a drooping tip. Not
exactly an image of potent authority. And the bird appeared
to be a crow whose tail feathers had been savaged by a cat.
He recalled the story that Shakespeare had been described
as an 'upstart crow' when he began making a name for himself in London. He looked at the balding man on the other
side of the table. The angle of the light turned
Shakespeare's eyes into sockets. Their usual benign brown
gaze was obscured.

'Can't you laugh it off?' he said.

'Yes, probably. Even if the word is spreading around town
that I wrote this thing, and people are repeating it out of
ignorance or malice, I could laugh it off.'

'Anybody who truly knows you, Will, must know that you
would not pen something like this. And this shield on the
title page is a plain mockery.'

'There is more and there is worse,' said WS, taking back
the book and flicking through the pages. He found the

passage he wanted and showed it to Nick, who read a couple of the lines aloud.

'"The Pictish king who rides his car to glories, Will be the theme for many future stories . . ." And there is more in similar style. I agree it's poor stuff but—'

'It's poor stuff, all right, only good to light a fire. But the Pictish king isn't some Scottish monarch from olden times. He could easily be construed as our own King James—'

Light was dawning for Nick and he interrupted, 'While "car" might be a chariot, but could also be a reference to Robert Carr, James's favourite.'

'His favourite companion, his pet courtier, yes. "The Pictish king who rides his car to glories . . ." We can imagine what kind of "riding" is intended here. These lines have been deliberately composed to cause trouble. I hear that the Privy Council is paying attention.'

Nick Revill suddenly felt chill, even though it was stuffy in the little back room of the playhouse. No one wanted to catch the attention of the Council. Nick might have said that William Shakespeare was protected. After all, he was one of the shareholders of the *King's* Men, enjoying the patronage of the monarch. Yet Nick was aware, as WS must be, of the various playwrights who'd been hauled before the Council after something unwise had been detected in their writings. The risks were severe. The offender might receive a whipping. He might lose his ears, or worse . . . It didn't matter that you had a patron or that you might have been a favourite.

'You don't know who wrote this?' said Nick.

'I have a notion.'

'Someone with a grudge against you?'

'If it's the person I'm thinking of, yes, he has a grudge against me.'

Nick was surprised. Considering that William Shakespeare was a successful author and – by players' standards – a prosperous individual, he seemed to be liked as well as admired by almost everyone.

'This is why I want to speak with you, Nick. In the years since you've been with our company I've come to trust your good sense and your ... enterprise. Your friendship.'

Nick knew WS was referring to the occasional errand or 'mission' with which he'd been entrusted. He should have learned caution by now but somehow the gratitude of the man sitting across the table always won him round. As it did now. The mention of friendship gave him a glow.

WS must have sensed Revill's willingness for he said: 'I know the printer of this piece, not well but slightly. George Bruton of Bride Lane. A man with a large family and an appetite for drink. I can only imagine that he was unaware of what was coming out of his press. Or perhaps he doesn't care.'

'But he will know who the author is?'

'He must do. Unless the real author used a go-between. At any rate, Bruton will have information.'

'The Privy Council may be looking at him as well.'

'In which case he will certainly disclose the author, probably under duress. I would rather go about it in a more roundabout way. And I do not wish to visit Bruton myself. He knows me. But not you, Nick. You may ask some questions. I have a further request. Do not say that you are from the King's Men but another company. Which company would you choose if you were not with us?'

Nick thought for a moment. 'The Admiral's.'

The Admiral's Men had recently acquired a new patron and become Prince Henry's Men but almost everyone continued to refer to them under their old name.

'And, as well as saying you are with the Admiral's, why not take an assumed name for yourself?'

'An assumed name?'

'To cover your tracks. It's an idea that should appeal to you as a player. It's what I would do in your place.'

There was a glint in WS's eye now. Nick thought again. Taking a different name was an appealing idea, for some reason. Why not do it?

'Then I shall reverse my initials and become Rick Newman – better still, Dick Newman.'

All WS's characteristic good humour was restored. 'Very good, now you are a new man,' he said. Nick smiled as though he had intended the pun (though in fact Newman was his mother's family name). Shakespeare continued: 'When our Richard Burbage wants to be taken seriously he remains a Richard, but when he requires a bit of swagger he turns into a Dick. So go to see Bruton as Dick Newman. Don't threaten him or hint at trouble from the Council. You might go so far as to say that the Admiral's are thinking of putting on this play, *The English Brothers*. Between ourselves, we might even stage it here at the Globe.'

'Surely not?'

'It has possibilities,' said WS. 'Besides, if this play is by the individual who I think wrote it, then I owe him amends.'

'Why?'

'I made some remark to do with another play of his, and the remark got about, as I perhaps intended it to.'

Shakespeare paused as if reluctant to say more. Nick kept silent.

'I described the experience of sitting through that play as "the happiest, most comical two hours I have spent in the playhouse".'

'What's wrong with that?'
'The piece was a tragedy.'

III

It was early in December and Christopher Dole was at the beginning of his last day on earth. By chance, it was the same day on which Shakespeare requested Nicholas Revill to look into the authorship of the play, now out in the world under the title of *The English Brothers*. As far as Dole was concerned, the piece was meant to draw down mischief on Shakespeare but it seemed to be causing more trouble for himself than anyone else. Under his direction, George Bruton printed about a hundred copies and Christopher caused them to be distributed round various shops and stalls, as well as simply dropping them in locations like the Inns of Court where they might be picked up by the curious or discerning reader. He spread the word among casual acquaintances that WS had penned a new piece.

It reached his ears that the word had not only been heard by WS but had come to the attention of the Privy Council. The Council was interested on account of some scurrilous remarks concerning King James. This was just as Christopher planned. But he had not planned carefully enough. Any investigation from the Council should initially be directed at WS but was then likely to turn towards the printer. Under pressure, George Bruton would name Christopher as the individual who'd brought him the play in the first place. It might not even be necessary to apply pressure. So Christopher needed to go back to the printing-house in Bride Lane and remind Bruton that, if questioned, he should refer to Christopher Dole only as an intermediary.

The real author was Henry Ashe. That might waste a bit of time, with the Council looking for the mythical Mr Ashe.

The truth was that Christopher Dole had not really expected to be alive at this moment, approaching Christmas. Convinced of his imminent demise, he gave little thought to the penalties the Privy Council might inflict on him. What could the Council do if he was in his grave? Nothing. Now the question was, what would they do if he was out of it? An ingenious revenge plot was threatening to turn on its creator.

Dole still owed money to George Bruton, and he decided to return to Bride Lane with a promise of the final payment. He'd also take the opportunity to remind George that it was not he, Christopher, who was the creator of *The English Brothers*. Definitely not.

As soon as Dole entered the ground-floor press in Bride Lane, he was attacked by Bruton. Attacked with words rather than blows, but the corpulent printer looked as though he might be ready to resort to those too. Perhaps it was only the presence of Hans de Worde and John the apprentice that restrained him. The two were on the far side of the room, getting on with their work, but they kept casting covert glances towards their master.

'You assured me there was nothing dangerous in this,' said Bruton, holding up a copy of the ill-fated drama. 'Nothing seditious, you said. But there are lines that are easily construed as mockery of the King.'

'Not so easily construed, George. You did not spot them when the play was being set up in type.'

'So you admit it?'

'Sedition is in the eye of the beholder.'

'*That* is a very foolish answer pretending to be a clever one, Christopher Dole. You had better tell that friend of yours, Henry Ashe, to watch out. He will have some questions to answer himself.'

Christopher was surprised, even amazed, to hear that Bruton still believed in the existence of Mr Ashe. He played along.

'Yes, yes. If the authorities want to know anything, you should direct them to Henry Ashe.'

'Where does he live?'

Christopher thought fast, though not so fast as when he had plucked Ashe's name out the air. He named a street at a little distance from his own. This seemed to satisfy the printer, for Bruton then moved on to the more pressing matter of money. Dole promised to pay him the final instalment.

'And how will you do that?' said Bruton, scornfully.

'I'll call on my brother,' said Dole.

'Much good that'll do you. I saw Alan very recently. He did not have a good word for you. He was still asking me about that Oseney text. Are you sure you don't have it?'

There was a crash from the other side of the press room. It was Hans de Worde. He had dropped a container full of type. Looking apologetic, he scrabbled around on hands and knees to pick it up.

Leaving Bride Lane, Christopher Dole had a thought. He had not seen his brother for some time, despite surreptitiously depositing a couple of copies of *The English Brothers* in Alan's shop. He'd mentioned his brother to Bruton as a way of warding off the printer's questions. Despite previous refusals, his prosperous sibling might advance him the money, enough to carry him over the next few weeks as well as to pay off his debts. If he should live so long.

He entered Alan's shop, grateful to get out of the cold. It was situated in Paul's Yard, where many bookshops and stalls clung to the skirts of the great church. There was no one inside, apart from Alan, who was sitting at a desk near the back of his store and making entries in a ledger. Christopher was glad to find his brother by himself. They were never friends but they had never descended to Cain-and-Abel-like levels of enmity either. Yet Alan greeted him with the same hostility as had George Bruton. Seeing his brother, he grabbed at a book and leaped up. Now he too began waving a copy of *The English Brothers*, presumably one of the two that Christopher had abandoned there so recently.

Alan Dole was, like his brother, a spare individual. But where Christopher's thinness seemed to be the result of some undisclosed sickness, Alan's lank frame was a reflection of his vigour. He was rarely still. He constantly looked for ways to expand his business. He possessed an intense stare. At the moment he was fastening that stare on Christopher. They were standing face to face. Alan Dole started speaking without any welcome or preamble.

'The word about town is that this was written by Shakespeare.'

'What is it, Alan?'

'Don't pretend you don't know, Christopher. It is a play. It is called *The English Brothers*. It appeared among my stock and I have no idea how it got here.'

'You have many books in your shop.'

'And I know the provenance and price of each of them,' said Alan. 'I know all their shapes and smells – except this one ... which smells fishy.'

'Written by Shakespeare?' said his brother.

'That's the rumour. But we are all aware of the hostility you feel towards Shakespeare.'

'I wouldn't know anything about this play.'

'That is most surprising of all,' said Alan, 'because when

I look through it, I find your handprint. I mean, the style of Christopher Dole, his tricks and turns of phrase.'

'Perhaps I have imitators.'

'Don't flatter yourself. More conclusive is that within these pages are fragments of an older play, to do with Cain and Abel.'

Christopher grew uneasy. Instinctively, his eyes flicked to the chest, barricaded behind piles of books, from which he had filched the manuscript of *The Play of Adam.* Alan noticed.

'Ah-ha. I thought so. Where is the manuscript now?'

Never much good at standing up to his more forceful sibling, Christopher gave a partial version of the truth.

'I might have borrowed it to have a look at it, just to see how they did things in the old days. Perhaps William Shakespeare also obtained a copy and included portions in that play you're clutching.'

'There is only one manuscript,' said Alan. 'And I have it. Or rather, I *had* it. It disappeared some time ago but I never suspected you, Christopher. You bloody fool.'

This seemed an excessive response and the playwright, realising that argument was futile, made to go. Outside flakes of snow were starting to dribble from a low-hanging sky. He wouldn't get any money from Alan now. He'd be more likely to obtain cash from the falling snow.

'Just a minute, brother. You do not realise the ill reputation of that old play.'

'No doubt you're about to tell me.'

'There was a seal on it, wasn't there? An unbroken seal?'

'Possibly,' said Christopher.

'It should not have been broken.'

Christopher was struck by Alan's tone. In it there was not just anger or indignation but something that sounded close to fear. Alan continued: 'If you'd examined the *outside* of the scroll before breaking the seal, you'd have seen a warning.'

'A warning?'

'Yes, you parrot, a warning. Written by a prior. If memory serves, it went like this: "In that this scroll contains Holy Writ, you shall not suffer it to be destroyed. Yet neither shall you break the seal upon it, lest fools and knaves make of it swords to slay the innocent and infect man's reason with the worm of madness."'

As he was reciting, Alan closed his eyes. Christopher was impressed that his brother recalled the words so exactly. Moreover, he began to feel the first tremors of alarm.

'The story goes that it was composed for a priory in Oseney near Oxford and that a murder took place before it could ever be performed. There are other tales of murder – in Wales, in Ely – all linked to presentations of "The Story of Cain and Abel", which you have been so foolish as to include in this – what's it called? – *The English Brothers*.'

'I never thought you were superstitious, Alan.'

Christopher Dole tried to keep his voice calm and even amused, but the fact was that, like most people who make their living in the theatre, he was the superstitious one. If he'd known of this warning beforehand, he'd never have picked up the manuscript, let alone copied out parts of it. But he'd been too eager to break the seal, to unroll the manuscript and then snatch gobbets of it for his own use. Eager to fill up the pages of his own play as fast as possible, with most of his attention being on those satirical jabs directed at King James and his favourites, and intended to bring down trouble on the bald pate of the man from Stratford.

'I am not one for old wives' tales,' said his bookseller brother, 'but these bad-luck stories don't spring from nowhere. I tell you, this old piece can bring misfortune or worse. You were foolish enough to write a play in the hope of somehow damaging Shakespeare, but you were downright foolhardy to include a cursed text in it.'

'Well, *The English Brothers* will never be performed on stage,' said Christopher. By now, he'd given up any pretence that the play was not by him.

'Performance on a stage does not matter. Printing and publishing is a kind of performance, isn't it? A sort of utterance. You still have the manuscript?'

Christopher nodded. He wondered whether he should destroy it, since the thing apparently brought such dangers with it. But it seemed that Alan was able to read his thoughts for he said: 'If you have the manuscript in that little upper room of yours, then go now and return here with it. Don't attempt to get rid of it. Worse luck will follow if you do. You know how the thought of destroying a book is abhorrent to me.'

More likely, thought Christopher, his brother was calculating what he might get for the original manuscript of *The Play of Adam*. He said nothing further. He nodded, turned on his heel and quit the shop. Although still early in the afternoon, dusk seemed already to be drawing in. The snow was falling sporadically. The upper reaches of St Paul's were hidden in the murk.

The chill struck Christopher to the bone. He pulled his thin coat tighter about him and trudged his way through the city and back to his lodgings. There was nowhere else to go. Head down, approaching the front door, he was stopped by a hand on his shoulder. He looked up. It was Stephen, the disagreeable son of his landlady.

'Why, Christopher, this is well met. I am on my way out.'

Not for the first time, Dole noticed how close-set were the young man's eyes. Even in the gloom they had a bird's glitter to them, a kind of malice. He shrugged Stephen's hand from his shoulder and did not reply.

'You have a visitor.'

'Who?'

'How should I know? I do not pry into other people's business.'

Christopher made to move past the insolent, lying youngster and get into his lodgings. Stephen said: 'I invited him in, seeing as the day is turning nasty. I directed him to your room and told him to make himself at ease up there. He has the appearance of a proper gentleman.'

Christopher hadn't imagined he could be any colder than he was but a fresh chill broke out along his body. He paid no attention to Stephen's parting words – 'Aren't you going to thank me for being nice to your visitor?' – and entered the lobby. He paused for a moment at the bottom of the stairs before starting up them. He felt dizzy and nauseous. Laboriously, he climbed to the top floor. There he hesitated again. A glimmer of light was showing under the lintel of his door. All at once, Christopher's apprehensions fell away to be replaced by anger. The unknown stranger must have lit a candle, one of his meagre supply.

The playwright did not have the advantage of surprise since the stranger would have heard his steps, but he turned the handle of his own door and pushed it open with as much force as he could muster. The first thing he saw was that the occupant had lit not one but two candles. The second was that his visitor was indeed a proper gentleman, or at least a prosperous one. He was sitting on Christopher's stool, which he had positioned against the wall so that he might rest his back against it. His arms were folded and his legs were fully extended and crossed at the ankles.

Christopher Dole saw the stranger's cloak, with its points,

or lace, gleaming a dull gold, and he saw the rich red lining where an edge of the cloak was casually folded back. He observed the gentleman's leather boots reaching almost to the knee, and it flashed through his mind that such well-made footwear must provide a good defence against the filth and cold of the streets.

What he could not see was his visitor's face, for the intruder was wearing a wide-brimmed hat that cast a shadow over the upper part of his body. He kept his head down, resting his chin on his chest. For an instant Christopher wondered whether he was asleep and, absurdly, felt guilty for having disturbed him. Next, he felt almost ashamed of the little space where he lived, with its simple bed, its desk, chest and stool. Then his eyes flickered back to the two – two! – candles burning on the desk and he moved a couple of paces further into the room.

So small was his chamber that this brought him almost to the outstretched feet of the stranger. If the gentleman had been asleep he was not asleep now, for the fingers of his gloved right hand, half concealed by the cloak, flexed and stretched. He looked up. Yet all Christopher could see under the shadow of his hat was a square, clean-shaven chin. Nevertheless Christopher had the feeling that he'd seen this individual before.

'Mr Dole?' This hardly amounted to a question for the stranger went on without a pause: 'Forgive me, but as it was growing dark I took the liberty of lighting your candles while awaiting your return.'

'Who are you?'

'Don't you recognise me, Christopher? You should recognise me. I am Henry Ashe.'

IV

Nicholas Revill made tortuous progress in his search for the author of *The English Brothers*. Carrying Shakespeare's copy of the play with him, he began the quest at the printer's in Bride Lane, saying he was Dick Newman, and that he came from the Admiral's Men. George Bruton was absent but his journeyman, an individual who introduced himself as Hans, reluctantly answered questions. He spoke with such precision that Nick would have known him for a foreigner even without being given his name. Dutch or German, he assumed.

Yes, it was in this workshop that they printed the play that was in the visitor's hand. The author? Hans fiddled with his spectacles and peered at the title page, which Nick held open for his benefit, even though the printer must have been aware already it didn't contain the information. Eventually he said, 'I am not sure but I believe that the author is an individual called Henry Ashe.'

Nick thought he knew the names of all, or almost all, the playwrights in London but he'd never come across anyone called Henry Ashe. Of course, Ashe might be a newcomer or a false name, rather like Dick Newman.

Hans did not seem to have any more information, and Nick asked whether he might talk to George Bruton if he was in the house. He cast his eyes up at the ceiling – there was the thumping of feet overhead – but Hans shook his head. No, Bruton was not available. Do you know where your master is then? The journeyman looked uncomfortable.

At that point the apprentice, who was hanging back in a corner of the room but attending to every word that passed between Nick and Hans, piped up: 'Are you really a player?'

'Yes,' said Nick.

'You'll find Master Bruton in The Ram, sir. That's where he is when he isn't here.'

Hans spun round so fast his glasses almost fell off his nose. He looked annoyed as though some family secret had been revealed. In this way Nick knew the information was reliable. He thanked the apprentice and left.

Nick was acquainted with The Ram although he had not stepped across its threshold for several years. He wondered why George Bruton habitually drank in a tavern that was quite a way from his work and his home, before it occurred to him that the distance was probably the reason.

He trudged through the slushy streets. The snow that had fallen the previous evening was lying in dirty, half-frozen pools in the road, and the white rooftops were now smudged all over with soot. Pulling his cloak about him and avoiding the other passers-by as they negotiated slippery corners, Nick thought about his 'mission'. He wasn't sure whether William Shakespeare was more worried because of the potentially treasonable lines in the play called *The English Brothers* or more outraged because someone – Henry Ashe? – was attempting to pass the piece off as his (WS's) work. Nick decided it was outrage rather than worry.

By now he had reached The Ram. The place showed no improvement in the years since his last visit. Still very dingy and disreputable. Despite the dim light, he observed a man sitting by himself in the corner. He recognised Bruton from Shakespeare's description: a man with a large belly pressed against the table before him and with the reddened nose of a drinker. Bruton looked up. When he saw that Nick was heading directly for him, he tapped with his fingers against his tankard. The gesture was clear. Since Nick needed him

to co-operate he ordered two pints before sitting down opposite the printer.

And he waited until the drinks arrived before announcing
that he'd come from the Admiral's Men.

'Oh, yes?' said Bruton, taking a big swig from his mug.

'We are interested in staging a play that you have recently
published.'

'Are you?'

'It is called *The English Brothers*.'

Nick was gratified to see a change come over Bruton's
hitherto impassive face. Not a positive change, since he now
looked both wary and irritated.

'You are sure you are from the Admiral's Men? You're
not from ... the Council.' Bruton lowered his voice as he
said the last two words, and in such an artificial way that it
would scarcely have been believed on stage. There was
nobody nearby, although a knot of men was sitting and
drinking in another corner. Bruton's manner told Nick that
WS's fears about the Privy Council were justified. He assured
Bruton that he really was a player and not a government
agent.

'What's your name?'

'Richard Newman,' said Nick promptly. He was pleased
not to have been caught out by the abrupt question. 'You
may call me Dick, if you prefer.'

'I have no preference over what to call you. I've never even
heard of you. You are sure the Admiral's want the play?'

'Absolutely sure,' said Nick, then went on quickly before he
could be asked any more questions. 'But there is no author
to go to, no one named on the title page.'

'The author is Henry Ashe.'

'I've never heard of him,' said Nick. 'Did he deliver the
play to you himself?'

Bruton paused before replying. 'No. Mr Ashe gave it to a friend – or an agent – I don't know which.'

It took another two drinks before Nick was able to prise the name of this supposed agent out of the printer. He was called Christopher Dole. This was a name that was familiar, or half familiar, to Revill. Wasn't Dole a bookseller?

'That's his brother, Alan,' said Bruton. 'Keeps a bookshop by St Paul's.'

Nick knew the bookshop. He tried again. Was Dole an actor? Or a playwright?

Yes, said George Bruton, he'd been both. Dole was an actor with Lord Faulkes's company for a time and he'd penned a few plays for them. Not very successfully. The last piece he wrote more or less finished him off. It was about the Roman emperor Nero and it was called *The Matricide*.

'A tragedy?' asked Nick.

'Meant to be,' said Bruton, 'but it was received as a comedy. Dole was humiliated. He blamed everyone but himself. Turned his back on the drama, which is why I was surprised when he presented me with this new piece, *The English Brothers*, even if it is by someone else.'

Nick thought that the play was probably by Christopher Dole, and not the elusive Henry Ashe. It was Dole he should be calling on. But if the printer knew where he lived, he was not going to reveal it. This might have been connected to the fact that Nick refused to buy him another drink. However, he did add, as Nick was leaving The Ram, 'And, if you catch up with him, tell that bastard – Christopher Dole, I mean – tell him that he owes me money.'

Nick thought that next he ought to visit Alan Dole. He would surely be familiar with his brother's whereabouts. Reflecting that he was having to go a long way round the town to carry out this task on behalf of Shakespeare, and warmed only a little by the thought of WS's friendship, Nick duly called at Dole's bookshop. At first the bookseller was reluctant to talk about his brother, but then he suddenly grew angry and made mention of Christopher's 'foolish crimes'. When Alan Dole calmed down, he was able to identify the street and house where Christopher lodged.

'The landlady is Mrs Atkins. Christopher occupies a meagre top-floor chamber and that is all he is entitled to,' said Alan. 'If you see him, ask him why he didn't return yesterday with the . . . the thing he promised to bring. He'll know what I'm talking about. And when he does return, I want a word with him, more than a word.'

So now, in the early afternoon and with the feel of snow in the air once again, Nick stood outside the house he'd been directed to. A young man opened the door to his knock. His close-set eyes scanned Nick without approval.

'I am looking for Christopher Dole, I believe he lodges here.'

'The world is beating a path to his door,' said the young man. 'You are the third visitor since this time yesterday.'

He stood aside to let the caller in, although in a grudging sort of way so that Nick had to squeeze past him. He pointed a finger upwards and said, 'Go as far as you can go.'

Nick groped his way up a dark staircase, which narrowed and grew more rickety as he reached the top of the house. Once there, he paused and listened. The house was silent and any street sounds were muffled by the snow outside. Suddenly Nick was reluctant to proceed with this. Yet he had his mission. He tapped on what, since it was the only door on this floor, must be the entrance to Dole's room.

No response. He rapped more loudly. Nothing. He reached out and twisted the handle, not expecting to get anywhere. But the room was not locked. His sense of unease grew stronger. Nick would have turned and gone back down the stairs but for the thought that he might find some evidence inside that Christopher Dole was the author of *The English Brothers*.

He pushed the door right open. It was a small room, even smaller than Revill's own lodgings. In the gloom he could make out the shape of a bed, a desk beneath the small window, a stool against the wall and a chest in the corner immediately to his left. Perhaps Nick looked at these things to avoid looking at what was in front of his nose.

Directly before him, so close that it was almost touching the door, was a body. Swaying very slightly in the draught from the open door, it hung from a belt or girdle looped round a beam in the low ceiling. The head was almost crammed up against the beam, and the feet pointed downwards so that they dangled a few inches above the floor. Not much of a distance perhaps, but even those few inches had been enough to ensure Christopher Dole choked to death.

It appeared the playwright had taken his own life. It looked like that. Yet he had not, Nick thought. He couldn't put his finger on the reason – he was too shaken, too confused at this moment – but Dole had not killed himself. This was a murder.

Nick took a couple of steps back from the body so that he was standing just outside the entrance to Dole's room. He twisted round as he heard footsteps rapidly mounting the stairs. His first thought was that it was the murderer returning to see that the business was complete, or to retrieve something he'd left behind, or to take care of an inconvenient witness . . .

Nick fumbled in his clothing. He sometimes carried a small dagger, even though it was against the law for a man of his rank to do so. Yet today he had nothing with him, no means apart from his hands of defending himself. He could have retreated into Dole's room, where the dead body, framed by the doorway, dangled from its makeshift noose. But he did not. Instead he shrank against the wall to one side of the tiny area between the top of the stairs and Dole's door. He readied himself to lash out with his arms and feet.

A shape, the head and shoulders only, emerged at the top of the stairs. It paused for an instant as though to take in the scene before it. Nick couldn't see who it was but he could hear breathing. Then the man made a kind of leap up the last couple of steps and whirled about as he reached the top. He was carrying something, a stick most likely. He struck out with it and, by chance, the blow caught Nick in the guts. He gasped in pain and doubled up on the floor.

He had no chance to defend himself properly. All he could do was to curl up and wrap his arms about his head for protection as the man rained down blows on him. From somewhere in the distance, among the blows and the attacker's grunts and his own involuntary cries, he heard a voice, a woman's voice. This seemed to go on for many minutes, although it was probably less than a single one. Then came the woman's voice, nearer at hand, saying: 'Stop, I tell you, stop!'

And, mercifully, the blows faltered and then ceased.

'There now, Mr Revill,' said the woman. 'That should ease your discomfort.'

Nick Revill winced as she applied the tincture to his face and bare arms and shoulders, which had borne the brunt of the blows. Nick was sitting, dressed only in his hose, on the bed in the woman's chamber. She was perched on a stool facing him, dabbing at the weals and bruises with a tincture which, she said, was a mixture of plantain and arnica. Sara

Atkins was the landlady of the house where Christopher Dole had lived and died. She was the mother of Stephen, the young man with the close-set eyes. In the aftermath of the attack Nick had forgotten his false identity and announced that he was Nick Revill of the King's Men. Sara Atkins was contrite, not because he was a player with a famous company but because she was a good-hearted woman. And perhaps because she felt guilt over her son's behaviour.

For it was Stephen Atkins who had attacked Nick. His story was that, after directing Revill to Christopher Dole's room on the top floor, he suddenly grew anxious that the visitor might be some sort of thief or ne'er-do-well. Without consulting his mother, and arming himself with a stave, he ran up the stairs, pausing at the top when he glimpsed the suspended body of the playwright through the open door. He could not see much more, since the only illumination came through the little window in Dole's room. Stephen's instinctive reaction was that the recent arrival at the house must have done this thing. At least that's what he claimed. To protect himself he went on the attack, winding Nick with a lucky stroke and then continuing to rain down blows on the player until Mrs Atkins appeared and commanded him to stop. This was the explanation he gave to his mother even as Nick was being helped to his feet.

Sara Atkins was more clear-headed than her son. She asked Nick for his name. She asked what he was doing in her house. ('Visiting Christopher Dole. I'm a player as he is – as he was.') Then she turned to her son and questioned how long had elapsed between the visitor's arrival and Stephen's rush up the stairs. When she heard that it was no more than a couple of minutes, she said that there would hardly have been time for their visitor – 'What is your name again, sir? Ah yes, Nicholas Revill' – hardly time for him to have disposed of their unfortunate lodger. After making sure that Nick could stand unaided, she went towards the body, which was hanging in the deep gloom of the room and put out a gentle hand, almost stroking the dead man's face. Then she pointed out that her lodger had grown cold, and so must have been gone for some time.

'Poor Christopher. This is a dreadful thing,' said Mrs Atkins, shaking her head and closing the door of the little upper room. She was quite composed, considering what had happened. Nick was ushered by her into her chamber on the floor below.

Stephen didn't comment on the corpse or apologise for his actions but continued to look at Revill as though the player might still be a thief or even a murderer. Mrs Atkins told him to go and fetch the headborough to report Dole's death. The snow was falling again and it was almost completely dark outside.

'A dreadful thing,' the landlady repeated after she'd finished with her application of ointments. She was referring to Christopher Dole, not Nick's injuries. 'A terrible crime.'

'Why do you say crime, Mrs Atkins?' said Nick, carefully drawing on his shirt again.

'Self-slaughter is a crime,' said the landlady. 'A crime against God. What are you doing, Mr Revill? Stay here.'

Nick was pushing himself off the bed while Mrs Atkins attempted to keep him there with a hand on his shoulder. She was quite an attractive woman, small, with a firm jaw and wisps of black hair poking from under her cap. Attractive enough that Nick had been conscious of sitting facing her while dressed only in his hose. Attractive enough that he shrugged off his hurts in a manly way rather than making much of them.

'I must look at the body again.'

240

'Why?'

'You say that Mr Dole killed himself and I admit it looks like that, but I will show you that it cannot be.'

Nick picked up one of the candlesticks that stood by the entrance to the bedchamber and clambered up the stairs once more, Sara Atkins behind him. The blows that Stephen administered were beginning to smart. Nick felt angry with the landlady's son even if, on the face of things, his suspicions might have been partly justified. At the top, he again opened the door of Christopher's room. By the light of the candle, he had his first clear sight of the playwright's swollen face, his head canted to one side against the beam, his tongue protruding from his mouth as the home-made noose bit into his neck. It occurred to Nick that he had not seen Christopher Dole alive. Now he would never have the chance to ask him whether he really was the author of *The English Brothers*.

Aware of Mrs Atkins close behind him, he raised the candle and glanced rapidly about the room to see if he'd missed anything on his first look round. But every surface was bare, apart from the top of the desk where stood the stubs of two burned-out candles and a pile of half a dozen books. He took the top one. A scrap of paper tucked inside it fluttered to the floor. Nick bent and picked up the paper. There was a scrawled line of writing on it. He couldn't read the words in the poor light but they didn't appear to be in English. Hurriedly, he stuffed the paper inside his shirt.

Then he examined the book. It was a copy of *The English Brothers*, identical to the one Nick was carrying. Not proof exactly, but a sign that Dole was the author. Nick remembered that the dead man's brother, Alan, was expecting some item to be returned to him. What was it? It couldn't be the disputed play, since the bookseller already had a copy. He

241

opened the dead man's chest but there appeared to be nothing inside apart from a heap of undershirts. There was no sign of anything of value in the room.

'How long did he lodge with you?' asked Nick. The landlady was at his shoulder.

'He was with me several years. He was no trouble.'

'When did you last see him?'

'Yesterday. Or perhaps it was the day before. I cannot recall. He kept irregular hours and he kept to himself.'

'Did he have many visitors?'

'I do not believe so.'

'Your son said that I was the third person to call on him in the space of a day.'

'Did he?'

'Mr Dole did not kill himself, Mrs Atkins. Look. To raise himself even those few inches above the floor in order to put his head in the noose he would have to be standing on something.'

'Yes,' she said doubtfully.

'The only way he could have hanged himself was to stand on a piece of furniture and then kick it away as he hung from the ceiling, but he did not do that. See.'

Nick spoke urgently. Once again, he raised the candle and shifted it from side to side so that its beams filled every quarter of the tiny chamber. Mrs Atkins was an intelligent woman. Surely she could see the situation for herself. Each of the few items in the room was several feet away from the hanging man, and each was neatly placed against a wall. Even the stool, which would normally have been by the desk, was against the wall facing the door. There was no way in which the man on the rope, who would have been struggling involuntarily for his breath even if he had chosen to do away with himself, could have ensured that whatever he balanced on (stool, chest) was tidied away after use.

'Perhaps he stood on the bed and somehow swung himself across,' said Mrs Atkins, who was reluctant to give up the idea that her lodger was responsible for his own death.

Christopher Dole had slept on a simple truckle bed, the sort without posts or a canopy, but equipped with wheels so that it might be pushed into some corner for a servant's temporary use. It was a melancholy sight, a reminder of Dole's lowly position in the world. Yes, it was possible he might have somehow used the bed as a makeshift scaffold. But there were no marks or indentations on the threadbare blanket, which was stretched tight across the thin mattress. No one could have stood on it without leaving a trace of his feet, as Nick showed with another sweep of the candle-light.

There were only two possibilities.

Either Christopher Dole, using the chest or stool to position himself under the ceiling beam, had taken his own life and then someone had come in to put the furniture back afterwards . . .

. . . or he had been murdered.

Any further conversation with Sara Atkins was prevented by the return of her son in the company of the local head-borough or constable. Both men tramped up the stairs with flakes of snow melting on their hats and capes. The constable, whose name was Daggett, and Stephen came crowding into the top-floor room, which was not large enough to hold five (including the dead man). Daggett seemed not to be as slow-witted as many London constables, or at least the ones that Nick had previously encountered. He greeted Mrs Atkins by name. He didn't ask Nick who he was. Perhaps he assumed that the player was a lodger in the house. He gestured that the others should leave the room while he examined the body.

After a brief time, and tugging at an ear-lobe as if to signify thought, Daggett came out onto the equally crammed space at the top of the stairs.

'This is a clear case of self-slaughter,' he said, echoing Mrs Atkins' words.

Nick saw that the general opinion was against him. There was no point in airing his suspicions of murder. Now the constable observed the fresh bruises on his face. His gaze flickered between Nick and the body hanging in the room behind him.

'I fell in the snow,' said Nick. 'Fell flat on my face.'

Everyone appeared satisfied with this explanation. Leaving Stephen and Daggett to take down the body, Nick and Mrs Atkins returned downstairs, this time to a ground-floor parlour, where a fire was burning. The landlady seemed relieved, perhaps because the story of Dole's killing himself was becoming the accepted version – so much more convenient than a murder – or perhaps because Nick explained away the harms her son had caused him.

She gave Nick some aqua vitae, saying that her husband had always used it as a restorative. From the wistful way she said it, Nick guessed she must be a widow. She took a nip herself, and then another one. The fiery liquid warmed Nick and took away some of the hurt from his injuries. Mrs Atkins talked about Christopher Dole, for whom she seemed to have a bit of a soft spot. Nick found himself agreeing to tell Alan Dole of his brother's death. Then he found himself thinking that perhaps Christopher *had* somehow brought about his own demise. After all, if that was the conclusion everyone else was coming to . . .

There was a bustle in the lobby outside. It was constable

Daggett departing. Mrs Atkins went out to see him off. Nick stayed sitting by the warmth of the parlour fire.

Gazing into the coals, he asked himself: who would want to kill a poor, out-of-fashion playwright?

Then Nick recalled that Christopher Dole had managed to incur the hatred or anger of several persons: the printer, George Bruton, who called Dole a bastard and said he owed him money; his own brother, who claimed that Christopher had committed 'foolish crimes', and who had uttered some threatening words against him. True, these individuals talked about Dole as if he were still alive, when it was evident he had died earlier. But this could just be clever talk, meant to hide their own guilt.

And then, to add to the list, there was William Shakespeare. As well as WS, there were probably others unknown to Nick with reason to dislike Dole. For an impoverished and neglected playwright, he certainly seemed to have a talent for making enemies.

Nick retrieved the fragment of paper he'd picked up from Dole's floor. By the better light of the parlour, he was able to read the words. They were not English, but Latin. There were only four of them, and they were easy to understand. What he read caused a chill to come over him, for all the heat from the fire.

The door to the parlour opened. Nick turned his gaze from the slumbering fire but his expectation of seeing Sara Atkins again was disappointed when Stephen entered the room alone. The landlady's son glanced briefly at Nick before pouring himself a good measure of the aqua vitae, which he swallowed in a single gulp. It crossed Nick's mind that he too might be a suspect for Dole's killing. Without saying a word, Stephen made to go out the door.

'A moment ... Stephen,' said Nick. 'Where is the body now?'

'Cut down and laid out upstairs.'

'I have a couple of questions for you, and I think you owe me some answers, after ...' He indicated the bruises on his face.

Stephen shrugged and leaned his lanky frame against the panel-work by the door.

'You told me that two other people came to see Christopher Dole recently.'

'Yes.'

'When?'

'There was a gentleman who called yesterday afternoon. I knew Mr Dole was absent but I directed the visitor to go upstairs to Dole's room since the day was turning nasty, and he was insistent on seeing our lodger. From his voice and manner, he was obviously an individual of refinement, not someone to be turned away into the cold.'

'So this gentleman waited for Christopher to return?'

'I encountered Dole when I was on my way out, and told him he had a caller, so they must have met upstairs.'

'What did he look like?'

'I cannot tell you. His clothes were good but he was wearing a hat with a wide brim and it threw most of his face into shadow.'

'He didn't give his name, I suppose?'

'You suppose wrong. He did give his name.'

Nick waited and said nothing. He let the silence stretch out. He looked at the fire. Eventually the landlady's son gave way: 'He said he was called Henry Ashe.'

Nick couldn't help starting in surprise. So Henry Ashe, the imagined author of *The English Brothers*, was real after all. To cover his reaction he said, 'You keep a close eye on the comings and goings in this house, don't you, Stephen?'

'I'm not sure what business it is of yours but, yes, I do. My mother is somewhat casual about callers.'

'And there was another caller, you said?'

'Yes.'

'Before or after the well-dressed man? Mr Ashe?'

'After.'

'What did this one look like? Was he wearing a broad-brimmed hat as well?'

Stephen shrugged. 'I did not see him, but I heard him. I heard someone going upstairs, not one of our lodgers, since I recognise them all by their treads. I was aware of steps mounting to the very top floor, therefore I assumed this person was on his way to visit Christopher Dole.'

'But you did not see who it was, even though you like to know who's coming and going here?'

'What I don't know is why I have to account to you, Mr … er, for what I do or do not do. You have no authority.'

No, I have no authority, thought Nick. No more than you have authority to rain down blows on me and then pretend to forget my name. But he could not think what else to ask. In his grudging way, Stephen had provided quite a lot of information. Nick was curiously relieved that Stephen had not been able to describe the second visitor to the house.

Mrs Atkins returned. She was carrying Nick's doublet and cloak, which he had left in her bedchamber. Nick was pleased to see her, quite apart from getting relief from her son's company. Stephen slipped out of the room. Nick promised again to inform Alan Dole of his brother's death. He didn't go over his suspicions that Christopher might not have killed himself. He was no longer so sure that he wished to pursue them anyway. Mrs Atkins told him he might return to her house, if he wished, to have more salves and ointments applied to his hurts. Was she saying this because her son had done the damage or because she wanted another visit from him?

Sara helped him on with the rest of his clothing. She was gentle, and she grasped him lightly but slightly longer than was needed. Nick felt warmer, from the fire, from the aqua vitae, from her attentions.

As he trudged back through the streets, which gave off a cold glow on account of the freshly fallen snow, Nick tried to sum up what he'd learned.

Henry Ashe really existed. Therefore Christopher Dole was his agent, presenting *The English Brothers* to the printer. Had Ashe fallen out with him and killed him? Or was it the second visitor, the one Stephen Atkins claimed he'd heard creeping up the stairs? No, he hadn't said 'creeping', had he? Nick was thoroughly confused. Perhaps it was the result of the blows he'd received to the head.

The real source of the confusion, though, was the four words scrawled on the scrap of paper from Dole's room.

Those words were: '*Guilielmus Shakespeare hoc fecit.*' 'William Shakespeare made this.'

Or as one might say instead: 'William Shakespeare did this.'

It was a claim of authorship. So WS was the author of *The English Brothers*, after all? No, that was Henry Ashe, the man who'd called on Dole the previous afternoon. But if the message on the scrap of paper wasn't a claim of authorship, then perhaps it was the finger of blame. William Shakespeare did this.

Killed Christopher Dole.

The thought crept into Nick's battered head that maybe WS had called on Dole in the person of Ashe, keeping his face hidden under the hat brim. Shakespeare was a gentleman, he possessed gentlemanly clothes. But you couldn't claim he spoke in a refined way. He still retained traces of

Warwickshire in his voice and he lacked the kind of courtly London tone that would impress a silly young man like Stephen Atkins.

Was WS the second visitor, though, the unseen one?

Nick was reluctant to think of WS in this harsh light but he had to. He could not remember seeing Shakespeare so angry as he was when displaying a copy of the play in the little office behind the Globe stage. Was it just that he was indignant over the feeble imitation of his coat of arms on the title page? Or was he frightened that the Privy Council were going to come calling, on the hunt for seditious satire against King James? Frightened enough to take action against anyone he thought responsible for causing him trouble?

V

'No, I am not familiar with Henry Ashe,' said Shakespeare. 'There is no playwright in London with that name. You are sure of it?'

'Yes,' said Nick. 'The name was given me by George Bruton, the printer in Bride Lane. And then I was told that a gentleman called Ashe visited Christopher Dole before he died.'

'Poor Dole,' said WS. 'For sure, he is the author of *The English Brothers*. Henry Ashe was just a blind. I always thought it was Dole. It was he whose play I mocked. It was called *The Matricide*.'

Nick studied him carefully. Once again, they were sitting in the small Globe office but this time it was the early afternoon, and shortly before the day's play was about to begin. Nick did not make his first entrance until the third act so he could delay going along to the tiring-room to put on his costume. In fact, his attention wasn't really on that afternoon's production, which was a drama of bloody revenge, but on the reaction of the man sitting across the table from him.

'Was your mockery of his play the only reason for his . . . dislike of you?'

'There were other causes. He thought I'd taken the idea for my *Romeo and Juliet* from him.'

'And did you?'

'No, Nicholas, I did not,' said Shakespeare, in a deliberate sort of way as if he were talking to someone whose understanding was slow. 'I took it from another and older source – several of them, perhaps. But not from Dole. Not poor Christopher Dole. He may have had the notion at the same time, of course. We all drink from the same well but some of us drink deeper than others.'

Shakespeare's sorrow for Dole was not profound, but Nick thought it was genuine. In fact, WS was showing more grief for the death of the one-time player than his own brother had. When Nick had called on Alan Dole in his St Paul's bookshop, as he'd promised Mrs Atkins he would, Alan had merely pulled a face as though he expected nothing better or more ambitious from his brother than to go off and die. Then the bookseller had started to complain about the funeral expenses. Then he'd asked whether Nick had seen the Oseney text in Christopher's room. Then it was Nick's turn to shrug. The Oseney text? He supposed this was the item that Christopher was meant to be returning to his brother.

By contrast to the brother's, Shakespeare's grief looked like the real thing. Shakespeare was an actor, of course, even if he played few parts these days. But he did not put on airs or false attitudes away from the stage. When he saw the marks on Nick's face and heard how he'd come by them in Mrs Atkins' lodging house, WS was so full of gratitude and apology that all Nick's suspicions began to fall away. Nick stuck to the story that Dole had done away with himself.

He said nothing of the scrap of paper that had fluttered to the floor. *Guilielmus Shakespeare hoc fecit.* William Shakespeare did this. No, it did not mean anything.

Richard Burbage, the principal shareholder and king of the players, now poked his head round the door of the tiny office and his presence brought to Nick's mind the name he had briefly assumed – Dick Newman. Much use it had been.

Richard Burbage evidently wanted to speak to WS but, seeing Nick, he said: 'You've been in a fight?'

'On my behalf,' said WS quickly.

Burbage raised his eyebrows and said, 'It's as well you're playing a villain and not the hero this afternoon. Bruises suit your part, Nicholas.'

'I could have painted them on with greater ease and less pain,' said Nick.

WS said: 'Richard, have you ever heard of a London play-wright called Henry Ashe?'

Burbage put his hand to his neatly tapered beard. He didn't seem so inclined to dismiss the name as WS had done. 'I do not believe so. But there are always new people coming into this town. I'll make enquiries.'

They went ahead with the performance that afternoon, with the pipe-smoke and the breath of the audience curling up into the freezing December air. Nick Revill threw himself into the part of the villain, forgetting his aches and bruises as he slashed and stabbed his way to his own inevitable doom. But he did not remember much about the play. What happened afterwards was much more significant.

Nick was leaving the Globe with a couple of his companions from the King's Men. He had changed into his day clothes in the tire house but had not bothered to wash off the dye that made his complexion more swarthy, nor to remove the false beard that he wore as the villain. Normally clean-shaven, Nick took pleasure in the fact that his neat, tapered beard was reminiscent of Richard Burbage's. It was made of lamb's wool and, quite apart from the fact that ungumming it from his face would take a little time, the soft fleece provided a little extra warmth in this cold period.

Evening was come. No fresh snow had fallen but the old stuff still lodged in street corners and on rooftops. The three players made their way down a street that ran past the Globe, known as Brend's Rents. They passed the entrance to the playhouse. Standing there was little limping Sam, a doorman who'd been with the company since the early days when they played north of the river. An individual was next to him.

'There he is,' the old man said to the person beside him. 'I told you he would be coming.' Then to Nick: 'Nicholas Revill, here is someone eager for a word.'

For some reason, Nick suddenly thought he was about to see Henry Ashe and the hairs rose on the back of his neck at the idea. But the person beside Sam was wearing not a wide-brimmed hat but a cap. Also, to judge by his clothes, this was no gentleman but a craftsman. The light from the entrance lobby fell on the face of the stranger and Nick was surprised to recognise the journeyman from George Bruton's printing works. He was not wearing his spectacles but he had that distinctive inky mole on the tip of his nose. It was Hans de Worde. As the printer came forward, Sam closed the door of the playhouse to signal that the day's business was concluded.

Nick's companions went on their way with scarcely a backward glance. It wasn't so unusual for a player to be waylaid

after a performance by someone wishing to give his opinion about the acting and how it might be better done, or
wanting an introduction to one of the shareholders. But
Hans wasn't interested in any of that.

'Can I speak to you, Mr *Revill*?' said Hans, stressing the last
word. Nick wondered why for a moment before recalling
that he'd announced himself as Dick Newman, of the
Admiral's Men, in Bruton's printing-house.

'I tracked you here,' said Hans. 'I do not visit these places
myself but John, our apprentice, is a keen attender at the
playhouse and other disreputable locations on this side of
the Thames, even though he should be occupying himself
with better things. I have told him so often enough. John
thought he recognised you when you came to Bride Lane.
He told me afterwards that you weren't with the Admiral's
but with the King's Men. He has seen you act.'

Nick ought to have been pleased to be recognised but the
accusation in Hans's tone put him on the back foot. Yes, he
had misrepresented himself at the printing-house. To be
more precise, he had told a lie.

'You want to talk with me now?' he said.

'Yes. It is important. But not here. We are too isolated.'

Hans looked about him as though he expected a gang of
knaves and cut-throats to emerge from the shadows. In the
district of Southwark it was not so unlikely. Nick felt a touch
of the other man's fear. Now that the theatre was shut up,
and with the players and the playgoers all departed, it was
cold and silent in Brend's Rents.

'We'll go to a tavern,' he said.

'I – I do not like to frequent taverns. I have rarely been
across the Bridge before. I am not familiar with this side of
the river even though my brother Antony lives over here.
He is a ferryman.'

This was an odd piece of information which Nick digested as he led Hans in the direction of London Bridge, only a few hundred yards from the playhouse. It was better lit and more crowded there. In any case, he had to go in that direction to return to his own lodgings.

Hans said nothing until they had reached the area at the top of the main thoroughfare known as Long Southwark People and vehicles emerged from below the great stone gate of the Bridge. Most of the traffic was southbound at this time of the evening. Almost drowning out the sound of cart wheels and the passers-by was the roar of the river as it forced its way through the many arches of the Bridge.

Nick and Hans stood to one side of the entrance to the street going towards Bermondsey and called Short Southwark to distinguish it from Long Southwark, from which it ran at a right angle.

'Why did you come to the Globe?' said Nick.

'I thought you could be found there, Mr Revill. But I had to see you and your fellows on stage before I was able to identify you for certain. The drama was full of blood and fury. Too much of it. It was not real, like that beard which you are wearing.'

Nick realised he was referring to the revenge play of this afternoon. Too much blood and fury? And not real? Oh, these things are real, thought Nick. Look around you. On the battlements of the gate-tower of the Bridge near where they stood were poles displaying the severed heads of traitors, including those executed after the powder treason of 1605. If no Londoner noticed them, even by daylight, it was only because the sight was so usual.

'It is cold, Mr de Worde, and I am tired and hungry after my day's work. Why did you want to see me?'

'I have something on my conscience.'

'I am not a priest.'

'There is something I should have told you when you came to the printing-shop yesterday. I knew more than I said.'

Even as he spoke, low and urgently, Hans's gaze was darting here and there. He was plainly frightened.

'I visited Mr Dole. I removed an item from his room. I should not have done so.'

'I don't understand,' said Nick. 'What item do you mean? Was Christopher Dole there?'

'Yes.'

'Did he allow you to remove this "item", whatever it was?'

'No. He could not have allowed me to do anything for he was dead.'

'Hanged?'

'It was a dreadful sight. He had killed himself.'

'You're sure of that?'

'Yes. There was a stool tumbled beneath his feet. He must have stood on it to reach to the ceiling and fix the cord up there. I replaced the stool by the wall and was going to take down his body so that his mortal remains should be displayed more decorously, but my nerve failed me at the last moment . . . and . . . and instead I found the item which I'd come for and ran down the stairs . . . '

Nick supposed that de Worde was the second visitor to the lodging-house, the one whose arrival Stephen Atkins had heard. Hans's description tended to confirm that Dole's death was not a murder after all.

'Did you see anyone else at the house?' he said.

'No. But there were men who came to the printing-house this morning. They spoke to Mr Bruton. They were—'

Hans's darting gaze suddenly became fixed on a point

over Nick's shoulder. He stopped whatever he was about to say. Automatically, Nick turned round. Coming up Long Southwark was a group of four men, wrapped up in capes, their faces muffled. They moved steadily across the slushy ground and with a gait that was almost military. Despite the poor light, Nick observed that one of the men, slightly in front of the others, was wearing a hat with a great brim. The group was heading straight for Nick and Hans.

He felt a touch on his arm and spun back. It was Hans de Worde. The touch was nothing more than a feeble parting gesture, for de Worde now took to his heels down Short Southwark. That was in the direction of Nick's own lodging, but the impulse to run away from the approaching band of four took the player not into the unreliable darkness of Short Southwark but towards the crowds and regular lights of London Bridge. Safety in numbers, Nick instinctively thought. The Bridge was always crowded from before sunrise until late into the night.

Not breaking into a run, although he wanted to, Nick walked rapidly towards the arch that pierced the Great Stone Gate. He glanced back. It looked as if the four men were not to be distracted by de Worde's flight down the side road. They were moving at a brisk pace after Nick. Why not go after Hans de Worde? he asked himself. This affair was nothing to do with him.

Nick felt his heart beating more quickly. He grew breathless, even though he was not yet moving very fast. There were watchmen on duty by the Great Gate but it was no use appealing for help to such timid, indolent men. These representatives of the law could scarcely bestir themselves to stop a fight on the Bridge, and they would certainly not interfere with a determined group like the foursome on Nick's trail. Besides, whoever his pursuers were, Nick

believed they were not robbers but something quite different . . .

He squeezed past a couple of closed carriages, the horses
shifting uneasily in the narrow pathway. Inside the carriages
would be well-to-do young men from north London on their
way to the gaming houses and brothels on the Southwark
shore. On either side of him were houses and shops, most of
them shuttered at this time of the evening. Parts of the
Bridge were more like a tunnel than an open lane since
many of the houses jutted out so far on their upper levels
that the occupants could have shaken hands across the
divide. There were even places where complete floors
extended right over the roadway between the sides.

Nick might have succeeded in losing himself among the
people and the conveyances if it had not been for a fellow
tucked into the shadow of a doorway. Drunk or exhausted,
he was sitting with his knees drawn up to his chin. As Nick
glanced momentarily over his shoulder to see where his pursuers were he stumbled across the other's feet. In an instant
he found himself winded and flat on his face. Behind him
there was a slurred curse from the figure in the doorway.
Nick started to push himself up again and was surprised
when helping hands raised him on each side. This was very
un-London-like behaviour, and he was turning to mumble
his thanks when he saw that his helpers were the caped men.
They had been moving more rapidly than he realised.

Two of the men were hemming him in, on the pretence of
helping him up. The one with the wide hat was already
ahead and now Nick felt a blow in the small of his back
from the man to the rear. These four persons were so muffled that almost nothing of their faces was visible apart from
the eyes. Nick was more surprised than fearful. Fear would
come later. No use appealing to any constable or watchman,

even had one been within sight. His captors had an authority that suggested they were above the law.

He was hustled forward, his feet scrabbling at the ground.
If they had been going any distance Nick might just have
had the chance to break away. But they were not. The group
moved under a wooden arch framed by columns and entered
a passage that ran straight through the newest and finest
edifice on the Bridge. This was Nonesuch House, which had
replaced a gatehouse and drawbridge that had stood a third
of the way across from the south bank. The drawbridge had
been an old defence for the city but one no longer needed in
these more peaceful times. So the gatehouse had been torn
down and Nonesuch put up in its place. Only the rich could
afford to take lodgings there.

Nick had often gazed up at Nonesuch House while he was
walking across the Bridge from the Southwark side. The glittering windows and the ornamental woodwork made for a
more agreeable prospect than the severed heads of traitors.
Nonesuch, with its corner towers topped with onion-shaped
domes, was grand enough to make most Londoners wonder
what it would be like to set foot over the threshold. Nick
Revill was about to find out.

There were lanterns hanging above the doors within the
tunnel-like walkway, through which people and vehicles
passed like shadows. The leader of the group rapped at a
door to the left. It was promptly opened and Nick was half
ushered, half pushed down a couple of steps and into a
lobby. A maidservant was waiting on the other side of the
door. She lowered her head as the group came in. A mark of
deference or fear? The individual with the wide hat said
nothing but gestured with a gloved hand and the two men on
either side of Nick, who had not relinquished their grip since
hoisting him up from the roadway, now escorted him down

a wide panelled passageway. The floor was so polished that their boots squeaked across it. At the end, one of them reached out, opened a door and nudged Nick as a sign for him to enter the room. The door closed behind him.

He had expected to see someone inside but the chamber was empty. It was lavishly furnished, with desks, small tables and upholstered chairs scattered about. The wall-hangings rippled slightly in the draughts of air penetrating even such a finely constructed dwelling as this. Candles burned in sconces on the wall and a fire flickered in an elaborate chimney-piece. Facing Nick as he stood by the door was an oriel window with a quilted bench beneath. He walked across and, leaning against the bench and shielding his eyes from the light in the room, he squinted through the thick leaded panes.

The view was to the west and upstream, with Southwark to his left and the city to his right. Extending away in front of him was the black river. There were glimmers of light from the little ferries still at work as well as from the buildings on either shore, but these feeble sparks served only to intensify the cold and dark beyond the wooden walls of Nonesuch House. From beneath Nick's feet came the unceasing rumble of the water. On this spot he was standing directly above it since the sides of Nonesuch House projected out from the piers of the Bridge. It occurred to Nick that, if it were daytime and the tide in full flow around the piers, it would be like standing on the prow of a ship. Then it occurred to him that he ought to feel afraid, taken against his will from the public street and confined in the grandeur of Nonesuch House.

Continuing to gaze at the dark river, although without really seeing it, Nick considered his predicament. He had a fair idea now of who was responsible for it. Hans de Worde, also, must have recognised the people striding towards him in Long Southwark. Recognised them not as individuals, perhaps, but for what they represented. They were surely the same ones who had called at George Bruton's printing-house. They were . . .

The door opened. A shadow cut across the candlelight reflected in the windowpanes. Nick turned slowly. It was the leader of the group. He was still wearing his broad-brimmed hat and Nick could not be sure whether this was for disguise or as an affectation. Nick saw only that he was clean-shaven. Behind him came the servant who had opened the front door. She was carrying a tray on which was a pitcher and two glasses, already filled.

The man indicated that Nick should sit and, when he did, the woman offered him a glass. He took it and sipped, wondering what fate he was being softened up for. The wine was spiced and warm. By this time, the man had sat down on a chair opposite and taken the other glass. The woman placed the tray and pitcher on a nearby table. Then she exited the room, quietly closing the door behind her.

Only when the man had swallowed some of the contents of his glass did he finally remove his hat. He did it with a flourish that would have done him credit on the stage. Nick had been expecting someone sinister or threatening but here was a man of about his own age, with a full head of straw-coloured hair and an open gaze. The man took another swallow from his glass.

'This is very welcome on a cold night, eh, Mr Newman?'

These were the first words he had spoken. His voice, like his manner, was easy, confident. Nick examined his glass, as if to savour the mere sight of the warmed wine. But his mind was elsewhere, working furiously. The man had addressed him as Newman, hadn't he? Not as Revill. Which meant that he was unaware of his real identity. As if to confirm the mistake, the man now added in a tone that was more of a statement than a question: 'You are Richard Newman of Prince Henry's Men.'

'That's right, although we still refer to ourselves as the Admiral's Men,' said Nicholas Revill in a tone that he hoped would convey slight surprise at how well-informed the speaker was. For an instant, it occurred to him to put the man right, to give his real name and to declare he was a member of the King's Men. But some instinct told him to stick with the assumed name. And, even as he decided this, he struggled to remember the limited number of people who knew him as Richard Newman.

Meanwhile, it seemed that the man wanted to test Nick's claims for he now said: 'So, if you are with Prince Henry's or the Admiral's, you must be acquainted with Thomas Downton and Richard Jones of that company?'

'Of course I know them, and I also know . . .' And here Nick reeled off half a dozen names of players with the Admiral's Men. He did know some of them personally, while the rest he had heard of. It was unlikely the man would detect the pretence, or at least it would take him a bit of time to do so. The big names in any group of players were familiar but there was quite a bit of coming-and-going between the London companies and no outsider would be able to keep track of all the latest arrivals and departures. For once, Nick was glad of his relatively junior status in Shakespeare's company. He decided to take the initiative.

'Since you know who I am, you ought to return the courtesy,' he said, pleased at the steadiness in his voice.

'You can call me Henry Ashe,' said the man, staring at Nick as if daring him to dispute the name. Nick's hold on his glass tightened. When he next spoke, it was harder to keep his voice even.

'Henry Ashe, the author of *The English Brothers*?'

'That's a seditious and satirical piece, so it is not likely that I would be the author.'

'Why is it unlikely you'd be the author, Mr Ashe? Who are you? Why am I here?'

Nick did not meant to ask so many questions but they came tumbling out. Be careful, he told himself.

'I said that you can call me Henry Ashe, Mr Newman. Let's be satisfied with that, as I am satisfied for the moment that you are who you say you are. As for the reason I keep sedition at arm's length – why, that is what any true-born Englishman should do. But, more precisely, it is because I work for ... because I am a Messenger of the Chamber.' This title was uttered with a little flourish, like the hat-removing.

Nick nodded. It confirmed his fears. The harmless sounding 'Messenger of the Chamber' was a title sometimes used by agents of the Privy Council. From the number and efficiency of the group that had apprehended him on the Bridge, as well as the opulence of the chamber in Nonesuch House, Nick already knew he could be at the mercy of only one particular arm of the state. This was the Council, operating under the direct control of its secretary, Robert Cecil. Diminutive Cecil, now the Earl of Salisbury. Cecil, the man with the crooked back, who had his finger in more pies than you could count and who ran a network of spies and informants in the name of national security. Nick had encountered Robert Cecil once at the end of Queen Elizabeth's reign. It was not a happy memory.

Nick's only weapon was that, for the time being, the man calling himself Henry Ashe thought he was someone else.

'If you are what you say you are,' he said to Ashe, 'then of course you cannot be the author of *The English Brothers.*'

'That was Christopher Dole. I hear he is dead – by his own hand.'

'And I heard,' said Nick, the blood thudding in his ears as he spoke, 'that Mr Dole was visited before his death by a gentleman who bore a great resemblance to you. He even gave your name.'

Ashe didn't reply straight away. He got up and refilled his glass, then came over to refill Nick's. It was if they were two old friends chatting in comfort. When he sat down again, he said: 'Yes, it's true, I did call on Dole. I gave the name of Ashe because it amused me to do so. I heard the name bandied about in a tavern called The Ram.'

Nick barely suppressed a start of surprise at the mention of the place where he'd gone in search of George Bruton. Ashe noticed Nick's reaction.

'You are probably thinking that The Ram is rather a low place for someone more used to Nonesuch House. But I tell you, Mr Newman, all kinds of information can be garnered there. People are less careful what they say in such places. It is a regular resort of ours. And of yours, I believe. Your voice sounds familiar.'

Nick remembered the recent occasion when he'd seen Bruton in the tavern. He had given his name as Newman, had claimed to be from the Admirals'. He remembered too that there was a group of drinkers in another corner of The Ram. Was Ashe one of them? He must have been. Perhaps it was not de Worde that the group was after but himself, under the assumed name of Newman. Perhaps they had been tracking de Worde but only in the hope that he would lead them to more valuable prey.

The man from the Privy Council continued: 'I went to

visit Christopher Dole because I was looking into some ...
careless comments that had been written about our sovereign. When I left him, he was still alive.'

Nick said nothing. Ashe's words agreed with what Hans de
Worde had said. It looked as though Dole had not been murdered, after all.

'It may be,' said Ashe, 'that something I said caused Mr
Dole to reflect on the continued worth of his existence. He
was not in good health, poor fellow. On the contrary he was
thin and shaking and in a very low mood. Perhaps he feared
further investigation. Not every conversation can take place
in such pleasant surroundings as this, Mr Newman.'

Henry Ashe gestured at the room where they were sitting.
His meaning was plain enough: we have other spaces to talk in,
other means by which we might interest you in talking to us.

Ashe suddenly said: 'What do you know about the Oseney
text?'

Nick had heard of the Oseney text from Alan Dole, but it
meant nothing to him. His look of confused ignorance must
have been convincing to Ashe since, for the first time in their
encounter, the other man appeared uncertain.

'It is the reason we have been keeping an eye on various
people – one of the reasons. The other is Mr Dole's unwise
mockery of the monarch. But it is the Oseney text we are
after. It is the old manuscript of a play reputed to have
unusual powers. Some phrases from the Oseney text were
used in that play called *The English Brothers*. The phrases were
recognised by ... those who are knowledgeable in such things.
It followed that whoever penned *The English Brothers* must also
be in possession of the Oseney text or know its whereabouts.'

'What do you mean by "unusual powers"?' said Nick,
genuinely curious.

'The Oseney text is reputed to be cursed.'

As a theatre man, Nick was familiar with stories about those dangerous phrases and spells that ought not to be uttered on stage. Hadn't an extra demon, one not accounted for in the list of players, appeared from nowhere during a performance of *Doctor Faustus*? And the thought of the devil suddenly explained why Secretary Cecil's man was concerned about a text with a curse on it.

'This is all on account of the King, isn't it?' said Nick. 'Everyone knows of his interest in witchcraft and devilry. He collects books on the subject. Why, he even wrote a book on demonology many years ago.'

'It may be so,' said Henry Ashe.

The man's guarded answer indicated to Nick that he was right. The order to lay hold of this dangerous manuscript – the Oseney text – must have come directly from Secretary Cecil, who in turn would have been given instructions by King James. Perhaps the King wanted it for his book collection. Perhaps he wanted it for some darker purpose.

'Are you telling me all you know?' asked Ashe.

'I know nothing.'

'You see, Christopher Dole assured me that he too knew nothing about it. I might have questioned him again but now he is dead. Yet you are still here, Mr Newman.'

Nick felt sweat break out on his forehead. It was not because of the warmth of the room or the wine, which suddenly tasted bitter on his tongue. He was aware of the rumble of the river below, although he had not noticed it for many minutes.

'Prince Henry's or the Admiral's Men, you said?' said Ashe. 'And to confirm it, you provided me with a string of names, a little too eagerly, perhaps. Suppose I summon a member of the company now to confirm that you are who you say you are, Mr Newman.'

Nick shrugged. Do as you please, the gesture said. He was thinking, the Admiral's are based in the Fortune theatre just outside the city walls. It will take a little time to lay hands on someone from the company and to bring them to Nonesuch House. A lot could happen in a little time. He might still be able to talk his way out of this.

'As it happens,' said Henry Ashe, 'I believe that Philip Henslowe is dining at another of the houses on the Bridge tonight. I'm sure he won't object to being interrupted at his table and coming along here to identify you. Not if he knows that he will be assisting the Council. I can see the idea makes you uncomfortable, Mr Newman, so I don't think I should leave you in here while I fetch Henslowe. Let us see if you can be lodged somewhere more secure.'

The sweat started to run down Nick's face. His beard itched. Henslowe was not a player but someone much more important: a builder of playhouses and a shareholder in the Bear Garden. He was closely associated with the Admiral's Men, now Prince Henry's. He would be familiar with every player on their books. He would not recognise the name of Richard Newman. More to the point, he would probably recognise Nick as one of the King's Men, despite the dye on his face and the lamb's-wool beard.

Henry Ashe got up, indicating that Nick should rise too. He stood aside to let the player go first through the door. It crossed Nick's mind to make a run for it. But immediately outside stood two of the caped men from the original group. Ashe, who seemed to employ gestures rather than words when giving orders to his underlings, nodded towards a second and smaller door to one side of the chamber they had just exited.

Once again Nick was grasped by the upper arms and, with more force this time, guided towards the second door.

It was opened and he was shoved inside. On the threshold he stumbled and fell to the floor. Behind him the door was closed, a key turned. He heard footsteps striding away, squeaking on that well-polished floor. Henry Ashe, no doubt, off in search of Philip Henslowe. There was some talk from the other side of the door, inaudible because of the background sound of the river, but it meant that the two men were remaining outside as guards.

Nick sat up. After the dazzle of the large chamber it took some moments for his eyes to adapt to what was an unlit, narrow area made more confined by piles of boxes and heaped-up sacks and bags as well as barrels.

He pushed himself to his feet. More by touch than sight he made his way around some obstruction in the centre of the room and across to a window. This was no more than an aperture giving a view onto a narrow slice of river and sky, though it was too dark to see the point where one became the other. The window was glazed but it seemed to have no catch, no means of being opened. Its function could only be to allow a little light into this side room.

The function of the room itself was clear to Nick. He could smell spices. There was a faint odour of fish. One of the smaller bags contained what felt like nuts – filberts from their size. An upright and open-topped barrel gave off no tang apart from a faint whiff of the river: water therefore. This was a storage area and sited here on the ground floor of Nonesuch House so that goods might be drawn straight up from the river rather than being brought to the Bridge on a long roundabout journey by road. Indeed, for a couple of items – fish and water – the river was the nearest and most convenient source. You might even catch your fish directly by dangling a line straight down.

As Nick's eyes grew more used to the gloom he could see

that the obstruction in the centre of the room was some kind of hoist, a sturdy wooden frame complete with a ratchet-wheel and handle, together with cords and a wicker basket. He got down on his hands and knees and fumbled for the trapdoor, which had to be close to the hoist. It took him only a few seconds to locate a metal ring, cold to the touch, and then the square outlines of the trapdoor itself, which stood slightly proud of the floor where it was embedded. He estimated it was about three feet on each side. The hinges were opposite to the hoist which meant that the door opened upwards and in the direction of the slit-like window over the river.

Nick was about to take hold of the iron ring when he heard noises outside the door. The handle rattled. Surely it was not Ashe come back with Henslowe so soon? No, for the rattling ceased almost immediately and Nick guessed that it was one of the guards testing that the door was fast. He would have to beware of noise, although the rumble of the river provided some cover. Fortunately, it seemed to be getting louder. The tide must be turning. Nick reached out for the ring and pulled at it. No movement. Making sure his feet were clear of the trapdoor itself, he craned over it and, using all the strength in his shoulders, tugged hard. The trapdoor came free so suddenly that, had he not been grasping the iron ring, he would have fallen over backwards. Even so, he put out his arm for balance and struck a pile of boxes, which toppled over with a crash.

He froze, still crouching and holding on with one hand to the ring on the trapdoor. No response from outside. No door flung open. He waited for as long as he dared and then gradually eased the trapdoor all the way open until it lay flat with its edge against the outer wall. There was an uprush of cold air and the noise of the river grew more insistent.

Nick kneeled down and, with fingers curled round the planking at the edge of the square hole, he peered below. What took his breath away was not the chill night air but the fall to the river. From this angle, it seemed an impossible, dizzying distance through the dark.

Nonesuch House, although built almost entirely of wood, was too heavy to rest on a span of the Bridge and so was set firmly on one of the great piers that thrust up from the boat-shaped foundations. The storeroom where Nick was imprisoned was on the north-west corner of the building and therefore half over a foundation, half over the water. Nick couldn't see them but he knew that there would be mooring rings on the wooden piles that held in the stone and gravel of the foundation-blocks. Here suppliers could tie up their boats while provisions were winched up to Nonesuch House. He glimpsed white flecks where the water broke against the pier. That, and the deep roar, showed the tide was ebbing. This was when the river was at its most turbulent since all of its upstream expanse was squeezed between the many arches of the Bridge, causing a dangerous, tumbling drop down to the far side.

For Nick, making a descent from the house on the Bridge was a frightening enough prospect. But a yet more frightening one was to stay and wait for the man calling himself Henry Ashe to return with Philip Henslowe. All too soon the Privy Council agent would discover that his prisoner wasn't Dick Newman, as he'd claimed to be. He would start to wonder what else Nick was concealing. The whereabouts of that item known as the Oseney text, for example. Ashe had already threatened Nick with a less comfortable conversation in a less agreeable place. That meant real imprisonment, and probably worse. The Council could authorise torture. Nick would have given up the secret of the Oseney text as easily and willingly as dropping a feather. They wouldn't even have to resort to torture. The trouble was that he had no idea what Ashe was talking about.

So, if it was a choice between the dangers of a sheer drop and the freezing river, and a dank cell courtesy of the Privy Council, he'd choose the drop and the river every time.

Even as these thoughts and fears were racing through his head, Nick had been testing the ropes that were heaped and coiled in the area of the wooden hoist. He was trying to select the longest by running stretches through his hands and extending his arms to either side. That amounted to between five and six feet, didn't it? But the ropes got tangled and Nick began to lose count. Besides, he had only a vague notion of how far it was down to the water and the pier foundation. The distance from the top of an arch in the centre of the Bridge might have been as much as thirty feet at low tide. But this corner-room jutted out below the level of the nearest arch. Then it occurred to him that, since these various ropes must be used for hauling goods up from below, they would all be of about the same length.

He could not afford to waste any more precious moments in choosing precisely the right rope. He untangled one that seemed a little more sturdy than the others, looped it around the frame of the hoist and tied a primitive knot. The very thickness and bulk of the cord made this awkward. He could not see clearly what he was doing and was forced to work mostly by touch. Once he thought it was secure, he pulled at it. Pulled hard because his life depended on that knot. Tugged twice more and then tossed the rope out so that it slithered through the gaping aperture in the floor. Even then he might have hesitated before launching himself into the air but, fearing he heard renewed noises outside the door of the storeroom, he grasped the rope in both hands. Lying on his front, he edged himself feet first over the lip of the hole.

Too soon he reached the point where more of his weight was outside than in. Almost convinced that the rope would not bear his weight or the knot would fail, Nick nevertheless started to clamber down. At first his legs swung free until, instinctively, he wrapped his feet about the rope. Nick was not fearful of heights. But he was very afraid of falling. Death was certain if he did, whether he struck the loose stone blocks and wooden piles of the pier-foundation or whether he plunged into the water.

For an instant, when he completely cleared the trapdoor opening and was out in the open, feeling exposed and insignificant beside the massive bulk of the Bridge, Nick found his bare hands refusing to unclasp themselves from the ridged rope. It was as if his fingers had a will of their own, locking themselves round the thin thread, which was all that prevented him from dropping down like a stone. With a great effort, he uncurled one hand, and swiftly placed it beneath the other on the rope. Then he prised that one away and positioned it beneath the first. And so on and on, until the action became almost automatic and his fear subsided slightly as, not daring to look down to see whether he was over ground or water, he concentrated on inching down the rope.

Careful hand over careful hand, feet and calves sliding down the coarse hemp strands, gusts of air plucking at his garments, Nick risked a look upwards and was disappointed to realise he had travelled hardly any distance. The trap-door entrance showed as a darker square against the jutting floor of the store room. At any moment, Henry Ashe would be returning with Philip Henslowe and finding the room empty. They could haul him up again, using the rope. Worse, they could simply untie or sever the cord, and allow Nick to plunge to his death. He was an escaper, he was an imposter, an enemy to the Council, whatever name he might adopt.

He started to move more quickly, much more quickly. And the rope started to sway because of his jerky movements and because he was emerging from the shelter provided by the bulk of the Bridge overhead. The swaying became more violent and Nick found himself twisting helplessly in the air so that one moment he was facing the stonework of the pier and the next confronting the open river. The end of the rope lashed around beneath him like a monstrous tail. At the conclusion of one swing his back struck the stone flank of the pier and the jarring force of the blow almost caused him to release his hold. He willed himself to be still, to keep gripping tight with hands and feet, and to wait until the worst of the swaying, sickening motions of the rope had diminished.

Only now did he look down and, this time, was surprised to see that he had less than twenty feet to go, as far as he could judge. By good fortune the rope would take him through that distance. But those twenty feet would also deliver him straight into the foamy water, whose smell filled his nostrils and whose roaring filled his ears. To one side was the edge of the foundation of the pier holding up Nonesuch House. At this instant, just when he needed to swing himself across to reach the foundation, he hung quivering, almost without motion. His arms and shoulders burned with labour, his bare hands were slick with sweat or blood or both.

One final effort. He jerked his body until he managed to gain some momentum and the rope was swaying now out above the current, now over the boat-shaped projection below the pier. At the same time he shifted himself lower. And then it seemed to Nick as though the rope began to slide down of its own accord before making an abrupt

descent of some dozen feet. It jolted to a stop. The knot
around the hoist in the storeroom was giving way. Or someone up there was attempting to loosen it. Without thought,
and as the arc of his swing brought him back once again
over the pier foundation, Nick let go his hold and, though his
feet struck the top of the wooden piles, he tumbled onto
solid ground. At the same moment, the rope sprang free and
snaked down behind him into the water.

For some time Nick lay where he'd fallen. The noise of
the river was thunderous. He scarcely dared to move for fear
that he would not be able to move at all. He tested his limbs
with slight flexing movements. There were some pains but
nothing beyond bearing. He scrabbled in the loose stone and
gravel and got to his feet. He looked up. Nonesuch House
hung above his head like a Jonah's whale brought to land. He
could not see the trapdoor hole through which he had
descended. There were no lights up there. Perhaps his escape
was not yet detected after all.

He huddled against the elmwood stakes that surrounded
the pier-foundation. He wondered what to do next. He had
escaped from one predicament into another. There was no
way off this place except by boat and, although there were
still lights showing a little traffic on the river, no means of
attracting anyone's attention in the cold and dark. He could
not even climb back into Nonesuch House since the rope
that had delivered him had disappeared, presumably to join
all the other rubbish in the river.

He didn't know how long he huddled there. It was bitterly cold and his hurts were beginning to trouble him. He
might even have slept for a few moments. He was afraid that
the winter's night might do for him. He staggered to his feet.
Keep moving, keep warm, keep alive. He stumbled over one
of the stone blocks beneath his feet. He cried out in pain

and anger and crashed to the ground. He lay there, wondering if this was his last night on earth. Then he saw two figures clambering over the piles.

One of them said: 'Mr Revill? Are you there? Please answer.'

VI

All was explained by Hans de Worde. He was very apologetic for having deserted Nick when the Privy Council agents strode into view in Long Southwark. It was pure fear. But after a moment or two his better and braver nature prevailed. Overcome by guilt, he turned back to follow the band of four as they took up Nick and ushered him into the ground-floor of Nonesuch House. There by the entrance he had hung about, in an anguish of indecision, watching the comings and goings, and unnoticed himself in all the busyness of the Bridge. After about an hour there was a great stir, with men rushing out of Nonesuch and word spreading like fire along the Bridge that someone had toppled into the river from the very wing of the house where Nick had disappeared. Convinced it must be Nicholas, and consumed twice over by guilt, Hans went to find his brother, the ferryman, so that they might go in search of Nick's— Here Hans stopped himself from saying 'body' although that was surely the most likely outcome of the search.

Nick and Hans were in the Southwark lodgings of Antony de Worde, ferryman and brother to the printer's journeyman. Antony was a rough-hewn version of the fastidious Hans. No attender at the Dutch church, he was, like other inhabitants of Southwark, and especially those engaged in the ferry-trade, almost indifferent to the law. He was not taken by his brother's suggestion. Not until Hans offered the ferryman enough money to take his boat out onto the river by night in this futile quest.

By chance, a miraculous chance, the brothers were about to give up and were navigating their way back to the dock by St Mary Overie's and so passing the region of the Bridge near Nonesuch House when they heard, above the roar of the river, a cry of pain coming from one of the foundations. Nick owed his life to the fact that he had fallen and shouted out in rage, in pain, in fear.

Once in the warmth and comfort of Antony de Worde's lodging – so much better than anything that Nonesuch could offer – Nick was revived with warm spirits. Salves were put on his scraped and bleeding hands. Finally, Nick removed his lamb's-wool beard, thinking that it had provided a useful disguise both on and off stage.

Words tumbled out of Hans de Worde's mouth as he described how glad he was to see Mr Revill alive and well, or at least fairly well. How he could not forgive himself for bringing down trouble on the player's head. How he could not wait to hand over the Oseney text, which he had retrieved from Christopher Dole's room, from its hiding place in the dead man's chest. He thought he recognised the text as he was setting it up in type for *The English Brothers* and the source was confirmed by a chance remark of George Bruton's, when Dole visited his printing-house the day he died. Hans was familiar with the stories about *The Play of Adam*. He did not believe that such a dangerous script should be allowed to roam free in the world. It was against religion.

More quick-witted than his employer, George Bruton, Hans had already worked out that Dole (and not the imaginary Ashe) was the author of *The English Brothers*. Believing that Dole must have the text of the old play as well, he went to his lodgings. Shaken to discover the hanging body – and wondering whether this was not another malign effect of *The Play of Adam* – he nevertheless persisted in his search and rapidly unearthed the scroll from among the few shirts and other items in Christopher's chest.

Hans now reached into his doublet and brought out an antique roll of vellum. He handed over the manuscript known as the Oseney text, saying, 'I don't want it any more. I should never have taken it. It is a play and you, sir, are a player. Do with it what you will, Mr Revill. There are words of warning on the outside of the scroll. Read them and ponder.'

The scroll was unexpectedly weighty, as though made of more than mere vellum. Hans tapped at some words on the outside, to indicate it was the warning he'd just mentioned. Nick thought, this is the very item for which Henry Ashe is searching, on behalf of the King. His first impulse was to hobble out of the Southwark lodging of Antony de Worde, to return to Nonesuch House, find the man calling himself Ashe and deliver the manuscript with some pithy comment. But a moment's further thought told him that that would be foolish. He'd be walking back into the lions' den all over again. No, he'd return the scroll to Alan Dole, who owned it.

Another small mystery was solved while he was being restored at Antony de Worde's. Hans produced a scrap of paper which, he said, had fallen from Nick's pocket. It was the piece Nick picked up in Dole's room, the one bearing the words '*Guilielmus Shakespeare hoc fecit*' or 'William Shakespeare did this'. Hans identified the writing as Dole's. It was the same writing as on the original foul papers brought to the printing-house. Christopher Dole was determined that Shakespeare should be taken as the author of this dangerous work. Not only had he spread rumours round town to that effect and provided a mocking version of Shakespeare's coat of arms on the title page, he had left a slip of paper claiming the false authorship inside a copy of the book. There was something pitiful in that little scrap of paper.

'So we are going to perform *The English Brothers*?' said Nick Revill.

'Yes,' said Shakespeare. 'It's a good story. It has rivalry between noble knights, the threat of battle and the drumbeat of patriotism, it has love unrequited and devotion rewarded. And we think it would be a fitting tribute to Christopher Dole.'

'As well as being likely to draw in an audience,' said Richard Burbage. 'In fact, the circumstances of Dole's death give off a whiff of tragedy and pathos so that alone will probably attract a few people. We'll put it about that *The English Brothers* was his final masterpiece.'

Nick was astounded to hear these things. They were sitting, the three of them, in the small, snug office behind the Globe stage. A fire was burning while the weather beyond the walls of the building was bitter. If it continued like this the river would freeze over. Every sight or thought of the river reminded Nick of Nonesuch House and his encounter with the Privy Council agent. Looking back, it seemed more like a dream, a bad dream, than reality.

Nick had not gained anything from his adventure on London Bridge, except a renewed respect for the power of the river. But nor had he lost anything of significance, such as his life or liberty. There had been no serious consequences. That is, no hue and cry after an individual by the name of Richard Newman. By now, Ashe must have discovered that no such person existed, at least not as a player with the Admiral's Men. And, presumably, Ashe would have concluded that Newman – whoever he was – had perished after making an ill-judged attempt to escape from Nonesuch House. It was not the kind of failure Ashe would be keen to enlarge on to his superiors, like Secretary Cecil. Nick had some anxiety that he could have been identified by anyone coming to see him at the Globe, but it helped that when Ashe questioned him he was wearing the false beard of lamb's wool; it also helped that his face was dyed a darker colour than natural. And, although Ashe had undoubtedly glimpsed him in The Ram, as well as hearing him give the false identity to George Bruton, the illumination in the tavern was little better than in the street outside.

So Richard Newman vanished as if he'd never come into being. It was fitting, really, since Henry Ashe had not existed either.

But now Nick could not understand why the shareholders of the King's Men were looking to stir up more trouble by staging a performance of *The English Brothers*.

Nick had already got rid of the original *Play of Adam*. He'd returned it to Alan Dole, only hinting at the trouble it had caused him. He did not say that it was possible that King James himself was interested in the Oseney text. That was none of his business. Dole was glad to have the manuscript back but only in the way that one might be glad to see a dangerous animal put back in its cage. What he said about the dubious provenance of the play, and its connection with murders in Ely and elsewhere, showed why he was wary of it.

Nick said a little more about his adventures to William Shakespeare, and was gratified at the look of horror that passed across WS's face and then the mixture of contrition and concern that followed it. But now, some time afterwards, they were talking about performing Dole's play, despite its connection with *The Play of Adam*.

'What about the warning?' asked Nick. 'The prior's words on the scroll about being infected with the worm of madness?'

'You are superstitious?' said WS.

'Well, you can hardly say that this *Play of Adam* has brought luck to those involved with it: not only the fate of Christopher Dole but those earlier stories of misfortune from Oseney and Ely.'

'The dangerous lines to do with Cain and Abel shall be removed,' said WS.

'While any references that nasty minds might think refer satirically to King James will also be cut,' added Burbage. 'There is no sense in offending our royal patron.'

'Or falling foul of the Council,' said Nick.

'I am adding a scene or two of my own,' said WS, 'as well as smoothing out some of Dole's.'

'I thought you believed him to be an inferior writer,' said Nick. 'Besides, it looks as if he wrote *The English Brothers* mostly as an act of revenge.'

A pained look seemed to pass across Shakespeare's face. He said: 'Christopher is dead and *de mortuis nihil nisi bonum*, you know. Let us speak only good things of the dead, in the hope that others will treat us in a similar style after we have departed. Now that I look more closely at the piece, I think better of it. I am even prepared to overlook the mocking coat of arms on the title page. Perhaps I was too harsh on Dole when he was alive. If so, I shall make up for it now.'

William Shakespeare did make up for it. He tinkered with *The English Brothers*, and a handful of other dramatists threw in some extra scenes and lines until the play became a strange, mingled affair, the work of several hands but growing out of

Christopher Dole's original conception and advertised as being by the late dramatist.

Burbage's commercial instinct was correct. Whatever the reason, whether it was the stirring quality of the story, or the melancholy tale of Dole's end and the hint that he'd left behind him a great work, *The English Brothers* became a palpable hit for the King's Men. It was performed several times and revived the following year. It was even published, in the revised form, and sold by Alan Dole, among other booksellers. From beyond the grave, Christopher Dole achieved his dream of being acclaimed – although all he had been seeking was revenge.

Alan Dole treated the returned manuscript of *The Play of Adam* with great care.

Unlike his brother, he did not study its contents carefully, let alone make use of them. But he did read several times over the warning penned by Alan of Walsingham, the Prior of Ely, wondering how Christopher could have neglected it. The bookseller was sufficiently alarmed to contemplate sealing the document up again. But the broken seal seemed like a broken egg, something that could not be restored to its former state. Nor could he bring himself to destroy the document, however dangerous it might be. He had too much reverence for the word, whether hand-written or printed, sacred or profane. Instead, he caused *The Play of Adam* to be bound into a book and put away, for good.

It is not quite true to say that Nick Revill gained nothing from the business. He acquired a new friend when he returned to Mrs Atkins' house, where the unfortunate Christopher Dole had lodged. There he found that Sara Atkins, who was indeed a widow, was happy to salve more than the wounds inflicted by her son. Stephen he could not persuade himself to like, but the attractions of his mother were sufficient to make Nick move north of the river. He did not live up in the garret but in a more spacious chamber close to Mrs Atkins' own. Sara offered Nick bed and board. The board was at a mutually agreed rate. The bed was free.

ACT FOUR

London, July 1821

Joe Malinferno peered at the lozenge-shaped figure again. The images wobbled in the flickering, yellow light of the single candle set on the surface that doubled as his desk and dining table. His eyes swam and his head ached. What did it mean, this little procession of pictures? He could make out the seated lion, the feather, and the two birds. Even the stylised palm of a hand was discernible. But what were all the other shapes for? And what did they all signify? He wrung out the wet cloth that had been soaking in a bowl of water at his elbow, and applied the cold poultice to his forehead. It eased the fevered ache, but did not bring enlightenment. A warm hand touched his hunched shoulder, and he looked up. It was Doll Pocket, a shawl wrapped around her bare shoulders and partly covering her high-bodiced muslin dress.

'Time for bed, Joe. You'll never figure it out, the state you're in.'

He patted her hand, and sighed deeply. 'I'll never figure it out anyway.'

Malinferno had set himself up as an Egyptological expert a number of years ago in the wake of the fashionable fervour for all things to do with that far-off land. Of course, it had been England's old enemy Napoleon Bonaparte who had started the craze after his expedition to Egypt in 1798. But that mattered not to London society, and soon there was a fashion amongst the wealthy for owning obelisks and statues plundered from the ancient past. Then more recently there grew a vogue for 'unrolling' mummies. At aristocratic soirées, Egyptian mummies that had lain untouched by grave-robbers for thousands of years were unceremoniously unravelling from their bindings. Their innermost secrets were exposed to the curious but ignorant stares of English lord and ladies in the name of entertainment. Malinferno had cashed in on the trend by selling his services as an expert 'unroller' to the élite. His decision to do so had not been entirely motivated by greed, though he did appropriate for himself some of the gems and scarabs hidden in the bandages wrapped round the mummies. He justified his actions by telling himself that someone less sensitive to the antiquarian value of the unrolling would destroy valuable finds on the altar of gross curiosity. He had recently found, in the process of unrolling three mummies, several small papyrus texts with Egyptian hieroglyphs on them, and salvaged them in the interests of scholarship. These curious symbols were inscribed on papyrus, carved on upright stones, and on walls and tombs all over Egypt. Malinferno, along with many other scholars and savants of the day, was fascinated by their mystery. It had become his fervent wish to be the first to unlock the mystery of these images. But two years of fevered thinking had brought him exactly nowhere.

Doll unwound the cold compress from his head, and stroked his damp and chilly brow.

'Don't despair, Joe. You'll get there.' She squatted before his hunched figure. 'Shall we go to Montagu House again, and see the stone?'

Malinferno knew that Doll was referring to the famous

stone classified as EA24 – Egyptian Antiquity 24 – that resided in the British Museum. Currently located in Montagu House, the museum had possession of the remarkable stone stolen from the French twenty years earlier. It was otherwise known as the Rosetta Stone. There was a text written in three languages on its broken surface, one of them being Greek, one an unknown language, and one being the mysterious hieroglyphs of the Egyptians. Over the years, many scholars had tried to decipher the pictograms found on Egyptian monuments and papyruses, and the Rosetta Stone was seen as the key. The physician and mathematician Thomas Young was the latest scholar in England to try his luck, but even he was struggling. Now Malinferno was beginning to wonder why he had had the temerity to imagine he could do it.

He looked down at Doll's remarkable cleavage, and shook his aching head.

'I think not, Doll. It will do me no good. This is a waste of time.'

He pushed the crackling papyruses on the table to one side. Though the sun was coming up through the dusty bow window of his rented rooms in Creechurch Lane, London, he realised Doll had only just returned home.

'Let's go and find a chop-house that's open and, over breakfast, you can tell me what kept you out all night.'

Doll Pocket looked away guiltily from his gaze.

'It was business, Joe. Honest.'

Malinferno hoped it was not Doll's old business that she was referring to. He wouldn't want that, even if they were stony-broke again. He had first met her in Madame de Trou's bawdy house in Petticoat Lane. A gold sovereign had been burning a hole in his pocket, and he had a similar heat in his breeches. But having been introduced to Doll, whose blonde tresses had been covered up by a black wig, he had lost track of his carnal desires. She had been fascinated by something more alluring about Joe than his privates, and it had all been his fault. Before getting down to business, he could not resist showing off his erudition concerning Egyptology. The night had flown by as this raven-haired doxy absorbed all he knew about the subject. Doll was what one might call a rabid autodidact, not only absorbing knowledge from whom she could, but interpreting it in the process. That night, she finally pulled off her wig, shook out her natural hair, and revealed her true self. From that moment, Doll's retirement from the business, and their friendship, was agreed. It was not long before she outstripped Malinferno in her understanding of many subjects, though she herself laughed at his description of her as a savant.

'An idiot-savant more like,' she once said, unfortunately mangling the French pronunciation. But he knew she was a natural talent, and indulged her. She refused to expose her erudition to anyone other than Joe, however, preferring to pass for a dumb-headed doxy in a male world that was only too eager to treat her as one.

Now she could see what was on Joe's mind, and came clean about what she had been doing all night.

'I was doing as you suggested a while ago, and trying to get a part in *The Taming of the Shrew* at Drury Lane. I met Kean himself.'

Malinferno gasped at Doll's audacity. Though he had expressed admiration at her ability to imitate the manners of the nobility in more than one of their escapades, she had had no theatrical training. And here she was approaching the great actor Edmund Kean, currently celebrated for his interpretation of Shylock, to ask for a part in a Shakespearean comedy. Malinferno hesitated before daring to ask Doll what the master's reply was to her enquiry. She grimaced, an unfamiliar blush appearing on her cheeks.

'I ... er ... persuaded the stage doorman to let me backstage after the play finished.'

Malinferno looked at her charming figure, and could easily guess how she had achieved that. His silence urged her to continue.

'I caught Mr Kean in his dressing room, and offered to clean the slap from his face.' She paused. 'That is the word we actors use for make-up, you know. Slap.' Her blush spread down her neck at this mild exaggeration of her experience to date. 'He allowed me to do so, and I wiped away the dark colouring of Shylock and teased the false beard from his chin. Of course I had to straddle his ... thighs to achieve this, and as he was in a state of déshabillé, I found myself in some intimacy with him.'

By now the roseate blush had spread to Doll's bosom, and Joe marvelled at the unfamiliar effect. He was also curious as to the result of her Herculean efforts.

'And was your ploy successful?'

Doll pulled a face, and wrapped her shawl around her exposed flesh.

'Nah. The bastard took me for that type of actress who is no better than a bawd. He groped me, and so I stuck my knee in his groin and beat a retreat.' She sighed. 'My days of being laced mutton are well and truly over.'

Malinferno burst out laughing, imagining the great tragedian turning an unusual shade of green and clutching his privates in agony. Perhaps the experience of exquisite pain could be drawn on when next he performed King Lear. But Doll Pocket was clearly in no mood to laugh.

'And that's my days as an actress over too. And before they'd even started. What am I going to do, Joe?'

Malinferno stifled his laughter and sympathised, stroking Doll's shoulder.

'There will be other parts, Doll.'

'Yes, I suppose I could be a mountebank, and go bareback trick riding in Astley's Amphitheatre.'

Picturing her in that famous circus bouncing along on the back of a horse, it was an image that Malinferno found irresistible. But he knew Doll was not of the same opinion. She so wanted to be a legitimate actress in one of the great theatres – either Drury Lane or Covent Garden. But it seemed the most she could hope for was to feature in one of the unlicensed theatres that had sprung up all around London.

Disconsolate, she idly leafed through the papyrus sheets that Malinferno had been poring over so unsuccessfully. She turned her head as though trying to see them another way than how Joe had been construing them. She stared, and then twisted the paper round.

'Which way do you look at these, Joe?'

Malinferno's stomach was beginning to rumble at the thought of a chop for breakfast, and tried to divert Doll's attention from the puzzle on the papyrus.

'Upside down, if you wish. Now, what about the chop-house?'

Doll airily waved her hand, and sat down in the chair Joe had been occupying.

'You go, Joe. I am not at all hungry.'

He sighed, knowing that, when her attention had been captured by something, Doll Pocket would not be moved by simple considerations of food and drink. He decided to let her be distracted from her disappointment about play-acting for a while. He was ravenous, if she was not. So, leaving her to gaze at the hieroglyphs, he grabbed his garrick, pulled the shabby but serviceable overcoat on, and went in search of food.

He eventually found himself trudging past the stench of Billingsgate fish market, and over the river at London Bridge. He had in his mind that he might find his old friend Augustus Bromhead at an unpretentious chop-house in Unicorn Passage just off Tooley Street, south of the Thames. Bromhead lived in a rickety tenement house in Bermondsey, and knew all the best eating houses on the south bank of the mighty river. He had introduced Malinferno to this establishment a year or two ago, but Joe had not been back since. He would not have walked so far, but was suddenly eager to conjoin good food with stimulating conversation.

On entering the low-ceilinged, smoky chop-house, he saw he was in luck. A curiously shaped fellow, resembling a tadpole because of his large, leonine head and stubby body, was perched on a high stool at the back of the premises. Augustus Bromhead was apparently breaking his fast with a steaming plate of well-cooked chops and boiled potatoes. Malinferno shimmied his way through the crowded room without disturbing the stolid transfer of food to the mouths of the numerous diners, and slid on to the bench opposite to his friend. The little man acknowledged his arrival with just a nod of his oversize head. His jaw was occupied with the mastication of his meal. When he finally swallowed, he wiped his lips with a stained napkin, and spoke.

'Giuseppe . . .' he always used Joe's proper name, reminding him of his Italian origins, '. . . dear boy, you look as though you have been burning the midnight oils. I have not seen such baleful, red eyes since I stared into the awful face of Ben Crouch of the Borough Gang.'

He was referring to the notorious resurrection man and

leader of a gang of body-snatchers who had nearly done for him and Malinferno both. Malinferno shuddered at being reminded of the incident.

'I have been working on the Egyptian hieroglyphs in my possession. All to no avail, I fear.'

'Ah.'

Malinferno could hear in the brief monosyllable the sound of Bromhead's disapproval. Augustus was an antiquarian of some repute, but his obsession was British history. He considered this unseemly fad for the artefacts and symbols of a far-distant land a temporary aberration and complete waste of time. He had told Malinferno so several times, attempting to bring him back to the right and proper course of study by pointing him in the direction of British history, particularly King Arthur and his putative bones, on more than one occasion. Bromhead was deprecating about the significance of the Egyptian pictorial images, and now said so.

'Take it from me they are no more than a rebus. A puzzle in pictures.'

'That is not what Champollion thinks.'

Bromhead snorted in derision.

'That upstart Frenchie? He knows nothing. And besides, has he not gone quiet the last few years?'

Malinferno had to admit that Champollion did seem to have disappeared off the face of scholarship after a brief blaze of early glory. Most English scholars now thought he had gone down a blind alley and, having failed miserably, hidden himself away in shame. The torch was now being carried in England by Thomas Young.

A waiter in a dirty long white apron, which betrayed the signs of several lost battles with the gravy on the plates he served, came and took Malinferno's order. Both men were silent as the waiter cleared Augustus' empty plate from the table. After he had gone, Bromhead reached down from his high stool, on which he had to sit to reach the level of the table, and groped for a leather satchel on the floor. When his outstretched fingers failed to reach it, Malinferno took pity. He lifted it up, noting how heavy it was.

'What do you have in there, Gus? It feels like a whole library of books.'

Bromhead ignored his companion's deliberate shortening of his first name. He hated being called Gus, and Malinferno knew it. And he knew it was said just to provoke him, so he kept calm. He stroked the battered leather satchel.

'You are not far wrong there, my friend. It is a whole series of plays in one, in fact.'

Bromhead lifted the flap of the satchel, and extracted a dusty tome from its interior. The leather was dry and cracked, and so old as to be of an indeterminate hue. He reverently tipped the book on its back and laid it on the table, carefully avoiding the wet ring left from the base of his ale mug. He brushed more dust from the book's surface.

'I found it in a poky little bookshop in a lane leading off Paternoster Row close by St Paul's Cathedral. I had never seen the passage before as it was so narrow. And it was only out of curiosity that I ventured down it this time. The only shop open in the lane was a dingy affair that looked as though it had not changed since Jacobean times. The sign over the door read Dole's Printers, and guessing that there might be some gems mouldering away inside the shop, I went in. The interior was a jumble of pamphlets and badly printed books, overseen by an old man who looked as antique as the shop itself. Indeed he blended so well into his surroundings that I did not see him until I had raised some dust by lifting a few tomes up. It caused him to cough like some diseased sheep. A sort of cross between a bleat and a death-rattle. I apologised and moved to the back of the shop, further away from his ink-stained desk. It was there I found this.'

He placed his hand on the book before them, patting it affectionately like the head of some favoured grandchild. Malinferno could bear the suspense no longer.

'But what is it that makes you value it so much?'

There were no words embossed on the front of the book or the spine to give away its secret. And Bromhead was clearly determined to keep his companion in suspense a little longer. He was also keen to impress Malinferno with the marvellous bargain he had come across, so he ignored the question and continued his tale.

'I could tell from the edges of the pages that it was old, because they are not made of paper but of vellum. Sheets of vellum stitched together at the edge, and bound in leather. I knew it would be something rare, but did not wish to reveal my interest to the old man in the shop. However, I could not resist a peep. I idly lifted the cover, and looked inside.'

He mimicked his action in the shop for Malinferno's benefit. But as Malinferno bent down to examine the contents thus half-revealed, Augustus snapped the cover shut again. A little puff of dust flew out from the edge of the tome, causing Malinferno to sneeze. Apparently, he was to be kept in suspense a while longer.

'What I saw convinced me I had to purchase the book. I lifted it up, aware for the first time of its weight, and walked across to the old man, who sat on his bench at the door like the guardian of Hell. When he saw what I had found, he sniffed disdainfully.

'"Why should you want that old thing? It's only some original manuscript for a set of plays my forebears printed off years ago. I was even told that bad luck follows those who enact the plays, especially that of 'Cain and Abel'. However, I can sell you a fair copy of the eleventh edition set in Baskerville. Here, I will find it for you."

'Before I could protest, he rose creakily from his post, and wove his way through the piles of books that rose like accretions of sea-eroded rocks by the shore. He disappeared for a quarter of an hour in the back of the shop, and I was all for grabbing the manuscript and running. But finally he returned, even more dust-covered than he had been when he left. In his hand he held an old book, poorly bound with gold blocking on it that had faded over the years. But it was still possible to read it. It was called *The Play of Adam*. He thrust the printed book at me.

'"Here it is. I knew we had a copy somewhere."

'Though I didn't want it, I saw that I was not going to leave without the book he had found for me. So after some dickering we agreed a price that included both the printed text, and the manuscript. And it was a rare bargain, I can tell you.'

Bromhead finally sat back with a smug look on his round face. Malinferno took his chance, and opened the book at last. Thinking he was going to see the crabbed hand of some Jacobean writer, he was filled with curiosity about the contents. What he saw astonished him, and he turned the crackling pages with great care. Finally, he dared to speak.

'It's a medieval manuscript, isn't it?'

Bromhead nodded eagerly. 'In a very educated hand. It is not illuminated, but must be the— Take care, you idiot!'

His cry of anguish was not due to Malinferno's handling of the book, but for the careless waiter who had finally brought Malinferno's meal. The man dumped the chops and boiled potatoes in gravy heavily on the table, spattering the brown, greasy concoction in which the chops swam perilously close to the precious manuscript. He grunted an apology and would have compounded his error by wiping the surface of the manuscript with his dirty apron. But Bromhead managed to stay his hand, and he retreated grumbling about gentlemen treating the eating-house as if it were a library. While Malinferno tucked into his meal, Bromhead explained his plans for *The Play of Adam*.

'I am seeking a theatre that might put on the plays included in this manuscript. It must be hundreds of years since they have last been performed. I have a little money available to me, though I shall need a rich sponsor too. I am to talk to Will Mossop, the manager of the Royal Coburg, this very day.'

Malinferno, who until this point had not paid much attention to what his friend had said, suddenly perked up. If Bromhead was prepared to pay to mount this play, maybe he would take on Doll in one of the parts. It did not need to be a major role, simply enough to assuage her desire to be an actress. Frankly, he thought she would not stick at it once she discovered how hard and repetitive the work was. He just needed to ensure she got the madcap scheme out of her system.

He swallowed a rather gristly piece of pork chop and, once recovered from the coughing fit it induced, enquired of Bromhead how far he had progressed in selecting a cast. The little man swayed on his seat, shaking his overlarge dome in such a way that Malinferno thought he might topple from his perch.

'I have not yet settled on the theatre, let alone thought of actors. That is why I am seeing Mossop. Anyway, I would leave the choice of actors to the theatre manager.'

Malinferno grimaced. It would not be so easy to persuade an experienced theatrical person to go along with choosing

293

Doll. On the other hand, the money man should carry some weight, so it was as well to keep in with Bromhead.

The Egyptological expert pushed his empty plate to one side, scrutinised the first page of the manuscript, and read the opening words out loud.

"'I am gracious and great God without beginning.
I am maker unmade; all might is in me.
I am life and way, unto weal winning.
I am foremost and first; as I bid, shall it be.'"

They were obviously the words of God, so that wouldn't be a part for Doll Pocket. He wondered if there was some small part for her to play. And as he turned the heavy, stiff pages he saw it. The next play was 'The Fall of Man', and he read aloud the dialogue down to the seductive words spoken by Eve to Adam as she offered him the apple.

"'Bite on boldly, for it is true;
We shall be gods, and know everything!'"

He looked at Bromhead with a winning smile on his face.
'I know just the actress for the role of Eve.'

The very person he had in mind was at that moment not thinking at all of her career as an actress. Doll had become engrossed in the puzzle of the Egyptian hieroglyphs that had so exercised Malinferno's brain. She had read his notebook, where he had recorded the discoveries of Thomas Young concerning the name Ptolemy. It had astonished Doll to learn from Malinferno that this ruler of Egypt wasn't really Egyptian, but Greek. And his name, according to Young, appeared on the Rosetta Stone at least three times.

The mathematician had even tentatively identified some of the symbols as spelling out Ptolemy's name sound by sound. And as Ptolemy had wed Berenice, Young assumed the next cartouche was her name, and identified some other sounds. But Young and many others still considered the signs and symbols on obelisks and papyruses as representing ideas not words. It was only the foreign Greek names that were different. So Doll spent the morning comparing Young's translated sounds with the cartouches in Joe's papyrus texts. The most promising name was frustratingly close to completion, and yet so far away. She looked at the word she had scribbled down in Joe's notebook inserting dashes for the letters Young could not supply.

-OLE I P KE—KE

It was not very promising, but it had fired her imagination. She could see another possibility if only the bird symbol was not the 'ke' sound from the end of Berenice. Just as she began to try other sequences of symbols, she heard the creak of the stairs up to the first-floor rooms that Joe rented from Mrs Stanhope. She knew his gait, and the way he took two steps at a time when he was excited. She pushed the pen and ink aside, and turned round in the chair that was one of only two in the sparsely furnished parlour. The door burst open, and Malinferno entered with a look of the deepest pleasure on his face.

'Doll. I have some news for you.'

She grinned, patting the papyruses on the table. 'And I for you. I think I have made a breakthrough with the hieroglyphs . . .'

She stopped in her tracks when she saw the dark look that came over his face at her news. She realised she had made a mistake by telling him she had potentially solved in a few hours a problem that had had him stumped for weeks, if not months. She changed tack, rising from the chair, and crossing the room towards him.

'But it's probably all wrong. Tell me what your news is.'

Malinferno, crushed by what Doll had said, looked cautiously at her. 'You're sure you want to know?'

She hugged him close to her ample bosom, and squeaked in the most mindless way she could muster, 'Ooooh, yes, kind sir. What treats do you have in store for me?'

He couldn't help himself, and a smile cracked his downcast features.

'I may have a part for you in a play.'

Doll Pocket gasped. Despite the distractions of her Egyptian studies, this was news indeed.

'Really?' Her voice, normally low and seductive, went up a pitch in genuinely uncontrolled excitement. She looked hard into Joe's eyes, however. 'You're not teasing me, are you? Only I wouldn't forgive you if you were.'

'Would I do that? No, Bromhead has found an old copy of some Biblical plays, and fancies to put them on in the West End.'

Doll gasped. The matter of the plays didn't sound alluring, but the idea of performing in the shadow of Drury Lane or Covent Garden certainly was.

'When can we talk to him about it? Which theatre has he booked?'

Malinferno saw he had run a little ahead of himself in his desires to cheer up Doll. She had pulled away from his embrace, and had grabbed the empty ewer on the sideboard. She was all for fetching some fresh water, and reviving herself with a wash and some perfume preparatory to meeting Bromhead in his new guise of impresario. But before she could dash out the door to get some water from Mrs Stanhope, Malinferno put a restraining hand on her arm.

'Hold on, Doll. He hasn't quite got there yet. He has only just found this medieval manuscript of something called *The Play of Adam*. It's all Adam and Eve, and Cain and Abel, and the Flood and such. But he hasn't sold his idea to anyone yet.'

Doll's shoulders slumped. 'I knew it was too much to hope for. Damn it, Joe, I was looking forward to it already. I could be the first woman, Eve.'

It was of course the very thought that Malinferno had had over breakfast, and which he had mooted with Bromhead. And the idea of Doll Pocket as the naked seductress still aroused him in a familiar way.

'It will happen, Doll. Only just not yet.'

His companion did not look convinced, and Malinferno wished he hadn't mentioned Augustus' idea. He rested his backside on the table edge, and the papyrus rustled beneath him. It gave him an idea of how to raise Doll from her sudden depression.

'Now, how about we follow your suggestion, and go to the British Museum, and take a look at exhibit EA24.'

Doll smiled, and immediately reached for her favourite headgear, an oriental turban in lavish brocaded material of the sort also favoured by Queen Caroline.

Montagu House was quite crowded, especially in the Egyptian Gallery, where everyone was hurrying to the far end of the room. As Malinferno and Doll Pocket approached the back of the tightly packed mob, they could see what all the fuss was about. Set between two tall windows in order to give it the best light stood the massive bust that was known as *Young Memnon*. One of Malinferno's countrymen, Giovanni Belzoni, had engineered its shipment from Egypt to London. There the Royal Corps of Sappers and Miners had used a huge block-and-tackle system set in an A-frame to hoist the head onto the plinth on which it now stood. It had been a Herculean task, and the bust was only recently cleared of its encumbrances of thick ropes and struts. It was now a glorious sight, despite the hole drilled in its right shoulder by the Frenchman Drovetti for the insertion of dynamite. It had been his idea to blast the colossus to pieces in order to reduce its mass for shipment. Belzoni, a hydraulic engineer and circus strongman, had managed the task without such drastic action being taken. It was now the latest wonder for the Egyptian-obsessed gentry to marvel at.

Doll and Joe, however, gave it only a cursory glance. There were no hieroglyphs on the bust, and so it was not a curiosity to hold their attention for long. They carried on down the gallery, lingering only to cast their eyes over the obsidian monolith that was Nectanebo's sarcophagus. It too was covered in hieroglyphs, and so merited passing attention. But EA24 was their goal.

The battered block of stone was almost black in colour. However, Malinferno had been told by his friend Thomas Elder, who worked at the BM, that it was so because someone had covered it with boot polish in order to make the whitened inscriptions stand out better. At the bottom of the stone, with only the right corner lost, was a text in Greek. Above it was a band of writing in an unknown script. Then above that stood the fragmentary section of Egyptian hieroglyphs. And in the midst of the puzzling symbols, there was the cartouche Malinferno and Doll had been trying to decipher. They were alone before the mysterious object, and stood in silence, examining its surface. Malinferno felt as if he were communing directly with the ancient scholar who had carved the stone. The man's lips were making the shape of words, but no sound was issuing forth. So he simply could not understand what the scribe was attempting to say to him. Meanwhile, Doll had leaned closer to the stone and her eyes moved from side to side along the Greek text. Malinferno could see that her lips, too, were moving silently. Puzzled by his companion's actions, he went to speak. But Doll held up her hand to stop him, and she carried on scanning the lines of Greek text.

After a while, she still ignored Malinferno's obvious signs of boredom, and turned her attention to the hieroglyphs at the top. So he ambled away to look at some more of the artefacts that had been taken from the French at the turn of the century. When the French in Egypt had surrendered to the English in 1801, one of the spoils of war had been a large collection of items gathered by French savants. The stone EA24 had been one, and Nectanebo's sarcophagus another. Malinferno drifted over to further spoils in the form of a row of lion-headed statues of the goddess Sekhmet. Then he heard a bitter voice ringing out down the long gallery.

'Look, Étienne. Yet more of the English plunder like that taken from us twenty years ago.'

Surprised by the familiar voice, Malinferno looked towards its source. Standing at the back of the mêlée that still clung around *Young Memnon*, he saw a figure he recognised. It was of an old man dressed in an antiquated form of court garb that had gone out of fashion years ago. And atop the fellow's head was a powdered, white wig only affected by footmen these days. He was leaning heavily on a cane, and favouring his left leg which, though sporting a well-shaped calf, Malinferno knew to be wooden. Thomas Chippendale the Younger would have been proud of its shape. Indeed, he may well have turned it in his workshop.

Jean-Claude Casteix was one of those savants who had collected Egyptian artefacts for Napoleon Bonaparte, only to see them stolen by the British. Swallowing his pride, Casteix and some of his colleagues had followed them to London. The French general Menou had been scornful of the scientists' behaviour, suggesting they could be 'stuffed for the purpose' of the voyage, along with their trinkets. Casteix reviled the English, and hated his exile, but had preferred to stay with the goods he had accumulated in Egypt. Now he stood sneering at the latest English out-rage: the huge statue of *Young Memnon* stolen by Belzoni from under the very nose of the French Consul-General, Bernadino Drovetti.

His remark, intended to carry through the Egyptian Gallery, and overheard by Malinferno, was addressed to his companion, an elegant and, in contrast to Casteix, fashion-ably attired young man. Casteix's disdainful gaze turned Malinferno's way, and fell on him just as Doll called out to him.

'Joe, I've just worked out something interesting.'

Malinferno tried to ignore Casteix, whom he had once consulted to learn more about Egyptology, only to be regaled with a tale concerning the loss of the Frenchman's left leg to the snapping bite of a crocodile in the Nile waters. He hur-ried back to Doll Pocket, but could hear the stomping thud of Casteix's wooden leg approaching up the gallery.

'What's that, Doll?'

Doll's eyes were bright. 'I've just calculated that there are some four hundred and eighty Greek words on the stone.'

Malinferno knew better than to question Doll's figure, even though he knew she could not have had time to count every word. But she was fearfully adept with mathematical calculations. So he confined himself to querying the import of this revelation.

'And what use is that in deciphering the words on the stone?'

'Indeed, young lady, what can be the import of such irrelevant knowledge?'

The second enquiry, disdainful in its tone, came from the breathless Jean-Claude Casteix, who had now joined them before EA24. The other man, fitter apparently, for his breathing hardly increased at all, stood at his friend's shoulder, his head cocked on one side like an alert hound.

Doll Pocket smiled enigmatically. 'It is meaningless. Unless you compare it with the number of hieroglyphs on the stone. By my reckoning, there are one thousand four hundred and ten of those.'

Casteix's companion looked puzzled, and, pointing with his silver-topped cane, spoke up in a distinct and, to Doll's ears, engaging French accent. 'Madame, what have all these numbers to do with decipherment?'

Casteix hurriedly interposed an explanation of the other man's interest, introducing him with a flourish of his hand. 'Monsieur Étienne Quatremain, here, is, like Champollion, a student of hieroglyphs.'

Quatremain waved away his friend's flattering description. 'I am no more than an amateur filled with curiosity. Not to be compared with Champollion, the future translator of hieroglyphs.'

Doll looked askance at Malinferno, who contained his disbelief over Quatremain's claim for his countryman. He merely raised his eyes to the ornate ceiling over their heads. The preening Frenchman meanwhile continued in his charming tones.

301

'But you have still not explained, Madame, your obsession with the numbers.'

Doll smiled sweetly, and fluttered her eyelids at the young Frenchman. Malinferno could see all the signs of Doll being in one of her moods when she pretended to be dim-witted to fool someone. Such a deception usually ended in the discomfiture of the other party. Surprisingly, though, she did not spring the trap on Quatremain this time. Instead she giggled inanely.

'I'm sure there is some meaning in them, sir. But for the moment I cannot see it.'

Casteix snorted, his opinion of womankind confirmed.

'Come, Étienne, let us seek more stimulating company elsewhere.'

His sweeping gesture was somewhat spoiled by his hand almost knocking his antique wig off his head. He clutched at it and, leaving it a little askew, stomped off down the gallery, scattering the idle gawpers in front of *Young Memnon*. His young companion bowed elegantly, his cane held to one side, and turned to follow. But not before he cast a wink in the direction of Doll. Malinferno wasn't sure, but he thought he saw a simpering smile of pleasure fleetingly play across her features. And it did not seem feigned to his jealous eye. With a proprietorial gesture, he took her arm.

'What was all that about numbers of words on the stone?'

'Don't you see? It's obvious.'

He always got vexed when Doll made it clear that he was slow in reaching what for her was an obvious conclusion. He might have walked away and sulked for the rest of the day, except he desperately wanted to know what she had concluded.

'No, I don't see. And I don't understand why, if it is so obvious, you didn't tell Casteix and what'shisname.'

He feigned not recalling Quatremain's name, as if the man was of no significance to him, when in fact he had got under his skin.

Doll squeezed his arm, pulling him close to her side. 'Is Joe just a teensy bit jealous of the elegant Monsieur Étienne? He is quite handsome, isn't he? But the reason why I didn't tell them my conclusion was so that the old man didn't rush off and beat us to it.'

'Beat us?'

'To solving the riddle of the hieroglyphs.'

Malinferno's curiosity overcame his exasperation at Doll's obtuseness. 'And how is the riddle to be solved by us?'

Doll stuck her fingers under her turban and scratched her head. 'Well, it's only a start, you understand.'

Malinferno growled, and Doll held up her hands defensively.

'If the Greek text is made up of four hundred and eighty words and the hieroglyphs amount to one thousand four hundred . . .'

'. . . and ten. You said one thousand four hundred and ten.'

Doll grinned conspiratorially. 'Oh, I added the ten to my estimate to make it sound more clever. But the point is, bearing in mind that the two texts are the same, then the disparity in numbers suggests that—'

Malinferno broke in. 'That each hieroglyph is a letter, not a symbol of ideas or a full word.'

'Give the man a prize!'

'But it still doesn't tell us their meanings.'

Doll's face fell a little. 'I know, but it's a start. Now we know each picture is a letter. Let's go back and see if we can decipher that cartouche. You see, I have an idea.'

*

They had hurried back to Creechurch Lane, intent on cracking the code. But an exciting message diverted them from
even looking at the papyruses left lying on the table. As they
climbed the stairs to Malinferno's rooms, a rotund figure
waddled out of the ground-floor parlour. It was their landlady. Mrs Stanhope's mobcap sat askew on her head, and
her face was flushed. When she spoke, her slurred voice
betrayed her having imbibed the best part of a bottle of gin,
despite it being not yet the middle of the day. She leaned
on the doorframe or she might have fallen over, and called
up the rickety stairs to her lodgers.

'Mr Mali . . . Manli . . . Joe, there is an urgent message for
you.'

Malinferno descended the stairs, and stood before his
landlady. She grinned inanely.

'A message you say?' he prompted her.

Mrs Stanhope tilted her head to one side as if pondering
the depths of his question. He observed in fascination as her
mobcap failed to tip with her head, slipping down until it
covered one eye.

'Yes. From a perfect tadpole of a man. I could have
wrapped him in a nappy and had him suckle at my breast.'

Malinferno recognised Bromhead from her description,
and cast from his mind the image of Augustus as a baby on
his landlady's large and fulsome tit. He prompted her again.

'May I have the message?'

Slowly, Mrs Stanhope's hand went up to her face, where
one long finger tapped the side of her nose. The other
hand slipped into the pocket of her apron, where it rum-
maged around interminably. Finally it drew out a slip of
paper, which was then offered to Malinferno. He took it,
and read it. Excited by its contents, he went back up to
Doll, who was hovering on the landing. She could tell by

the look on his face that the message bore interesting news.

'What does it say, Joe?'

'That we should go directly to the Royal Coburg Theatre, where Augustus Bromhead is casting his play. He says there is a part for you.'

Doll Pocket gave out a whoop, forgetting all about ancient hieroglyphs. This was the chance of a lifetime, and she was not about to give it up. She grabbed Joe's hand, and dragged him back down the stairs. Mrs Stanhope gave them a befuddled wave as they dashed out into the lane and past the church on the corner to find a cab.

They managed to hail a small fly and, having given the cabby the theatre's name, they settled back under the flimsy hood. The driver turned south, and they crossed the river by the grand new Waterloo Bridge, named for Wellington's great victory six years earlier. For some reason, Doll was beginning to have doubts about the scheme. The Thames looked grey and oily as it roiled around the Doric pillars that divided up each of the nine arches of Waterloo Bridge. The journey to the south bank seemed to take for ever, and the far side looked most unwelcoming with looming rain clouds racing towards them. She clutched Joe's arm.

'Is this the right choice to make, Joe? I mean, the Royal Coburg is not Drury Lane or Covent Garden. It is south of the river, and is not even allowed to put on serious drama. What is this play of Gus's like?'

Malinferno knew that Doll yearned to be an actress in what she called the 'legit' theatres she had mentioned by name. All other theatres in London were restricted to melodrama or burlesque. And it wasn't as if the theatre they were now approaching was even in the West End. But it was a grand theatre, and had taken its name from Princess

Charlotte, King George's only child with Queen Caroline, when she had married Leopold of Saxe-Coburg. Charlotte's death in childbirth had been a terrible tragedy, but had not marred the Royal Coburg Theatre's reputation as a popular place for entertainment. Malinferno tried to reassure Doll.

'The play is . . . a classic. You shall see.'

He knew it was stretching the truth to call 'a classic' the ancient set of mystery plays that he had seen only a brief part of. But it seemed to mollify Doll, and she perked up despite the splashes of raindrops hitting the soft cab roof. Then, as the cabby, who sat behind them to drive, turned off the Waterloo Road into The Cut, she saw the façade of the theatre straight ahead. It was an imposing and classical structure, all arches and pediments. A sudden thrill of pleasure ran up her spine, and her doubts disappeared.

Descending, Malinferno passed a silver sixpence to the driver of the fly, and he and Doll dashed across the pavement in the sudden downpour that blew over their heads. Under the cover of the theatre's portico, they paused while Doll rearranged her turban with its long ostrich feather. She reasoned she would have to look her best for the audition for the part of Eve, even if the character she might play would have originally been as naked as the day she was born. A sudden thought came to her, and she hesitated on the threshold of the auditorium, grasping Malinferno's arm.

'Joe. Was Eve born, or was she created?'

Malinferno gave her a puzzled look. 'Born of Adam's rib, of course.'

That still didn't answer Doll's question, and she felt full of confusion. How was she to play Eve, if she didn't even know the slightest thing about her? She saw that this acting lark was not as straightforward as she had anticipated. Well, she would have to rely on her manifest charms to see her through. They had served her well in the past, after all. Resolute once more, she pushed the heavy oak doors open.

Inside, the auditorium all was dark, save for a blaze of light on the stage, which must have been lit by a hundred candles. And in the light was a bevy of pretty young girls, most showing off well developed décolletages. Doll heard Malinferno sigh deeply at the array of cleavages, and suddenly she felt very old. After all, her thirtieth birthday was fast approaching. Someone in the dark of the auditorium called out a name, and the girl first in line stepped forward. She pouted and posed with her breasts thrust out, looking friskily at the huddle of figures seated in the front row of the stalls.

A male voice rang out. 'No. Next.'

The girl stamped her slipper-clad foot, and stormed off-stage. The next buxom offering stepped up, only to receive the same short shrift. This one burst into tears, and ran into the wings. A flurry of 'no's accompanied Doll's walk down the aisle to the front of the auditorium. Malinferno spotted the large head of Bromhead at the end of the front row, and he slipped into the seat next to him. Doll sat too, as the queue of hopefuls was whittled down inexorably. She began to slump in her seat. What hope did she stand if such young pulchritude was being discarded? Bromhead looked at Malinferno, and patted him on the knee. Then he turned to the young man who sat on his other side. He was a well-formed young man with a head of black curls, and was the source of the negative responses to the procession of girls on the stage. He listened to Bromhead's whisper, and held his hand up as the final girl stepped to the front of the stage. He leaned forward in his seat, and looked along at Doll. A smile broke out on his handsome face. He waved a dismissive hand at the girl onstage.

'No. You may go, Bess. I have found my Eve.'

'Gawd, Will. You said the part was mine.' The girl was clearly annoyed at the man. 'I even—'

Will rose quickly from his seat, and strode to the front of the stage. He leaned on the edge, and whispered words that seemed to mollify the angry actress. Malinferno guessed that future promises were being made in response to what he assumed was the girl's amorous offering to Will. She walked away into the darkness of the wings with a disdainful look at Doll, who still sat on the end of the front row. Bromhead rose from his seat, though his doing so didn't increase his height much from when he had been seated. He took Doll's hand, and raised her up.

'Doll Pocket, this is Will Mossop, manager of the Royal Coburg, and producer of *The Play of Adam*.'

Will tossed his curly head, and bowed elegantly, kissing Doll's proffered hand.

'Mistress Pocket, I am delighted to meet you at last. Augustus has told me much about you, and until you appeared I was fearful that we would never fill the part of Eve. Now I am a happy man.'

Once again, Malinferno witnessed Doll's simpering. This time it was at Mossop's complimentary tones, just as it had been when the Frenchman, Quatremain, fell all over her. He slumped sulkily in his seat, and wished some of the buxom young girls were still on display, so that he could simper over them and make Doll jealous. For the first time, he took note of the pile of newspapers and caricatures strewn on the crimson carpet. They were mostly of Queen Caroline and the King. The farce of the Queen being kept out of George's coronation ceremony, and their independent sexual adventures had caused a storm of cartoons in magazines like *John Bull*. And printers like George Humphrey had produced a whole series of denigratory caricatures aimed at the royals. Some of them lay at Mossop's feet now, and he picked one up. It showed a corpulent Caroline sitting at a table surrounded by her advisors, one of whom was Alderman Matthew Wood in the form of a naked, hairy devil. On a pile of books on the table stood a little mannequin Pergami, the Queen's lover who had been abandoned on the continent. The caption read: 'The Effusions of a Troubled Brain'.

Since the Queen had been turned away from the coronation of her husband due to their estranged relationship, Caroline had been a figure of great debate. These caricatures lampooned her and her Italian lover, a handsome courtier, who had been bought a defunct baronage by Caroline. The cartoons did show him to best effect, though. In the caricature, as in life, he was tall, with an enviable physique and a full head of curly black hair, luxuriant moustachios and side whiskers.

Malinferno was about to replace the caricatures on the stack of papers, when Bromhead, noticing what his friend had seen, whispered in his ear, 'Doll will make a fine Queen, do you not think?'

Malinferno was puzzled. 'I thought she was to be cast as Eve.'

Augustus waved his hand at the cartoon in Malinferno's hand, his face reddening slightly. 'Did I not explain in my note to you?'

Malinferno brought out the piece of paper given to him by Mrs Stanhope. He realised that his landlady, in tucking it securely into the pocket of her pinafore, had folded it several times. Malinferno had omitted to open the last fold, and beneath it he read the explanation for Bromhead's words. He looked his friend in the eye.

'You are to give *The Play of Adam* a topical twist to suit the present mood for matters royal?'

Bromhead pulled a face. 'Yes. It was the only way I could get the play accepted. I tried several theatres without any luck, before Will Mossop suggested that each scene should be brought bang up to date by having the characters resemble the royals. So Adam himself will look like Baron Pergami; the snake will be King George, and Eve, Queen Caroline. Each scene will be performed in that way. The Prime Minister and the Attorney-General will appear in "The Fall of Man", and Cain and Abel will be George and Pergami once again.'

Malinferno laughed out loud. He realised now why all the pretty girls had been rejected in favour of Doll. They had all been too young to bear any passing resemblance to the Queen, who was over fifty, and overweight. He wondered when the truth would dawn on Doll, and he cast a glance over at where she and Mossop were talking animatedly. As he looked on, he saw her face cloud over, and annoyance spread across her normally buoyant features. She stormed over to where Malinferno and Bromhead sat.

'I am to play Eve, because of my apparent resemblance to the Queen, Joe.'

Malinferno tried to keep a straight face. Both he and Doll had seen Caroline at closer quarters than most of the common crowd. Only a few months ago, they had been embroiled in a murder and scandal at a soirée on Solsbury Hill. The Queen had attended incognito under the name Hat Vaughan, and they had both received personal thanks from her when they had saved her already tarnished reputation from further scandal. The consequence was that neither could tell anyone of their intimacy with Caroline, having been sworn to secrecy. But they both knew that the Queen's unusually liberal lifestyle had told on her. Doll had at first taken the buxom and blowsy lady for an aging trollop, employed to amuse the titled gentlemen at the soirée. It was only later they had learned she was the Queen. Now Doll was being selected because of her likeness to Caroline.

Malinferno strove to find words to soften the blow.

'I am sure it is because of your shapeliness and not because of any reference to her age. The leading lady of a play must still be a great beauty, Doll.'

Bromhead's great leonine head nodded vigorously in agreement. 'Indeed, Doll. You will portray her obvious charms ... ' he described two orbs with cupped hands, '. . . so well, and win over the mob in the pit, hungry to view great beauty.'

Doll narrowed her eyes, trying to guess whether the two men were mocking her. Satisfied they weren't, she dipped her eyes in an exaggerated show of modest concurrence with their sentiments. She turned back to Will Mossop, who looked anxiously on. He had, after all, sent away all the other actresses, including apparently one to whom he had already promised the part of Eve.

'I will do it, Mr Mossop.'

Malinferno could already detect in her tones something of the prima donna, and sighed. She would be insufferable if this mad scheme came off, as well it might. The coronation, so very recent, was already being performed in pageant form at Drury Lane with Robert Elliston impersonating the King so well that it played to full houses. Mossop was all smiles.

'Excellent, Miss Pocket. We begin rehearsing tomorrow.'

'So soon?'

'Oh, yes, the play must open in two weeks' time, if we are to benefit from the topical nature of its presentation. And tomorrow is when you will meet Mr Morton Stanley – your Pergami.'

Malinferno didn't like the broad wink that accompanied this declaration from the theatre manager. He felt this Stanley fellow would be another seeker after Doll's attention. His comfortable position as Doll's paramour seemed to be under siege from all sides.

If Malinferno had witnessed on the following day the meeting at the Royal Coburg of Doll and Morton Stanley, he would have been really worried. The actor bore a striking resemblance to Baron Pergami, being around thirty, over six foot tall, and with a splendid physique and black curly hair, which extended down into luxuriant muttonchop whiskers. Doll, still new to the ways of theatrical folk, almost swooned away when Stanley gave her an exaggerated bow, and lifted her hand to his full red lips. Her normal perceptiveness was swamped by his manner, or she would have noticed his obvious vanity. He twirled his moustachios, and Doll simpered like one of the young girls she had seen auditioning for the role she was now to perform. Then a deep and resonant voice came from the depths of the auditorium.

'Ah, I see you have won over another beautiful lady, Stan.'

The young actor's face contorted into a mask of sheer hatred at the sound. He turned away from Doll to peer into the darkness of the rows of seats, and spoke in a baritone voice.

'I wondered who Mossop would get to play the part of *fat* King George. I might have known it would be you, Percy.'

Doll watched as a rotund, and cheery-faced man made his way down the central aisle of the ornately decorated auditorium. The man Morton called Percy did indeed resemble the King, or at least the popular caricatures of George, being portly and red-faced. He lumbered up the steps leading on to the stage, giving Doll a bow and a buss on the back of her hand. He winked conspiratorially at her.

'Perceval Tristram at your service, madam. But beware, beautiful lady, Stan will break your heart, take it from me.'

Stanley's face darkened, and he strode off into the wings, calling for Will Mossop.

Malinferno, meanwhile, had called on Augustus Bromhead in his rickety tenement in Bermondsey. The tall, narrow building, squashed between its newer neighbours was a structure from an older age. In fact, its foundations were built on the footings of an even older building. Bromhead's cellar revealed part of the arched ceiling of the crypt of Bermondsey Abbey. The antiquarian revelled in the thought that his very residence was piled up on the foundations of something so old. It matched his own life, which was built on the quest for the keys to ancient Britain. It was no accident that his study lay at the very apex of the old house, for he saw himself as at the peak of antiquarian studies. He worked surrounded by a very blizzard of old manuscripts and printed books, perched on a high stool to bring him to the height of his sloped work desk, a former accounting bench.

Malinferno sat in a more comfortable armchair by the high gabled window that let the sallow light of fog-bound London into the attic room. He had in his lap the printed version of *The Play of Adam*, purchased from Dole's Printers. In front of Bromhead the precious original manuscript itself lay open. He had stopped at a point where his fingers had felt a rough spot on the reverse of a page. Peering closer he thought he could see the remains of red sealing wax. The wax had all but gone, leaving only a roughened red patch, but he could also see some faded writing. He turned back the page and read what was written on the correct side. Puzzled, he ran his finger down the page again, before calling out to Malinferno.

'Read the ending of "Cain and Abel" to me.'

Malinferno turned the stiff pages of his printed book until he came to the relevant passage.

'It's Cain's final speech after the angel hands down God's curse on him. It ends,

"The devil take both Him and thee!
Foul may you fall!
Here is a crooked company;
Therefore, God's curse upon you all!"'

Bromhead tapped his original gleefully. 'I knew there was something different. There are two more lines attributed to the angel at the end here in the manuscript.'

'What do they say?'

Bromhead intoned the extra lines in his most solemn voice, though it cracked a little and somewhat spoiled the effect.

'"Beware the sins of envy and vainglory,
Else foul murder ends your story."'

Malinferno rose from his chair and leaned to look over his friend's shoulder.

'Let me see. Oh, yes. And yet they look like an addition done in a different hand. Could they have been added at a much later date?'

Bromhead frowned, peering closely at the intruders on the neat page of handwritten text.

'I don't think so. The script is still very old, and I would swear that it has been done by the same hand. The only

314

difference is that the two lines are in a quickly written bastard script, whereas the rest is a more formal book hand. The whole of the rest of the book was carefully inscribed in a way suggesting the author wished his work to last down the ages. These words were stuck at the bottom of the page, below the lines drawn for the proper text. As though they were an afterthought. And a warning.'

Malinferno laughed. 'A warning? Have you been reading Mary Shelley?'

Bromhead gave him a scandalised look for suggesting he of all people would be reading such modern Gothic rubbish as Malinferno referred to. He shrugged.

'I suppose it's nothing really.'

'Of course it's not. The writer of the play was a monk, yes? He probably had second thoughts about finishing Cain and Abel on a curse, and made a late addition. A salutary lesson to avoid ... what does he say? ... "envy and vainglory".'

Bromhead nodded at Malinferno's wise words. But a nagging doubt remained in his mind. If he had known what was going on at the first rehearsal of *The Play of Adam* at the Royal Coburg, he might have been more worried.

'I'll kill you, Jed Lawless, you incompetent nincompoop.'

Morton Stanley had been in a bad mood since realising he would have to share the stage with Perceval Tristram. Doll noted that, when he came back from talking to Will Mossop, his temper had been unalloyed. The first run-through of "Adam and Eve", with Tristram as a rather corpulent serpent, had gone badly. It had terminated when a canvas backcloth, painted with a scene more reminiscent of a prim English woodland than the Garden of Eden, came tumbling down into a crumpled heap close on the heels of Stanley.

He had leaped away just as the wooden beam at the top of the backcloth crashed to the ground. With years of dust rising in clouds, and a shocked silence hanging in the air, the tall actor had laid into the chief stagehand. It must have been Lawless's grip on the cloth that had failed.

Lawless himself, a wizened but wiry old fellow with a club foot, had emerged from the gloom of the wings, ashen-faced, but determined not to be railed at by a mere actor. He cast a glance into the auditorium where Mossop sat giving his instructions.

'He can't talk like that to me, Mr Mossop. It was a genuine accident. The rope gave way.'

Will Mossop gave a deep sigh, and waved a hand in his stagehand's direction.

'Just tidy up the mess, Jed. Anyway, haven't we got anything better for the Garden of Eden. I'm sure that backdrop was last used as Birnam Woods in the Scottish play.'

Lawless grinned toothlessly at the theatre manager. 'It's true, what you say. We could always use the backdrop of *Jack and the Giant*.'

He ambled offstage and, as he passed Doll, shot her a comment out of the side of his mouth: 'He won't like that. It's got a ruddy great beanstalk in the middle of it.'

Mossop called the cast to order as the offending backcloth was hauled back up into place. The collapse had creased the painting badly, and Birnam Woods was now mottled with gashes of bare canvas and flaking paint. The effect was most surreal.

Mossop clapped his hands to gain everyone's attention.

'Look here, everyone. I want to move on to the Cain and Abel scene, and block it in before we call it a day.'

He pointed at the quiet, middle-aged actor who had already played several minor roles as angels. He had been so self-effacing that Doll had not yet learned his name. Mossop now provided it.

'Harry, you are the yokel, Brewbarrel, and you come on from stage left.' He waved his hand disdainfully. 'Do your usual moping and leering.'

Harry blushed, and nodded as he walked off into the wings. Doll followed him offstage as she was not needed in this scene.

Standing by him in the darkness of the wingspace, she whispered in his ear, 'What's blocking?'

He cast a curious glance at her, thinking she perhaps was trying to take a rise out of him. But the genuinely puzzled look on her face showed him that this attractive, voluptuous woman with whom he was sharing this intimate little space was truly ignorant of theatrical jargon. He guessed that she had probably had to provide her services on the couch in Mossop's office to get the part, rather than by dint of her acting skills. He glanced onstage, and saw that he had time to explain. Mossop was still manoeuvring Stanley and Tristram around the vast open space. He put his mouth to her pretty shell of an ear, and pointed onstage.

'That is blocking. Giving the actors their moves, and hoping they will remember them at the next rehearsal.'

Doll breathed a sigh of relief. 'Thank goodness. I thought it was going to be something quite painful.'

Harry grinned, observing how Morton Stanley was stumbling around the stage, much to Mossop's exasperation.

'Oh, for some actors of limited brain it is very painful, I assure you.'

Mossop's harassed voice coming from the auditorium broke off their conversation.

'Harry, that's your entrance.'

*

The blocking lasted another full day, and then on the third day work began in earnest. Mossop wished the actors to concentrate on the tale of Adam and Eve, and Doll, Morton Stanley, and Perceval Trsitram, who played the part of King George/Satan, went over their lines again and again. Doll had spent the previous night learning her words with Malinferno, who had had to read both Adam and Satan. He had seemed to have taken great relish in the speech after the eating of the apple.

"'Alas, my wife I blame, for so she to me said—'" He broke off. 'This text is quite up-to-date, is it not, Doll?'

Doll cuffed him around the head with her copy of the play. 'I shouldn't need to remind you, Joe Malinferno, that I am no wife of yours. Thanks to your reluctance to make an honest woman of me.'

Malinferno's face went a little pale at the mention of marriage, but he diverted Doll's sally into the running battle between them concerning making of her an honest woman.

'What are you going to do about the fact that Adam and Eve are naked, my dear?'

Doll leered at him. 'I shall be clad in the sheerest of muslin, and Morton will be bare-chested and wearing the tightest pair of breeches you have ever seen.'

That had shut Joe up, and now at the rehearsal, Doll examined the aforesaid actor's shapely form from the wings, as she awaited her next entrance.

'No good looking at that, dearie. Didn't you know that Morton Stanley plays backgammon with the boys?'

It was Jed Lawless who had spoken out of the gloom where all the ropes for the backdrops came down to a series of cleats on the wall. It reminded Doll somewhat of a ship at sea, with taut ropes holding masts and sails in place. At the Royal Coburg, they disappeared into the space above the stage that she had learned was called the flies. This wing-space was Lawless's domain, and he was often to be seen hauling on ropes and tying them off again. Usually, his crude comments were spoken *sotto voce* to his crew of scene shifters, but this time he had aimed his comment at Doll. He had also spoken too loud, and a red-faced Stanley stormed into the wings, brushing against Doll as he passed. He grabbed the unrepentant Lawless by the neck.

'Make such unfounded allegations again, and I will kill you.'

The stagehand seemed unworried by the actor's violent behaviour, and simply grinned at him. The even-tempered Harry, who had been playing an angel to Stanley's Adam, hurried over and prised his colleague's hand from Lawless's throat.

'Come, Morton, let's get on. We have less than two weeks to opening night.'

Stanley growled deep in his throat, pushing Lawless back against the row of cleats.

As he strode back on to the stage, Doll heard the stagehand whisper to himself, 'Kill me, Molly? Not before I have killed you first.'

Doll wanted to ask Lawless how he knew about Morton's preference for boys, but before she could say anything, she heard her cue, and she was onstage. Strangely, the rehearsal progressed well after the altercation. Morton Stanley's anger appeared to bring his performance to a higher pitch. And when they came to the expulsion from Eden, which was now represented by a field with a large beanstalk in it, he took hold of Doll in a feverish embrace.

'"Oh, Eve, to see us is a shameful sight.
We both, who were in bliss so bright,
Must now go naked, day and night."'

As he held her to him, she felt his manhood hard against
her thigh. Her eyes flashed at him, and he grinned in a way
that belied Lawless's allegation. Then the spell was ruined as
sporadic applause broke out in the auditorium. Doll held
out her hand to shield her eyes from the light of the candles at her feet, and peered out to see who was watching.
Two gentlemen were seated side by side in the stalls a few
rows back. One was rather languid, with curly hair, and
handsome in a rather feminine way. The other she recognised immediately. His silver-topped cane and elegant pose
gave him away.

'Why, Mr Quatremain! How did you find me?'

The charming Frenchman, whom Doll had last seen in
the British Museum, rose from his seat, and bowed gravely.

'It is a miracle, Mam'selle Pocket. I was invited by my
friend, here . . . ' He indicated the man at his side, who
nodded her way but remained seated. ' . . . to view a play he
was funding. He knows I have some interest in the theatre
due to my uncle, who was temporarily the commissioner for
the Comédie Française in Paris. So I know they call such
backers as my friend "angels" in theatre parlance. And an
angel he is, for he has brought us together again.'

He walked down the aisle and leaned with his left elbow
on the front edge of the stage. His cane remained extended
to the right in a foppish pose.

'And this time I will not let you go so easily.'

A light cough from Will Mossop interrupted the tête-à-
tête, and Doll gave Quatremain a winning smile.

'We shall meet after the rehearsal, Mr Quatremain.'

'Oh, please. It's Étienne. And, yes, I shall be waiting. My
friend Mr Bankes and I are completely enthralled by your
performance.'

He retreated to his seat, sliding down beside the handsome

man, who was part-funding Bromhead's endeavour. His
teeth flashed a smile, and Doll turned reluctantly back to
the task in hand. Morton was staring out into the auditorium, and she wondered what he felt about Quatremain's
presence. She felt a flush warming her face at the thought of
choosing between these two rivals for her attention. Though
whether the rampant Stanley, or the suave Quatremain was
the devil or the deep sea, she was not sure.

Malinferno, meanwhile, had returned to Creechurch Lane
with thoughts of the doom-laden *Play of Adam* racing around
his brain. He had hoped Doll would be back from the theatre, but his rooms were in darkness. The only sound was
that of Mrs Stanhope's gin-soaked snores from below. He
lit an oil-lamp, and slumped down at his table, at a loss as to
what to do with this new information. Would he put off Doll
from chasing her dream, if he mentioned Augustus' comment about the warning in the old manuscript? Or would
she merely laugh at his worries? He idly drew the papyrus
sheets towards him, and looked at the cartouche in the centre
of the top one again. Recalling that Doll had suggested she
had made some progress, where he had signally failed, he
reached out for his notebook in case she had written something in it. After the last page of his own notes, there was a
single word in her sprawling hand.

-OLE I P KE—KE

It was gobbledegook, and he sighed, having hoped for more.
But despite having felt annoyed when she had intimated that
she had made a breakthrough, he knew Doll was more likely
to solve the riddle than he was. Maybe using her latest idea
of single letters for each hieroglyph, rather than Dr Young's

idea of sounds, would pay dividends. He began scouring her other notes for inspiration.

It was only when the oil lamp wick burned low and the room was plunged into darkness, that he realised how much time had passed. And that Doll was still not home. He stepped over to the bow window, which looked down onto the narrow street, and saw two figures approaching the end of Creechurch Lane. Turning in past St Katherine Cree, they were lit momentarily by the yellow light of the new gaslamps on Leadenhall Street. Such illumination had not yet crept down Malinferno's little lane, and the two people were soon enveloped in darkness again. But he had seen who they were. One was Doll Pocket with her favourite turban perched jauntily on her head of blonde hair. And the other fellow, identifiable from the silver-topped cane that swung on the end of his elegantly clad arm, was surely the Frenchie Étienne Quatremain. As the two figures approached Mrs Stanhope's house, his fears were confirmed. Quatremain was fashionably dressed in a rich blue tailcoat and brown fall-front trousers topped by a white waistcoat, shirt, and cravat. And Doll hung on tightly to his arm with both hands.

Malinferno stayed by the window but hugged the shadows of his darkened room. From there he observed Quatremain escorting Doll to the very front door of Mrs Stanhope's house. He doffed his tall hat, and kissed Doll lingeringly on her outstretched hand. Malinferno could see the simpering look on her face from where he stood. As Doll entered Mrs Stanhope's front door, the Frenchie looked up at the first-floor window, and his gaze locked with Malinferno's. He smiled triumphantly and turned away, striding down the lane back to the lights of Leadenhall Street.

The stairs creaked familiarly, and Doll, apparently a little drunk, reeled into the room where Malinferno stood. She clutched her head, tilting the turban over one eye.

'Joe! Are you still up? You gave me quite a shock, lurking in the shadows, there.'

'I have been working. How about you?'

Doll puffed out her cheeks, and slumped in one of the two dining chairs. It groaned in protest.

'Oh, it is such hard work being an actress, Joe. You can't imagine.'

'So hard that you have to spend the rest of the evening relaxing, I suppose.'

Doll gave Malinferno a peculiar look, until enlightenment dawned.

'Oh, you mean my drink with Étienne? He was at the theatre, Joe. It would have been rude not to accept his invitation. We ain't married, after all.'

Malinferno pulled a sour face, knowing how his continuing aversion to such a commitment irked Doll. He sat on the other dining chair, set at the table where he had been working until the lamp wick had died.

'Now it's all my fault, I suppose.'

Wearily, Doll rose from her chair, and plonked herself in Malinferno's lap. The chair beneath the two of them groaned more ominously than its partner.

'Silly boy.' She twirled a hank of Malinferno's dark locks in her slender finger. 'Étienne was at the theatre with another gentleman, who was putting money into the play. I had to be good to him, didn't I?'

Malinferno pouted, twisting his head away from Doll's wheedling.

'Why?'

She laughed. 'Because his name was Mr William Bankes.'

Malinferno gave her a blank look. Then the truth dawned.

'William Bankes of Kingston Lacey?'

Doll nodded eagerly. 'Yes, the same William Bankes who has just returned from Abu Simbel and Philae in Egypt. He's brought an obelisk back, and will show it me. It lies at Deptford right now.'

Malinferno pondered this exciting news for a moment before anxiously questioning Doll further.

'What did Bankes demand of you for this favour?'

Doll hugged Joe gleefully, causing the chair almost to collapse beneath her onslaught.

'Why, it's nothing like that, Joe. William Bankes is, as Jed Lawless puts it, a backgammon player.'

'Why should I care about his gambling propensities?'

Doll guffawed. 'No, you sweet innocent. In the business,' Doll always used this expression to mean her former trade of doxy, 'that means he likes to enter through the back passage.'

Malinferno gasped, never comfortable with Doll's relapses into crudity.

'You mean he frequents molly-houses?'

'Yes, Joe. He likes to dress as a woman, and is more likely to be interested in Morton Stanley than me.'

Even though Malinferno had been reassured by Doll's innocent explanations of her various beaux, he still managed somehow to be at the Royal Coburg for the next few days. But the endless repetition of the short religious scenes from *The Play of Adam* began to pall. Even the topical references to the Queen's love life, and the meetings between the King and Pergami in the guise of Cain and Abel – meetings that had never happened in real life – failed to stimulate his interest. And Mossop was ever prone to changing his mind about the location of the actors onstage. He prowled around the auditorium like a shaggy-maned lion, examining the stage from all angles.

'It is to observe all the sight-lines, do you see?' he explained when Augustus Bromhead taxed him on his restlessness. The antiquarian nodded wisely, though he had not understood a word, and was still perplexed by Mossop's actions. Just as he was about to ask for clarification, the manager broke away. He rushed down to the front of the stage, and berated the stagehands. They had dragged a large hip-bath on the stage, and had clearly not located it in the correct position.

'No, no, no, Jed. Can you not see the cross I chalked on the stage? The bath must be there. Dead centre.'

Jed Lawless grumbled under his breath, and took the reprimand out on his two assistants. He cuffed the ear of the nearest youth, a spotty-faced lad with wire-rimmed glasses hooked over his protruding ears.

'Tom, you stupid idiot, can't you see the mark?'

Tom clearly couldn't, and blushed. The other boy grinned and pushed the bath in place.

Malinferno leaned across the seats to where Bromhead was sitting, and whispered in his ear, 'Isn't this supposed to be the Garden of Eden? Where does a bath come into it?'

Bromhead shrugged wearily. He had tried to persuade Mossop not to use the pantomime backcloth for the scene, but had withdrawn his objection when asked for some more money for a new backcloth. Now, Mossop had inserted a bath into the scene. He began to explain to his friend.

'Will is taken by Theodore Lane's cartoon showing Queen Caroline and Pergami frolicking in a bath together. He is determined to reproduce it in the play, and insists "The Fall of Man" is the best place. God knows how he plans to show Adam and Eve in all their nakedness.'

Malinferno had a good idea how from what Doll had told him, and his fears were realised immediately. Doll and Stanley emerged from the darkness of the wings in their

attire for this scene. The handsome Stanley was stripped to
the waist, showing off a hairy chest and a tight waist. His
nether garment was no more than a tight pair of breeches
that did little to obscure his well-endowed manhood.
Malinferno thought he heard an indrawn breath from
behind him where William Bankes sat. This was followed
by a long-drawn-out expression of admiration in French
from Quatremain, who sat next to Bankes. Of course, the
Frenchman's salute was not for Stanley, but for Doll. She
was clad in nothing more than a thin muslin shift, which did
nothing to hide her manifest charms. Especially when the
candlelight shone on her.

Stanley led Doll over to the bath, and held her hand as she
stepped into it.

Mossop then called out to Stanley, 'Morton, kneel behind
the bath. It will mask your lower half.'

The actor did so, and the rolled edge of the hip-bath all
but obscured his breeches. He looked naked. Stanley flicked
some imaginary water at Doll, just as in the cartoon, and
they recited their lines, Stanley first.

> '"Ah, Eve, you are to blame;
> To this you enticed me –
> My body gives me shame;
> For I am naked, it seems to me."'

Then it was Doll's turn as Eve.

> '"Alas! Oh, Adam, so am I!"'

That was as far as she got, for she burst into a fit of the gig-
gles, and covered her breasts with her hands. Mossop rushed
down to the front of the stage.

'Eve! Doll, what is the matter?'

Doll could not stop her laughter, merely pointing into the wings. Everyone turned to see what had amused her. The hot faces of the two young stagehands, formerly agog at Doll's nakedness, suddenly disappeared into the darkness.

That interlude proved the highlight of a long and arduous day's rehearsal. When the only short break they did have arrived, Doll was steered to one side by Étienne Quatremain, and Malinferno was left to talk to William Bankes. It could have been very enlightening for Malinferno, as he knew Bankes too was a student of hieroglyphics, but the man seemed distracted by Morton Stanley's deliberate avoidance of him. The actor first complained to Mossop about some minor matter, then deliberately joined Quatremain and Doll rather than talk to Bankes or Malinferno. Bankes was obviously put out, and all he did in response to Malinferno's questions about the obelisk he had brought back from Egypt was wave a hand and sigh. Malinferno was actually glad when the rehearsal began again in earnest.

Soon, only Doll, Morton, Perceval and Harry were left onstage, and the auditorium was empty but for Malinferno. All the other onlookers, including Bankes, Bromhead and Quatremain had long since gone, driven out by the tedium of actors repeating the same scenes and words over and over again. Mossop had been particularly irritated by Morton Stanley, who seemed unable to remember his words from one run-through to the next. At one point Mossop stalked towards Malinferno cursing under his breath, and making his feelings clear.

'I would get rid of him if I could. In fact I would murder him, if only I had a replacement.'

But he concealed his annoyance, and patiently called out to the actors to begin again.

Malinferno eventually gave up too, and returned to Creechurch Lane, where he sat down on one of the creaky chairs and awaited Doll's return. When evening drew on, he sent out for chops and gravy, which a skinny boy delivered on a tray almost as big as he was. But there was no sign of Doll, and Malinferno did not feel like eating alone. Both meals eventually lay cold and congealed on their respective plates. He looked to pass the time until Doll's return with some more research into hieroglyphs, but was unable to find his notebook. He assumed Doll had misplaced it, as it was she who had been scribbling in it the previous evening. He remembered because she had been excited and had wanted to show him something, but he had been too sulky. He wished he had let her reveal her secret now.

When she finally came in, and flopped on the other chair, much to its creaky consternation, he taxed her with the missing notebook. She flapped a hand wearily.

'Lawks, Joe, I don't know where it is. My brain is all a muddle of "move stage right" and "avoid masking the other actor". Why can't they use plain English in the theatre?'

Malinferno knew he was being a little hard on her, and knew why too. He was resentful how Doll had become the centre of attention lately, on stage and over the cracking of the hieroglyphic code. But that didn't stop him chiding her.

'You had the book last. Where did you put it?'

Doll sighed, knowing that, when Joe was in this sort of mood, he would not give up. She got up and crossed the room.

'I hid it behind the sherry bottle. I put it there for safety. That sherry-wine is so awful no one would go near it.'

She groped behind the dark brown bottle in question.

'It's not there.'

Malinferno groaned. 'I know it's not there. That was the first place I looked. It is my hidy-hole too, after all.'

Doll's face lost the grey weariness that had spoiled her looks when she entered the room. She was now concerned, and peered sharply at the shelf where the bottle stood.

'The bottle's been moved. Look, you can see its original sticky ring on the shelf. The bottle is not where it was before. And I had an idea about the bird symbol I wanted to share with you.' She looked around the room. 'The papyrus sheets have been disturbed too. I left them stacked up at the back of the table. The one with the cartouche I copied into the notebook was on the top.' She shuffled through the crackling sheets. 'It's gone. The one with the cartouche is gone.'

Malinferno held his head in his hands.

'All my notes . . . and yours . . . gone. We shall have to start again.' He looked up at his worried companion. 'What was the idea you had that you wanted to tell me last night?'

'Oh, yes. The bird symbol. I think Young was wrong, and if you substituted an "a" for the "ke", you had—'

Suddenly, Doll held a finger to her lips. Joe looked at her quizzically, and she pointed at the door to their rooms.

'The stairs creaked. There is someone out there,' she whispered in his ear.

Malinferno tiptoed to the door, and with a glance at Doll, flung it open.

'Oh, sir, sorry, is your meal finished. I've come to fetch the plates.'

It was the chop-house boy, come back with his vast tray, which he now held like a shield. Doll laughed, and ushered him in.

'The meal, I am afraid, is uneaten. But you can take it away.' She scanned his skinny frame. 'Do you think you could find someone who could eat it up, all cold and congealed as it is?'

The boy's eyes widened at the feast on offer, and nodded eagerly. Once he had cleared all the crockery and left the room, Malinferno turned the key in the lock of the living room door. It was too late, but he knew he would feel safer with no possibility of further intrusions. He still wanted to know Doll's theory, though, and followed her to the bedroom. But she was already snoring by the time he entered.

The month end had come, and with August arrived, there were only three more days to go before curtain up on *The Play of Adam*. Rehearsals at the Royal Coburg Theatre were taking on a very serious mood. It was Friday, and the hangers-on were no longer in attendance. Even Malinferno had avoided going, but then he had other concerns. He was trying to resurrect his and Doll's notes on the papyrus documents, especially the one with the cartouche on it that Doll had almost deciphered. He wracked his brains to recall the sequence of letters she had noted down. Was it '-OLT I M KE—KE'? That didn't look right, but the letters were borrowed from the ones assumed to spell out Ptolemy. He scribbled something else down – '-OLE I P KE—KE'. Yes, that was it. It didn't make sense, but then she had wanted to substitute another letter for the final two. The trouble was, he couldn't recall what the letter was. He began to retrace his steps through other papyri, searching for other cartouches – those little clusters of hieroglyphs that were supposed to be names from the past. He reached for a damp cloth to cool his throbbing head.

One of the young stagehands hadn't bothered turning up to the rehearsal, and Jed Lawless had sent a message to the theatre saying that he himself was sick. Will Mossop assumed it was a hangover. Lawless drank too much gin, and he had a mind to fire him again. The trouble was, Lawless knew the ropes inside out at the Royal Coburg – literally. The ropes and pulleys that raised and lowered the backcloths and the counterweighted ropes used to cause actors to seem to fly were Lawless's private domain. No one knew them better, and besides, he was the best stage manager this side of the river. Mossop was aware that firing him would necessitate re-hiring him the following day. And that would be an exercise in humiliation for Will that he did not wish to undertake.

The rehearsal had started without Jed, and the boy with the glasses was just about coping on his own. But the next scene was 'The Fall of Man', and required the Garden of Eden backcloth and the hip bath. The boy scurried on stage and pushed the heavy bath roughly into position. Doll, in her thin muslin gown, stepped into it, and Morton Stanley kneeled behind it. There was a pause while everyone waited for the Garden of Eden to descend. It didn't, and Mossop called out to the boy to set the correct backcloth. His head popped out from the wrong side of the stage, his face red, and his glasses askew. Then he rushed across stage into the opposite wing-space where all the ropes were cleated up. There was a short pause. Then a squeal of pain rang out from the wings, quickly followed by a strange whirring sound, fast and high-pitched. Doll was half-aware of something large descending from above, and she instinctively closed her eyes and flinched, throwing her arms over her head. There followed a huge thump, and the stage under the bath shook as though from an earthquake. A snake-like form draped itself suddenly over Doll's upraised arms, and she screamed, struggling to cast it off as it wrapped itself around her. When her scream stopped, a deathly silence hung over the theatre for a long moment.

She opened her eyes to see a cloud of dust rising around her. She coughed, choking on it, and fought the snake that had entangled her. It turned out it was merely a rope, and she pushed it off her, grasping the side of the bath. Beside the bath was the humped form of a filled sack, the sort of sack used as a counterweight to a human body in the flying device. This time, though, an actor was not at the other end of the rope. It now lay on the floor, where Doll had cast it. A body, however, did lie underneath the heavy, sand-filled sack that had plummeted from the heavens. It was the body of Morton Stanley and, judging by the blood that was seeping from under the sack and being absorbed by some of the sand that burst from it, the actor was dead.

Doll heard a whimpering noise coming from the wings. She clambered out of the bath, and ran across the stage. Everyone else seemed stunned into immobility by the catastrophe. In the darkness, she could just make out a small shape – someone kneeling in front of the morass of ropes leading down to the cleats on the wall. It was the bespectacled boy – Doll was ashamed she didn't even know his name – and he twisted round, holding out his hands to her. She could see that the skin on his palms was red and torn.

'The rope just ran through my hands, lady,' he blubbered. 'It should not have been that heavy. It was only the backcloth.' He looked up at her with reddened eyes. 'What happened?'

Doll grimaced, thinking the poor boy had made a mistake. He had been hurried into doing a job he knew nothing about, and had dropped the counterweight.

'It was the wrong rope, lad.'

This was Will Mossop's voice coming from the stage. It shook with anger and emotion. The boy looked up at Doll, ashen-faced.

'It wasn't, lady. Look. The cleats are all marked.' He pointed at the clear, hand-painted black letters on the cleat that no longer had a rope attached. The deadly rope. Doll read the letters: 'US3.'

'Upstage backcloth number three,' the boy explained.

Mossop by now was in the wings too. He strode over to the cleats, and yanked on the rope secured round the next cleat to US3. Following the angle of the rope as it soared into the flies, both Mossop and Doll could see the Garden of Eden backcloth shuddering in response to his tug on its rope. Mossop pointed at the cleat the backcloth was on.

'FL1. Fly one. The ropes have got crossed over. This is Jed Lawless's fault.'

Doll peered back onto the stage, where a small knot of actors stood around the heavy sack.

'Is Morton . . .?'

Mossop nodded.

'Dead for sure. I shall have to call for the magistrate, but it is surely nothing more than a tragic accident.'

Doll was about to offer a different opinion, but saw the far-off look in Will's eyes. She knew he was already thinking of the implications for the play. She took his arm and drew him to one side, casting a glance at the whimpering boy.

'Will, look after the boy.'

Mossop shook his head, as though trying to clear his thoughts.

'What? Oh, Tom, you mean? Yes, I will get a doctor to put some salve on his hands. He will be fine.' He looked at his disconsolate band of actors onstage, then at Doll.

'You had all better wait for the magistrate, and when he is finished, you can all go home. I will send a message round telling what I propose to do when I know myself.'

Doll could see her chance at stardom slipping away. But

for now there were other matters to deal with, and she didn't propose to be held up by some interfering magistrate. She threw a cloak over her diaphanous shift, slipped out the stage door of the theatre, and called a cab.

'Morton Stanley has been murdered?'

Malinferno had reacted in shock at Doll's pronouncement. Bromhead's dire prediction was still uppermost in his mind, and now it seemed the warning had not been for nothing. He was pacing the landing that separated their two rooms, trying to convince himself that it wasn't so. He called out to Doll, who was changing into something more decent in the bedroom.

'Couldn't it have been an accident? If the kid released the wrong rope, then it was just unlucky that Stanley was underneath the sack of sand.'

Doll stepped out of the bedroom, and would have spoken, but she noticed that their landlady, Mrs Stanhope, was hovering at the bottom of the staircase all agog, so she steered Joe back into their living room. She closed the door, and leaned against it. Her bosom, now clad in more demure white cotton, heaved.

'It was no accident. The boy knew what he was doing, and chose what should have been the correct rope.'

Malinferno frowned, still unconvinced.

'He wore spectacles, didn't he? That may have caused his confusion.'

'No. He chose the correct cleat. But the ropes had been switched, and I think it was done deliberately.'

'Who would have cause to murder Morton Stanley?'

Doll barked out a laugh. 'Nearly everyone who had been in the theatre the previous day. Percy Tristram and Morton have been at each other's throats for years, apparently. Percy used to get the leads, but now he's older and fatter, Morton has replaced him. He gets Morton's goat by calling him Stan. It seems that when he started out on the boards, Morton Stanley was plain Stan Morton. When his star began to wax, he suddenly emerged as Morton Stanley. Percy doesn't let him forget the old days.'

Malinferno held up a cautionary finger at this point. 'Yes, but if they have been old enemies, why kill him now, and so openly, too?'

Doll sighed. 'The very same thought had occurred to me. And I can't give you an explanation. But it had to be someone theatrical, who knew about all the ropes and pulleys.'

'Will Mossop must know.'

'What makes you think Will murdered Morton?'

Malinferno recalled the rehearsal he had attended when Stanley's ineptitude had driven Mossop to distraction.

'He actually said to me something about wanting to get rid of him if he could. I can recall his very words. He said, "In fact I would murder him, if only I had a replacement."'

Doll shook her head. 'Nah. That's just theatre-speak. They all go to excess like that.'

Malinferno was not so certain.

'We should not rule him out nevertheless. Who else is there with a motive?'

Doll grimaced, thinking of the exchange between Morton and the chief stagehand.

'The obvious suspect has to be Jed Lawless.'

She told Malinferno of the incident in the wings when Morton threatened to kill Lawless, grabbing the club-footed stagehand by the scruff of his neck.

'It was when Jed accused him of being a player of backgammon in a rather loud voice. Morton threatened him with violence, and Will had to separate them. They cooled down, but I heard more than I was supposed to when Jed stalked off. He made a threat, spoken in a whisper.'

'What was it?'

'"Kill me, Molly? Not before I have killed you first."'

This time, she didn't have to explain to Joe that 'molly' was a derogatory name for a man who liked to dress as a woman. The euphemism 'playing backgammon' had been sufficient education for him.

'But doesn't the same apply to Lawless as to Will Mossop? Could that not just have been all wind and bluster?'

'Not the way he said it.'

Malinferno gathered up his garrick greatcoat, and tossed her cloak at Doll.

'Come on.'

'Where are we going?'

'To the theatre, of course. I need to see the scene of the crime.'

Doll groaned, and was about to complain that the last place she wanted to go right now was the Royal Coburg. In fact, she wanted to say that she was heartily sick of the place, but Joe was already halfway down the staircase.

She called after him. 'Go to the end of the lane, and find a Tilbury. I'm not walking there this late at night.'

The little Tilbury cab came to a halt outside the imposing front of the theatre. A mist had risen from the river, and it drifted down the Waterloo Road, turning the façade of the Royal Coburg into something from a Mary Shelley novel. Malinferno paid the cabby, and watched as the Tilbury disappeared back over the river. Despite his heavy coat, he shivered as the cab was swallowed in the swirling fog. Doll grabbed his arm.

'Come on. It's bleeding cold out here. Job will have a nip of something in his cubbyhole.'

'Job?'

Doll dragged him down a dark side street that ran between Waterloo Road and Webber Street.

'Job is the stage-door man. He always has some gin tucked away somewhere.' She grinned. 'I call it his little comforter.'

Malinferno groaned at the pun, but allowed himself to be led to a dingy door set deep in the recesses of the grimy brick wall at the rear of the theatre. Doll pushed it open, and it creaked theatrically.

'Job? It's only me, Doll Pocket. Are you there?'

There was no reply, and the little office with its window on the corridor that led backstage was empty. Doll frowned.

'That's odd. He should be here. He practically lives in that office.'

Malinferno glanced nervously over his shoulder. There was something eerie about an empty theatre, devoid of actors and the noise and bustle of performance.

'Shouldn't we just go?'

Doll laughed. 'Nah. You wanted to see where Morton snuffed it, and see it you will. It's only along here.'

She led the way confidently down the darkened corridor, and Malinferno followed, groping along the wall uncertainly. At the end of the corridor, which he presumed led onto the stage, there was a glimmer of light. The yellowish glow of candles. As they got closer, Doll suddenly stopped. Malinferno came up behind her.

'What is it, Doll?' he whispered into her ear.

'There's someone on the stage, and he has candles lit.' She looked around the wings. 'Where the hell is Job when you want him?'

Malinferno peered over Doll's shoulder.

'Could that be him lying in the middle of the stage?'

Doll turned her gaze where Joe had indicated, and gasped.

The body of an elderly, unshaven man lay face up right where the sack had plummeted down onto Morton Stanley. She turned to Joe, and was about to speak, when he held a finger up to her lips. He pointed towards the wings on the other side of the stage. Jed Lawless limped out of the darkness, his club foot clomping on the boards. He bent over the body of the stage-door man, and peered at his face. Doll gasped involuntarily.

'Poor Job, what's Jed gone and done to him?'

'It's easy to find out,' Malinferno responded decisively. 'He can't run far with his gammy leg.'

He rushed out of the wings towards the murderer. His approach surprised Jed, who fell back from the body. But just before Malinferno could grab him, the body reared up.

'What the hell ...?'

Malinferno was stunned, and stared at Job, who appeared to have come back from the dead. It was Jed who broke the deadlock.

'What you doing here? And who are you, anyway?'

Doll emerged from the wings to settle the impasse.

'Jed, this is Mr Malinferno. He has been to see the rehearsals, don't you recall?'

Jed waved a dismissive hand. 'Ahhh. I don't have time to look out beyond the proscenium arch. I'm too busy backstage.'

Malinferno couldn't help himself, and threw out an accusation: 'Setting up traps to kill innocent actors?'

Lawless gaped at Malinferno, and then he barked out a derisive laugh. 'You don't think I did for him, do you?'

Doll added her voice to Malinferno's. 'You did say you would kill him before he killed you.'

The diminutive stage-hand frowned. 'Did I? When?'

'When you cast that slur on his masculinity, Jed.'

'Oh, that. You mean when I called him a backgammon player and a molly.' Lawless was unperturbed. 'That was just talk. But if you think his murder has to do with his private proclivities, you should look at that Bankes fellow. Him what put up all that money, and got Stanley the part.'

It was Malinferno's turn to frown.

'William Bankes, the MP? What has he to do with Morton Stanley?'

'I don't know if he is a Member of Parliament or not. What I do know is that him and the molly-man was close friends.' He winked. 'Very close friends, if you take my meaning.'

Malinferno suddenly recalled the frosty atmosphere at an earlier rehearsal between Bankes and Stanley. The actor had deliberately snubbed Bankes. Was that the start of a row that had led to murder?

Lawless turned his back and proffered a hand to Job, who was still on the floor. The old man was having difficulty getting back to his feet, though apparently not having been murdered at all. When Doll asked what they were up to, Jed explained that he wanted to find out what had been done with the counterweight and the fatal rope. Job had been lying where Stanley had been in order to see up into the flies. The old boy turned to Lawless, and pointed upwards as if to God.

'You were right, Jed, the pulleys have been moved.'

Jed snapped his fingers. 'I knew it. And the counterweight reversed.'

Malinferno was puzzled. 'Reversed?'

Lawless snorted at Malinferno's ignorance of matters theatrical. 'The sack should have been in the wings, and the other end hooked onto the actor, who would have been onstage. That's how the flying rig works. We manipulate the weight in the wings and make the actor rise or descend onstage. The weight should never have been above the stage, so someone deliberately put it there, if you ask me.'

Job pointed at the chalked cross drawn on the stage.

'Right above where Stanley was due to hit his mark.'

Doll stared at the scuffed mark, and felt a chill run down her spine. She clutched at Joe's arm.

'Come on, Joe. We won't get any further standing here.'

'But—' Malinferno wanted to share his suspicions of William Bankes, but Doll was determined to go.

'Come on!'

She dragged the puzzled Malinferno off the stage, leaving Jed Lawless to sort out his tangled web of ropes and pulleys. As they retraced their steps along the dark corridor leading to the stage door, Malinferno asked her what the hurry was, bursting with his new idea.

'We were just getting somewhere there. Just imagine if it was a . . .' He sought the right word. '. . . a lover's tiff between Bankes and Stanley. Or if Stanley was about to let society know of Bankes's leanings, it could have destroyed his reputation. That makes it a very good reason for Bankes murdering Stanley.'

Doll remained silent until they had escaped the gloomy confines of the backstage area of the Royal Coburg. But once they were out again in the street, she took a deep breath, and the words tumbled out of her mouth.

'You're exactly right, Joe. It makes a good reason for murdering Morton. But the problem is that we aren't looking for someone who set out to kill Morton.'

Malinferno stared at Doll, not comprehending her meaning. 'We aren't? Why not?'

'Because Morton Stanley wasn't the intended victim.'

She pointed over her shoulder at the large and looming

edifice that was the Royal Coburg, still shrouded eerily in mist. Malinferno was completely lost.

'Then who was?'

Doll Pocket pulled a grim face. 'Me.'

Doll promised to tell Malinferno all if he first bought her a meal.

'The truth has made me feel famished.'

Now, they sat in the anonymous chop-house in Unicorn Passage, just off Tooley Street, where Malinferno had first become acquainted with Bromhead's copy of *The Play of Adam*. He was beginning to feel that the warning written at the end of 'Cain and Abel' had some meaning to it after all. And that it was his fault that Doll's life had been placed in jeopardy. It was he who had suggested that she should audition for a part in the play. As they ate, he confessed to Doll that the play was cursed, but that he'd only learned this much later. He wanted to know why she thought the deadly trap had been set for her. But Doll refused to enlighten Joe until she had finished the food placed before her. Finally, she wiped the brown gravy from her lips with a napkin, and dabbed the splash that had marred the pristine white of the front of her gown.

'I hope that doesn't stain. I paid a lot of money for this gown.'

Through gritted teeth, Malinferno begged Doll to explain why she thought she had been the target of the heavy bag of sand.

'It was when Job pointed at the chalk cross marked on the stage.'

'Yes. He said it was Morton Stanley's mark. You yourself told me he couldn't remember all his positions. Mossop must have put it there to make sure he was in the right place.'

Doll smiled fleetingly.

'Yes, we thespians call it hitting your mark.'

'And the sandbag certainly hit Morton's mark. With deadly results.'

Doll spat on her napkin, and worried at the gravy stain that marred the material over her cleavage.

'But that is the whole point. It wasn't a mark placed there for Morton to hit. It was there to show young Tom where to put the bath.'

'Tom, the stagehand?'

'Yes.'

Doll watched as understanding blossomed in Joe's eyes.

'The bath in which you were to sit. Then if Tom hadn't missed the mark in his haste, you would have been right under the counterweight.'

Doll nodded, and Joe squeezed her hand.

'You would have been crushed to death. Just as Morton was.'

'Yes. So you see, we are looking for someone who wanted *me* dead, not Morton Stanley.'

'But ...'

Malinferno didn't want to believe what Doll was telling him. He wanted another explanation for the falling sack that had taken Stanley's life. Then he wouldn't feel so guilty.

'But, why would anyone at the theatre want to kill you? Unless Bankes was jealous of the attentions Morton was paying you.'

Doll gave up trying to remove the gravy stain, and patted Joe's hand.

'I think he would have known that Morton's embraces onstage were all for show – a pretence for everyone else. But I believe that you are right to point the finger at William Bankes. Remember the other incident that occurred this week?'

342

Malinferno frowned, and then recalled what had vexed him so earlier.

'The theft of my notebook with all the workings you and I had made on hieroglyphs?'

'Yes. The murder took place after that notebook was taken, so perhaps something in it drove the killer to set the trap up at the theatre.'

'But very few people were there when Stanley was killed, apart from the actors and Will Mossop. Do you think it was one of them?'

'No. The beauty of the trap was that someone else would spring it unwittingly. It could easily have been Jed Lawless, and maybe that was what the murderer intended. To shift the blame on to Jed. As it turned out, Jed was ill and poor young Tom released the rope that was supposed to lower the Garden of Eden backcloth. But it was the rope that now held the counterweight of the flying rig. With the bath in place and me sitting in it . . .'

Doll brought her hand down on the table with a crash, and their cutlery rattled. A few heads in the chop-house turned to look at them. But Doll just stared back brazenly, and the onlookers' eyes fell back to their own meals.

She leaned towards Joe, and hissed in his ear, 'I'd've been squashed as flat as a pancake.' She looked around for the waiter. 'And talking of food, do you think we could get some plum pudding? This evading death by a whisker makes me feel starved.'

Only when the puddings were laid before them would Doll continue with her diatribe.

'No, I reckon it's what I wrote in your notebook that almost did for me.'

'And you think Bankes was responsible?'

Doll inclined her head. 'Something like that.'

She shovelled a spoonful of plum pudding in her mouth, and winked at Joe. He felt ill, pushed his bowl aside, and pursued the line of thinking.

'He is, after all, an Egyptian scholar himself. If he saw that you had cracked the code of the hieroglyphs, he had every reason to kill you and claim the breakthrough for himself.'

Doll waved her spoon in the air as if about to say something, but her mouth was still full of sweet pudding. So Malinferno pressed on.

'I think we should follow up your suspicions, Doll. We know that he has shipped an obelisk to London from Philae on the ship *Dispatch*. And that it has just landed. He told you so. The obelisk lies on the quay at Deptford, and it is likely Bankes will be there to view his prize. We should confront him there immediately. And even if he's not there, we may at least learn something of his plans.'

Malinferno pulled on his garrick, and was almost out the door before Doll could spoon the last of her pudding into her mouth. She grabbed her hooded cloak and followed him. Once in Tooley Street, they searched in vain for a cab of any sort. The night was cold and it began to drizzle, causing Doll to doubt the urgency of their mission. But Malinferno was not to be put off.

'Come on, Doll, it's not far from here. We can walk it.'

He strode off towards Deptford, and Doll sighed, wrapping her cloak close around her. Her satin slippers were not the most appropriate footwear for the weather, and soon her feet were soaked and frozen. The rain began to come down more heavily, and soon a rising wind was driving it in their faces. But finally the dreary sight of the Royal Dockyards came into view. Ten years ago, this had been a bustling area where ships bound for the Napoleonic Wars were built. Now, with the threat from the continent over, and victualling the only use for the dockyards, it was a run down and almost deserted place. The stench of rotting food drifted on the wind along with the rain, and any night watchman worth his salt would be snug and warm out of sight. Malinferno led the way to the main wharf where he guessed the *Dispatch* was moored up. The obelisk it had brought back from Egypt had to be so big that it would be hard to miss. Even in the gloom of a dreary London night.

Suddenly the persistent drizzle turned to a downpour. The quay was inky black, and merged with the sky as the sullen rain clouds scudded over. Malinferno stumbled on a loose coil of ropes, losing his footing. Doll grabbed his arm and he regained his balance. It was so dark, he could barely make out the location of the quayside, but thought he saw the outline of masts and rigging. Holding on to Doll's arm tightly, he groped his way towards the ship. A long, dark shape, lying on its side, loomed out of the pelting rain, blocking their way to the *Dispatch*. Malinferno could see that it was fully six foot high and square, but it tapered away evenly to their left. He touched its surface, and he could feel carvings all along its length. It was the Philae obelisk, lying where it had been offloaded onto the quay. Fascinated, he took a step along it, but Doll held his arm, stopping him.

'Listen,' she hissed under her breath, and held a cupped hand to her ear.

He did so, and discerned a sound like someone chipping at the stone. It was coming from the other side of the obelisk. Malinferno indicated that he would go to the left, and that Doll should go to the right around the base of the prostrate pillar.

'Just position yourself at the end,' he whispered in her ear, 'but don't show yourself until I have had time to get close to Bankes.'

She would have asked how Joe knew it was William Bankes who was chipping away at the obelisk, but he disappeared into the darkness before she had a chance. She shrugged, and pulled her cloak tighter around her shoulders. Somehow the rain was penetrating her cloak, and a cold dribble was running down her neck. She tiptoed towards the end of the mighty monument, stroking her fingers along the cold stone, admiring the hieroglyphs that disturbed its surface. She was almost stopped in her tracks by a familiar cartouche, but realised that if she examined it she would not be in place to trap whoever it was on the other side of the obelisk. She pressed on. The base of the stone was smoothly cut, and as she rounded it she could now see the ship at its mooring and the grey surface of the Thames beyond. The water was like a wide, undulating grey ribbon caught between the darkness of the sky and the quayside. Raindrops pockmarked its otherwise dark and mysterious surface. She peered cautiously around the end of the stone, knowing that Joe would not yet be in place.

Despite the gloom, she could make out a tall elegant figure, shrouded in a heavy coat similar to Joe's garrick. He was apparently poking and prodding with one hand at the surface of the obelisk. He held a cane in his other hand, which was pressed against the surface of the obelisk for balance.

As Doll observed him, he looked nervously down the length of the obelisk towards where Joe would emerge. He must have heard something. She decided to act before he got worried and ran for it. She stepped out from the base of the stone and strode towards the figure.

'Hello, Étienne. What have you found? Cleopatra's car-touche?'

The Frenchman spun round, astonished at Doll's pres-ence.

'Cleopatra? What do you mean?'

'It was you, wasn't it? Who stole Joe's notebook with my translation of the cartouche in it. You could tell from the different handwriting that it was my discovery, not Joe's. And that my experimental replacement of the two "ke"s at the end of the word with "a"s gave me most of a familiar name. Cleopatra. That is why you decided to murder me at the Royal Coburg. You could not bear the thought that a mere Englishwoman would beat you to the great prize of deci-phering Egyptian hieroglyphics. Unfortunately for you, and Morton Stanley, the bath I was in was misplaced. So your heavyweight trap fell on the wrong person. You even absented yourself from the theatre at the moment the appar-ent accident was to take place so as not to be suspected of foul play.'

Quatremain sneered, recovering his sang-froid.

'Yes, I invited myself to Bankes's celebration of the arrival of the obelisk to these shores.' He patted the prostrate stone. 'So neither of us was at the theatre when the ... accident happened.'

He took a step away from the obelisk, and closer to the quayside.

'No one could accuse either of us of dropping the coun-terweight on you. And neither of us would be suspected of knowing enough of backstage matters to set the trap, if it was seen as something more than a mere accident.'

'Except you made the mistake of telling me that your uncle was once the manager of the Comédie Française in Paris.'

Quatremain poked with his cane at the gaps in the stone slabs of the quay. His right hand was behind his back.

'Ah. I had thought that you would not remember me saying that. Now I have two reasons to kill you.'

'Before you do, do tell me what you were doing to the obelisk.'

'I was trying to obliterate the Cleopatra cartouche so that neither you nor Bankes would see it and get to decipher hieroglyphs before I did. Now I must use this hammer for another purpose.'

He brought his hand from behind his back, and swung the hammer he held in it high in the air. But before he could bring it down, Malinferno, who had been sneaking up behind Quatremain as Doll diverted his attention, grabbed at his arm. However, the Frenchman must have seen the look in Doll's eyes, betraying her accomplice's presence to him. He twisted round at the last moment, and Malinferno missed Quatremain's upraised arm. Instead he caught his shoulder, and the Frenchman stumbled sideways. He dropped the hammer, and reached out to break his fall. But there was nothing behind him but air. He teetered on the brink of the quay, and his elegant shoes slipped on the wet, rainy surface. The edge of the dock was curved and did not help him regain his balance. For a long moment he hung in the air. Then he moaned and, still clutching his cane, fell into the waters below.

Cautiously, both Joe and Doll stepped to the edge of the quay, and peered into the inky Thames. The tide was fast flowing out to sea, and Quatremain had already disappeared into the river's depths. Malinferno ran up and down the quayside for a while, but could see nothing of the Frenchman.

Then Doll cried out, 'Look!'

She pointed downstream at the middle of the torrent. Malinferno gazed hopelessly into the teeming rain, the gap between the downpour and the river hardly discernible. Then he spotted what Doll had seen. An elegantly clad arm was raised above the waves holding on to a silver-topped cane. To Malinferno, it resembled the outstretched arm of the Lady of the Lake holding Excalibur. But then, he had been embroiled in several Arthurian escapades lately, and his fevered fancy was aroused. As they both watched, the arm slid slowly beneath the waters, still clutching the cane.

Malinferno and Doll Pocket met Augustus Bromhead in the eerily silent Royal Coburg Theatre the following day. Will Mossop was supposed to be present, but had left a note with Job, the stage-door man. It apologised for his absence due to 'pressing matters'. Bromhead sighed.

'He means he is busy finding a replacement for *The Play of Adam*, which has been cancelled.'

Doll joined her sigh to Bromhead's as she scuffed at the chalk cross on the stage that was to mark the place of her death.

'I suppose that, after losing the leading man, today's news was the final straw for the production.'

Everyone knew to what she was referring. Since the farce of the King's coronation, and her failure even to gain access to the Abbey, Queen Caroline had taken to her bed. She complained of persistent stomach pains, for which she took copious amounts of milk of magnesia laced with laudanum. Late on the previous night, when Joe and Doll were struggling with Étienne Quatremain in Deptford Docks, Caroline had given up her struggle to live. Her death had put an end to Mossop's topical version of Augustus' rediscovered play.

No one was in the mood to satirise a dead queen. Actually, Doll was not too disappointed.

'I don't think I'm cut out to be an actress, Joe. It's too much like hard work.'

Bromhead also expressed some relief at the demise of the project.

'My heart ceased to be in the production ever since Mossop changed it into a modern satire, I must say. And as for the curse of "Cain and Abel", it has convinced me to lock the manuscript and the old book in a box well away from prying eyes. As I have no children, I have bequeathed all my books to the boy of my second cousin. Thackeray by name. Young Will is a bit of a ne'er-do-well and I don't suppose he will amount to much, or even read any of my collection. Though he may pass it on to a library, if he has any sense. Personally, I hope *The Play of Adam* is never found again, or if it is, that no one tries to revive it. The first murder in history should be the only one associated with this cursed play.'

EPILOGUE

Surrey, July 1944

He limped into the Senior Common Room and tossed a file of dog-eared lecture notes onto the stained table near the door. This held a kettle simmering on a gas ring, a collection of odd cups and saucers, a battered tin tea-caddy, a large brown china tea pot and a tin of National Dried Milk donated by the assistant librarian, who had small children.

'Harry's had another of his brain-storms,' the newcomer announced glumly, as he poured himself a cup of over-stewed Brooke Bond and stirred it vigorously to break up the lumps of milk powder. 'He's decided the college needs a diversion from the Second Front, so we have to put on a medieval play to entertain visitors at the Open Day next month!'

The only other occupant of the SCR groaned.

'Why the hell can't Harry stick to *The Importance of Being Earnest* or *Jack and the Beanstalk*, like any normal person?'

'Harry' was the covert nickname for Dr Hieronymus Drabble, the Reader and Head of the History Department at Waverley College, beloved by none of his small staff. The first man sank into a sagging armchair of worn Rexine and sipped his tea as he stared around the room. The grand title of Senior Common Room, which conjured up visions of a sedate chamber in a venerable Oxford college, seemed misplaced for this seedy place more suited to an inner-city secondary school. But Peter Partridge was not looking at the familiar décor and furnishings, but was casting a critical eye at the windows. In charge of Air-Raid Precautions at the college, he stared at the wide strips of sticky tape that crisscrossed the panes of glass to minimise the possibility of blast injuries and then at the heavy curtains of black cloth that had to blank out the slightest glimmer of light after dark. Obsessive about his responsibilities, he satisfied himself that a broken hook on one rail had been replaced by the college caretaker.

'What's brought this on all of a sudden?' demanded Loftus Maltravers, Senior Lecturer in the History Department. 'Harry's not angling for a professorship again, is he?'

'Only God knows how his mind works!' growled Partridge. 'But you might be right. No doubt some of the members of Council will turn up for it. Anyway, he's called a meeting for three o'clock to discuss it. Every one has to be there, it's a three-line whip.'

Peter was a big man in his late twenties, with red hair parted in the centre and Brylcreemed down flat on either side. A lecturer with a special interest in the plays of Molière, he had heavy features and an aggressive manner, which made him unpopular with his colleagues, who tried hard to make allowances for his club foot and the consequent three-inch-thick sole on his left boot. Like most of the college staff, either on health grounds or from being overage, he was exempt from military service.

Loftus, who suffered from bouts of severe asthma, was a thin, morose fellow nearing fifty, with black hair and a Clark Gable moustache. He was an expert in the history of stage scenery and pantomime throughout the ages. The two men always seemed ready to snipe at each other, contradicting and arguing over trivialities.

'So what play do we have to do?' he demanded. 'Not another bit of the Townley Cycle, surely? We were stuck with that two years ago. I'm not building another bloody Noah's Ark for it.'

Partridge sighed and shook his head. 'No need to get yourself in a lather, Loftus! Harry said he'd found something very interesting in an old journal. He seemed quite excited about it, said we ought to follow it up and maybe get up a paper for one of the Yank publications.'

'Nice to see that plagiarism is still alive and well,' observed Loftus, with his habitual cynicism.

They broke off their conversation as the distant ululations of air-raid sirens began broadcasting their warning to a wide area of northern Surrey and South London. The college was a few miles south of Croydon, having been evacuated in 1940 from the main university campus in Lambeth to this shabby Victorian mansion in the supposedly safer Green Belt.

'Bit early for them, isn't it?' asked Loftus, uneasily. With part of the northern coast of France already liberated following D-Day the previous month, the Luftwaffe air raids had almost ceased, but the unmanned V-1 missiles were still coming from launching ramps in the Pas de Calais.

The wailing sound faded and nothing further disturbed the peace of the morning, though until the steady tone of the All Clear sounded forty minutes later, both men had half an ear listening for the throbbing drone of the pulse-jet engine that signalled the approach of a 'doodlebug', to use the derisory but fearful term for Hitler's no-longer secret weapon.

Loftus carried on reading some essays he had set during

term time to the few undergraduates that had either escaped the call-up or had been invalided from the Forces. In the armchair, Peter Partridge scanned the four thin pages of the morning newspaper. As a drama historian, he found the news that Stalin had once more attacked Finland and invaded the Baltic States of less immediate interest than reports of the London premiere of Laurence Olivier's film of Shakespeare's *Henry V*.

The door opened again and a very thin elderly woman came in, hugging a briefcase under her arm. She had a severe face devoid of make-up and wore old-fashioned pince-nez on a cord pinned to her mannish grey costume. Dr Agatha Wood-Turner, Senior Lecturer in Religious Art, was inevitably known by the nickname of 'Lathe', from both her surname and her body shape.

Scorning the motley collection of crockery on the table, she sat on an upright chair and delved into her case to retrieve a tartan Thermos flask. Unscrewing the Bakelite cover, she poured some murky brown fluid into it and then produced a small bottle of milk, two sugar cubes and a paper bag containing three digestive biscuits. Only when she had organised her 'elevenses' did she acknowledge the presence of the two men.

'I hear that Doctor Drabble is intending to put on a play for Open Day,' she said, as if she was reading the one o'clock news on the BBC Home Service.

Maltravers nodded. 'We're on parade at three o'clock. A hundred lines for any absentees,' he added sarcastically, but the prim and proper woman ignored his attempt at levity.

The door opened again and a very different sort of female entered. Christina Ullswater was the archetypal fluffy blonde – petite, blue-eyed and shapely. She wore a fussy pink floral dress with ruffles at the neck, a white cardigan thrown artfully over her shoulders and unsuitably high-heeled shoes. At twenty-six, she was a postgraduate working on her doctoral thesis, and in spite of looking like an escapee from a Chelsea tennis club, was in fact a very clever young woman, already making her mark in the rarified world of early medieval poetry.

It was a matter of covert speculation in the college as to why she was not a Waaf or Wren, and opinions varied from having a daddy who was 'something in the War Office', to having being the mistress of the Chancellor of the Exchequer. The most popular theory at the moment was that her first war job had been filling shells at a munitions factory, but that she had been asked to leave after a fortnight, due to fears for the safety of the establishment!

Christina gave a big smile to the others and dropped into another mismatched armchair. Though technically not on the teaching staff, the exigencies of war allowed her to use the SCR, as out of term time the students' meagre facilities were closed down.

'Hear the sirens earlier on?' she asked brightly. 'Less often now than last month, thank heaven. Why they bother with sirens, I can't imagine. When the motor stops, we've got only half a minute left, so what's the point?'

Listening to doodlebug engines was now a serious pastime. If the noise continued when directly overhead, you were safe, but if it cut out before it reached you, you could well expect half a ton of high explosive to be dropped at your feet.

Agatha Wood-Turner preferred not to dwell on instruments of violent death, unless they were medieval tortures portrayed in stained-glass windows.

'I suppose you'll be cast as the Virgin, and I'll get Noah's wife, as usual,' she said bitterly.

The blonde batted her long eyelashes at the speaker in a parody of puzzlement.

'What on earth do you mean, Agatha?'

'Haven't you heard yet on the college grapevine? Our lord and master wants to put on a Miracle Play for the Open Day.'

Christina shrugged philosophically. 'Oh well, it beats having to listen to Harry making more speeches about how studying art history furthers the war effort!'

She groped in her own document case and pulled out a shapely bottle of orange Tizer and a glass. Filling it and raising it to the others, she proposed a toast.

'Here's to Adam and Eve, then. On with the motley, the paint and the powder!'

'I thought we needed something essentially British in these dangerous times,' said Hieronymus Drabble, doing his best to sound Churchillian. 'Something from our glorious past, like a medieval play from the Old Testament.'

'That would be essentially Hebrew, not British,' muttered Partridge, but Drabble ignored him. He was a fat man with a bald head and a double chin, having a passing resemblance to the Prime Minister, which he cultivated. Approaching sixty, he saw his coveted professorship slipping beyond his grasp, and this soured his whole nature.

'Are you talking about another bit of the York or Chester Cycle?' demanded Agatha, referring to a couple of the well-known collections of religious plays from the Middle Ages. 'We've done a few of those over the years, even going back before the war,' she pointed out, to emphasise her seniority in years of service.

Drabble shook his head, his jowls flapping above his spotted bow tie.

'No, no! I came across something new quite recently.'

He reached across his paper-strewn desk and picked up a few pages of foolscap, pinned together in one corner. 'I was in Oxford the other day, as an external examiner for a dissertation, and took the opportunity to call into the Bodleian to look up a few references.'

He looked at the fifth member of his captive audience, who were all seated on hard chairs around the other side of his desk. This was Blanche Fitzwilliam, the assistant librarian, a short, dumpy lady with a pleasant manner.

'As you know only too well, our own library is woefully short of many historical journals,' he said heavily.

Blanche was a war widow, having lost her RAF husband in the Battle of Britain, and was not going to be brow-beaten by the likes of Harry Drabble

'And it will remain woefully short until the war is over!' she said spiritedly. 'We lost half our stock when that incendiary bomb came through the roof three years ago.'

The Reader raised a hand in surrender. 'Of course, dear lady! I'm not blaming anyone, apart from Adolf Hitler – just stating a fact. Anyway, I found one of the papers I was looking for in an 1894 volume of the *Quarterly Journal of Historical Research*, but serendipitously noticed another title on the Contents Page that was of even more interest!'

He waited for an excited reaction, but there was a sullen silence.

'It was a translation and a commentary by Austin Dudley Price of something he found in the London Library archives the previous year. An Early Middle English script – the twelfth-century original and a Jacobean translation of *The Play of Adam*.'

This time, Loftus Maltravers showed some reaction, albeit negative.

'*The Play of Adam*? Never heard of it. Not in any of the well-known Cycles, is it?'

Christina chipped in, 'Couldn't be, it's too early. Where did it come from originally?'

'Oseney Abbey, according to Dudley Price,' said Drabble. 'It's got the usual subjects in it – the Creation, the Fall of Lucifer, Cain and Abel, the Flood.'

They all pondered this for a moment.

'How much of it do you propose doing? Some of these went on for hours, even days,' objected Agatha Wood-Turner.

'About an hour would suffice, I think,' replied Harry. 'Just to show people that even five years of war can't abolish academic scholarship.'

'And to impress the Dean of the Faculty with his genius!' murmured Peter Partridge under his breath.

The pages that Drabble had copied out from the journal in Oxford were passed around and after a quick scan, no one could think of any valid objection, if the boss was really set on this idea. The Open Day was an annual event as inescapable as Christmas, and something had to fill in the time to divert the few dozen people who felt obliged to attend. A discussion developed and, with it, mild enthusiasm for the project.

'It looks as if three of these short sections would fill the hour,' suggested Agatha. "The Creation", "The Fall of Lucifer" and "Cain and Abel" seem most suitable.'

'Great!' said Loftus with relief. 'That means I don't have to make another damned Ark.'

Hieronymus leaned back in his chair, put his thumbs in his waistcoat pockets and nodded his agreement. 'I'll get this typed up and make half a dozen stencilled copies for you all. We can get some of the post-graduate students to help with scenery and take a few of the parts.'

'Where are we going to do it?' asked Maltravers. 'Not on the back of a cart again, I hope.'

The last attempt at medieval authenticity several years earlier had been a disaster due to a sudden thunderstorm soaking the outdoor audience, making them run for cover just as Noah had announced the start of the Deluge.

There was a discussion about the best venue and eventually all agreed that the Large Lecture Theatre would be most suitable. Though as with the SCR, the title suggested serried ranks of polished benches climbing a curved auditorium, it was actually a First World War military hut that had been erected in 1917 when Waverley House had been commandeered on a previous occasion. A rectangular wooden structure similar to a small parish hall, it stood in the yard at the back of the main college building, whose red brick formed a U-shaped embrace around the hut. It had a raised platform at one end, ten rows of chairs and very little else.

'Who's going to organise the casting?' asked Blanche Fitzwilliam.

With no sign of embarrassment, Hieronymus produced a sheet of paper. 'I took the liberty of drawing up the dramatis personae. I thought Mr Partridge, being in the prime of life, could play Adam, and also portray Cain, alongside Doctor Maltravers as Abel.'

'So who will be Eve?' demanded Agatha, clipping on her pince-nez to glare at Drabble.

'Perhaps Miss Ullswater would oblige,' said Drabble in his most oily voice. 'It would be more consistent with the age of Adam.'

'And who's going to be God?' wondered Peter aloud, silently adding, *As if I didn't know!*

'I think that part would best suit me,' said Hieronymus brazenly. After some more wrangling, they agreed that

Agatha Wood-Turner, Christina and Blanche would make suitable angels.

Hieronymus made some notes on a pad as they went on with their plans.

'Dr Maltravers, would you dragoon a few senior students to fill the other roles? We need the Devil, the Serpent and few extras to stand around and look either sinister or beatific.'

Loftus also grudgingly agreed to knock together some simple scenery, pointing out that the materials were almost impossible to obtain in these hard times. The meeting broke up after half an hour and the members drifted away. Peter Partridge and Maltravers went back to the Common Room to put the kettle on, and by the time they had brewed another pot and started an argument about Christopher Marlowe's death, Christina had arrived.

As they sat drinking their rationed tea, she handed them each a chocolate biscuit, with 'US Army' printed on the wrapper. The blonde offered no explanation, but the treat was accepted graciously. But she did have something to say about the meeting they had just left.

'I'm sure I've read something about this play somewhere, not all that long ago.'

'Harry said it was in the *Q. J. Hist*,' said Peter. 'We all read that; perhaps what you saw was in there?'

She shook her golden curls. 'I've never looked at any issues from half a century ago. He said it was in the 1890s. No, I've read a much shorter piece somewhere else. I think it was a commentary on medieval writings that had some stigma attached. I'm sure there was a reference to *The Play of Adam*. The name stuck in my memory.'

Loftus shrugged. 'As Blanche said, half our library was destroyed, so it would be a devil of a job to follow that up.'

Christina agreed. 'It doesn't matter, anyway, but I was just curious. Next time I go up to town, I'll call in at the London Library to have a root around.'

'Take your tin hat and gas mask, then,' advised Peter. 'Though these days, it's probably more dangerous down here than in the City!'

The following week, the attractive Miss Ullswater took the train up to Waterloo. Looking through the carriage windows at the hundreds of bombed-out buildings on the way through South London, she could only be thankful that the History, Language and Theology Departments had been evacuated early in the war to Waverley, even if the old Victorian mansion was gloomy and inconvenient.

After her business at the surviving part of the mother college in Lambeth was done, she went across to St James's Square in the heart of the West End, to what was left of the venerable London Library, for which she had a personal subscription at four guineas a year. Founded as an independent institution in 1841, it had been bombed earlier that year and much of the most precious material had been evacuated to safety deep in the countryside. However, many of the periodicals from recent years were still there and as her speciality was quite circumscribed, she knew which journals she would have been combing for her thesis in the past eighteen months. Going down into the dank subterranean chambers that held the stacks of past issues, too deep for even the air-raid sirens to penetrate, she scanned the shelves for her familiar old favourites.

Thankfully, these half-dozen regular academic publications had annual index lists, which indicated the titles and authors of each new paper published during that year. In her document case she had her own draft thesis with all the references she had culled from the journals and now she systematically revisited each one in the indices. Though the article she sought was nothing to do with her own particular field of expertise, she recalled that it had immediately followed one of them, and that it had caught her eye and she had read it out of curiosity.

It took her forty-five minutes to find it again, but her methodical mind was used to such literary dredging exercises and with a quiet whoop of triumph, she moved along the stacks to find the correct book, the 1936 volume of the *Transactions of the British Society for Medieval Studies*. Taking it to a nearby table, Christina sat down and read the article again. Then she took a pad from her case and started making some notes.

'Now then, Hieronymus,' she murmured to herself, 'let's see if I can put the wind up you with this message from the past!'

The next meeting of '*The Play of Adam* Steering Committee', as the pompous Dr Drabble insisted on calling it, was held a few days before the performance. They quickly went over the relatively straightforward arrangements, as everyone claimed that they were already word-perfect in their short parts. The costumes were simple, mostly cloak-like drapes made from odd lengths of fabric, Peter Partridge's stock of blackout curtain material being prominent. Loftus's scenery was primitive in the extreme, but he claimed this was quite authentic: a few cardboard trees straight out of the Bayeux Tapestry, as well as a plywood mountain and part of a castle left over from a pantomime put on for local children the previous year. After they had hammered out the few glitches with only a mild degree of the bickering traditionally associated with all academic committees, Harry Drabble shuffled his papers together as a signal that he had had enough.

'I think I can safely say that I have guided us all to a satisfactory conclusion on all matters that will ensure our venture is a success,' he said, in his best Winstonian impression.

'All he needs now is a bloody cigar,' muttered Peter to Blanche, who was sitting next to him before the magisterial desk. As Harry began to rise in his seat, Christina Ullswater put up a finger and smiled sweetly at him.

'Excuse me, Dr Drabble, but before we break up, I think there is one matter that should be brought to your attention.'

Hieronymus sank back into his chair and stared suspiciously at her.

'And what might that be, Miss Ullswater?' he grunted.

'Did you know that *The Play of Adam* is alleged by some to be cursed?'

'Nonsense! Where on earth did you get that idea?' rumbled Harry.

'From the *Transactions of the BSMS*. It discusses, amongst other plays, this one you found in the Bodleian.'

The other four members, whom Christina had briefed beforehand, sat back to enjoy Drabble's discomfiture.

'There was nothing about this in the article I showed you,' he said dismissively.

'No, but that was only based on a copy of the seventeenth-century translation.' Christina handed across a short transcript she had typed up from her study of the article in the London Library. 'The original parchment still exists and that has a postscript by the author that warns of the perils of performing the play.'

Drabble put his half-glasses back on his nose and scanned the brief extract, before handing it back.

'Very interesting, Miss Ullswater. You are to be complimented on digging up such an obscure gloss on the Oseney play,' he said patronisingly. 'In fact, I might mention it to the audience in my introduction before the actual perform-ance, just to lighten the proceedings.'

'Do we know what sort of ill fortune followed exhibitions of this drama?' asked Agatha Wood-Turner, being deliber-ately provocative.

When Christina admitted that there was no information on this point, Harry Drabble snorted his derision. 'Interesting, of course – but a lot of nonsense! Like the old chestnut about it being unlucky to mention *Macbeth*, and having to call it "The Scottish Play" instead.'

'I never understood the origin of that,' ventured Blanche Fitzwilliam. 'But I know several actors who are very serious about sticking to the tradition.'

'No mystery about it,' advised Loftus. 'When a lousy play nose-dived at first night or was pulled after a short run, it was common for the theatre management to rustle up a quick *Macbeth* to fill in, as every actor worth his salt knew it off by heart, so to mention the play when something else was run-ning was held to be a bad omen.'

Peter Partridge immediately contradicted Loftus with a rival *Macbeth* theory and their difference of opinion was soon in danger of becoming quite acrimonious, until Drabble loudly declared the meeting over and cleared them from his room.

As Christina Ullswater and Dr Wood-Turner walked together to the bus stop opposite the college gates, the younger woman sought to delve into Agatha's long-standing knowledge of their colleagues.

'Why do Peter and Loftus always seem to be at each other's throats?' she asked, turning her innocent blue eyes on the older woman. 'They never seem to be easy in each other's company. Sometimes it gets a little embarrassing to be with them, when they are busy putting each other down.'

They reached the bus stop, alongside which was a red postbox, its top painted dull green, which Christina knew would allegedly change colour if poison gas was around. Ignoring the reminder that they were permanently in a war zone, Agatha's sharp face turned to look quizzically at the blonde.

'I think you're rather taken by young Peter, my girl! Yes, there is some friction between them, but it's not that serious. All I can tell you is that Peter feels resentful that he was beholden to Loftus Maltravers over a matter some years in the past. I can't say more, as it would be betraying a trust.'

With that, Christina had to be satisfied, as the single-decker bus came towards them, looking oddly blind with its headlights blanked off by slitted metal masks, which at night reduced their illumination to a point where the poor driver would have been better off leaning out of his cab with a white stick!

As the two women climbed aboard, the kindly young academic decided that she would somehow find a way of trying to heal the breach between the two men. But perhaps Fate already had the same idea.

The morning of the Open Day started bright and sunny, and remained so as the dozen visitors from the parent establishment in Lambeth arrived on the 11.37 train. Much to Dr Drabble's contentment, this year these included the vice principal, the dean of the Arts Faculty and the bursar, all influential people when it came to bucking for a Chair. As Waverley College also housed the Theology and the Language Departments, History had to share the glory of displaying the talents available in deepest Surrey. By noon, spectator numbers were swollen to about thirty by families, non-teaching staff, some curious local residents and a few waif-like students who had projects to complete or examinations to resit during the summer.

The academic staff went through the ritual of parading the visitors through each department to show them the mediocre facilities worsened by the privations of wartime. Unlike Faculties of Engineering, Science or Medicine, there was little of visual interest to show visitors and it was with relief that they adjourned at one thirty to the lecture theatre, where some meagre refreshments were laid out on two trestle tables.

After five years of rationing, the days of buffet lunches on Open Day were a distant memory, but the staff had scraped together enough from their weekly allowances to provide the makings of a few fat- and sugar-free sponge cakes, sandwiches of home-made jam, tomato or tuna, and a fruit salad culled from the produce of their own gardens. Agatha Wood-Turner had contributed wafer-thin margarine sandwiches containing either cucumber or reconstituted egg powder, and Blanche had made patties of mashed potato and corned beef. Christina's bowl of chocolate biscuits, the American Army wrappers diplomatically removed, was emptied in a flash. All these victuals were washed down with either tea, instant coffee or 'pop', while the visitors and staff gossiped, recalled better days in the past and looked forward to better ones in the future.

Some looked curiously at the large black structure occupying much of the dais at the front of the hall. Loftus Maltravers had simulated the medieval stage which had been built either in a town square or outside a priory gate – or on the back of a hay wagon. He had erected what resembled a room-sized four-poster and surrounded it with long curtains, again borrowed after some wrangling from Peter Partridge's blackout stores. At half-past two, Dr Hieronymus Drabble mounted the two steps to the platform and stood importantly centre stage, in front of the Black Box. After coughing himself hoarse to call the audience to order, he began a tedious monologue of welcome, then extolled the virtues and academic excellence of Waverley College, emphasising the pre-eminent position that the History Department occupied. Before the muttering objections of the other departmental staff became too obvious, he shifted to the high spot of the day's entertainment, as he called it.

'You may wonder why we have not provided you with chairs, Vice Principal, ladies and gentlemen, but we always strive for authenticity. Imagine yourselves back when this *Play of Adam* was first performed in the twelfth century. Then you, as the audience, would have stood in the street, perhaps in front of a crude ox cart or a makeshift stage such as this.'

He swept a hand dramatically at Peter's black out material behind him, then launched into a reasonable account of mystery and miracle plays and the part that the religious establishment and then the guilds played in the evolution of the theatre.

'One of my gifted postgraduates, who you will see onstage in a moment, discovered an interesting legend, in that the author of this play, the prior of Oseney Priory in Oxford, added a written warning on the original script that performing this play could lead to some unspecified disaster. So perhaps we should have done it two years ago, when some of you will recall having a soaking when we suffered a cloudburst in the middle of an outdoor performance of part of the York Cycle – appropriately when Noah announced the start of the Deluge!'

He waited for a titter of amusement, but there was only

stony silence. Having rounded off his speech with some further platitudes, he bowed himself offstage to put on his robe as narrator, the other members of the cast having already assembled inside the box, through a door at back of the platform.

When the front curtain of the box was hauled up by strings, the Creation was displayed and, with Hieronymus now downstage left in a voluminous cowled cloak, the drama penned eight hundred years earlier began, with Harry filling in the gaps between the actors' dialogue with a sonorous Latin narration. It went without a hitch. Then Drabble could not resist giving a summary in English of his Latin commentary. The next pastiche was 'The Garden of Eden and the Fall of Man', with Christina tempting Peter Partridge with a large Cox's Orange Pippin.

The format was as before and appeared to be well-received by the audience, other than the small son of the lecturer in Spanish, who in a strident voice, demanded to know when the Demon King was going to pop up through a hole in the floor. The final act was 'Cain and Abel', performed with enthusiasm by Peter and Loftus, who after their initial lukewarm acceptance of Harry's dictat to put the play on, seemed to have vied with each other to inject life and drama into the ancient words. Each was essentially a frustrated actor, turned aside by circumstances into the academic study of the theatre, as an alternative career to treading the boards. With Loftus traditionally in a white robe as the good innocent brother, and the evil Peter swathed in one of his own blackout curtains, they pranced about the stage declaiming the Jacobean translation, while Hieronymus spewed out streams of Latin at one side.

The action began building up to the climax, Cain bitterly complaining about Abel's better fortune and ability to offer higher quality sacrifices to God. The lethal weapon was already in his hand – for lack of an ass's jawbone, one of the college archaeologists had loaned a Bronze Age shin-bone from his departmental collection – and Cain was beginning to brandish this threateningly as the acrimonious dialogue reached its peak.

Suddenly, Hieronymus became aware that the attention of the audience had been diverted, some looking about them, others whispering and several edging out towards the exit at the back. The actors on stage also felt that they were losing their grip on the spectators and their speeches faltered, as did Drabble's haughty stream of Latin.

Above the words as penned hundreds of years before by the prior could now be heard the all-too-familiar 'thrum-thrum' of an approaching pulse-jet. Even more menacing was the fact that a moment later, the engine was heard to cut out.

The sudden silence in the hall was far more sinister than the previous droning from above, but was abruptly broken by Peter Partridge's shouts from the stage. Now incongruously waving the three-thousand-year-old bone, he yelled for everyone to take cover. The cellars of the college were designated as air-raid shelters and the entrance was within a few yards of the lecture hut. Those on stage began to clamber down from the platform and join the orderly but hasty stream of people, now shepherded by Peter as ARP boss and by other members of the staff. Even Harry Drabble dropped his usual posturing to help the older members of the audience to hobble a little faster to the door.

'How long do you reckon we've got, Peter?' shouted Blanche, as she helped the aged wife of the bursar towards the exits.

'Can't tell. Sometimes it's a couple of minutes, but it can be much less. But it may land a mile away, if we're lucky.'

As if to mock his hopes, there was a tremendous explosion and a blast of air that blew out many of the windows, though Peter's sticky tapes prevented a storm of flying glass. Thankfully, the flying bomb had struck three hundred yards in front of the college, so that the big U-shaped building sheltered the hut from the worst of the blast, though it suffered badly itself.

Then, amid screams of fear and terror, came another ear-splitting crash as one of the tall brick chimneys of the college teetered over and fell onto the roof of the lecture hall. It landed on the near end, squarely above the stage. The rafters gave way and the roof structure, plus half a ton of masonry, folded down on to the 'black box'. By now almost everyone was at the other end near the doors, many already having gained the entrance to the shelter opposite.

Peter Partridge, like the captain of a sinking ship, was last to leave the hut, in his capacity as ARP supremo. He was shepherding out the last straggler and could not resist a last backward glance at the ruination of Loftus's primitive medieval scenery, just visible in a cloud of cement and brick dust. But also just visible was a shod foot sticking out from under a pile of collapsed blackout curtains – and even more ominous was the flickering of flames at the side of the stage, where the mangled electricity distribution-board had short-circuited and ignited yet more curtains that had fallen onto it.

Though the centre of the roof was now groaning and ceiling plaster falling like snowflakes in anticipation of a further collapse, Peter turned and hurried back to the stage end as fast as his gammy leg would allow. He was alone, as the last of the geriatric visitors had left for the shelter.

'Loftus!' he yelled as he hauled his heavy surgical boot up the steps to the platform. He knew who it was, as Maltravers had worn a pair of Clark's open-toed sandals on his bare feet, to imitate Abel's antediluvian footwear.

'Loftus, are you all right?' Even in such fraught circumstances, Peter realised what an inane question this was. The victim would hardly be lying in a burning disaster zone out of choice!

He limped across to the heap of curtains and debris, feeling the heat from the rapidly increasing fire a couple of yards away, which was avidly devouring more of the cardboard, plywood and fabric substance of the stage set. Pulling off some shattered rafters to reach the mound of black fabric, he found Loftus lying on his back, gasping and blue in the face, in the throes of a severe acute asthmatic attack.

'Are you hurt, old chap?' Peter asked urgently, kneeling and lifting the victim into a sitting position. Afraid that he had been struck by a falling beam, Peter rapidly scanned Loftus's body, but saw nothing sinister, and between his wheezing paroxysms Loftus managed to shake his head.

'We'd better get you out of here pronto, chum! There's a bit of a fire starting upstage.'

His own leg defect made it difficult, but he managed to drag the other man to the edge of the platform and then stumbled down the steps himself to grab Loftus in a clumsy fireman's lift and stagger halfway back down the hall, just in time to avoid the collapse of another section of roof. Running out of strength, he was forced to lay Loftus on the floor and bend panting over him until he got his own breath back.

By this time, several of the staff who had escaped to the air-raid shelter had noticed that Peter and Loftus were missing and had returned to look for them. Hieronymus Drabble pattered along behind them and soon was organising everyone, but by then Peter Partridge had delved into Loftus's pockets and found his asthma inhaler. A few puffs began to improve his breathing and colour, but as soon as the Auxiliary Fire Service and Red Cross ambulance arrived, Peter insisted that he be shipped off to hospital for more effective treatment, along with a few others who had minor injuries, mostly from flying glass.

A few minutes later, Agatha Wood-Turner stood with Christina Ullswater, watching as Peter climbed into the back of the ambulance with his colleague. The two women were both shaken, but unhurt and unbowed by the afternoon's events. The blonde postgraduate stared after the retreating ambulance as it left the college.

'Well, looks as if the prior's curse has struck again, after eight hundred years!' she said uneasily. 'Yet Cain and Abel seem to have made up their differences in a rather dramatic fashion.'

The wise old Agatha nodded. 'Young lady, I think that possibly this may at last have lifted that stigma from *The Play of Adam.*'

Christina looked enquiringly at Agatha. 'Why do you say that?'

'You asked me not long ago why Peter and Loftus always seemed at odds with each other. Well, I happen to know why, because I was there. When Peter applied for the lecturer's post here, Loftus, as a senior lecturer, was on the appointment committee and it was his vote that swung it. Paradoxically, Peter has always resented that, feeling that he should have been appointed solely on merit, not by a favour, and since then he's always been difficult with the very man that got him the job.'

Christina looked puzzled as she used her handkerchief to dab away a smear of blood from a small glass cut on the older woman's cheek. 'I don't understand why Loftus should have been shown him such partiality, Agatha.'

The expert on religious art smiled at her knowingly.

'Because I happen to know that although Peter and Loftus had different fathers, they had the same mother! So they really are brothers – at least, half-brothers. Though Peter felt guilty about this bit of nepotism, being siblings, they were well cast as Cain and Abel. Now that at last a performance of *The Play of Adam* has had a happy result, maybe it always will!'

Historical note

The V-1 terror offensive against Britain began a week after D-Day in June 1944 and continued until October, when Allied troops overran the launching sites in France, though the last one to reach England was as late as March 1945. A total of over nine thousand of these jet-engined missiles were launched at South-East England, up to a hundred a day, though many never reached their targets. The 2,419 that exploded, killed over 6,000 people and injured over 17,000.

After the French sites were captured, the offensive was directed at Antwerp then in Allied hands, at which 2,448 V-1s were launched, with great loss of life.

Following the V-1 campaign, the Germans used the large V-2 rockets, which were far more destructive. Over 3,000 were launched, killing over 7,000 victims.

After the war, these were the basis of both US and Soviet intercontinental missiles and space programmes.